Reason and Romance

DEBRA WHITE SMITH

HARVEST HOUSE PUBLISHERS
EUGENE, OREGON

Quotes from *Sense and Sensibility* are taken from Jane Austen, *Sense and Sensibility*, in *The Complete Novels of Jane Austen*, vol. 1 (New York: Modern Library, 1992).

Cover by Koechel Peterson & Associates, Inc., Minneapolis, Minnesota

Cover photo by Tom Henry

Published in association with the literary agency of Alive Communications, Inc., 7680 Goddard Street, Ste #200, Colorado Springs, CO 80920.

This is a work of fiction. Names, characters, places, and incidents are products of the author's imagination or are used fictitiously. Any resemblance to actual persons, living or dead, or to events or locales, is entirely coincidental.

REASON AND ROMANCE
Copyright © 2004 by Debra White Smith
Published by Harvest House Publishers
Eugene, Oregon 97402

ISBN 0-7394-4526-**X**

All rights reserved. No part of this publication may be reproduced, stored in a retrieval system, or transmitted in any form or by any means—electronic, mechanical, digital, photocopy, recording, or any other—except for brief quotations in printed reviews, without the prior permission of the publisher.

Printed in the United States of America

*For my wonderful Vietnamese princess,
my daughter, Brooke Debra Smith.*

Cast

Anna Woods: Based on Marianne Dashwood from *Sense and Sensibility*. Flighty yet innocent, Anna is Elaina Woods' younger sister.

Bryan Brixby: Based on Colonel Brandon from *Sense and Sensibility*. Bryan is a medical doctor and harbors a mysterious past.

Pearl Farris: Based on Mrs. Ferrars from *Sense and Sensibility*, Pearl is Ted Farris' mother.

Elaina Woods: Based on Elinor Dashwood from *Sense and Sensibility*. A recent Ph.D. graduate, Elaina begins her teaching career at Southern Christian University in Lakeland, Oklahoma. She is Margaret Woods' daughter and Anna's elder sister.

Faye Woods: Based on Fanny Dashwood from *Sense and Sensibility*. Faye is Elaina and Anna Woods' sister-in-law.

Joseph Woods: Based on John Dashwood Sr. from *Sense and Sensibility*. Joseph is Elaina and Anna's father and Margaret Woods' husband.

Jake Woods: Based on John Dashwood Jr. from *Sense and Sensibility*. Jake is Elaina and Anna Woods' half-brother.

Jeanna Harley: Based upon Mrs. Jennings from *Sense and Sensibility*. Jeanna is a wealthy and fun-loving cousin to Margaret Woods.

Lorna Starr: Based on Lucy Steele from *Sense and Sensibility*. Lorna is Ted Farris' fiancée.

Margaret Woods: Based on Mrs. John Dashwood Sr. from *Sense and Sensibility*. Margaret is Elaina and Anna Woods' mother.

Noah Harley: Based upon Sir John Middleton from *Sense and Sensibility*. Noah is as merry as his wife, Jeanna.

Robert Farris: Based on Charles Ferrars from *Sense and Sensibility*. Robert is Ted Farris' elder brother and president of the family aviation business.

Ted Farris: Based on Edward Ferrars from *Sense and Sensibility*. Ted is a concert pianist and Elaina's student.

Willis Kenney: Based upon Willoughby from *Sense and Sensibility*. Willis is a handsome model who enchants Anna Woods.

One

Elaina stepped into her father's ICU room. The smell of antiseptic did little to assure her that her dad had awakened from the coma for good. She paused before approaching the white-swathed bed. A haunting precognition insisted this would be the last time she spoke with her childhood hero. He struggled for every breath with a rasp and wheeze that nearly took Elaina under. Two days ago, Joseph Woods Sr. had slipped into a coma after a massive heart attack. This morning the doctor hinted that Joseph wouldn't survive the night.

By a divine miracle, her father burst from the dark mysterious an hour ago. The initial report elated Elaina and her family. Optimism flared, and for the first time in two days she hoped her father might recover. Soon after the doctor announced his consciousness, Joseph insisted upon talking to Margaret Woods, his second wife and Elaina's mother.

Margaret came from the brief conference, settled in the waiting room's corner, and gently wept. She shared no news with either of her daughters, only choked tears and the claim, "He's going…he's going."

Elaina's hopes disappeared.

Then Joseph summoned his first child, Elaina's half-brother, Jake. The 45-year-old man returned from the visit, his face white and stony, as if he were a marble statue filled with a bilious brew that could find no release.

"He wants you next." Jake had dropped the tightly spoken words in front of Elaina as if he were choking on them.

Now Elaina moved farther into the room. She stepped to the bedside, gripped the cool, metal rail and stared into the graying face of the man she called Daddy. Her eyes stinging, Elaina wadded the hem of her cotton blouse. She placed her unsteady fingers upon his forehead and whispered, "Daddy?"

His head tilted toward her voice; then his eyes slid open. "My favorite redhead," he mumbled with the shadow of an adoring smile.

"Hey there, you gave us all a terrible scare," Elaina chided.

"I'm leaving, Elaina," he whispered.

"But—"

"No, l–listen," he continued, and barely lifted his wrinkled index finger off the bedspread.

Elaina covered his hand, as weak as a newborn's, and smiled through a veil of tears that threatened to fog her glasses. "Always the one in charge, aren't you?" she teased as the hiss of oxygen in plastic tubing testified to his frailty. *You're being bossy, even on your deathbed,* she thought. Her smile vanished.

"I—I saw the c–city," he said, his hazy gaze taking on an uncanny sharpness. "H–He was there, hold–holding out His hands." Joseph reached forward, as if he still saw the vision. "I was about—about to step over." He coughed and wheezed. "But I asked to come…to come back and say…say goodbye." The final words slurred out. His gaze dimmed. His thin gray brows twitched.

As Joseph's eyes shut, Elaina felt as if the walls were pressing all oxygen from her lungs. Finally she understood her brother and mother's reactions.

In her mind, the limp man before her was replaced by the vigorous father from her youth. Joseph had been 50 when Elaina was born, but that didn't stop him from jumping into fatherhood with the zeal of a 20-year-old. He coached her little league ball team… took her to girl scouts…and treated her and her friends to every kids' movie that released. He cheered her through high school tennis, urged her into college, and thought a Ph.D. was the only natural choice. Last month, when she'd secured an assistant professorship at Southern Christian University, her father wrapped her in his lanky embrace and promised to visit her first class this fall. Even then Elaina had been stricken with his growing frailty.

Joseph stirred. The crumpled sheets murmured about his imminent death. And Elaina was almost certain she heard the brush of angel wings. He swallowed and frowned as if his every move were an unforgiving leech sucking the life from him.

Joseph's eyes drooped open. "Do you—you remember what I t–told you last year about the—the prenuptial agreement?" he rasped, his purplish lips crinkling like crepe paper.

"Yes, I remember." As Elaina squeezed his hand, she recalled the day he'd insisted on explaining the existence of the legal agreement between him and her mother. Elaina never knew of the document and was grieved by her father's regret of it.

"It's okay, Daddy," she now assured. "I understand. I know you would have never intentionally deprived Mother and Anna and me."

A shroud of relief swept his pinched features. "I would have never pr–promised my first wife if I'd—if I'd known…"

"I know. I know." Elaina rubbed her thumb across the back of his wrinkled hand, spotted with age. When Joseph's first wife, Angela, died of a rare liver disease, she made him pledge to leave the family estate and import business to their son—no matter what. At the time, Joseph had been so distraught at losing his wife he never imagined marrying again, let alone having more children.

"But really, I can't blame her for making you promise, and I can't blame you for agreeing," she said with as much calm assurance as she could feign. Elaina would do anything to bring her father peace—even pretending no resentment for a first wife she'd never met.

"It was her—her money—" he broke off.

"Yes, I understand." Elaina prepared to repeat the facts, as if by restating them she could validate the merit of her half-brother inheriting the mansion, millions of dollars, and a thriving import business. Her mother didn't receive half as much. "It was her family inheritance that started your business and bought the estate," Elaina said. "Daddy, please don't let that worry you now. N–not now," she choked over the last words and wiped her clammy hand along the side of her walking shorts. All at once the will's unfairness meant nothing to her.

"Do you—do you remember what I told you about the private account for your—for your mother—where it is and how to get to it…and what—what lawyer to use in case…so no one will…"

"Y–yes." Elaina sniffled. She had tried to resist her father's information last year because she dreaded the thought of his death. Elaina stroked the gray wisp of straw-like hair near his temple and bit back a sob.

"I told—I told Jake about it all…all…and that—that he needs to—to make sure Margaret and—and you and—and Anna are taken care of."

"But I don't need anyone to take care of me."

"He—he promised. He promised to do—do more than the will ev–even. But I don't trust—" A gurgled cough wracked his body, and his hospital gown sagged across his shoulder. "I don't trust *her*," he finished.

She understood all too well who he referred to. Her half-brother's wife, Faye, had proven her self-interest far out of balance. Fifteen years ago, Joseph predicted as much when his son announced their engagement. But Jake declared that his mother and her best friend had paired him and Faye from their childhoods. He would honor his mom's wishes and marry the woman she had chosen for him. Of course, Faye's huge inheritance hadn't hurt her appeal. Elaina suspected Jake's love of money had demanded he turn a blind eye to his wife's antics.

Elaina comprehended her father's worries all too well. Once Faye learned that there was $500,000 in an account that her husband wasn't allowed to touch, she would probably explode into a screaming fit—despite the fact that Jake would be a millionaire at his father's death.

"M–make sure your mother gets all—gets all of her things out of the house." Joseph kneaded the covers. "And—and the money. I won't be here to fight for her. And she—she won't fight for herself."

"I'll stand up for her, Daddy," Elaina promised, and straightened. "I'll do it for you."

The faint squeeze on her hand sealed the deal. "I…I love you," Joseph whispered. His dimming gray eyes took on the glimmer of fond memories too poignant for words.

"I love you, too, Daddy," Elaina squeaked and released his hand. She pretended to fuss with his IV pole in order to hide the tears that slipped beside her nose and pooled at the corners of her mouth.

"Anna," he whispered, confirming Elaina's suspicion that he'd ask for his youngest daughter next.

Elaina clamped her teeth together in an attempt to stifle the evidence of her grief. The sob leaked out anyway. She yanked off her narrow-framed glasses, snatched a tissue from the sink counter, and jabbed at the hot tears.

"Don't—don't cry for me, 'Laina," Joseph encouraged, his voice a mere echo from a distant land. "I've seen the city. It's so… so beautiful."

Two

"I believe that concludes the course overview. Before we go further, does anyone have any questions?" Elaina skimmed her syllabus one last time and laid it on the lectern.

The class of 23 graduate students eyed the taxing schedule as if they were entering academic death valley. Elaina resisted a smile. No one had ever let her off easy when she was pursuing higher education. She saw no reason to lower the standard.

The sight of the austere room painted "college eggshell," along with the smells of chalk and ink and notebooks, only heightened the heady sense of accomplishment this first week of school had ushered in. With professional flair, she straightened her knit pantsuit's jacket and thought, *Finally! I'm a professor!*

Southern Christian University consisted of only a thousand students, which meant a tight-knit literature department and opportunities for Elaina that wouldn't have come so soon at a larger university. Already, the seasoned staff had been more than welcoming and gracious to the "new kid" on board. Several times today, Elaina had been struck with how proud her father would have been of her. During those minutes, she was hard pressed to believe he died two months ago. She shoved aside that forlorn day and all the family and financial complications it had ushered in, including the vulture's gleam in her sister-in-law's eyes.

"Okay, if no one has questions," Elaina looked at her gold watch, "we have an hour left of this class. Since we meet only once-a-week, we need to go ahead and begin our first lecture. It will be an introduction and overview to the English Romantics, which is, of course, early nineteenth century lit. You'll need to have the first reading assignment finished before next class. Next week we'll be getting down to specifics."

"Excuse me, Dr. Woods?" A man in the back of the room raised his hand.

Elaina nodded toward him. "Yes, Mister…" she paused long enough to bring his name to the front of her memory. This was her third class today, and she had yet to get a name right. "Mr. Farris," she concluded with a sheepish smile. "That's Ted Farris. Am I correct?"

"Correct." He leaned to one side and offered Elaina a better view of him. Ted Farris was several years older than most of the students in the class. He looked closer to 30 than 25, and he seemed oblivious to the fact that several of the younger women had intermittently investigated the "more mature guy in the back of the room." Dressed in a pair of classic worn jeans, a striped cotton shirt, and a pair of new Reeboks, he wasn't the most handsome man Elaina had ever met; but he was the only person whose name she'd remembered all day. While Ted's respectful smile suggested he was a perfect gentleman, there was an air of resigned desperation in his brown gaze that reminded Elaina of a tortured artist.

Despite her bent to the practical, Elaina had always loved the tortured artist appeal—right down to Ted's prominent chin and dark, shoulder-length hair slicked into a ponytail.

"I was just wondering about the due date on the first research paper," Ted continued. "It says April third."

"What?" Elaina grabbed her syllabus, adjusted her glasses, and scanned the top lines.

"I'll take that due date," a young lady quipped from the front row.

The rest of the students chuckled.

"In your dreams," Elaina challenged with a good-natured smile. "That is supposed to be October third. Sorry. I typed this up last night at midnight." She started to explain the reason she'd been so pressed for time—that she'd been helping her mother make arrangements to move from Oklahoma City to Lakeland. Margaret Woods had just wrapped up the purchase of a small cottage from her first cousin, Jeanna Harley. The home proved perfect because it was only 15 minutes from Elaina's new apartment, and it gave her mom and sister the benefit of living near relatives on their family estate. Elaina would be helping with the move this weekend.

After deciding not to bore the class with the details of her life, she offered an assuring smile to Mr. Farris. "Thanks for catching my error," she said. "Here's hoping you don't make as big a blunder on your paper. The outcome would probably *not* be pretty," she teased.

"Ouch!" a guy groaned from the next row over. "This is going to be a killer class," he mumbled, and Elaina figured he hadn't intended for her to hear.

"I promise all my papers will be flawless," Ted Farris claimed.

"Yeah, right," someone responded, and the class enjoyed another round of mirth.

All the while, Ted observed Elaina as if they'd bumped into each other in a crowded room and he was about to ask, "Haven't I met you somewhere before?"

A wisp of recognition tickled the back of Elaina's mind, and she wondered if they really had encountered each other at some point. She also entertained the idea that they might relish encountering each other in the future. Discreetly she checked Ted's left hand. No wedding band in sight. A troublesome passage from the employee handbook flopped into the center of her mind…something about not fraternizing with students. A flutter of caution demanded she focus on the task at hand.

Without further consideration of Ted and his ringless finger, Elaina jumped into the lecture with precision and zeal. Halfway through, three of the students stopped taking notes, and she figured she wouldn't see them back. By the time nine o'clock arrived, she had wrapped up her closing remarks and dismissed the class. As she was gathering her notes and portfolio from the desk, a student textbook slid into her line of vision. Elaina glanced up to encounter the man attached to the book—Ted Farris, his dark eyes glimmering with realization.

"It took me the whole class, but I finally figured out why I know you," he said.

A trio of young women walking toward the door cast an envious glance toward Elaina as if they'd be thrilled for Ted to use that line on them.

For a second Elaina wondered if he really *were* using a line. But the earnestness of his gaze belied her assumption.

"Oh really? Where?" She gathered the portfolio into her arms and tried to maintain as professional a distance as possible.

"You're my brother-in-law's sister, aren't you? My sister is Faye Woods. She's married to your brother, Jake. Am I right?"

Her mouth fell open. She forgot all about professional distance in the wake of trying to squelch the irritation at the mention of her sister-in-law. The last two months had *not* been pleasant. Elaina wouldn't be surprised if Faye secretively arranged a yard sale in her mother's absence to dispose of all her household treasures—right down to the fine china. The vixen had been trying to force Margaret Woods out of the mansion for the last month.

Elaina masked all hint of disdain before finally answering, "Yes. You're exactly right. My brother is Jake. And Faye's maiden name is Farris. I should have made the connection," she continued and wondered if Ted Farris was as greedy and manipulative as his sister. She deposited her portfolio on the desk and sharply assessed the man. What she encountered was nothing but honesty and an ocean of the silent despair she'd noticed from across the room.

The tortured artist, she thought again. This time the turn of phrase brought snatches of lines from Poe and Coleridge and Blake, and she wondered if Mr. Ted Farris hid a wealth of brilliant prose or poetry in a remote closet of his home. In the middle of Elaina's grandiose literary musings, a misty memory swam into her mind. She recalled a lanky adolescent whom she and her friend had giggled about during her brother's wedding reception. The two 12-year-old girls had dubbed Ted cute. This evening, the word cute didn't do him justice.

She squinted and tilted her head. "Did you and I meet at Faye and Jake's wedding?"

"As a matter of fact, I believe we did." Ted nodded his head.

"But that was 15 years ago!" Elaina claimed. "I can't believe you remembered me from all that time ago. I was only 12!" She resisted the urge to remove her dark-rimmed glasses. Her father always told her and her sister that blue-eyed girls were his favorites. Maybe Ted would feel the same—if he could better see her eyes. A no-nonsense voice reminded her that she shouldn't care whether Ted appreciated her blue eyes *or* her bobbed red hair.

"Well, my brother-in-law has your family photo hanging in his office," Ted admitted. "I've seen it a few times." He shrugged. "It's harder to believe that you would actually remember seeing me at the wedding. I was only 15," Ted said. "Hopefully, I've changed since then." He rubbed the side of his shaven jaw, and Elaina stopped herself from blurting that all changes had been for the better—right down to the sideburns and broadened shoulders.

"But how could I forget?" she said instead. "Remember at the reception? You dumped your cake in my lap."

"Yes." He pointed at her and laughed. "And when you stood up, you spilled your punch down the front of my suit."

Elaina covered her mouth and felt like an embarrassed 12-year-old all over again. She and her friend had both been mortified that Elaina doused the best-looking guy there. "Oh my word!" she exclaimed. "Yes, I remember! And your suit was white, wasn't it?"

"Yes, I was an usher!" he claimed. "Actually, I turned out to be a *pink* usher! I'm just glad all that happened *after* the wedding."

Elaina shook her head and said, "I am *so* sorry!" as if she'd just baptized him in pink.

"It's okay." He shrugged. "The suit doesn't fit anymore anyway."

"Well, for all that's worth, neither does the dress you spilled cake on."

"And wasn't the cake chocolate?"

"Yes, it was." Elaina paused as the memory continued to unfold. "Didn't you keep wiping at my sleeve and licking the icing off your fingers or something?"

"Oh my." With a groan, he stroked a sideburn. "I honestly forgot that part."

"Seems like you said something like, 'No use wasting perfectly good cake.'"

"Now you're starting to tell lies on me," Ted claimed and leaned toward her, his face alight with hilarity.

"Not on your life," she shot back. "I remember like it was yesterday." Their chortles mingled as one.

Elaina couldn't deny that she would have liked to move a little closer to Ted and the sweet memories they shared. Instead, she leaned away and reminded herself that Ted Farris was her *student*. She discovered some stray copies of her syllabus and made a major task of placing them inside her neatly organized portfolio. As the seconds ticked on, Elaina gathered her things and turned toward the doorway. Ted stepped in beside her, as if he planned to continue their conversation. Immediately she sensed that if they'd been in seventh grade he would have offered to carry her books. But that didn't quite fit the professor–student scenario.

As they exited the room, the klatch of young women who'd enviously eyed Elaina pointedly noticed that their professor was leaving the room with Ted. She considered shriveling into the short-piled carpet but decided to hold her head high instead. Elaina had nothing to hide and refused to be intimidated by her own students.

Ted eyed Elaina and wondered how he'd managed to choose the prettiest professor on campus for his final class. On top of all that, they had mutual relatives they could freely discuss while he admired the woman he'd once mopped chocolate icing off of. He sensed that Elaina might have let herself enjoy their conversation a little more than professional etiquette allowed. In the room, when she pulled away from him and picked up her portfolio, Ted took the opportunity to remind himself that he was an engaged man. For whatever it was worth, he and Lorna would get married this time. No more turning back—regardless of the fact that he wasn't in love with her and never had been.

Despite his relationship with Lorna, there was no harm in chatting with a relative of a relative—especially one as attractive as Dr. Elaina Woods. As things stood, they were nearly related; it would be rude not to be as nice as possible.

While they walked down the hallway together, Ted debated how best to extend his apologies for her father's recent death. Finally he blurted what was on his mind. "I was really sorry to hear about your father." He turned toward her as they continued their trek down the hallway.

"Thank you," Elaina responded and looked up with a hint of warm appreciation. "I guess I knew Daddy couldn't live forever, but it's always such a shock."

"Yes. My dad was killed in a boating accident three years ago."

"Yes, I remember Jake being really disturbed. He admired your father," Elaina said with a hint of empathy.

"None of us were expecting that one. He was only sixty." Ted shifted his books to his other arm.

"My dad was seventy-seven." Her coppery hair swung forward to hide Elaina's features, but the tremor in her voice suggested her eyes were misty.

Ted decided a subject change might be in order. He wouldn't dare mention his next thought—that from his viewpoint his sister had been a little too eager to settle the estate. He'd heard his mother on the phone with her daughter several times over the last two months. While Ted's late father would have called his mom's advice "taking care of business," Ted thought her guidance was more avarice than good business tactics. Thoughts of his mother and Faye nearly made Ted wince.

Oh well, he thought as they approached the student lounge near the professor's offices, *when I announce my engagement to Lorna, Mom and Faye will probably both disown me. Then I won't have to worry about what they're doing with anyone's money ever again.* Meanwhile, Ted needed to stay in his mother's good graces—at least until he wrapped up this second master's degree. Then he planned to escape from the cage of control in which she'd kept him locked his whole life. He'd finally gotten to the point of wanting his freedom more than the millions he'd inherit were he to continue as his mother's lapdog.

"So is this your first professorship?" Ted asked. "You really don't look old enough to be a prof."

Elaina looked down as if she were trying to hide her smile. "That's exactly what I wondered if everyone would think," she replied and tucked her bobbed hair behind her ear. "And, yes, this is my first position. I just wrapped up my doctorate in May—a month after I turned twenty-seven."

"Oh, I remember twenty-seven," Ted teased, "in the far, distant past."

The corners of her mouth quivered, but no smile arrived. "You're not *that* old," she claimed.

"Actually, I'll be thirty-one in December," Ted said, wondering if Elaina were always so controlled. "So I guess I really don't have too many years on you. Faye is actually thirteen years older than I am."

"Jake is eighteen years older than I," Elaina said.

"Does he still try to boss you around like you were a kid?"

Elaina shrugged. "Not really. He was on his way to college by the time I was born. We aren't very close and never have been." She turned her attention to Ted and then looked away again, as if she might have continued but chose to halt. Ted had listened to his sister complain enough about Jake's stepmother and half-sisters to suspect there must be friction on both sides of that relationship.

Ted attempted to detect a whiff of some perfume Elaina might be wearing. His efforts weren't rewarded, and he wondered if she might think such indulgences weren't practical for a new professor. An unexpected fantasy unfolded within Ted, and he imagined offering her a tiny bottle of Eternity perfume—his favorite—on their first date. Ironically, Eternity made Lorna sneeze.

He grimaced and wondered if he were testing fate by being so chummy with this new prof. Whether she was a near-relative or not, she was an attractive, single female. Ted wasn't above temptation. Nobody had ever told him that being engaged could be such a lonely experience.

"There she is!" a young woman yelped. "Elaina! We're over here."

Ted glanced toward the voice to see a blue-eyed, dark-haired female who looked to be sixteen. Like Elaina, Ted recognized her from the family portrait in his brother-in-law's home office. The silver-haired woman sitting nearby resembled Elaina and her sister—both in the contour of her face and the attention to stylish clothing. Vigorously, Elaina's sister waved as Mrs. Woods laid her open magazine on the couch cushion and prepared to stand.

"Hello, you two," Elaina said. "I wasn't expecting you here." She hurried past a potted palm tree and around a pair of chairs as her relatives stood. Ted saw no reason to avoid a family introduction, so he followed close behind Elaina.

"What are you doing here?" Elaina questioned as her sister eyed Ted with enough speculation for three women. "I thought you were going to be waiting on me at home."

"Well, we've got some good news and some bad news," Mrs. Woods said. She, too, curiously observed Ted and then looked back at her daughter with deflated resignation. "I finally got 'the phone call.'" She used her fingers to draw imaginary quote marks in mid-air. "So which news do you want first?" she continued, and a sixth sense told Ted the bad news might involve his sister.

Three

"Oh, first let me introduce my new friend...uh...one of my students," Elaina rushed before her mother blurted out any information that might incriminate Ted's relatives. Neither her mother nor sister had ever been as discreet as Elaina preferred.

Earlier today Margaret had reported that she received a voice mail from Faye after lunch. Elaina's sister-in-law claimed the message was urgent, but when Margaret attempted to return the call all she got was Faye's voice mail. The exasperation oozing from Margaret convinced Elaina that the phone call was indeed from her daughter-in-law.

Anna stepped forward and extended her hand toward Ted. "Hi, I'm Anna Woods," she said and smiled at him with the artless grace of an adolescent. But the truth was, Anna had turned twenty-two a month ago. Nevertheless, with her straight, dark hair and hip-hugger jeans, she still managed to attract as many high school guys as men her own age. The way she was looking at Ted, Elaina wondered if she might be finally maturing enough to appreciate the stability of an older man.

"Pleased to meet you, Anna," Ted said. "I'm Ted Farris. Your sister-in-law's brother."

Elaina widened her eyes at her mother and mimicked turning a lock on her lips as Ted repeated the handshake with Margaret.

"Oh...oh...well, hello!" Margaret exclaimed as she pumped Ted's hand. "It's good to meet you." She fidgeted with the reading glasses hanging from her neck by a thin silver chain. "I guess we've probably met in passing a couple of times through the years," she babbled as if she didn't quite know how to make room in her mind for bad news involving Faye and the introduction of Faye's brother.

"Ted is taking one of my classes," Elaina explained. "We met as a result of a botched date in my syllabus."

"Yes," Ted added, "I didn't put two and two together until the end of class. I just kept thinking that Dr. Woods looked *so* familiar."

"Just call her Elaina, dear." Margaret patted Ted on the arm with the familiarity of a long-time friend. "I almost can't stand hearing her referred to as Dr. Woods." She wrinkled her nose as if Elaina's title were the bane of her existence. "She still ought to be in pigtails as far as I'm concerned."

"Oh, Mom," Elaina complained and touched her temple. "I haven't worn pigtails in twenty years."

The group indulged in laughter. Soon Ted cast a questioning gaze toward his latest acquaintance, as if silently asking permission to follow Margaret's advice and drop the title.

While debating her options, Elaina decided to have a chat with her mother. She couldn't make a habit of dissolving professional convention between her and her students. But Ted Farris was practically a family member. Not granting his request would seem rude.

"Please *do* call me Elaina," she offered, "except when we're in class."

"Sure, no problem." Ted nodded as if he fully understood.

"You know," Anna said. "I think I might have heard Faye mention you not long ago. Are you the brother who is the pianist or is that your brother?"

"No, that would be me," Ted acquiesced with a hint of a shy smile. "Robert is my elder brother. He took over my father's aviation business when Dad passed away a few years back. He couldn't find middle C if it bit him, and I couldn't fly a plane if my life depended on it."

"So..." a simmering excitement sparkled in Anna's eyes. "Are you the one who played the piano in Washington D.C.?"

"Yes." Ted glanced at his feet and touched the tip of his sideburn with slender fingers that Elaina imagined merging with a keyboard. She pictured him wearing an exquisite black tuxedo. Ted's slicked back hair hung in a simple ponytail at his neckline and added a debonair dash to the whole suit. The man walked onto a massive stage, settled upon the bench of a lacquered grand piano, found her in the audience, and offered a flirtatious wink. Then a rapt audience held its breath as he stormed the piano.

The whole scenario proved a little too appealing for Elaina's wayward pulse. That annoying section in the employee handbook resurrected itself anew. "Did you play for a political event?" Elaina asked and was ready to predict this might be a long semester.

"A political event!" Anna snorted. "He played for the president of the United States—and got a return invitation last spring!" She eyed Elaina and added a silent, *How could you be so dense?*

"Well, how was I supposed to know?" Elaina defended.

"Don't feel left out." Ted rested his hand on Elaina's shoulder. "Faye never once offered to introduce me to you all, and I would have insisted years ago had I realized what a captivating group of ladies I was missing out on." Elaina would have wondered again if Ted were using a line on her if he hadn't included Anna and her mother in the compliment.

Margaret Woods looped her fingers around Ted's arm, and Elaina assumed her mother nearly started purring. "We were just going downstairs. Would you like to walk down with us?" she questioned. "Maybe we even have time to grab a soda somewhere before we leave town."

"Sure!" Ted agreed.

Elaina blinked. *Leave town?* she thought. There had been no plans for her mother to leave town tonight. *I wonder if this has something to do with Faye's phone call.* Elaina's head threatened to start hurting. The faint scent of popcorn floating from the employee lounge did little to assuage her tension.

Anna grabbed Ted's other arm while Elaina stepped aside. Her mom and sister began walking Ted toward the elevators as if he were the most scrumptious morsel they had encountered in years. Briefly Elaina wondered if the two of them had decided to just take him out of town with them.

"I know why Faye hasn't introduced us," Margaret's claim mingled with the elevator's ding. "You're so delightful, she wanted to keep you all to herself!" The door sighed open and the trio stepped inside.

"Don't mind me," Elaina mumbled and noted that both her sister and mother had left their purses where they were sitting. "Figures," she said as the elevator door shut behind them. There were days when Elaina felt like her mom and Anna were the most absent-minded people on the planet. Presently Elaina debated if her mom and sister had forgotten they were even waiting on her.

Elaina adjusted the weight of her portfolio, retrieved the purses, and moved toward her office. The mellow smell of popcorn grew more intense as she rounded the corner to enter the office alcove. She had been involved with her colleagues long enough to assume that Dr. Cecilia Johnson was indulging in her usual weakness of double-butter microwave popcorn and a Diet Coke. Like Elaina, Cecilia was young and single. The two were forming a new friendship. They had discovered many similar interests—including the popcorn and Caffeine-free Diet Coke. The professors lounge was well-stocked with both treats. Given the stress of Faye's looming demands, Elaina wouldn't mind munching away her tension. She dismissed the idea.

"No time," she stated as thoughts of Faye evolved into thoughts of Faye's brother. Images of Ted reminded Elaina that her mother and sister had just stolen him from right under her nose.

Well! Elaina huffed to herself. *I guess that teaches me to think about tuxedoes and pianos and winks. Looks like the guy will be more interested in Anna than me.* She stepped into the small office that bore the title "Dr. Elaina Woods, Assistant Professor" on the frosted-glass window. After a swift glare at the title, Elaina's reasonable side insisted that Anna would by far be the best choice for Ted's interest. Despite the man's good looks and winning personality, Elaina refused to ponder frivolous romantic fantasies about a student—at least not for long, anyway.

With a determined thud, she placed her portfolio on the neat desktop and dropped the extra purses nearby. Elaina grabbed her purse from one of the bookshelves that lined the walls and double-checked a manila folder near her phone. The notes for the Advanced Composition class were still in place and ready for ten o'clock tomorrow morning. After that, she, her mother, and Anna planned to drive to Oklahoma City to spend the rest of the weekend packing and moving.

She reached for her mother and sister's purses and stopped. Margaret Woods had mentioned leaving town tonight instead of tomorrow, as planned. Elaina stared at her sister's Gucci handbag until it blurred. The pieces of the puzzle clicked into place. Her mother had received a phone call—most likely from Faye. Margaret mentioned some bad news she never told Elaina because of Ted's presence. On top of that, she was leaving town tonight. Elaina deduced that Faye had called and was making demands for her mother's imminent departure from the mansion that was no longer legally hers. So Margaret and Anna, as accommodating as ever, were undoubtedly rushing to Oklahoma City tonight to do whatever they must to keep Faye happy.

The purse came into sharp focus, and Elaina narrowed her eyes. She slung the strap of her practical sling purse upon her shoulder and snatched up the other two bags. She locked her office doorknob, slammed the door, and hurried up the hallway. Within seconds, she was rounding the corner near the elevator and nearly bumped into her mother.

"Oh!" Margaret exclaimed, her blue eyes round. "We left our purses up here!" She worriedly looked toward the student lounge. "I hope nobody got them."

Elaina lifted the purses. "Somebody did, and it was *me*," she said with an assuring smile.

Margaret placed her hand over her heart. "Oh my goodness," she breathed. "We were scared stiff that somebody might have taken them. What would I do without you?" she asked and took both purses from her daughter.

With a good-natured shrug, Elaina smiled. "I guess you'd be as lost as I would be without all those meals you spoil me with," she said as the elevator door sighed shut. "Are Anna and Ted still downstairs?"

"Yes. I left them talking." Margaret hung Anna's purse on her shoulder and began scratching through her leather bag. "He is *so nice*, Elaina." She pulled out a lipstick pouch and unzipped it. "Too bad Faye can't be as nice as he is."

Elaina stepped toward the elevator button and stopped before pressing it. "Speaking of the devil," she drawled, "I'm assuming the phone call you got was from her? And you're leaving town tonight instead of tomorrow because Faye wants your things out of the house ASAP. Am I right?"

Margaret, posed with a pink lipstick inches from her mouth, peered at Elaina as if she were awestruck. "How do you always do that, child?" she asked. "It never ceases to amaze me!" She shook her head. "You're just like your father, that's how," she answered herself.

"So I'm right?" Elaina repeated the question and didn't wait for an answer. "Mom, why do you always jump to her demands? Why didn't you *tell* her that we would be there tomorrow afternoon, *as planned*, and she could just cool it until we get there?"

A couple of male students walked toward the elevator, and Elaina stepped out of their way. Her mother followed, and Elaina detected a faint whiff of Opium perfume, her father's favorite. Thoughts of her dad heightened her determination to stand firm against Faye.

"Oh dear, I could *never* be so feisty," Margaret claimed.

"Why not?" Elaina crossed her arms.

"Because it would make her and Jake both mad, and I want as much peace as possible. Faye wasn't really mean about any of this." Margaret waved the lipstick as if it were a director's baton. "She just requested that we get started as early in the morning as possible instead of waiting until the afternoon. She's going to be doing some remodeling, and the workers need to do some measuring. She wants at least the den free of furniture by noon. I don't see anything too terribly unreasonable about all this."

Unless you count the fact that Faye and Jake promised they wouldn't rush us. Elaina tapped her toe as her mother slathered on a layer of the lipstick that matched her blouse. "So was this the good news or the bad news?" Elaina questioned.

"I guess that's *part* of the bad news," Margaret said and rolled down the lipstick. "The good news is that my cousin Jeanna called today and said that she and Noah discussed it and have decided to put a new roof on the cottage for us. Isn't that delightful? I was all set to call the roofers Monday, but they're going to take care of it."

"Great!" Elaina shook her head and smiled. "I always liked her! I think she and Noah are going to make great neighbors."

"Yes," Margaret popped the gold lid back on the lipstick and dropped it into the pouch, "and the more I think of it, the more I think this little two-story cottage is going to suit Anna and me *so* much better than that three-story elephant of a house!" She zipped the pouch, placed it back into her purse, and secured the flap.

Elaina patted her mother's shoulder. "Leave it to you, Mom, to always find the bright side of every situation—even being booted out of your own home."

"Don't put it like that," Margaret pleaded. "I knew when I married your father chances were high this would happen one day. I went in with my eyes open. He was a man of his word, and I didn't expect him to break it for me." She looked across the lobby, as if talking to one of the artificial palm trees. "Besides all that, he provided for me nicely. Five hundred grand is not anything to sneeze at. I'll invest it, and I won't starve by any means." Margaret's eyes grew red, and Elaina regretted having pushed the issue.

"Was there any other bad news?" she asked as gently as she could. While Elaina hadn't planned this conversation taking place by the elevator, she needed the information and certainly didn't want to discuss it in front of Ted.

"Oh…" Margaret tugged on a curly strand at the base of her neck. "I almost hate to bring it up now."

Elaina's headache would no longer be denied. It erupted with a vengeful thud in her temples. She narrowed her eyes and cautiously posed her next question, the question she knew she would eventually have to ask. "Is Faye trying to cheat you out of something?"

"She wants the Renaissance furniture." Margaret fidgeted with her reading glasses' silver chain.

"What!" Elaina erupted and then covered her mouth with her fingertips. She looked across the lobby. Only a handful of students remained at a corner table, and they were so focused on their notes they never wavered from their scholarly pursuits.

Margaret nodded, and her blue eyes took on the pathetic defeat of a resigned victim too fearful to press for what was rightfully hers. "She has offered to pay for it, but—"

"Let me guess…at half the value?" Elaina questioned, determined to keep her voice void of any more unseemly displays of emotion.

"At about two-thirds of what Joseph paid for it. She claims its value has gone down since we've used it."

Elaina stifled a caustic laugh. "Yeah, you and a whole bunch of other people in the last 400 years. Mom, you and she both know that's not true."

"I know," Margaret worried.

"You *did* tell her you weren't interested in selling, didn't you?" Elaina checked her watched and noted that it was nearly nine-twenty. She didn't relish the idea of her mother driving so late in the evening.

"I told her I'd think about it," Margaret answered.

"Are you serious?" Elaina asked. "You don't want to sell it, do you? I mean, Dad bought that whole room full of furniture for you for your twentieth anniversary. What about that table that belonged to Queen Anne herself? Some of those pieces are one-of-a-kind. You can't replace them."

"Yes, you're right!" Margaret rose to her full height, and Elaina recognized a spark of determination that made her hopes soar.

"You need to tell Faye that is *your* furniture, and that it perfectly fits the decor of your new home. As a matter of fact," Elaina tugged on the collar of her jacket, "why don't we tell the movers to load those pieces first. I want to make sure one of them doesn't mysteriously come up missing."

"Okay," Margaret slung her purse strap onto her shoulder along with Anna's purse. "And what time did you say you'll be there tomorrow?" she questioned with a worried undertow to her words.

"I should be there no later than one o'clock," Elaina said, infusing extra assurance into every word. This was not the time for her mother to grow weak and crumple under pressure. "Would you please do me a huge favor until I get there?"

"Sure." Margaret nodded.

"If Faye tries to get pushy about the furniture—or anything else for that matter—would you tell her you'd like to talk to me about it first? That way, you will have some time to think and make up your mind. So whatever you do decide, it will be what you really want." Along with the dull thud in her head, the balls of Elaina's feet began to ache. She reminded herself never again to wear such tall heels to teach in.

"I think that will work!" Margaret squared her shoulders and showed a renewed hint of spunk.

"Good." Elaina reached to press the elevator button, only to have the button light up as the elevator dinged. Half expecting Anna and Ted to be inside, she checked her watch again. When the doors wheezed open, Anna and Ted were indeed on the lift.

"What's going on?" Anna questioned as she and her companion stepped into the lobby. Her dark hair swayed with the rhythm of every move. "Did you find our purses?" She worriedly glanced toward the chairs they had vacated.

"Yes." Margaret fumbled with the straps on her shoulder and extended Anna's purse. "Elaina got them for us."

"Oh good." Anna covered her heart with her flattened hand. A gold band with a tiny row of diamonds twinkled in the room's recessed lighting. Elaina used her thumb to stroke the band of a similar ring on her own finger. Their parents had given each of them a ring the year they graduated from junior high. With the bands, they asked that their daughters take a vow of purity. Now the gift was more precious than ever.

"When the two of you didn't come right down," Anna continued, "I was scared someone had stolen them."

"We just got caught up in discussing some family business," Elaina claimed and shot an apologetic glance toward Ted. "Sorry for the delay."

"Oh, that's perfectly fine," Ted said, no hint of irritation in his dark-brown eyes. "Anna and I were just talking about the move this weekend, and—"

"Ted has offered to help us!" Anna, giggling with delight, grabbed Ted's arm as if the two of them were already a pair. "Isn't that just the coolest?"

Elaina refused to allow her mouth to drop open. Instead she schooled her features into a pleasant yet bland expression and said, "What a wonderful gesture."

"The only problem I have," Ted continued, "is that my Corvette is in the shop."

"I offered to have him ride down tonight with Mom and me, but there's so many reasons that won't work." Anna wiggled her fingers as if she expected everyone to fill in the blanks. "One of them is Ted's schedule."

"Well, I think it was wonderfully gallant of you to offer," Margaret said and smiled at Ted with enough warmth to melt a candle.

The four of them walked into the elevator. As Elaina pressed the button for the first floor, she imagined what a weekend with Ted around would have been like. Elaina stole a glance at his profile. His slender, straight nose and the kind tilt of his lips hinted at the artist's heart beating within the man. *At least the scenery would have been greatly improved,* she thought with an impish, inward laugh.

"Oh!" Anna placed her palm against her forehead. "I just had a great idea!" She looked at Ted and then Elaina. "Why don't we just get Ted to ride to Oklahoma City with you tomorrow, Elaina? Don't you think that would work out?" she rushed. "And then he can ride back to Lakeland with you Sunday afternoon."

Ted's eyes widened, and a faint flush tinged his tan. He cast a dubious glance toward Elaina that said, "I had no idea she was going to say that."

With an unexpected surge of anticipation, Elaina imagined two hours alone in her Honda with Ted Farris. *Don't forget! He's your student!* she reminded herself and then decided that would only be until December. While Elaina had never been one to entertain illogical fantasies concerning the opposite sex, she knew herself well. She couldn't deny that she had already experienced enough sparks with Ted to create a slow-burning blaze. That flame could easily become an inferno by the semester's end

While Elaina had never been a believer in love at first sight, she would never again doubt a woman who claimed an instant attraction to a man. Despite her rationale that Ted would be more appropriate for Anna, Elaina could not dispute that he was *her type*—right down to the slender fingers that must possess some magic when they caressed a keyboard. The idea of Anna and Ted as a couple now struck her as the oddest match of the century.

When Elaina refocused upon the conversation at hand, her mother was saying, "I agree, Anna. That's a perfectly wonderful idea." Margaret's cheeks glowed with expectation. "And then we could all get to know one another so much better." She eyed Elaina with enough encouragement for a dozen matchmakers.

"That's fine with me," Elaina said and offered Ted a reassuring smile she hoped encouraged familial friendship and nothing else. The last thing she needed to do was come across like a man-chaser—especially since she *was* his prof…and the teacher handbook hadn't changed in the last hour. "I'm always game for somebody to talk to on a drive. I get bored by myself," she claimed with as much nonchalance as she could muster.

"You know, I guess I could always rent a car," Ted said and touched his temple with his index finger. "Oh, duh! I didn't even think of that until now."

"No, no—oh no," Margaret said and patted his arm. "Now that we've found you, we wouldn't dare allow you to do such a thing. We're family, right?" She looped her fingers around the crook of his arm. "We must take care of each other." Margaret leaned behind Ted and directed a discreet wink at Elaina.

Four

By twelve-thirty the next afternoon, Elaina understood what it meant to be charmed all the way to her toenails. Ted Farris proved to be a more pleasing male companion than any Elaina had ever encountered. Her commitment to academic achievement had left little time for the opposite sex. None of the few gentlemen Elaina had fancied herself attracted to even touched the thrill she enjoyed in Ted's company. All morning she anticipated picking him up at his apartment, only six blocks from her duplex. Now, with the family estate thirty minutes away, Elaina whimsically wished they had all afternoon to drive.

"I still can't believe your sister is twenty-two!" Ted said as Elaina slowed for merging traffic. "I promise, last night I thought she was sixteen. I was thinking that biologically I was nearly old enough to be her father!"

"A lot of people think she's way younger than she is," Elaina asserted and glanced toward the passenger seat. Ted claimed his side of the car like a prince sitting on his throne. With his sleek, dark ponytail and thick brows, the man certainly had presence. She reveled in knowing that Ted wasn't interested in her younger sister, who was by far more beautiful than Elaina—by her estimation anyway.

"Some of the people who think Anna is so much younger are male and eighteen," Elaina added as a string of cars whizzed past them in the left lane. She reset her cruise control and didn't budge off of seventy.

"Yes, I can see that happening," Ted said, and Elaina sensed his appraisal. "I guess you and she both were blessed with young looks."

"Let's just hope you didn't think you were nearly old enough to be *my* father," she said and kept her attention firmly on the white stripes as they slipped by.

"That's the *last* thing I was thinking," Ted admitted. "Actually, when I figured out who you were, I was trying to decide how my brother-in-law could be so average-looking and have a sister who is so—" He stopped and cleared his throat.

The unspoken compliment hung between them like a sizzling prediction of their future relationship. Elaina upped the air conditioner a notch and then clutched the floor gearshift until her palm protested. Who knew what kind of aftershave the guy put on before settling into her car. Elaina had never been a connoisseur of fine fragrances, but this woodsy scent plus Ted's appreciative attitude proved quite distracting. The Honda's perpetual purr seemed to insist that Ted's growing regard went deeper than just friendship…and transcended that of a student trying to schmooze his professor.

Elaina stared straight ahead into the cloudless horizon and didn't quite know what to do or say. She rubbed her hand along her knit slacks and picked up the conversation where it seemed safe. "Maybe my youthful looks will be a blessing when I'm forty-five," she babbled, "but right now, it can be annoying. I believe I was slighted at a few job interviews before I got the position at SCU. One university wound up hiring a woman with gray in her hair and the other one hired a man who really *could* have been my father."

"Do you think some of the reason they hired the others might have involved their experience?" Ted asked, his voice now void of the "admiring male" inflection.

Elaina shrugged and relaxed a bit. "I'm sure. But, as things turned out, I guess the Lord knew what He was doing. So far, I'm thrilled to be at SCU. The staff is great and super supportive. Nobody has even once made an issue of my youth. They've all had a very professional attitude." Elaina clicked on her left blinker and accelerated around a lumber truck.

"Well, I'm wrapping up my final class there, and I'll be glad to get it over with." Ted hesitated and then continued, his voice mellow with humor. "I think the professor I've got in this Romantics class is going to be as tough as nails, though. She's new and I'm afraid her mind is too fresh for any of us to pull any tricks on her."

"Ooh, she sounds wicked." Elaina dashed a sly grin his way. "What's her name?"

"Dr. Elaina Woods. Ever heard of her?" While Ted's impassive face suggested he was serious, his merry eyes denoted a sense of humor hard at work.

"No, never," Elaina said. "But she certainly *sounds* mean." She adjusted her glasses. "Probably wears glasses an inch thick so she can see all the way to the bottom of your brain."

"Yes. You've pegged her perfectly. And she's got these blue eyes that will pierce you to the bone! One of the guys in the class even said he heard she's so dedicated to her job she sleeps in her office."

"If I were you, I'd do my best to butter her up. Maybe she'd give you a good grade for your charm alone." She pressed her thumbnail into the steering wheel and wondered where that little flirtatious ditty came from.

"Nah, not me," Ted claimed. Elaina sneaked a peak toward him as he shifted his weight and crossed his arms. "I'll work hard for my grades and let her decide what it's worth."

"Hmmm, good game plan." She cut him another smile and stopped herself short of winking. Things were warming up between them…and fast. Presently, there was no trace of casual friendship from Ted Farris—only the fervent intensity of appreciative brown eyes.

"Are you planning to go on for a Ph.D. yourself?" Elaina squeaked out and cleared her throat in an attempt to cover her increasing amazement. Never had she been so distracted with a man—and certainly not so soon into an acquaintance.

"No way," Ted answered as if she'd asked him to walk into a cloud of killer bees. He grabbed the neck of his stone-washed shirt and fanned his chin. "Let's don't *even* go there," he said. "This is actually my second master's degree. I'm stopping here—no matter what!"

"And the first one was in?" Elaina purposed to keep her attention upon the highway that cut through miles and miles of wide-open prairie.

"Piano performance."

"Ah, makes sense." She nodded and hoped she didn't sound like a seventh-grader with her first crush. Elaina thought back to her brother's wedding. She wondered what Ted would think if he knew she'd watched him the whole reception and prayed he'd talk to her. Three months ago, she would have dubbed such reminiscing as childhood foolishness. Now Elaina could only wonder if she had sensed the chemistry between them even as a youth.

A growing sense of nervous anticipation crept through her veins. The weekend stretched forth like a vast unknown, full of all sorts of unspoken surprises. With the press of a button, she turned on her radio and welcomed the instrumental pop music that was her constant road companion. However, the tunes produced the opposite effect of what Elaina had hoped. Instead of taking her mind off of the masculine entity in her passenger seat, the music enticed her to imagine the two of them twirling across a ballroom like the hero and heroine from a fairytale.

Elaina gripped the steering wheel and commanded herself to stop thinking like Anna. This was the twenty-first century. She was a mature woman. There were no such things as fairytale princesses—not in the real world.

"And you really played for the president?" she asked, forcing her voice into an even tenor.

"Yes, I guess I did," he said, his mellow tones full of mirth.

Elaina eyed him and discovered he was smiling, just as she'd predicted. "What?" she asked.

"I was just thinking of you and Anna last night," he said. "When you asked about my playing for a political event, your sister acted like she thought you'd had your head stuck in a book one day too many."

She chuckled. "How close you are to the truth. She never made it past her second semester in college and thinks I'm just a dull, hopeless bookworm."

"I guess that's a matter of opinion," Ted answered without a hint of hesitation.

A delightful shimmer teased Elaina, and she wondered if Ted's words were purposefully weighted or if she were reading more into his every syllable than he ever intended. After searching for any distraction, she finally turned up the instrumental music—only to hear the first few measures of the classic ballad "I Only Have Eyes for You."

Oh great, she thought. *Before this song is over, I'll probably be watching Ted so much I'll have a wreck.* She reached to turn off the radio.

"Do you mind leaving that on?" he asked as his fingers wrapped around hers. "I have an arrangement of this tune. It's one of my favorite pop numbers."

Her focus rested upon a diamond ring claiming Ted's pinky. A golden lion head held a glistening stone in its open jaws. She'd seen a similar one upon Faye and wondered if it were a family signet. Elaina felt like that diamond—clutched in the jaws of an insane attraction. A ripple of apprehension replaced anticipation. She thought of the respectable people who had gone goofy over a person of the opposite sex and done something really stupid—

like jeopardizing a new professorship for the thrill of a romance with a student.

"Oh sure," Elaina finally answered and couldn't quite remember what she was agreeing to. As she pulled her hand from his, a clammy film covered her palms.

The song's mellifluous lyrics worked exactly as Elaina had suspected. By the time the final stanza was floating around the vehicle, she wondered if Ted had ever played that song for any other woman or if he one day might play it for her. Out of a desperate attempt to rein her mind back to the logical, Elaina decided to be as practical as possible in her next statement.

"So do you and your piano tour often?" she squeezed out and conjured a crazy mental image of Ted boarding a plane while dragging a grand piano with him. "I mean," she corrected, "do you go on tour to play the piano very often?"

"No," he said with an indulgent nuance to his words. "I've only played where my mother or family have managed to book me. I've never gotten an agent or pushed for bookings."

"Your family has connections at the White House?" Her brows raised, Elaina darted him a glance.

"Well, yes. My elder brother, Robert—he's the one who took over the family aviation business when my father died—anyway, he has contacts with several political figures. My dad secured a contract with the government several years ago. We provide charter flights here, there, and everywhere for presidential cabinet members and all sorts of other important people. I guess it all boils down to who you know and all that. Anyway, the presidential team requested that I play for a banquet a year ago. Then they had me back last spring for a private party." He shrugged. "It's really not that big of a deal. They're just people like we are."

"Not that big of a deal?" Elaina wiggled her fingers. "I imagine there are pianists who'd give their fingertips for that chance."

"Maybe so. I guess I'd be lying if I said I didn't enjoy knowing that everyone—even the president—was very pleased. And it *was* an honor. But I think my mother and sister got a bigger charge out of it than I did. Sheesh! If they had their say, I'd be doing the international tour scene, playing for the Queen of England, recording a new CD every year, hiring a bodyguard, and having a limo entourage."

"So you and the piano must really get along well." Elaina looked at him again.

He averted his gaze and toyed with the seam of his slacks. "I guess I've been told that a time or two," he said. "Problem is, my mother and I haven't been able to see eye to eye about what I and my piano should do. Once I finished my first master's degree, Mom arranged for me to have high-profile bookings that have gotten me major exposure, whether I wanted it or not. Finally I enrolled in a second master's degree program three years ago just to give me a reasonable excuse not to be on the road. She has not been the happiest with me ever since. Neither has Faye for that matter. Faye, I can handle. My mom is a different story."

"Maybe they're just proud of your talent and want you to be the best you can be?" Elaina offered, and she couldn't believe she was actually suggesting her sister-in-law's motives might be pure.

"Maybe." He propped his elbow on the window ledge and caressed his sideburn. "And maybe they just like the strokes themselves," he mumbled. "The problem is, regardless of their motives, I hate life on the road. I have no desire to be an international great." He waved his hand as if he were about to bow before a burgeoning audience. "All I want is a simple life."

"Doing?" Elaina checked her rearview mirror and noted a clear highway.

"Don't laugh, okay?"

"I promise I won't laugh," she said and imagined all sorts of crazy scenarios.

"I want to be the minister of music at a church that needs me. I've got the education to do it, and I know I could really help bring a spirit of worship into a congregation."

Elaina lifted one corner of her mouth. "Why did you ask me not to laugh?" she asked. "I think that's a *wonderful* aspiration."

"You do? Really?" Ted questioned.

"Well, yes." Elaina nodded and rubbed the hem of her sleeveless shirt. "And you don't?"

"*I* do." Ted's eyes widened. "But my mother and sister think it's a waste of my talent."

"I thought they attended church," Elaina countered and noted that the car was growing chilly. She clicked the air conditioning back to low.

"Of course they do," Ted affirmed. "But they have this vision of my impacting millions of people and won't let it rest. They don't seem to want to accept that being on the road all the time is just not my cup of tea. I mean, I don't mind playing for some significant engagements—several a year maybe. I don't even mind producing my own CD and selling it myself. But this business of being sent on international tours by a record producer and then having engagements on top of that—essentially living out of a suitcase—would get really old for me."

"You don't like to travel?"

He laughed. "Yep, I love traveling—but not forty-eight weeks out of the year. Would you like that?"

Elaina thought of her journey to Europe last summer—a study trip that involved a tour of Jane Austen's house and many other literary historic sites. When the month was over, she'd been thrilled to get back into her own bed even though she immensely enjoyed the trip.

"No, I wouldn't like being gone all the time," she finally said.

"And then, when…*if* I get married and have kids—un unh," he said and shook his head. "There's no way I'm going to be gone all the time. My dad did that, and I can tell you from experience it's no fun graduating from high school when your father is on the road…or in the air."

Watching Ted from the corner of her eye, Elaina sensed his shrinking away into an internal passage where he brooded over his plight in life. As they continued to drive in silence, Elaina was hit with the impression that Ted Farris was on the verge of changing his plight. How, she could not say. Nor did she feel it proper to ask. Nevertheless, the perception was so strong she could in no way alter it. Fleetingly, she wondered if their new relationship might be part of the catalyst that would alter his life. Perhaps the weekend would answer that question…and many more.

Five

Ted looked out the window. With a cheerful rendition of "Music Box Dancer" spilling from the speakers, he chose not to add to his complaints—like the fact that his mother had threatened to disinherit him if he didn't follow her music dreams and also choose a wife from the top of society. For years, Ted had let his inheritance of 5.3 million dollars dictate his life. Little did his mother know he'd stopped letting the money rule months ago. He planned to prove that when he wrapped up this final graduate class. For now, he needed the financial backing his trust fund supplied. He and his mother held joint custody of that account. Ted didn't doubt she might withdraw every penny were she so inclined. While he did have a private nest egg hidden away, Ted wanted to reserve that for the future.

He pinched his lower lip. *No, I won't burden Elaina with any more of my family's dysfunction.* Given Faye's usual negative behavior, he figured Elaina's impression of the Farris clan could have stopped her from befriending him. But she hadn't judged Ted based on his elder sister. Instead, Elaina had been kind and generous in setting aside her professor role and treating him as an equal.

Maybe a little too *kind,* Ted mused and realized he hadn't thought of Lorna all day. He imagined her photo in his billfold warming in silent reproach. But the truth was, Ted couldn't remember ever being as taken with Lorna as he already was with Dr. Elaina Woods. Ever since yesterday after class, Ted had been increasingly distracted by the attractive professor—so much so that he could barely sleep for anticipating the trip. What the weekend would bring was anybody's guess. Ted had already fantasized about kissing Elaina a dozen times and dismissed the idea of mentioning his engagement an equal number of times. He wondered at the logic of placing himself—a committed man—in such close proximity to a woman he found increasingly alluring.

Nevertheless, Ted had stepped forth like a gallant knight, determined to assist and protect the three women he'd just met. Last night, an inexplicable precognition urged him to accompany the Woods ladies for the weekend move. He understood from the second he offered that the whole trip might be a divine appointment. He knew his sister well. She would likely cause the Woodses enough irritation for an army full of difficult in-laws. Maybe if he acted as buffer, she would curb her overbearing tendencies.

Ted figured Lorna, the ever-jealous fiancée, would not be happy if she knew where he was heading this weekend. Thankfully, she was visiting friends in Kansas. *What she doesn't know won't hurt her,* he thought seconds before Beethoven's Fifth flowed from the backseat.

"Oh man," Elaina moaned. "That's my cell phone. I guess I must have left my purse in the backseat when I was loading my luggage."

"Want me to get it?" Ted asked.

"Do you mind?" Elaina darted him a thankful glance, and Ted wondered what those gorgeous baby blues looked like without the dark-rimmed glasses.

"Not in the least." He unclipped his seat belt, swiveled, and followed the sound until he spotted a sling purse beside an overnight bag on the floor. He retrieved the purse and pulled the cell phone from the side pocket.

"Go ahead and answer it," Elaina said. "I'm afraid it's going to stop ringing any second."

As Ted flipped open the top, he noted the caller ID read "Anna cell." He placed the receiver to his ear as Elaina turned down the radio. After grappling with what to say, he finally blurted, "Ted Farris speaking."

A female voice from his recent past floated over the line. "Hi, Ted!"

"Hello, Anna," he replied.

"I'm assuming you're with Elaina?" she questioned, and Ted thought he detected a strained thread in her words. He often noticed the same nuance in his own voice after a weekend with Faye.

"Either that or I've highjacked her phone," he teased. He mouthed "Anna" toward Elaina. She nodded and refocused on driving. A déjà vu aura cloaked Ted, as if he and Elaina had been together for years, and for years he'd been answering her phone and performing all sorts of other "honey-do's." He rebuckled his seat belt, focused on Elaina's profile, and fell into rapt admiration. While no one would claim she was drop-dead gorgeous, Ted liked everything about her, including her upturned nose and the faint scar above her arched brow.

It gives her character, he thought.

"May I speak with her?" Anna's question held an impatient edge.

Ted was so distracted by the woman next to him he nearly said, "Speak with who?"

"Uh, sure," he said instead. After covering the mouthpiece he extended the cell. "She sounds a little stressed."

"Doesn't surprise me," Elaina mumbled. She offered a sheepish grin as she took the phone.

Ted tapped his index finger against the door's armrest and deduced clues as he listened.

"Uh huh," Elaina said stiffly. "Yes...okay," she nearly growled. Ted discreetly observed her and couldn't miss her right eye twitching. "We're about..." she checked the dashboard's digital clock, "...about ten minutes away. Do you think I need to talk with her or will ten minutes be too late?"

"Sure," Elaina continued. "I'll talk to her now, then." Her contrite look at Ted suggested she was now uncomfortable with his presence.

Ted pretended interest in a pasture full of cattle and wondered if he could conjure a means to disappear. Simultaneously, he reminded himself that part of the reason he offered to help the Woods ladies was to protect them from his sister.

"Hello, Faye," Elaina purred into the phone as if she were an unhappy lioness. "I understand you're interested in buying Mom's Renaissance furniture?"

Ted felt as if he were a German Shepherd, and his ears had just pricked straight up. One thing his sister loved was purchasing priceless antiques at a fraction of their cost. For years, he'd listened to her brag about the steals she'd found. Often Ted wondered if her conscience ever suffered from the number of little old ladies she'd ripped off at estate sales. He also wondered if the thought ever occurred to Faye that there were times when paying full price was the honorable thing to do—especially when you had the money and the person selling did not.

He watched as Elaina's knuckles turned white around the phone. Finally she broke the stony silence with a firm, "I'm sorry, Faye, but my mother is not going to sell that furniture. I don't care what you've managed to get her to imply or tell you. She told me last night that she wants to keep it."

Yep, she's up to her usual tricks, Ted thought. As he concentrated on the thickening traffic, he suspected that the divine appointment was about to bear fruit.

"But it's *worth* a hundred thousand dollars!" Elaina blurted.

Ted frowned and shifted his attention solely toward her. His pulse thrashed against his ribs as he recalled the years Faye had bullied him in his childhood and beyond. He was tired of being the brunt of her domineering attitude and wasn't prepared to silently sit by while she attempted to force her wishes upon Elaina and Margaret.

"No, she doesn't *need* the money," Elaina snapped as if she'd just been insulted. "She *needs* to keep her furniture! It was a gift from my father!" A red veil crept up Elaine's neck and splotched her cheeks.

Ted decided now was as good a time as any to fulfill his purpose for the weekend. On an impulse, he snatched the phone from Elaina and accidentally bumped her glasses in the lurch.

"What are you doing?" she croaked. With her glasses sitting cockeyed, she looked at him as if he were crazy.

Ted would have laughed out loud if not for his sister's persistent voice faintly floating over the phone's speaker, "Hello! Hello! Elaina? Are you still there?" He placed the receiver to his ear. "Hello, Faye, this is your brother, Ted," he drawled into the phone.

Elaina straightened her glasses and spent the next several seconds intermittently focusing on Ted and the road. After wondering if he had lost his mind, she considered stopping on the highway's shoulder. But Elaina decided they didn't have time to spare. She had some furniture to rescue!

"I'm here with Elaina, in her car," Ted continued, his voice firm. "I'm coming this weekend to help her mother and sister move."

Once the shock of Ted's snatching the phone subsided, Elaina drummed her fingers on the top of the steering wheel and glowered his way. Ted looked straight ahead, as if he were a warrior on a mission to rescue a damsel in distress.

But I didn't ask to be rescued, Elaina groused to herself.

"I *didn't* know them until last night," Ted said. "Elaina is teaching this last class I'm taking. We realized after class that we have a family connection. Anna invited me to come help them move, and I agreed." As Ted shifted in his seat, Elaina read a sign announcing their exit was a quarter mile away.

"Listen, Faye," Ted said, his tone permitting no argument. "I believe Mrs. Woods wants to *keep* her furniture. Let's not push this issue, shall we? I'm sure you can find some similar pieces if you look hard enough." As the silence stretched, Ted tapped Elaina's arm. When she looked at him, he extended the thumbs up sign.

"Okay, good," he continued. "Thanks for agreeing."

Elaina stopped drumming her fingers. Her shoulders relaxed while Ted spoke his farewells. When he flipped the phone closed, gratitude replaced her irritation.

"My sister can be a pistol when she wants to be." Ted stuffed the cell phone back into the purse's side pocket. "I'm not sure she ever learned the meaning of the word 'no.'"

"Thanks." Elaina clicked on her blinker and slowed. She debated a variety of things to say, including kindly asking Ted never again to grab a phone from her. But Elaina decided to remain positive and not address the issue unless he made a habit of it. "I have a hunch I was about to make Faye really mad," Elaina said. "Then, Mom would have gotten exasperated with me. I think she'd sell the family jewels for a buck just to keep the peace."

"Hmmm," Ted said and toyed with the shoulder strap of her sling bag. "She seems like a very good-hearted woman."

"Oh she is! But she wouldn't lift a *finger* to defend herself."

"So you act as her watchdog?" He teased.

Elaina rubbed her forehead. "And you've decided to act as mine?" she asked and scrutinized him. "Exactly why did you agree to come help us move this weekend?"

Ted peered toward the county highway on which Elaina was merging. "Let's just say I had a hunch you ladies might need me for a little more than shoving around boxes."

"But you just met us," Elaina asserted. "How do you know you shouldn't be protecting your sister from us?"

"From *you* maybe," he joked.

Elaina chuckled under her breath. "That's probably truer than you know," she said and slowed at a four-way stop.

"Uh…" Ted continued as she turned right, "do you mind my asking *why* it looks like my sister and brother-in-law are inheriting everything and your mother is getting the short end of this stick?"

Grimly, Elaina eyed the long line of brick fence posts that marked her father's extensive estate. "It's called a prenuptial agreement," she said and couldn't deny that she sounded as if she were gnawing nails. "Just before my father's first wife died—that was Jake's mother—she made him promise that he would leave the family estate and his business and all operating capital to Jake. You know he was their only child, right?"

"Yes." Ted stretched his legs.

"Daddy told me that his first wife's inheritance is what bought this estate and started his import business." She pointed left toward the 300 prime acres that now belonged to her half-brother. "Anyway, my father promised to leave everything to Jake because he never imagined marrying again—let alone having children. When he fell in love with my mother, he explained everything to her and told her he was duty-bound to keep his word." Elaina clicked on her left blinker and slowed. She drove between a pair of massive brick pillars that marked the estate's paved road, which was lined in august oaks.

"Of course, my mother, being the cooperative sort, never complained," Elaina said as they bumped into a speed dip. "She's told me over and over again since Daddy died that she loved my father and that was all she needed."

"Did you and your mom and sister get *anything*?" Ted questioned.

"My mom got a decent cash account that should provide her income until she dies if she invests it right." Elaina tempered the vehicle's speed and rolled beneath a canopy of oak branches.

"Of course, you'll make sure *that* happens." Ted stated.

"I'll try my hardest," Elaina agreed as she spotted the pillared mansion nobly residing upon a small prairie hill. She noted a large moving van sitting in the circular drive behind her sister-in-law's glistening red Mercedes.

"My sister and I each got a small trust fund—enough for a nice new car or a down payment on a house," Elaina continued, her words tight. The site of the place where she'd been raised twisted her heart and made her ache for her mother's situation. She wondered how her mom could bear handing over her home of thirty years to her stepson. She also wondered how Jake and Faye could take everything in good conscience, without even a hint of generosity. Before he died, her father had mentioned Jake's promising to monetarily assist her mother and sister and Elaina. But neither Faye nor Jake had offered a dime.

Instead, Faye has tried to cheat Mother out of her prized possessions! Elaina thought and shoved a strand of hair behind her ear.

"This all seems so unfair," Ted said. "Does any of it bother you?"

"Who me?" Elaina laid her hand over her chest as if she were a scandalized southern belle. "Why-*evah* would you ask that?" She laced her stare with a heavy dose of sarcasm.

Ted rolled his eyes. "Not only did Jake and Faye inherit everything, now Faye is trying to essentially steal the antiques," he said and shook his head.

Elaina tapped the accelerator and rolled into the circular drive lined with beds of ferns and roses. She stopped twenty feet behind the moving van, put the vehicle in park, and turned off the engine. Two meaty men dressed in jeans and black T-shirts hauled a claw-footed table to the back of the truck.

"There's a piece of the famous furniture now," Elaina said. "My mom's favorite, as a matter of fact." She released a silent sigh.

"I really appreciate your intervening, Ted. I'm afraid I was about to say some things that would have caused the rest of the weekend to be unpleasant, to say the least." She reached for her sling bag and popped open the door.

"I was glad to interfere," Ted said with a sheepish grin. "Sorry about knocking your glasses coo-coo. I guess I jumped right in there, didn't I?"

"It's okay…really," Elaina asserted and was thankful she really meant it.

"Just so you know, I've never ripped the phone out of anyone's hand before like that. But I was overcome with…" He lifted his fist. As he pressed his lips together his nostrils widened. "Sometimes I really don't like my sister, you know? I love her. She's my sister. I'd do anything in the world for her. But she has some serious issues that have a way of leaking all over me and anybody else who gets in the way. It gets *really old*. I get exasperated when she tries to push me around, but it makes me downright mad to see her doing something like that to three women who've been— been stripped of nearly everything, and—" He yanked on his ponytail and stopped in mid-sentence.

Elaina followed his gaze. Faye Woods rushed past the moving van and straight toward the Honda. *Speak of the devil,* Elaina thought and wondered what the next few minutes might hold.

Six

Although Elaina had never told anyone, her sister-in-law reminded her of Cousin Jeanna's Pekinese. Her pudgy nose, bugging eyes, and flat cheekbones made Faye look so much like a canine that Elaina half-expected her to bark every time she saw her. Today was no different.

"Hello! Hello! It's so good to see the two of you!" Faye squealed. As she approached the vehicle, her linen duster jacket billowed behind with every gust of the humid breeze.

Yes, I'm sure that's really *how you feel*, Elaina thought and never remembered Faye issuing such a friendly greeting. She watched Ted as he stepped from the vehicle and neared his sister. The two exchanged a quick embrace that surprised Elaina with its genuine affection.

The only things the two shared in looks were their dark hair and olive skin tone. In character, Elaina had detected no similarities. Once again, she marveled that Ted could be so enchanting and sincere when his sister was such a shrew.

Wondering what kind of greeting Faye would extend to her, Elaina stepped from the vehicle and snapped the door closed.

"And you, Elaina!" Faye said as soon as she spotted her sister-in-law. "It's *soooo* good to see you!" Fully expecting Faye's approach to stop within a few feet, Elaina widened her eyes with Faye's embrace. She backed away and looked Elaina in the eyes. While her smile spoke friendship, her cold gray eyes stirred with contempt.

This is all a show for Ted, Elaina thought.

"I'm so glad you and Ted have gotten to know one another," she continued and squeezed Elaina's hand. "Isn't this just so cozy?" She wrinkled her pudgy nose.

You are lying, Elaina thought. "Yes, I guess so," she drawled and glanced toward Ted.

However, he had already spotted a need and was assisting a third mover in hoisting a wing-backed chair into the van. From the looks of Ted—dressed in casual slacks, a stone-washed denim shirt, and a pair of Reeboks—Elaina would have never guessed that he was from such a wealthy family or that he was an acclaimed pianist.

She made a mental note to ask him to play the piano for them this weekend. Anna had already arranged for her baby grand piano to be moved into the cottage's formal living room. Tomorrow morning, the instrument was to be serviced and tuned by the same music company who transported it from the mansion.

"You know, Elaina," Faye said as if they were the most intimate of confidantes. "If I were you, I wouldn't get my hopes up about Ted." Each word was weighted with mockery. "My mother will never allow him to marry anyone who isn't his economic equal."

Elaina swiveled toward her sister-in-law and leveled a flat stare at her. Faye's eyes narrowed as if she were issuing a challenge. The wind tousled Faye's loosely curled hair, and Elaina was reminded of Medusa, the mythological fiend who had serpents for hair. A hundred possible retorts twisted through Elaina's mind. She chose none of them. Instead, she stiffened her legs and continued to observe her sister-in-law as if her claim were of no concern. The triumphant tilt of Faye's lips soon stretched into a straight line.

After slinging her purse upon her shoulder, Elaina walked toward the moving van with as much nonchalance as she could feign. Despite the slow burn that consumed her gut, she refused to be baited…or to give Faye the satisfaction of a reply. The woman had lost precious few opportunities to demean her—especially once Elaina announced her doctorate candidacy. While the verbal jab came as little surprise, Elaina detested the comments as much for Ted's sake as her own. She had a hunch that Ted Farris just might be his own man, despite his mother and sister's claim to control. She had been sorely tempted to tell Faye that Ted possibly wanted a choice in his wife. But that would have only led her to believe that Ted and Elaina really were an item. And that wasn't true—not yet, anyway.

When Elaina passed the truck, Ted turned from his completed task. "Hey, wait for me!" He trotted to Elaina's side and casually placed his hand on her shoulder.

Elaina could only imagine what Faye might think. She considered slipping her arm around Ted's back and giving him a squeeze. Elaina refrained. Aside from fearing what Ted might think of her, affection for the sake of spite was not the mature reaction.

Faye, her back stiff, marched around them and stomped toward the mansion. *Well, at least one of us is taking the mature path,* Elaina mused. Faye whipped past the massive pillars that claimed four corners of the porch and paused only long enough to wrench the knob and step inside. She slammed the door with so much force the mammoth, floral wreath flopped in protest.

"What's the matter with *her?*" Ted asked.

Elaina smiled up at him. "I don't think she's happy that we're together."

"Humph," Ted said. "She might as well get used to it. It's going to be a long weekend." He nodded toward the doorway. "C'mon. Let's go see how we can help your mom and sis. I'm sure

Faye is probably safely in hiding by now. Whatever you said to her, the coast is probably clear."

"I didn't say a word to her," Elaina explained as they stepped onto the porch that featured two giant urns full of geraniums. Their acrid smell and cheerful blooms befit the bittersweet emotions that played upon Elaina's spirit.

"Ooooohhhhh." Ted raised his brows as he opened the mansion's door. "That's even *worse*. She hates that."

"I'm assuming you're speaking from experience?" Elaina entered the marble-tiled entryway and was reminded why this house made the cover of *Better Homes and Gardens* two years ago.

"You guessed it," Ted replied with an obstinate gleam in his eyes.

"There you two are!" Margaret Woods exclaimed from the formal dining room.

With the smell of take-out burgers heavy in the air, Elaina peered into the room, past piles of boxes and askew furniture. She first spotted her mother beside the china hutch. Nearby, Anna fussed with her sloppy hair caught into a clip. Beside them sat two large sodas with the golden arches on them. An open box and a pile of newspaper claimed the floor between them. Margaret, dressed in a smock top, held a silver-rimmed white platter. Anna gave up on her hair, reached into the china hutch, and pulled out a delicate cup.

"Hey, you two!" Anna's grin revealed twin dimples at top advantage. "Great to see you! Hope you wore your working pants." She patted her denim capri pants.

Ted looked down at his casual attire and extended his arms. "I'm at your service," he said as if he were a gallant knight. "Tell me, dear ladies, what you would have me do."

Anna giggled as Margaret feigned a swoon. After rolling her eyes, Elaina mumbled, "Oh brother."

"What?" Ted asked with an innocent expression.

"What indeed," Elaina returned. She dropped her purse into a settee and walked into the dining room. "Looks like you guys have this room packed up," she said. Hands on hips, she pivoted to scan the room full of boxes. "What about the kitchen?"

"Oh yes! The kitchen." Margaret placed her hand atop her head. "The maid and the movers got the cookware, but I told them to leave the glassware. I want to make sure it's wrapped tightly." She laid the platter on the floor.

"Consider it done!" Ted claimed.

"The prize awaits you behind door number one!" Her eyes merry, Margaret pointed toward the swinging door that led to the kitchen. Elaina marveled that her mother could be so cheerful when she was essentially being turned out of her own home. "The boxes are ready to be filled. There's even newspaper in there as well."

"Whatever shall please the lady is my bidding," he said with a deep bow.

"Well, aren't you the sweetest thing I've ever seen?" Margaret exclaimed. "If you keep this up, I'll have to get up and hug you."

"Hold that thought." With a wink, Ted hurried through the door.

"Whoa!" Anna whispered as soon as the door stopped swinging. "Is he turning it on thick or what?" She finished wrapping the china cup and gingerly placed it into the box. "He acts like he's trying to impress *somebody's* mother because he really likes *somebody*." She wiggled her eyebrows in an exaggerated manner.

"I don't think it's an act—not really." Margaret shook her head and reached for a piece of packing paper. "I knew from the minute I met him, he's got a good heart—a million times bigger than that of his sister's," she added with a sniff.

Elaina neared her mother and squatted beside her. The smell of long-closed cabinets and musty newspaper made her ache for her mom's loss. Elaina lovingly stroked her back. At a closer vantage she detected a few more lines around eyes that still held shadows of sorrow.

"Speaking of Faye," Elaina began, "she just met Ted and me outside and wasn't exactly thrilled to find out Ted and I are new friends."

"So that's why she came slamming through here like a bull moose," Margaret said.

Elaina started to repeat the degrading things Faye said, but she decided those details would only disturb her mother all the more.

"Well, Faye's been on a tear all morning," Anna said. "I promise, I think she was ready to force Mom to sign an intent to sell the furniture before I called you." Anna feigned a shiver. "I think she must have been a vampire in a former life. I don't see how Jake or Ted puts up with her." She pulled several cups and saucers to the cabinet's edge and retrieved one.

"It's because she doesn't treat them the way she treats us," Elaina said. "Although, I don't think she's completely fooling Ted. Before we got here, he said there are times when he doesn't like her." Elaina reached across the box, removed two cups and saucers from the hutch shelf, and placed them beside Anna. The fine china clinked as if it were applauding Elaina's words. "Then after saying that, Ted turned around and hugged her as if he thought she hung the moon." Elaina shrugged. "Go figure."

"Blood is thicker than water," Margaret said.

"Well, I know it's thick with me," Anna declared. "And I promise, there's no will in the world that would make me take Mom's house or antiques away. None!" Her pout turned into a scowl that reminded Elaina of a toddler's. "We can't get away from her soon enough, as far as I'm concerned." She fussed with her lopsided hair and clip atop her head. "I'm just glad you were able to get her to back down, Elaina."

"I wasn't the one." She pointed at her chest. "Ted snatched the phone from me and essentially said, 'Down, girl.'"

"He's wonderful, Elaina! Just wonderful!" Margaret exclaimed. "I promise, if you don't marry him by Thanksgiving, I will." Her blue eyes shown with certainty as she retrieved the silver-rimmed platter from near her leg.

"Oh, Mom," Elaina chided and stood. "I just met him."

Anna looked up at her. "Like I've always said, no sense in wasting time."

"Marriage is a lifetime commitment," Elaina said as if her younger sister were six. "You can't just—"

"Blindly jump in without properly getting to know someone." Anna straightened her spine, puckered her lips, and narrowed her eyes. She looked as if she had either just eaten a lemon or was mimicking the prude of the century.

"Oh brother," Elaina mumbled. "Give it a break. I've got to go help Ted." She turned for the swinging door as Anna released a wolf whistle.

Margaret's snicker prompted Elaina to pivot. "Mom!" she exclaimed. "Who's side are you on, anyway?"

"There are no sides," she said. "Your sister just makes the most ridiculous faces of anyone I've ever seen." Her words tumbled out over more laughter. "Oh dear."

"Now you're making faces behind my back, are you?" Elaina feigned a glower as Anna repeated the buck-toothed, wide-eyed gesture. A giggle escaped Elaina despite her attempts to remain somber. "You people are crazy," she mumbled and stepped through the swinging doorway.

The kitchen welcomed her with an abundance of childhood memories that spilled into her soul. Elaina would have vowed she could smell her mom's chocolate chip cookies—just as they baked them for Santa every Christmas Eve. The oversized room, replete with stainless steel appliances and a tiled island, was every chef's dream. Next to the island stood Ted, talking with Elaina's half-brother, who sipped a cup of aromatic coffee.

"Jake!" she exclaimed the second he looked up.

His welcoming smile radically contrasted Faye's greeting. "Hi," he responded. "I just walked in and found this cat scrounging around in the shelves." He nodded toward Ted. "I didn't realize until just now that Ted rode over with you. At first, I assumed he'd come to help us. He was just explaining that he came to help you. This guy's a moving machine—works like a dog when he wants to. Now, aren't *you* the lucky ones?"

Jake, whose dark hair and high cheekbones favored Anna more than Elaina, observed his sister. He squinted as if he were trying to solve a perplexing mystery. "I didn't know you guys knew each other," he finally said.

"We didn't—at least not until last night," Elaina said before the two of them explained their recent acquaintance.

"That's great!" Jake said. "Faye's around here somewhere. She'll want to know Ted's here." He looped his thumb in his cotton shorts pocket and looked toward the doorway that opened onto the back hallway. "The remodelers are due soon. But I decided maybe Margaret could use some help several hours ago. So here I am in the kitchen now."

He set his coffee mug on the island and pointed toward the counter. A box with newspaper sticking out the top sat next to the sink, filled with afternoon sunshine. Beside the box rested a row of cups. "I was just threatening to take over that box, as a matter of fact."

Elaina masked her surprise. At this point, the last person she expected help from was her half-brother. While Jake wasn't nearly as haughty as his wife, Elaina assumed he had written off his half-sisters and stepmother as an unnecessary part of his past. She managed a discreet "thanks" that sounded genuine but not insulting.

"Maybe that explains why the dining room is ready to go," she added.

"Yes, and so's the living room," Jake explained with a proud smile. "And your mother's room. We've really worked hard this morning. Your mom is worried the maid and movers won't pack the fragile stuff well. She also refused to let anyone touch her personal items."

"I can understand that," Ted chimed in and moved toward the industrial-sized coffeemaker. "When I moved into my apartment, Mom tried to get me to let the maids and movers take care of everything, but I couldn't." He picked up a thick mug. "I wanted to know my stuff was taken care of," Ted added and placed his index finger against his chest, "especially the music-related stuff."

"Oh, I wasn't *complaining!*" Jake extended his hand, palm outward. "I'd probably be the same way myself. I was just saying that…" He shrugged and looked at his sister. "I really don't know what my point was," he said with a smile. "I guess I was just telling you guys about the morning."

Jake scrutinized Elaina as if searching for any trace of animosity. If Elaina weren't certain that he and Faye lacked even a scrap of conscience, she might have assumed Jake was masking a guilt complex.

The quick tapping of shoes against polished hardwood sent a cringe through Elaina. She recognized the rhythm of that gait all too well. As suspected, Faye marched from the back hallway into the kitchen as if she were immensely enjoying her status as queen of the manor.

"There you are, Jake," she said without acknowledging Elaina. "The remodeler is here *finally,*" she huffed, "and she wants to talk with you about your office."

"Oh sure," Jake said. He retrieved his mug of coffee before walking toward his wife.

"She's waiting for you in the office," Faye said as Jake meandered out the doorway and down the hall.

"Why don't you come with us, Ted?" Faye asked and slid a sly glance toward Elaina, who refused to acknowledge the silent affront. Instead, she glimpsed Ted, who finished filling his mug with the dark brew. Elaina moved toward the counter and started wrapping a cup in thick layers of newspaper.

"The remodeler brought color swatches with her this time," Faye explained. "You've got such a good eye for color, brother, dear," she said in a voice so sweet Elaina almost gagged, "I don't know if we should make the choices without your help."

"Thanks for your vote of confidence," Ted said as if he were genuinely fond of his sister.

Elaina peeked at Ted and was amazed to see no trace of the former irritation. Her mom's cliché, blood is thicker than water, took on new meaning. Elaina thought Ted might even agree to his sister's request. A tinge of disappointment wouldn't be denied. Somewhere between Lakeland's rolling hills and the mansion's prairie, Elaina developed a deep respect for Ted Farris. He was choosing his own path in life and not bowing to the whims of an overpowering mother and sister. He certainly hadn't been afraid to stand up to his sister over the furniture. But Elaina sensed that he was far less strong when facing the compliments of his sibling. Now she wondered what cooperation the allure of a doting mother might produce.

Maybe that's the reason he's done so many public performances, she thought as she crinkled a wad of newspaper into a cup's center. *He was charmed right into it!* With a resigned wilt of her shoulders, Elaina recognized that she had strongly anticipated working side-by-side with Ted Farris. As every nuance of his personality unfolded today, she had never wanted to get to know a man more than she did him.

Nevertheless, some of Elaina's desires were now replaced with doubts. If she ever got serious about a man, she wanted him to *be* a man—not a child who bent to his mother or sister's every whim. As she crammed the final mug into the box, Elaina fully expected Ted to trot after Faye like an obedient little boy...and dissolve all hopes of their romantic involvement.

Never had Elaina been so glad to be proven wrong. Ted deposited his mug on the counter. "I'd enjoy the redecorating, Faye," he continued while rolling up his shirt sleeves, "but I promised Elaina and Mrs. Woods I'd help them. I wouldn't be much good to them if I went into a decorating huddle with you."

Elaina's lips twitched. As much as she wanted to witness Faye's reaction, she turned her back on her sister-in-law and opened another cabinet full of her mother's everyday glassware. The kitchen reverberated with a silent scream, and Elaina would have vowed the temperature rose ten degrees. Faye's only response was the clap of heels on wood as she stomped out of the kitchen.

A box appeared on the cabinet next to Elaina's elbow. She observed the man who'd plopped it there. Ted took a draw on his black coffee and said, "I guess she's having a bad hair day or something."

"I guess," Elaina agreed and decided not to tell him that his sister was always this crabby around her.

Jake lifted his coffee mug. "Want me to fix you a cup?"

"No, thanks." Elaina shook her head. "I never touch the stuff—or anything else caffeinated, for that matter."

"No way!" Ted teasingly scoffed and then shook his head. "So that explains the problem."

"What problem?" Elaina challenged.

"I knew there was something the matter with you when we first met, but I couldn't quite put my finger on it. Now, I know."

Elaina silently prompted him to expound.

"You're decaffeinated!" he claimed with a flirtatious smile.

"Oh brother," Elaina said. "Actually, I love anything caffeinated, but it doesn't love me. It gives me chest pains and makes my heart palpitate." She touched her upper chest. "I promise, a year ago I thought I was having a heart attack. There I was, twenty-six-years-old thinking I was going down for the count!" She shook her head, retrieved a pair of glass tumblers from the shelf, and set them on the counter.

"I went to the emergency room first. They ran all sorts of tests that came back normal. So they referred me to my general practitioner. She diagnosed the problem as caffeine intolerance." Elaina picked up a stack of newspapers from the other side of the sink. "I can't drink anything with chicory in it, either. It's a stimulant, like caffeine."

"Wow! I never heard of such a thing." Ted observed Elaina as if she were an odd cell under a microscope.

"Well, get a load of this, then," Elaina continued, "once I got off caffeine, I was able to sleep all night for the first time in my life. Until then, I had been a chronic insomniac my whole life. Even as a child, I drank iced tea at night with supper. It's got caffeine, too, you know." She dropped the stack of newspaper near the box.

"What's next," Ted questioned, "chocolate? Doesn't it have some caffeine, too?"

"Actually, hot cocoa *does* bother me. But so far, small amounts of chocolate candy don't phase me in the least. As a matter of fact, let's don't even go there." Elaina raised her hand and turned her head. "I don't want to discuss the candy thing anymore. I'd *die* if I couldn't have some Hershey's kisses every now and then."

Ted leaned closer. "Chocolate has caffeine…chocolate has caffeine…chocolate has caffeine," he chanted while bobbing his head.

With a playful shriek, Elaina covered her ears and the two fell into mellow laughter.

The dining room door swung open, and Anna peered into the kitchen. Her concerned blue eyes soon softened. "It looks like you two are having *waaaay* too much fun in here," she said and then called over her shoulder, "Elaina's fine, Mom. They're in here laughing." As Anna turned back around, her hair collapsed and the clip clinked onto the tile.

Ted and Elaina laughed again. "You people need to get a life," Anna playfully groused. As she bent to retrieve the clip, her hair fell into a cascade of dark silk.

"It's time to get buuuusssssyyyyy!" Margaret's jovial call from the dining room prompted Elaina to grab a sheet of newspaper.

"We are! We are!" she bleated and began wrapping one of the tumblers.

Ted set his face into a serious mask and deposited his cup on the counter. "Ma'am, yes, ma'am!" he crowed, while Anna snickered.

Seven

So the day progressed—hours in which Elaina and Ted worked side-by-side to complete the packing. By Friday evening, the movers pulled away from the mansion, fully loaded with Margaret and Anna's furniture and belongings. Elaina and Ted drove back to Lakeland in weary, contented silence. Saturday morning Ted retrieved his Corvette from the mechanic, and they met at Margaret's new country cottage. He and Elaina worked with her mom and sister all day Saturday as if they were lifetime friends.

By the time the sun was sinking west, Margaret called a halt to labor. "We've all worked like a bunch of dogs," she claimed.

Elaina turned from the brick fireplace, where she was adjusting a portrait of their family now hanging over the mantel.

Margaret collapsed onto her beloved antique sofa. "I for one have *had* it!" She placed her hand on her head, leaned into the couch, and gazed at the ceiling.

"Me, too!" Anna gasped. She slumped near the floor-to-ceiling bookcase, mere feet from Elaina. After dropping a handful of books back into their box, Anna flopped into the closest recliner. "All we lack now is unpacking the nonessentials. I say we quit for a day or two."

Elaina rubbed her stiff neck and couldn't argue that she was as tired as her mother looked, but neither could she ignore reality. "The problem is, I'm here now," she firmly stated.

"That's okay, dear." Margaret raised her hand as if she were the prime minister. "We'll take care of the rest. I promise, we'll be just fine."

"Okay," Ted said as he breezed into the formal living room. "All the study stuff is in place." He rubbed his hands together. "Now, what's next? I could take care of the extra bathroom upstairs if you like."

"Looks like the chief is quitting on us," Elaina said as she settled onto the grand piano's bench.

Ted leaned against the imposing oak instrument and stroked the front of his designer T-shirt, stained with ketchup from their fast-food lunch. "No way," he said as if he were scandalized. "I thought you were like the Energizer Bunny."

"Well, this bunny is pooped," Margaret declared. For the first time, Elaina noticed the intensity of the dark circles under her mother's eyes.

"So's this one," Anna claimed, but Elaina hardly heard her.

Instead, she gazed at her mother with a sinking, sick feeling in the pit of her stomach. Only two months had passed since she buried her father. Losing him had made Elaina all the more aware of her mother's mortality. Margaret was only sixty-two, and her vibrant complexion suggested she had many full years left. Nevertheless, Elaina didn't want her to work herself into an early casket. She resisted the urge to sit beside her mom and check her pulse.

"I say we *do* call it quits," Elaina said. "And I'll do my best to come back over Monday night and try to help. I have choir practice Tuesday night, church Wednesday night, and a class to teach Thursday night. But Monday, I'm free."

"Oh, I couldn't impose—" Margaret began.

"Please, Mom." Elaina held up her hand. "I insist."

Ted straightened. "So do I. I'll be over Monday night, too."

Margaret looked from one to the other. "You two are really a great pair," she announced.

Elaina looked down at the Persian rug—one of her father's imports. As her mom's statement took on romantic implications, the rug's colors mingled into a kaleidoscope of burgundy and black and forest green. The truth was, Elaina had thought all weekend what a great pair she and Ted made...how well their personalities complemented each other...how nicely they worked together...how much she was looking forward to seeing him every Thursday night...and what possibilities the future might hold.

As she grappled for something to say to ease the awkward moment, Elaina was certain she sensed Ted's appraisal. But she wouldn't dare look at him—not even a stolen glimpse. While she hoped his regard for her was growing as rapidly as hers for him, she would never make him think she was chasing him—absolutely never. Furthermore, there was still that pesky section in the employee handbook. At the very least, Elaina would be forced to keep a new relationship with Ted top secret until the semester's end.

"Ted," Anna began as she kicked back in the recliner, "if you've got enough energy to keep unpacking, surely you've got enough to play the piano for us worn-out women."

"Only if you'll join me," Ted replied. "From what I understand, this beauty belongs to *you*."

"Well," Anna hedged, "it does, actually. But I wanted to hear *you* play."

"Nonsense," Ted said and motioned toward the bench. "Maybe we can share duties." He stepped toward Anna and extended his hand.

With a groan, she placed her fingers in his and stood. "Slave driver," she teased.

"I think this is a *lovely* idea," Margaret exclaimed.

Elaina stood from the piano bench and moved toward the fireplace. She removed her glasses and slid them onto the mantel.

Everything took on a mild blur, but Elaina was ready for a reprieve from the lenses. Rubbing her eyes, she turned her back to the empty fireplace, as if this were the chilliest of winter nights. Yet the temperature had shot to ninety degrees today, and the air conditioner was now running.

As Ted settled onto the piano bench with his back to her, Elaina reveled in the freedom to watch him unguarded. His graceful fingers began caressing the keys, and she hovered like an eager bee, ready to savor the honey of his genius. Elaina closed her eyes and allowed the ballad to pour into her spirit, bringing the nuance of poetry and carefree, summer days. His art was everything she had expected...everything and more. Ted Farris was more than talented. God had blessed him with an amazing gift. She wouldn't be surprised to learn that he, like Mozart, had been a child prodigy who perhaps played and composed from the time he was four or five.

And on top of that, Elaina thought, *he has studied his art and polished his gift.* By the time he touched the ballad's final chords, Elaina fully understood his mother's obsession with pushing Ted into the limelight. Undoubtedly, Mrs. Farris was exploding with pride over her son's abilities and wanted to show him off to the world.

Nevertheless, Elaina was beginning to see the heart of the man with the gift—an uncomplicated soul who simply wanted a peaceful life. No prestige. No honor. Just his music and a means to release it to the glory of God. When he leaned toward Anna and mumbled something, Elaina realized she was more taken with this man than she had been any other. She liked everything about Ted Farris. Everything, right down to the ketchup streaking his T-shirt.

Elaina considered the weeks to follow—weeks when she would see him every Thursday night. She wondered how she would ever hide this fascination for Ted that had sprang out of nowhere. The power of her growing attraction nearly forced her to collapse into Anna's vacated recliner.

When the next song started, Elaina soon realized that Anna was now playing. Ted slid from the bench and stepped toward her mother. He bowed before her as if he were a gallant gentleman from the 1800s. "May I have this dance, Madame?" he requested with a British accent.

"Who me?" Margaret fidgeted with her dusty smock top. She picked up her reading glasses, hanging around her neck by a silver chain, and then dropped them again.

"Yes, you." Ted encouraged her hand into his and gently pulled.

While Anna chuckled, she never missed a note of "I Only Have Eyes for You."

Elaina, worried that the exertion might be too much for her mom, stepped forward to suggest Ted wait until his next visit. However, the glow on her mom's face stopped her; that, and the voice of reason suggesting that Margaret Woods was a healthy sixty-two-year-old and a long way from feeble.

Margaret soared to her feet and stepped into a simple waltz. While Ted sang the lyrics, Elaina relived their ride yesterday from Lakeland to the mansion. As Ted's baritone voice blended with Anna's melodic rendition, Margaret twirled around the spacious room as if she were twenty again. Elaina hadn't seen her smile so freely in months. She even detected a trace of the dimples that so resembled Anna's. Elaina decided she would be indebted to Ted Farris for years to come.

Soon the song neared its close and the smiling couple rotated toward the fireplace. Elaina didn't suspect her mother's intent until Margaret whirled under Ted's arched arm and then lifted Elaina's hand to his. Her eyes widened, and she encountered Ted's round-eyed stare that lasted a second. A grin followed, and Ted drew her into his embrace as if this was the best idea he'd encountered in weeks. Margaret whispered something in Anna's ear which prompted her to begin the song all over again.

A rational voice suggested that Elaina should resist such a frivolous indulgence, but another side of her insisted she'd been far too reasonable far too long. *There's a season for everything,* she quoted to herself, *even for romance.*

As the music wove a mellifluous ribbon around them, Elaina revisited her fantasies from yesterday—fantasies of her and Ted at a magical, fairytale ball. For a few seconds, Elaina even wondered if her running shoes might have become glass slippers, her slacks and cotton shirt, a glittering gown. Finally, the waltz was forgotten, yet the music still lingered.

Elaina, oblivious to the room's other occupants, didn't resist when Ted offered to simply sway to the music. For the first time since Margaret placed Elaina's hand in Ted's, he began to sing the timeless lyrics. Now, he wasn't smiling. Instead, his dark, sensitive eyes stirred with the conviction of every word. And Elaina felt as if her insides were dissolving into a warm pool of enchantment.

Ted never dreamed when he volunteered to assist the Woods ladies that his good deed would culminate to this moment. But here he stood, within kissing distance of a woman he longed to hold all evening. Ted felt as if the two of them were engulfed in the rich, ardent aura of first attraction that was stronger than anything he had ever experienced.

All the while, a certain hunch insisted that Elaina Woods was "the one," and Lorna was not. Nor had she ever been. Something in the center of his soul clamored that he and Elaina might have been made for each other. For the first time, he was privileged to look into her candid blue eyes without the glasses to block a single trace of her musings. And Ted encountered the same awe he experienced from their first rotation around the room.

Heaven help me! he thought as he considered the binding force of his engagement. *What have I gotten myself into?*

He broke Lorna's heart once ten years ago. She had married a jerk on the rebound and wound up as his punching bag. Sobbing uncontrollably, Lorna had arrived on Ted's porch nearly a year ago and vowed she never stopped loving him. Ted felt completely responsible for the horrible circumstances Lorna fell into. After all, he had given the lady his word of honor, only to renege. When he promised her he would marry her *this* time, Ted took a vow before God to keep his word—even if it meant losing all 5.3 million dollars of his inheritance.

The cold hiss of reality swept away that rich, ardent aura of first attraction. And Ted was left with nothing. Nothing but the chilling fact that he was flirting with the unfathomable seas of danger...and luring Elaina into the enticing waters with him.

An irritating chime pierced his reverie. Ted realized the piano had fallen quiet and had been for awhile. He looked around the classically decorated room to find that he and Elaina were alone. When Margaret and Anna left, how long they had been gone, or what they must be thinking was anybody's guess. The chime erupted anew, and Ted recognized the doorbell. He awkwardly released Elaina, who stepped from his embrace. She averted her gaze as if she didn't know what to say.

"I normally don't, uh..." She crossed her arms and cautiously looked back up at him.

"Yeah, me neither," Ted said as a chorus of female voices erupted from the entryway.

"Elaina! Guess who's here?" Margaret's claim accompanied an entourage of nearing footsteps.

Eight

"It's Cousin Jeanna," she exclaimed as she burst into the room. "And she has a simply delightful new neighbor, Dr. Bryan Brixby. He runs the family health clinic just inside Lakeland."

Still trapped in hazy wonder, Elaina struggled to focus on her mother, Cousin Jeanna, and the newcomer, who all appeared a tad blurry. She remembered her glasses on the mantel.

"Let me get my glasses so I can see you better!" Elaina said with a wry grin.

She used the walk to the mantel and back to gather her scattered senses. With her glasses in place, Elaina hurried toward the guests. She first hugged Cousin Jeanna, a plump, rouged lady with bleached-blonde hair. As always, she smelled like musk perfume, wore a flaming red moo-moo, and carried a Pekinese named Kay-Kay under her arm. Recently, Anna snidely reported that she wanted to call the dog Faye-Faye.

Elaina turned toward the sandy-haired Bryan Brixby and extended her hand. As he shook her hand, Elaina noted his broad shoulders and tall frame ensconced in a black sports jacket. She assumed he had seen a football field or two during his academic career. His sedate smile and alert green eyes bespoke a man of high intelligence and reserve.

"Nice to meet you, Dr. Woods," he said in a calm voice that must have soothed many patients' nerves.

Elaina was about to ask him how he knew of her title when Cousin Jeanna said, "Oh my! Oh my! Two doctors in one room! Whatever shall we do? Just like I told you, Bryan, the two of you are like two peas in a pod. I guess the rest of us are just podless!" She fell into high-pitched giggles as Kay-Kay licked her lips and wagged her whole body.

Margaret covered her mouth with her fingertips and stifled a snicker. "Oh Jeanna," she cooed, "you haven't changed a bit—not since we were teenagers."

Elaina glanced toward Ted, standing nearby. He looked as if he didn't know whether to proclaim Jeanna absurd or heartily laugh. That was exactly the effect Jeanna Harley always had on Elaina, and she had known the lady her whole life.

"And this is our new friend, Ted Farris," Margaret continued the introductions. "He has helped us move all weekend. He's actually my daughter-in-law's brother, but we're all only just now meeting."

"Oh! All these handsome men in one room!" Jeanna exclaimed and placed her hand over her chest. "Whatever shall we poor women do! Well," she batted her short lashes, "I *know* what I'll do. I'll just remember I'm an old married woman and leave all the fine pickings to you single gals!"

Elaina fixed her gaze on the ornate grandfather clock in the room's corner and didn't dare look at Ted. First, her mother had nudged them into that waltz, and now Cousin Jeanna was unfolding matchmaking schemes. Elaina hoped Ted didn't think her every relative was bent upon placing her in his arms.

"Oh, Jeanna," Bryan chided with only a hint of a smile, "as many times as I've tried to get you to elope with me, you would think you would have some grace and not mention you're already taken."

Jeanna arched her back and exploded into more hilarious shrieks. Her Pekinese yelped and howled as if she were attempting to mimic Jeanna's laugh.

Shaking her head, Margaret chuckled with her cousin. Bryan's eyes revealed a hint of subdued merriment. Jeanna blotted at her tear-laden lashes and slapped at Bryan's arm. "I wish you'd stop that nonsense," she said as if she didn't mean it. Her heavy chest bobbed with her every gasp.

Out of nowhere, a snicker escaped Elaina. Shaking her head, she looked at Ted whose indulgent smile suggested Cousin Jeanna had found another conquest.

"Now, where is that Anna?" Jeanna blurted and turned off the giggles as quickly as they had erupted.

"She went to the little girl's room and should be right back," Margaret claimed.

"Oh good, oh good!" Jeanna said and nodded. "Bryan and I brought a deli platter full of all sorts of cheeses and meats and goodies for your dinner tonight. I don't want Anna to miss out on it."

"Did someone mention my name?" Anna asked from the doorway.

"Oh there she is!" Jeanna said. "Come here, *hooooney*," she crooned and scooted toward Anna. "I'm just *tickled pink* you're going to be my neighbor." She engulfed Anna in a bear hug that trapped the Pekinese in the middle. Elaina expected the poor canine to come out looking like a furry pancake.

"And look! I brought a handsome neighbor for you and Elaina to meet. He lives a quarter of a mile that way." She pointed west as Anna extended her hand toward Dr. Brixby. "Just over the hill. He's single and *desperately* needs to get married. I was hoping one of you girls would oblige him."

"Why not have the wedding tonight, then?" Ted growled under his breath. When Elaina looked at him, she suspected Ted Farris wasn't enamored with the idea of her marrying the handsome neighbor. A delicious thrill couldn't be denied.

When she observed Bryan and her sister again, all thoughts of Ted's comment vanished. While Anna seemed polite, yet distant, Bryan had gone pale. After gazing at Anna as if she were an apparition from another life, he abruptly released her hand.

"If you'll excuse me," Bryan mumbled. "I'll go to the car and get the food."

"Oh sure, dear! Why don't you just *do* that?" Jeanna exclaimed. "What a *thoughtful* young man," she continued the second he left the room. "I promise, Elaina, I think the two of you would make a fine match." She shook her finger at Elaina's nose. "He's terribly fascinating and has traveled all over the world volunteering on mission fields. Two doctors in one family—that would have to be a good thing."

"But I'm really not the same kind of doctor he is," Elaina tried to explain. "Mine is a Ph.D. It's totally different than an M.D."

"Doesn't matter!" Jeanna shook her head. "Doesn't matter! A doctor is a doctor."

Margaret cleared her throat and cast a wary glance toward her daughter and Ted. "Why don't we all go into the dining room? If Bryan is bringing in food, that's where it needs to go. I don't know about my daughters and Ted, but I am hungry. I feel like I could eat the whole deli platter—plate included."

"Yes, yes, *ooohhh* yes!" Jeanna raised her hand and waved as if she were having a shouting spell in an old-time gospel meeting. "That's exactly what Bryan and I thought. So we've got everything—sodas and chips and croissants. We even have paper plates and cups!"

Within minutes, Bryan retrieved nearly everything from his vehicle. While he and Ted made the final haul, Elaina looked at enough food to feed twenty people...the promised deli platter full of meats and cheeses, vegetable and fruit platters, a shrimp ring with cocktail sauce, croissants, and chips. The tantalizing aroma filled the box-strewn room just as the food filled the massive dining table.

She couldn't imagine where Bryan and Ted would fit the sodas they were bringing in.

"Look at all this!" Margaret exclaimed. "How will we *ever* eat it all!"

"I'm going to start trying now," Anna said and reached for a plate. "I've worked up a ravenous appetite."

"Oh dear, yes," Jeanna oozed. "And here you are." She picked up a pair of tongs, gouged into a mound of olives on the vegetable tray, and plunked six on Anna's plate. "Let's make sure you get plenty of olives before I eat them all. Oh!" She grabbed one and popped it into her mouth. "I just *love* olives! I could eat them all day."

"Thanks." Anna's desperate expression said, *She tainted my whole plate with the things!*

Jeanna retrieved another olive and extended it toward her dog, still clutched under her arm. "Here you are, Kay-Kay," she crooned as the Pekinese gobbled the treat. "I don't want to leave you out."

"I think you're absolutely right, Jeanna!" Elaina claimed with a broad smile. "Why don't we fix Kay-Kay her own dinner." She grabbed Anna's plate and started adding more olives. "Since she likes olives so much, let's give her these and add a few slices of meat and cheese."

"Oh, sure! What a *great* idea!" Jeanna exclaimed and never noticed that Elaina had relieved her sister of the green monsters.

Anna eagerly snatched up another plate and began choosing the items she preferred. Jeanna, distracted with her pooch, ignored Anna. Soon, Bryan arrived in the dining room's arched walkway, carrying a cooler full of sodas. Elaina looked toward the entryway, but saw no sign of Ted.

"Where's Ted?" she asked.

"He ran to the store," Bryan explained and scooted the cooler onto the table's end.

"Whatever for?" Margaret asked as she removed cellophane from the fruit tray.

"He checked out the colas, and said since they were all caffeinated he needed to go get something for Elaina." Bryan smiled toward her. "He said you have a caffeine intolerance."

"Yes, yes, I do," Elaina affirmed.

"I told him we brought some bottled water, too, but—" He lifted his broad shoulders.

"He didn't have to… Whatever possessed him? I would have been glad to just drink water." Elaina stepped toward the door as if she could stop Ted and then halted. "Oh well, if he's already gone, I guess that's that."

Anna moved beside Elaina, nibbled a chip, and mumbled, "*I know what possessed him.*"

"What's that supposed to mean?" Elaina whispered.

"You're smart." Anna quipped on her way toward the cooler. "You figure it out."

Elaina watched her sister as she sashayed toward the cooler, retrieved a soda, and began her trek toward the living room. With a flirtatious wrinkle of her nose, Anna looked over her shoulder, winked at Elaina, and blew her a kiss. Elaina gripped her styrofoam plate until it crackled. She studied the infamous pile of olives as if Anna's actions were of no concern to her. Desperately, she sneaked a peek at Bryan and her mother. The two of them were hovering over the deli platter, locked in conversation about whether the cheese was sharp cheddar or mild. Elaina relaxed her grip on the abused plate full of doggy goodies, and set it on the floor for Kay-Kay.

While Jeanna focused on her dog, Elaina retrieved another plate. Quickly, she constructed her croissant sandwich and chose a few pieces of melon. She didn't want to be the brunt of any more of her cousin's matchmaking comments and decided to cruise toward the living room. Hopefully, Cousin Jeanna would settle at the kitchen bar.

"I'm sorry about all that stuff Jeanna said," Bryan's kind voice broke into Elaina's escape plans.

Nine

She pulled her hand from a bag of pretzels and deposited the treats beside her croissant. "Oh!" she said and wondered if Jeanna's vocabulary was swiftly becoming hers. "It's okay."

Elaina really didn't know *what* to say. The last thing she wanted was to make Dr. Brixby think she was a frantic female bent on chasing every pair of pants in the community. By the same token, she didn't need to insult his masculinity by emphatically denouncing Jeanna's assumptions either. In the middle of all her mental floundering, Elaina hoped her smile didn't appear as stiff as it felt.

"I had no idea she brought me over here to marry me off," Bryan continued. His reticent grin accented tiny crow's feet and struck Elaina as both boyish and endearing. "I thought we were just welcoming a new neighbor. I never intended you and your sister to think…" He studied the trio of shrimp on his plate.

Elaina cleared her throat. "I was just thinking the same thing," she admitted with an assuring grin. "I hadn't planned on a wedding tonight, either."

Bryan's shoulders relaxed. "Good," he said. "Jeanna means well," he gazed toward the plump matron as she rose from dealing with Kay-Kay, "but she's a little overbearing at times." Cousin Jeanna, bent upon pummeling Margaret with a battery of questions, followed her hostess toward the kitchen.

"Truth is," Bryan continued, "my practice is my life. That, and my volunteer work abroad." He shook his head. "Jeanna can't seem to understand that I'm content with my life."

As Bryan spoke, Elaina began to wonder why such an attractive, successful man had escaped matrimony all these years. She estimated he was in his mid-thirties. By this conversation she assumed he wasn't dwelling on marriage.

She reached into the open cooler, scooted aside a layer of ice, and pulled out a bottle of water. Bryan made no effort to add more food to his plate. Instead, he hovered beside Elaina, head bent, as if a debate warred within.

"Your sister reminds me of someone I once knew," Bryan finally released the tormented words.

"Oh really?" Elaina queried and chose not to mention that the man had gone pale when he met Anna. Her stomach rumbled, and she hoped Bryan hadn't heard. While his admission intrigued, her appetite was demanding appeasement.

"Yes, she does. Very much." He stared at the vegetable tray. "It's been years since…" He trailed off as ghosts from the past gyrated across his features. "She's dead," he stated, his voice flat and empty.

"I'm so sorry." Elaina laid her hand on his arm. She doubted his heart was released from the deceased lady. She stopped wondering why he wasn't married and began to speculate if perhaps he was a widower.

Bryan shook his head as if clearing the ghosts. "I'm sorry," he countered. "I shouldn't have brought it up." His lips settled into a strained line. He grabbed at the food as if he were angry with it, and Elaina postponed her journey to the living room.

She hated to just meander off with the poor guy in such a state. Simultaneously, she felt similar to an impostor upon reverent ground. Her rumbling stomach bade her forget Dr. Brixby, his past, and any future conversation. Elaina placed a pretzel in her mouth and chewed. The salty snack did little to counter her need. Nevertheless, Bryan held her captive. Try as she might, Elaina could not leave.

"How old is she?" he squeezed out.

"Who, Anna?" Elaina asked and added that comment to her "most inane questions I've ever posed" list.

He nodded and pinched a strip of lettuce drooping from his plate's edge. "Yes, Anna," he repeated, as if the name were symbolic of all that was pure and right and lovely in the world.

"Twenty-two," she answered.

"Really?" Bryan made eye contact, and Elaina almost stumbled back with the intensity of his torn soul.

"And you're older than she is?"

"By five years."

"I was thinking you must be the youngest Ph.D. in history," Bryan chided, and the pain in his eyes dulled. "I was marveling that I had never met an eighteen-year-old professor before."

Elaina crunched another pretzel. "You aren't the first person who's thought that," she explained.

"I'm thirty-five, by the way," he added with a lift of his mouth. "I guess since I'm being so nosy about your ages, I should reveal mine as well."

"Thanks." Elaina adjusted her glasses and decided that a little humor might do the melancholic doctor some good. "I can sleep more soundly tonight now that I have the piece of information." She allowed her voice to reveal her smile.

One corner of Bryan's mouth quirked. "Maybe you should stop by my office next week. I have a new prescription available for a sinister sense of humor."

"Does it by chance have hemlock in it?" Elaina queried and decided that she and Dr. Brixby stood the potential of becoming good friends.

"Yes, as a matter of fact it does," he purred. "How did you ever guess?"

Jeanna's voice neared from the kitchen. "It does feel so good to wash my hands. Kay-Kay is such a sweetie, but sometimes she has *odors*," she continued as if Kay-Kay were the first canine with such a problem. "Now, I'm ready to eat, eat, eat!"

"I guess I better scoot. The last thing we need is for Jeanna to catch us talking. She'll start throwing rice at us or something."

"Hurry!" Bryan whispered while eyeing the kitchen doorway. "I'll keep her in here."

"Thanks!" Elaina rushed toward the doorway and didn't even look over her shoulder for fear of being fitted for a wedding dress on the spot. By the time she neared the living room, Elaina detected strains of Jeanna's words as she drilled poor Bryan on the virtues of "those wonderful young Woods ladies."

"At long last," Anna drawled the instant Elaina stepped into their mother's antique haven.

With a backward glance, Elaina slowed her pace. Soon she observed Anna perched on the bay window's cushioned ledge.

"Whew!" Elaina whispered. "That was a close call. I barely got out of there before she hit the scene again." While grasping the chilled water bottle, she nudged a strand of hair away from her glasses.

"You mean Jeanna "Olive" Harley?" Anna questioned.

"In the flesh." Elaina neared her sister.

Anna feigned a cringe. "I *hate* those salty green things. I don't even want to think about my food being on the same *plate* with them."

"I know," Elaina said as she settled on the padded window seat, next to her sister. "I think she means well, poor thing, but…" She didn't expound, but chose instead to look at the cottage's front yard. While her mother's new home didn't match the opulence of her former house, the setting was equally serene. Margaret declared it even more appealing, due to the scenic pond across the country lane and the rolling green pastures filled with grazing cattle. The setting sun, which announced that eight o'clock was near, cast long shadows upon the lush oaks and rose garden that graced the home's west side. Elaina detected the faint shrieking of crickets and a distant moo. The mild tinge of Anna's floral perfume seemed to complete the late summer splendor.

But such a scene could not detain the attention of one so hungry. No sooner had Elaina's stomach complained than she crammed the end of her croissant sandwich into her mouth.

"Woof, woof!" Anna teased. "I'm going to hide my hands, in case you decide my fingers are looking yummy." She placed her hands beneath her thin thighs.

Elaina ferociously chewed and nodded. After her first swallow, she said, "Might not be a bad idea," and then scarfed down another bite.

"Now, to the issue at hand," Anna drawled and picked up her bottle of Pepsi, sitting near her empty plate. "Are you the queen bee this weekend or what?" She swallowed a mouthful of cola and winced as it went down.

"What?" Elaina muffled over a mouth full of bread and meat and cheese.

"You've got a music genius chasing all over the countryside for caffeine-free sodas just for little ol' you," she batted her eyelashes, "and while *he's* gone, a medical doctor is flirting with you. I'm starting to wonder if the two of them will be in a duel over you by sunrise."

She narrowed her eyes and produced her best John Wayne imitation, "Meet me by the water tower at sunrise. That is, if yer man enough."

Elaina shook her head and munched a pretzel. "You missed your calling," she claimed, "you should go into theater."

"What? And miss the wild and adventurous life of a secretary?" Anna exclaimed, referring to the part-time job she was interviewing for Monday at Elaina's church.

Try as she might, Elaina couldn't interest Anna in signing up for any courses at Southern Christian University. Anna seemed perfectly content to live at home and work part-time until she married a rich husband who would support her for life. Since their mother was their father's secretary before they got married, Anna believed that must be the best way to nab a well-heeled husband. Elaina couldn't get Anna to understand that if no wealthy man ever proposed she would be hard-pressed to support herself without some form of education. And their mother wouldn't be around forever to support Anna. Elaina was so tempted to embark upon her "sermon," as Anna resentfully dubbed it, that she decided to get back to the subject at hand.

"Bryan and I *weren't* flirting, if you have to know," she firmly claimed. "If you had listened, you would have known—"

"I *did* listen," Anna bobbed her head as if she were the final authority on Elaina's love life. "I was walking in there to see what was taking you so long, and I heard every syllable of the hemlock episode."

"It wasn't an *episode*." Shaking her head, Elaina rolled her eyes. "We were just…" She shrugged.

"Flirting," Anna leaned closer and batted her eyelashes, "dahling!"

"Well if you must know," Elaina continued, "he started out asking about *you!*" She examined her croissant and prepared for another bite.

"Me?" Anna's face scrunched up. "Whatever for?" she asked.

Elaina lowered her sandwich. "I guess you didn't notice Bryan's reaction when he met you?"

Anna crossed her legs. "What do you mean 'reaction'?"

"He went pale, sister dear," Elaina explained and jammed the end of the sandwich into her mouth before she was delayed again.

"Maybe he just needs to get out more," Anna said. "He's probably pushing forty and needs blood pressure medicine or something."

"Humph," Elaina grunted, vigorously chewed, and then swallowed. "He's only thirty-five." She patted her mouth with her napkin.

Her sister waved her hand and shook her head. "Thirty-five…forty…what's the difference? He's one step away from the nursing home."

"I beg your pardon!" Elaina straightened her spine. "He's not *that* much older than *I* am."

"Just like I said," Anna teased, "nursing home material!"

"Oh stop it!" Elaina complained. "You're just so used to robbing the cradle, you can't imagine a mature man being interested in you."

"Robbing the cradle? Since when have I robbed the cradle?" Anna sipped her soda.

"Does the name Barry Walton mean anything to you?"

"Oh, Barry," Anna scoffed. "He was—"

"Eighteen!" Elaina stated.

"Well…" Anna set her soda near her empty plate and shrugged. "Can I help it if younger guys are sometimes attracted to me?"

"Robbing the cradle," Elaina repeated.

"Do you mean that old man was *really* interested in me?" Anna asked, and Elaina deduced the subject change was not an accident. "Like, boy–girl stuff?"

"Well, it appeared that way, yes." Elaina nabbed a tidbit of melon, popped it into her mouth, and reveled in the explosion of moisture and flavor. "He said you reminded him of someone he once knew. By his reaction, my guess is she was someone he once *loved*."

"Well, I can't help him there!" Anna quipped. "He's thirteen years older than I am."

"Dad was fifteen years older than Mom."

"So what! That was *their* problem." "Besides all that, I don't like sleeping with electric blankets," Anna said as if that alone were enough to seal Bryan's doom.

Elaina narrowed her eyes. "Electric blankets?" she questioned. "What does that have to do with anything?"

"He's so old he probably uses one!" Anna observed her sister as if she were daft.

"Oh brother," Elaina complained, "I use an electric blanket in the winter, and I have since I was a teenager. That doesn't have anything to do with—"

"Yeah, but you're a *woman!*"

"Yes, I am." Elaina shook her head. "Thanks for noticing."

"Don't you get it?" Anna leaned toward her. "*Real men* don't use electric blankets."

Elaina relaxed against the window frame and snickered.

"Laugh all you want to," Anna complained with a pout. "But I'm not interested in nursing a weak old man years down the road when I'm still young."

"Okay," Elaina said in a singsong voice, "but you might just be slamming the door in the face of a wonderful opportunity." *At least the guy would be able to support you,* Elaina thought, *unlike Barry Walton, et al.*

"If I didn't know any better, I'd say you were turning into Cousin Jeanna." Anna angled her head and allowed her hair to fall around one shoulder. She stroked the shiny strands as if her hair were a pet.

"If you ever say that again," Elaina threatened, "I'll sit on you and cram olives down you."

Anna opened her mouth and inserted her index finger as if she were about to gag herself. "That would be grounds for sisterly divorce," she teased.

"All I was trying to do was make you believe I wasn't flirting with the doctor, okay?" Elaina said.

"Okay, okay!" Anna held up both hands, palms outward. "I believe you. But you'll have to talk a *year* to convince me you didn't just spend the weekend flirting with Ted."

"I won't lie. I *did* enjoy Ted's company," Elaina admitted with as much reserve as she could muster.

"Enjoyed his company?" Anna wilted her hand across her forehead as if she were about to swoon. "Oh *puuuullllleeeezzzze!* The two of you have been drooling over each other *all weekend!*"

Elaina placed her half-empty plate next to Anna's. "*Now* who's acting like Cousin Jeanna?" she asked.

"Are you going to sit there and tell me that you aren't already smitten with Ted?" Anna's voice rose with every word. "Because if you are, I'll be forced to call you a liar!"

Elaina looked over her shoulder and detected no visual signs of the home's other occupants, only the rise and fall of voices from the dining room. "Hold your voice down," she complained. "I'm not saying I'm not interested in Ted. I am beginning to have a... a...high level of regard for him. He appears to be a very respectable man and very much unlike his—"

"A high level of regard? Respectable?" Anna rocked back and shook her head. "Oh, sister, sister, sister! You've read one too many of those old-fashioned novels you lecture on. Either you've got the hots for him or you don't." She pointed at Elaina's nose. "Now, which is it?"

"Why do you have to be so uncouth about it?" Elaina asked with a frown.

"I would rather be uncouth all day than be without feeling one second," Anna claimed as if Elaina were completely out of touch with her own heart.

"Who said I'm without feeling?" Elaina demanded and popped another piece of melon into her mouth.

"I do, my dear," Anna said and placed her index finger in the center of her chest. "When *I* meet the man of my dreams, *I* will know it."

"As in the second you meet him, you're going to know that he's the one you've been waiting for your whole life?"

"Of course." Anna lifted her chin. "It will be love at first sight. And after that, we'll get married soon. Why wait when you know you've met the right person?"

"Now who's been reading too many old novels?"

"*You* have!" Anna accused and slurped down another swallow of her soda.

Elaina halted any new comments. Long ago she had learned that arguing with Anna was a fruitless endeavor. Why she attempted it now was anybody's guess.

The faint hum of a high-powered engine zooming along the country lane drew Elaina's focus from her sister. She sat straight and strained to catch the first glimpse of what she hoped was a red vehicle. As suspected, a scarlet Corvette rounded the final bend in the road and neared the cottage's driveway. Elaina swallowed hard and carefully peeked at Anna, who was petting her hair again. She looked down at the bottle of water she never opened and smiled. Ted was by far one of the most thoughtful men she had ever met. If things continued to progress, maybe she *would* consider marrying him.

Of course, she reasoned, *we'll have to spend plenty of time getting to know each other first.*

"Well, here he comes now," Anna cooed and Elaina sensed her scrutiny.

She masked every scrap of anticipation and serenely rose from the window seat. The last thing she needed was for Anna to see just how distracted she was by Ted's arrival. From childhood, her younger sister had been known to release information at the most inopportune times. Elaina certainly didn't want her turning such a private issue into public information.

"I'll let him in," Elaina said in an even tone.

"I think I'll go up to my room and watch the TV's blank screen," Anna taunted. "Even *that* would be more exciting than you."

Ten

Ten weeks later Anna put her new Ford Escort into park. She eyed the distance between her car and the covered entry to Lakeland Community Church. Cold rain pelted her windshield as if to mock her lack of an umbrella. When she left the cottage fifteen minutes ago, her mother insisted rain was imminent. Anna ignored her because she couldn't find her umbrella and was running late. She eyed the dash's digital clock.

"Nine-sixteen," she rasped and felt as if Father Time clamped his rigid fingers on the back of her neck.

Anna never understood the world's preoccupation with time. In her estimation, as long as she arrived the time of arrival was immaterial. Her new boss, Grace Livingston, wasn't of the same mind. The merciful director of single's ministries lived up to her name. However, Anna realized early in their relationship that Grace preferred to start the day promptly at nine o'clock—not nine-sixteen. So far Anna had been late only nine mornings during the nine weeks of her employment. That averaged out to one day per week. Nonetheless, Grace's tolerance wore thin all nine of those mornings. This week, her tenth, Anna hadn't been late once. She had hoped to set a new precedent.

Still, Anna toyed with her keys and fretted over the damp distance. Dubiously she observed the concrete parking space bumpers installed last week. Yesterday, she almost tripped over one of them. In an exasperated fit, she abused the thing with a swift kick before stomping to her car. The parking lot now became an obstacle course grueling enough to challenge the best Olympian. She imagined the new church's modern design taking on a surreal, gothic quality through the haze, as if the structure were a forboding, moss-covered sanctuary miles removed from Anna's reach.

The new car smell seemed to beckon her to enjoy the vehicle's warm comfort until the rain subsided. She rubbed at a smudge on the windshield with the hem of her trench coat's sleeve and recalled Elaina's reaction to her recent vehicle purchase.

"You mean you *paid cash* for it?" her sister had queried as if Anna were squandering her inheritance. "I thought your other car was still working fine!"

Anna wondered if her elder sister would ever loosen up. "I still have $10,000 left," she mumbled as if Elaina were present. "I don't know why she has to act like Mother Superior every time I sneeze."

The rain's rhythm increased from a steady drip to an insistent staccato. Anna eyed the darker bank of clouds moving from the north with the promise of an even heavier downpour. After a frantic groan, Anna grabbed her purse, opened the door, and lunged into the parking lot. The car door slammed behind her as she hunched her shoulders and raced for the church office.

So much for my hair, Anna thought and attempted to cover her head with her Gucci bag. A gust of cold wind whipped a sheet of rain into her face and she squealed.

The awning-covered entry loomed only ten feet away. Anna focused on the light, welcoming and warm, that beckoned her indoors. She upped her speed for the final dash. But her pointed-toed pump struck an obstacle that tilted her off balance. Anna flailed her arms and fought the pull of gravity as she tried to correct the mistake with a giant step. The over correction proved her downfall. Before Anna crashed to the pavement, she spotted one of the parking space bumpers. As her right ankle wrenched and her knee ground into the pavement she wished she could rip up the concrete offender with bare hands.

A whimper escaped Anna. She dropped into a soggy heap. The parking lot's oily smell engulfed her. The dark, northern cloud stretched across the parking lot and released a new velocity of rain, as if in sadistic applause of Anna's plight. Although her ankle protested with a dull ache, she grabbed her throbbing knee and groaned. The knee cap felt as if shards of gravel were ground into it. She examined her bloody, torn stockings. As chilling rain dripped against her thighs, Anna decried her decision to wear a short skirt today rather than slacks. Her tears mingled with the moisture on her face as she searched for her purse. The leather bag lay out of reach, eight feet away. Using the cell phone to call Grace for assistance was not an immediate option.

After telling herself to be brave, Anna decided to act like Elaina and just deal with the situation. She clamped her teeth and attempted to struggled to her feet. When she placed her weight on her right foot, spears of pain shot from toe to knee. With a dismayed cry, Anna plopped back onto the sidewalk so hard her derrière burned.

An approaching vehicle roared from nowhere, and Anna looked up into the headlights of a black sport's car, aimed right at her. She felt like an innocent rabbit in the shadow of a buzzard, and her ankle and knee now seemed a minor concern. She imagined herself smashed flat. A scream lodged in her throat. The vehicle skidded to a stop six feet away. As the word "Jaguar" slammed against her vision, she wilted onto her elbow.

A tall man emerged from the car and hurried toward Anna, his dark raincoat billowing.

The cold rain now drenched her face and hair. A trickle slipped down her spine, and a shiver penetrated Anna's bones. The resulting tremors rattled her teeth.

The man lowered himself and placed his face inches from hers. "Where are you hurt?" he asked, his ginger-brown eyes full of concern.

"M–my knee and—and ankle," Anna rasped and managed to inch her throbbing foot forward.

He placed slender fingers upon her injury and gently prodded. "Do you think it's broken?"

"I...I..." Anna groaned and shoved the back of her hand against her mouth. "I don't know," she moaned and closed her eyes. But even with her eyes closed, she could not blot out the impression of a drop-dead gorgeous male with curly dark hair, a tan, and a mouth that begged to be kissed. That's when she decided her ankle must not be broken. Surely, if a bone were fractured she wouldn't have noticed if her rescuer were ancient or the perfect image of manhood.

"I think it's just twisted," she whispered and allowed her eyes to droop open. Her feminine instinct suggested this was *not* the time to be strong.

"Do you think you can walk?" the stranger questioned.

"Oh no," Anna protested. As she vehemently shook her head, she checked the man's left hand for any sign of gold. No band circled his third finger. Anna welcomed his comfort as he wrapped his arm around her back.

"I'll have to carry you inside, then." He hesitated, backed away, and looked her in the eyes. "Is that okay?"

"Y–yes," Anna said and was thankful for the spontaneous hard shiver that couldn't have been better timed.

With a nod, the stranger pulled her closer. "I'm going to support you while you see if you can stand on your good foot. Once we're standing I'll pick you up, okay?"

"Okay," Anna rasped. *You can carry me to the moon,* she added to herself.

"Now, I'm going to count to three, and we'll see if we can pull this off. One...two...three."

Anna gritted her teeth, tried to cooperate, and considered her straight hair, plastered to her head. She also didn't deceive herself into believing that her makeup wasn't running to her chin. When the strong stranger hoisted her into his arms, she hoped he could look past the moisture to find *something* attractive about her.

Even though her knee's initial protests was diminishing, a new arrow of agony pierced her ankle. Anna momentarily forgot the dynamics of her handsome rescuer. Amid a fresh onslaught of shivers, she groaned, closed her eyes, and rested her head against the man's shoulder.

The trek to the doorway proved swift. "You're going to catch pneumonia if we don't get you warm soon," he mumbled as he stopped. A series of hard thuds accompanied Anna's rocking in her handsome knight's arms.

She opened her eyes as he kicked the dark glass door again. He backed away from it just in time to miss being whacked when the door swung open. Grace stood on the other side. Her mouth formed an "o," which accented the pouty line of pink lips against creamy Asian skin.

"Anna!" she exclaimed. "What *happened?*"

"I...I...tr–tripped over—over the new—the new—"

"I saw her go down," the man explained. "I was afraid she'd broken something."

"Here!" Grace hustled toward a sitting area near Anna's office. "Let's put her on the couch." She rushed forward, and the kind stranger followed.

The earth-tone decor of Anna's office streamed into a blur, and her tense stomach rolled. She swallowed another moan and hoped she didn't lose her breakfast on her gallant rescuer.

Grace fussed over plumping pillows on the striped couch and then turned toward the man. "There. That's as good as I can make it," she proclaimed.

With a nod, the man began lowering Anna toward the cushions. But all Anna could envision was wallowing in her wet coat against polished cotton.

"Wait! Wait!" she protested. "Let's see if we c–can get me out of...out of this wet—wet coat first." Another drop of water sashayed down her back. Anna tried to stop the tremors, but to no avail.

"Good idea," Grace agreed.

"If I hold you up, can you rest your weight on your good foot again?" the stranger asked.

After a nod, Anna looked the man square in the face. Beads of rain dotted his tanned skin. A lone droplet shimmied down his cheek, and she was struck by his resemblance to a classic Greek statue carved to celebrate the finest masculine beauty.

Soon she was stationed upon the sofa, and Grace's black wool cape served as a blanket. Her boss fussed over her drenched hair with a plethora of paper towels from the ladies' room. The kind stranger bore a cup of steaming hot cocoa with extra marshmallows, just as Anna requested.

"Oh, thank you," she cooed and smiled as sweetly as her aching ankle would allow. Now that Anna was relaxing, her stomach had long stopped clenching. The cocoa smell proved inviting.

The man finally took the time to slip out of his damp coat and gingerly hang it on the coat tree near the entry.

When he turned back toward them, Grace extended several paper towels. "Want some of these for *your* hair?"

"Sure," he replied and accepted the gift.

As he rubbed his damp hair, Anna sipped her sweet cocoa. She reveled in the warm trail of pleasure which seeped into her stomach. The chills were finally subsiding enough for her to think clearly.

The masculine image before her proved more distracting than she had even realized. The man looked as if he belonged on the cover of a magazine. The wet hair and tan pressed Anna with images of a summer TV commercial. A lean male erupted from the depths of a pool, walked up the steps, and bespoke the superiority of Dr Pepper to quench summer thirst.

When the man stepped away to deposit the paper towels in the trash can, Grace whispered, "How did you manage to get the best-lookin' guy in the south to rescue you?"

Anna, swimming in the aftermath of pain and surprise, found herself without words. Instead, she was overcome with the suspicion that the male before her *was* the Dr Pepper model. Elaina had even teased her one day and said, "Why don't you just marry *him!*" Anna had responded, "For all you know, I just might!" She eyed the expensive cut of his sweater and slacks, pondered his Jaguar, and wondered how much male models earned these days.

"Now," the man said as he approached again, "we probably need to see about getting you to a doctor."

"Uh…" Anna grappled for words.

"Do you have a regular physician or should we go to the emergency clinic?" he asked.

"I haven't lived here long," Anna explained and welcomed another sip of cocoa. She winced with a new stab of pain and downed another generous gulp of the warm liquid.

"What about Dr. Bryan Brixby?" Grace questioned. "He's new in our singles program here. Didn't I see you talking with him after church last Sunday?"

He was talking to me, Anna thought and recalled trying to duck out the glass doors to escape him. "Okay, call him," she choked out before she considered the complications of including Bryan Brixby.

"I'll just be a second then," Grace claimed and rushed toward Anna's office.

Ever since Anna and her mom moved into the neighborhood, Dr. Brixby had paid regular visits. While he spent a good deal of the time chatting with Margaret, Anna felt as if he watched her through every visit…and through every church service. Last week when she spotted his Lexus pulling into their driveway, Anna crammed her feet into her walking shoes and rushed toward the back door.

"I'm going for a walk, Mom," she had called and stepped from the house as the doorbell rang.

Now Anna imagined Bryan smothering her with flowers and chicken soup. *And don't forget the electric blanket!* she snapped to herself. Anna eyed her rescuer. *This hunk of manhood doesn't look like he's* ever *used an electric blanket,* she thought.

He sat on the couch's arm and silently adored her as if she were the only woman on the planet. "I don't believe I know your name," he claimed with a smile that nearly made Anna forget her ankle and stinging knee.

"Anna," she demurely supplied, "Anna Woods."

"Anna...Anna Woods," he spoke the name as if it were luscious. "My very own Annabell Lee," he crooned and then began quoting the famous poem.

> It was many and many a year ago,
>   In a kingdom by the sea
> That a maiden lived there that you may know.
>   By the name of Annabell Lee;
> And this maiden lived with no other thought
>   Than to love and be loved by me....

As the poem unfolded, word for precious word, it calmed Anna. At the end, she join him on the final stanza. When their voices caressed the poem's last line, Anna sighed and felt as if she were melting into the couch's soft folds.

"You like Edgar Allen Poe, too?" she asked.

"So, you know the author as well as the lines." His dark brows rose.

"Yes, he's one of my favorites," she said.

"Really?" the man asked. "Mine, too."

Anna would never have admitted her literary preferences to her elder sister, for fear of Elaina forcing her into a literature class at SCU. While Elaina seemed convinced that Anna was only inches from illiteracy, she immensely enjoyed reading a variety of authors. Anna simply couldn't tolerate college life's stiff structure.

"Okay, I got Dr. Brixby," Grace said as she approached from Anna's office. "He's coming here, believe it or not!" she exclaimed and lifted her arms as if her team just scored a touchdown. Her golden skin glowed with more than just the complement of her pink sweater.

"Whoa!" the gentleman exclaimed. "I thought the days of doctors making house calls was over. You must rank highly on his list." He eyed Anna's left hand.

She strategically placed her left hand around her cup and demurely smiled. "Whether I do or not is no concern of mine," she claimed and held her ankle perfectly still.

Grace cleared her throat and added, "Dr. Brixby also said it would be okay for me to go ahead and give you four ibuprofen." So focused was Anna upon her gentleman that Grace's words barely registered. "He said that's prescription strength," the singles pastor continued. "I'll just go get them from the first-aid kit."

"Now, you never told me *your* name," Anna said as Grace scurried away.

"I am Willis Kenney," he said, "at your service." Willis bowed his head, and the fluorescent lights seemed to sprinkle silver dust upon his damp locks. Anna was reminded of a similar gesture by Ted Farris the day he arrived to help them move.

These past few weeks, Elaina had sidestepped every hint Anna dropped about Ted. Furthermore, Anna hadn't seen them together once. Lately, she began to wonder if her sister and Ted weren't going to be a hot item after all. Faced with Willis' blatant charm, Anna dismissed all thoughts of her sister's love life. Presently she had her own romance to consider.

She tilted her head and conjured the most flirtatious grin she could, despite her smeared makeup and wet hair. "Were you by chance ever in a Dr Pepper advertisement?" she queried.

"Ah, you've discovered my secret," Willis teased with a seductive wink.

She stirred at the pleasant discovery, and her ankle complained. Anna gulped her hot cocoa to hide her wince. Despite all complications, she was beginning to look forward to Bryan's visit.

"Oh man!" Willis smacked his forehead with the heel of his hand. "I forgot! I left my car running in the middle of the parking lot. I better go move it before somebody either hits it or steals it."

"Oh no!" Anna exclaimed as she recalled an oversight of her own. "My purse! It's still lying out in the rain." She wondered if water could seep through leather or seams and imagined all the contents damp and limp.

Willis retrieved his wrap from the coat tree. As he shrugged into it, he moved toward the doorway. "I'll get your purse before I move my car." His grin made Anna wonder if he'd also done toothpaste advertisements. "I'll be right back, darlin'," he called over his shoulder, and Anna strained to catch the very last glimpse of him.

Under normal circumstances, she would have giggled, but all she could muster was a wilting smile. Soon Grace appeared to offer the ibuprofen. Anna gladly swallowed the painkillers and decided she would have cheerfully endured a broken leg for the attentions of Willis Kenney.

Just as she told Elaina, Anna knew beyond doubt she had met the man of her dreams...her knight in shining armor...the fulfillment of all her hopes. By the time Willis swept back into the church office, Anna saw no reason the two of them shouldn't be married by January.

Eleven

Ted stood outside Elaina's office door and gazed through the frosted glass for any signs of life. A nondescript movement coupled with a slight bump suggested the professor was at work. He eyed the name and title on the window and reminded himself that Dr. Elaina Woods was his teacher. Simultaneously, Ted grappled with several excuses for his visit and couldn't conjure one that sounded legitimate. The truth was Ted just wanted to talk with his alluring prof.

A rational voice suggested that he shouldn't do anything to move closer to Dr. Woods. After all, he and Lorna had agreed to announce their engagement not long after graduation, just four weeks away. But his engagement hadn't stopped him from waltzing Elaina across her mom's living room, gazing passionately into her eyes, or racing to the store like some devoted slave for decaf soda. Ted had even honored his promise to go back to her mom's and help them finish the move. That memorable Monday evening, he shamelessly flirted with Elaina to the accompaniment of her mom and sister's approving giggles. Elaina herself had done nothing to discourage him.

Therefore, her behavior the next time they had class momentarily confused Ted. Elaina treated him with the curt respect a student should expect from a professor—and nothing more. After class, Ted hurried from the room without a backward glance. Only when he arrived home did he realize she must be establishing some boundaries for their university relationship. He knew some colleges prohibited student–professor alliances. He recalled that one of his profs even lost a job because of a forbidden attachment with a student. So Ted had decided to back off and do nothing to threaten Elaina's new position. Ted further told himself her attitude was for the best since he was, after all, an engaged man.

The result had been days full of torment, days in which Ted thought of nothing but the forbidden relationship with the forbidden professor. Like a moth darting toward a deadly flame, Ted could no longer inhibit the compulsion to make contact with Elaina. Ten weeks had passed since they enjoyed a personal conversation. Ten weeks of nothing but professional, in-class interaction. Ten weeks in which Ted had begun to wonder if Elaina viewed their special weekend as a casual game and nothing more.

As of this evening, he could stand the torture no longer. On his drive to the university, Ted convinced himself he must end his misery. He even told himself that the outcome would probably be better for Lorna. If Elaina cared nothing about a relationship with him, then Ted could more peacefully endure his engagement.

He eyed the corner of his latest research paper, peeking past his folder's cover. Elaina had written, "98 Great Work!" at the top. After the struggle for an explanation of the visit, he decided he should thank her for the good grade.

Ted wrapped his fingers around the cool knob. Another thud from within accompanied his releasing the knob. He balled his fist to knock and then gripped the door facing. Ted eyed the cuffs of his sweat pants touching his Reeboks.

Lorna would not be happy with this visit. *Oh well*, he thought, *what she doesn't know won't hurt her.* Somewhere in the back of his mind, Ted wondered if he could somehow convince Lorna to hold off announcing their engagement awhile longer.

A tall, thin woman carrying a bag of microwave popcorn and a Caffeine-free Diet Coke rounded the corner. Ted recognized her as Dr. Johnson, the Medieval English professor. He had seen Elaina talking with her several times and speculated they must be friends. He wondered what Dr. Johnson would think of a student hovering outside Dr. Woods' office with no apparent intent. Straightening his back, Ted knocked on Elaina's door.

A louder thump preceded a faint, "Yow!" A pained "come in" followed.

Ted twisted the knob and stepped into the office. "Everything okay in here?" he asked with a concerned smile.

Her face tense, Elaina yanked off her glasses. She hobbled toward her rolling chair, shoved against a loaded bookcase. "I just dropped the edge of my desk on my toe. That's all," she growled. Elaina tossed her glasses to the center of her desk and plopped into the chair with the squeak and roll of wheels.

"Were you trying to move it?" Ted eyed the oak desk. The thing looked to weigh at least a hundred pounds.

"Yes." She slipped off her low-backed loafer and rubbed her big toe.

"Do you think you broke your toe?" Ted closed the door and plunked his book and folder into a nearby chair. He stepped toward Elaina and examined her stockinged toe which sported a red blotch below the nail.

She wiggled it. "No. I really don't think so. I think I just did a grand ol' job of smashing the living daylights out of it." She lowered her foot to the floor and flexed her toe. "The pain is already diminishing some," she added with a weak smile.

"Here, let me help." Ted stepped toward the desk. He had never claimed to be the body-building sort, but he was always glad to use his upper body strength to help the ladies—especially one as delightful as Elaina. "Tell me where you want this elephant."

"I was just trying to angle it in front of the corner." She pointed toward her projected destination. "That way, my chair fits in the corner and I'll still have room to roll. I was hoping it would open up a little more office space for me."

"Consider it done," Ted said and began the heave-ho process. Soon the desk was exactly where the lady desired.

With no signs of a limp, she squeezed her chair into the corner, sat in it, and rolled within inches of the desk. "There!" Elaina's grateful grin reminded Ted of the heartfelt thanks she'd extended after they finished unpacking her mother's belongings. Focusing on the subject in tonight's class would prove a challenge.

"Now, what can I do for you?" She replaced her glasses as if she were dedicated to resuming business as usual. Despite her attempts at remaining professional, Ted sensed the undercurrent of attraction from weeks ago. As if he were watching the rerun of a favored movie, Ted relived those moments when Anna stopped playing the piano. He and Elaina were left to sway in each other's arms with only the music of two hopeful hearts.

"Uh…" Ted turned to pick up his book and folder, moved the extra chair toward the desk, and then sat down. "I came to contest this grade." Forcing back a smile, he slipped the research paper from his folder.

With a frown, Elaina adjusted her glasses and accepted the paper. "But this is a 98," she countered, "and the highest grade I gave on any of the papers."

Ted's soft chuckle instigated her looking up. "I was teasing," he said, and her expression softened. "I really wanted to say thanks."

"No thanks needed for me," she said without the hint of humor. Elaina extended the paper across the desk. "You're the one who did all the great work."

Wrestling with what else to say, Ted accepted the paper, placed it atop his book, and then checked his stainless steel watch. Still an hour before class started. If it weren't for the trace of warmth in her baby blues, Ted would have vowed the woman didn't even remember they'd shared a memorable weekend.

He glanced back at Elaina and couldn't get past the effect of a cobalt-blue sweater against coppery hair and blue eyes. "So, how are your mom and sister these days?" he finally asked.

She looked down. "Fine, as far as I can tell. I got a call from Mom about an hour ago. Anna had a nasty fall this morning at the church where she works. Looks like she's sprained her ankle. I'm tied up tonight, obviously," she waved toward the stack of notes in the desk's center, "but I'm going to go see her tomorrow night. You know," she shrugged, "take her some chocolates and a good book."

"Ah, chocolate!" Ted teased. "The caffeinated cure for everything."

Elaina tugged on the neck of her sweater. One corner of her mouth lifted, and Ted sensed that maybe she was forgetting she was his professor.

As the room fell into another awkward silence, Ted observed the Thomas Kinkade painting on the wall behind her. The country cottage sent forth a beckoning welcome and reminded Ted of Margaret Woods' home. "If I didn't know any better, I'd say Kinkade used your mom's new place as a model for that painting."

"I thought the exact same thing the first time I saw her cottage." Elaina swiveled to observe the painting. "It's amazing, isn't it?"

"Yes," Ted agreed and drummed his fingers on the chair's arm, "amazing."

The air seemed too heavy to breathe, and Ted wondered if someone had upped the heater. A thousand possibilities cavorted through his mind, including his politely taking leave. Finally, he decided to be honest.

"I guess I should come clean, Elaina…" He hesitated and searched her face for any new encouragement. "I really stopped by tonight to tell you…" Ted fidgeted with the research paper and felt as if he were a junior high kid in the throes of a crush on his favorite teacher. Crinkling the paper did nothing to help him form a coherent statement.

"I haven't called since your mom's move because I picked up on your vibes and had a hunch you were probably under some kind of policy against fraternizing with students," he explained. "But now that the semester is getting close to an end, I thought maybe..." When Ted observed Elaina again, the controlled reserve was replaced with the uncertainty of a woman on the precipice of adoration.

"I thought maybe you just didn't..." she started.

"Oh, but *I did*," Ted answered. His book and folder slid off his lap and banged on the floor. He ignored them, leaned forward, and said, "I did *very much*. I just thought you probably needed to keep things distant for professional reasons. I didn't want you to think I was pushing myself off on you," he said and forgot to remember Lorna.

She nodded and glanced behind Ted toward the door, as if she feared the "professor police" would explode into the room. "I thought about calling you a few times," she said in a low voice, "but I..." Elaina averted her gaze and picked up a pen. "I've never been one to do the chasing," she said and Ted read between the lines.

"Or you just didn't want me to think you were chasing me. Is that it?"

"Well..." Elaina opened the desk's center drawer, dropped the pen inside, and snapped the drawer shut.

Ted detected feminine reticence in the midst of all Dr. Woods' self-confidence. Masculine instinct invited him to enjoy the thrill of pursuit. "You know," he said, "some of us guys do enjoy a little encouragement. I was beginning to think that maybe *you* didn't..."

"Oh, but *I did*." She leaned forward. "I did *very much*." Elaina hesitated and observed her office door again.

Ted nearly suggested that they wait until after the semester's end to pick up where they left off. *But I'll be announcing my engagement then,* he told himself. Ted suppressed a groan. Never did he anticipate such complications when he promised Lorna he'd stand by his word this time—no matter what. Ted tried to make himself relive that cold night when Lorna knocked on his door. She'd been weeping and was covering a black eye. By the evening's end, he had been as enraged with himself for breaking his word as he was with her husband. While that brute had bruised her face, Ted had bruised her heart.

"Would you like to meet me tomorrow night at my mom's?" Elaina's question annihilated all images of Lorna and her problems. "Earlier on the phone she said she'd have dinner ready for me when I go to visit Anna. I'm sure she'd be thrilled to see you again."

"Are you sure?" Ted asked. "I don't want to do anything to compromise your position here."

Elaina's thoughtful expression hinted that she did possess some doubts. "I think if we keep a really low profile between now and the end of the semester we'll be okay. I don't think it would be very wise for either of us to be seen riding with the other one again. Once probably wouldn't raise any questions—especially since you're nearly a relative and were helping Mom move. But other than that…" She shook her head.

"Right," Ted said, "I fully understand. Now, what time do you think your mom will have dinner ready?"

Elaina's unrestrained smile reminded him of all the reasons he'd wanted to kiss her ten weeks ago.

"About five, I believe," she said. "She's always an early bird on the evening meal."

"I'll be there!" Ted blurted before even considering what he would tell Lorna. He vaguely remembered her mentioning traveling to Dallas with a friend to shop for a wedding dress. If the heavens were smiling on him, that trip would be scheduled for this weekend, not the next.

Twelve

By four o'clock the next evening, Elaina was pulling her Honda into her mother's driveway. The pleasing drive through eastern Oklahoma's rolling pastures and woods culminated in the scene before her. As Elaina cruised along the winding, paved driveway, she thanked God for the quality home Cousin Jeanna and her husband had offered her mother at such an affordable price. The wintry sun, tilting toward the west, christened the yard's golden-leafed oaks in an explosion of color. Even the white wicker furniture sitting on the porch took on a flaxen hue. Elaina was hard-pressed to realize that yesterday had been so drab and wet...or that the current temperature was so bitterly cold.

As she rolled closer to the two-story cottage, she recalled Ted's comments about the home resembling the Thomas Kinkade painting in her office. Thoughts of Ted instigated an anticipating smile. Seeing him week after week in class, yet not knowing what the man was thinking, had so thoroughly distracted Elaina she was barely able to concentrate on her lectures. Having Anna and her mother periodically inquire about Ted only increased her discouragement. Nevertheless, Elaina gracefully sidestepped their questions and hadn't allowed either to detect her heightening dejection.

With the onslaught of autumn, Elaina grew more intensely attached to Ted than she ever had any other gentleman. At last, she wondered if she were in the clutches of new love. No other option proved reasonable.

Ted's visit yesterday had so surprised and delighted Elaina that she had been hard pressed not to fall into giddy chatter. Nevertheless, she purposed to maintain the calm aura which served her well in every situation. By the time Ted agreed to tonight's dinner, a renewed surge of confidence left Elaina breathless. All doubts vanished; only expectation remained.

Elaina pulled her car around the side of the house and parked outside the closed garage beside a black Jaguar. The distraction of the vehicle jolted her thoughts from Ted to Anna's latest news. Elaina examined the vehicle and deduced that it must belong to her sister's recent acquaintance. Yesterday when her mother called to detail Anna's accident, she incessantly praised Willis Kenney, the "perfect gentleman" who rescued her sister from the parking lot.

"Not only is he the kindest person you'll ever meet," Margaret had continued, "he's also the most handsome! I nearly melted into a puddle when I met him yesterday, and I'm an old widow woman!"

As she retrieved her sling bag and got out of her Honda, Elaina dubiously scrutinized the classy sports car. Once she pressed the button on her keys that locked her vehicle's door, Elaina dropped the keys into her coat pocket. She hugged herself against the bone-biting breeze and stepped closer to the vehicle. The sun's bronze aura cloaked the Jaguar in a surreal glow, as if the owner were a mythological god whose vehicle radiated with supernatural powers.

A suspicious imp suggested that the guy behind the car might be superficial, conceited, and immature, just to name a few of his "better" traits. Elaina had watched too many men who fit Willis

Kenney's description break the hearts of too many women to ever offer blind trust to his type—or any type, for that matter. She also knew Anna, and knew her well. Elaina wouldn't be surprised to learn that her sister was already declaring herself in love with her new champion.

Shaking her head, Elaina hunched her shoulders against the wind. The smell of smoke drifting from the cottage's chimney promised a warm fire and a welcoming hearth. Elaina hurried past a pair of decorative cedars onto the front porch. After a light rap on the red door, adorned with an autumn wreath, she tried the knob. It turned with little effort.

Elaina hurried into the balmy entryway and snapped the door closed against the frigid air. The aroma of her mother's mouthwatering pot roast sent a rumble through her stomach. Elaina stuck her thumb into the waistband of her size-ten slacks and reminded herself she didn't want to expand into a size twelve any time soon.

Margaret Woods emerged from the formal living room, her hair spiraling around her face in a new style *and* color. "Is Ted with you?" Margaret asked, her face aglow.

"No. He's—he's coming later," Elaina stammered as she attempted to absorb the changes in her mom.

Last Sunday Elaina had enjoyed a noon meal with a graying mother who fretted over whether or not Elaina ate all her vegetables. Today, she gaped at a woman who had dyed her hair the same shade as Elaina's. That, plus the new look in cosmetics, peeled ten years off Margaret's age. Speechless, Elaina came to the conclusion that Margaret Woods had morphed into a sassy fifty-year-old overnight.

"Mother!" Elaina finally gasped. "What have you *done* to yourself?" She dropped her sling bag on a coatrack hanger and then attempted to loop her leather coat atop it but kept missing. Elaina stopped gaping at her mother to examine the rack and finally hook her coat.

"I decided it was time for a new look!" Margaret plumped the back of her spiral curls. "I wanted to tint my hair when I first started turning gray, but Joseph said he liked the gray better. Now," she shrugged, "I decided I was ready to be a redhead again, I guess."

"Wow!" Elaina said and circled her mom. This time she also noticed her mother's new blue pantsuit. While Elaina and Margaret agreed that Anna looked good in any color, they readily admitted the two of them were best in blue.

"You look great!"

"Do you really think so?" Margaret asked and touched her cheeks.

"Yes!" Elaina shook her finger at her mother's nose. "If you don't watch out, there will be *two* Jaguars in the driveway!"

"Oh stop it!" Margaret slapped at her daughter's hand. "You know your father was the only man for me! I just started feeling…" she shook her head, "I don't know, dowdy, I guess. This week I just knew it was time to do something different."

"Well, I'm glad." Elaina embraced her mom in a tight hug. She detected a light, floral fragrance that meant Margaret had even changed from Joseph's favorite—Opium. Elaina squelched the emotions that threatened to well in her eyes. Seeing her mother mourn for her father had been nearly as painful as losing him. Tonight was the first time since the funeral that the shadows of loss didn't mar her mother's blue eyes.

"Well, enough of this!" Margaret said as they parted. She squeezed Elaina's hands. "You've got to meet Anna's new friend! He is just too scrumptious for words!"

The sound of footsteps neared from the living room seconds before a long shadow fell in the entryway. The man appeared next. Willis Kenney observed Margaret with a fervent urgency that suggested Anna must have fallen into the gravest of fevers and was on the brink of death.

He glanced toward Elaina and then peered at Margaret with an apology in his ginger-brown eyes. "Anna is asking about the ibuprofen," he said as if he were requesting the preservation of her life. "And now she's also wanting a Pepsi."

"Oh! Of course!" Margaret lifted her reading glasses from her chest and allowed them to plop back into place on their chain. "I got sidetracked with my other daughter here."

She laid a hand on Elaina's arm. "This is Elaina, by the way," Margaret said and then looked back at Willis. "And this is Anna's angel in disguise," she oozed, "Willis Kenney."

"Pleased to meet you," Elaina said as Willis neared.

"And you as well," Willis answered. He offered a considerate smile and shook her hand.

While Margaret flitted away for the medicine and soda, Elaina was struck with the reason her mother had threatened to melt into a puddle when she first met Willis. The man was every bit as arresting as her mom had vowed. She released his hand and was certain she had seen him or his look-alike in TV and magazine ads. The car in the driveway coupled with the expensive cut of his navy jacket and clay-colored slacks suggested he wasn't lacking for funds. A high-profile modeling job would most likely explain his cash flow.

"How's Anna?" Elaina asked and began analyzing the man's character. Surprisingly, Willis didn't possess the air of conceit Elaina would have suspected from someone as attractive as he. *But I just met him,* she thought, *he might hide it well.*

"She's going to live," he answered as they turned toward the living room, "but her ankle is giving her plenty of grief. I'm just glad I was there to help her. I'm afraid if she'd stayed out in that cold rain too long she might have come down with ammonia."

Elaina stopped walking and glanced up at him. "Don't you mean *pneu*monia?" she queried with a mild smile.

"Of course." He faced her, his forehead wrinkling. "What did I say?"

"You said *ammonia*," she said through a chortle.

Willis joined her laughter. "Believe it or not, I'm the great, great, great nephew of none other than Lady Malaprop."

"Ah, the famous neoclassical character who mixed her words up like a bag of potpourri. And how do you so readily know of her?" Elaina asked.

"I minored in English in college," Willis explained and clasped his hands behind his back.

"Where did you go to college?" Elaina asked and began to wonder if all her assumptions about Willis Kenney might prove incorrect. Not only was he not conceited, the man had an education. Elaina's mind raced with the possibilities that Willis might one day influence Anna to attend college. *Only time will tell about that…and his character,* she reminded herself.

"Don't sound so surprised," he teased. "Do I strike you as only an eighth-grade graduate or what?"

"No, of course not." Elaina looked down. "It's just that I didn't—" She stopped herself from saying, "I didn't expect Anna to bring home someone educated or mature enough to appreciate education." Elaina glanced toward the living room. At this angle, she barely glimpsed part of Anna's dark hair scrunched against a mound of pillows. Facing the fireplace, she lay on the claw-footed couch. Even though her face remained hidden, Elaina suspected her sister was straining for every word of their conversation. Not only did she not want Anna to hear something negative, Elaina preferred not to criticize Anna to Willis.

"I know." Willis crossed his arms. "You expected the Jag to belong to some fast-mouthed, slow-thinking hotshot, didn't you?"

"Weeelllll…" Elaina dragged out the word in hopes of diverting Willis from her original assumptions.

"If it's any consolation," he continued, his eyes dancing, "I attended Oklahoma State University and majored in acting."

Before they began their trek into the living room again, Elaina asked, "If you majored in acting, then you must be in the business."

"A little," Willis answered with a secretive smile.

"Were you by chance in a Dr Pepper advertisement last summer?" she asked and recalled telling Anna she should marry the hunk who stepped out of the pool and spoke the praises of

Dr Pepper. Anna had stuck out her bottom lip and said, "For all you know, I just might!"

"You and your sister must have really liked that ad," Willis said with an unaffected grin. "Yes, that was me—or should I say that was I. I understand you have a Ph.D. in English. I would hate to trample our beloved language in your presence." He bowed his head as if in deference to her superior knowledge.

"You won't offend me in the least," Elaina assured. "I would have said 'that was me.' We all do. If I get too starchy about grammar, I'll be no fun and short on friends."

Willis stepped into the living room. "Well, I will *gladly* be your friend any day," he claimed with brotherly generosity.

Following close behind, Elaina sensed herself genuinely liking Anna's new acquaintance, despite her initial reservations. *Maybe I was too quick to judge,* she mused and remained near the entry as he stepped closer to Anna.

Willis sat in a wing-backed chair scooted close to Anna's side. He picked up a familiar-looking book from the seat and then indulgently smiled at something Anna said.

Elaina narrowed her eyes and determined not to be swift in pronouncing Willis trustworthy—not until time proved him so. A man with his looks most likely lived through women chasing him since he was old enough to shave. Elaina wasn't naïve enough to think the guy's past wasn't dotted with a long string of broken relationships. Many of his girlfriends may have even been models and actresses who were far more beautiful than Anna. While Elaina's sister had always turned more heads than she, Anna typified the sweet girl-next-door, not a camera-friendly femme fatale. All Elaina could do was pray that Willis would eventually prove her worries wrong and that her little sister wouldn't get hurt.

Thirteen

Accompanied by the crack and sizzle of the fire, Elaina strode forward and settled onto the edge of Anna's couch. The sweet aroma of burning wood spawned childhood memories of her and Anna sitting in their father's lap by the fireplace.

"Some people will do anything for a little attention," Elaina teased and squeezed her sister's hand.

"Who me?" As Anna touched her chest, Elaina noted the dark circles under her eyes that even a skillful application of makeup could not hide.

"You're a fine one to talk." Anna feigned a glare. "I heard you flirting with Willis. I just told him you were a shameless flirt and not to take anything you said seriously."

"What?" Elaina sat straight. "I'm not the flirt."

Anna turned her head toward Willis. "She tries to act all staid and boring," she claimed, "but I've personally seen her flirting with two men this very fall. *Three* counting you." She touched Willis' fingers, and he covered her hand with his. "No telling how many men I've missed!" Anna wrinkled her nose and lowered her voice. "It's a shame to society, you know."

Elaina released a good-natured laugh. She didn't bother to suggest that Anna was projecting her own behavior onto her elder sister. Instead, she patted her shoulder and said, "How are you feeling today?"

"I hurt," Anna pouted in the most pitiful voice Elaina had ever heard.

Willis placed the familiar book on the coffee table, which Faye had tried to swindle from Margaret. The priceless antique was covered with stationary and teacups in saucers. Neither Anna nor Willis seemed to notice the mess as he lifted her fingers to his lips. Elaina, tempted to gawk over Anna and Willis' intimacy, was equally distracted at the book title: *America's Best Loved Poets*.

No wonder I recognized the book, she thought, *it's mine!* Elaina had chosen to leave some of her volumes in the family library in hopes that Anna might discover the joys of classical literature and go to college. She assumed Willis must have been reading Anna classical poetry.

"I wonder where Mom is with my ibuprofen and soda," Anna whimpered.

"She probably started fussing over something she's cooking and forgot all about the medicine," Elaina said. "I got her off track when I arrived."

"I'll go—" Elaina and Willis simultaneously spoke and rose.

"It's okay, Elaina," Anna said and gripped her sister's hand, "let Willis go. You've got to be tired after working all day." She threw in a discreet wink.

"Yes, I'll go," Willis gallantly agreed.

The second he stepped from the living room, Anna giggled and raised up on one elbow. "Oh, Elaina," she whispered, "isn't he the most drop-dead gorgeous man you have *ever met?*"

"Well, I hadn't thought of him in *those* terms," Elaina admitted. "But yes, he does appear to be," she raised her brows and nodded, "better looking than most of the men I've encountered."

"Most?" Anna huffed and flopped back onto the couch. "Most?" she repeated. "How can you say most? Try *all!*" Anna's cheeks flushed with the excitement of a child at her first circus.

"Looks aren't everything," Elaina said and anticipated Anna's scandalized response.

"Oh, you're just jealous because he's better looking than Ted." Anna tugged the bright afghan up to her chin and sniffed. "That is, if you and he are even an item any more. You won't even tell Mom and me *that* much. You might be jealous because you don't even have a boyfriend."

"I am *not* jealous," Elaina denied and assumed her mom must not have told Anna that Ted was coming for dinner. "I'm just saying that a man can have all the looks in the world, but without good character—"

"Are you suggesting Willis doesn't have good character?"

"No, of course not. He seems really nice and genuine, but I can't know for sure about his character at this point. I just met him!"

"Well, *I* know." Anna lifted her chin.

"You do?"

"Yes."

"But you've only known him a day." Elaina inserted her finger through an opening in the afghan's weave.

"But my heart told me from the moment he scooped me into his arms that he's sterling through and through." She silently dared Elaina to refute her. "Just this evening I've discovered that he's the nephew of Nancy Moncleave, whose estate is just a few miles from us. He lives in Tulsa and travels all over the place for his modeling agency. He says he spends time with his Aunt Nancy several times a year. She never married and doesn't have any children." Anna tucked her hand beneath her pillow. "Willis is the closest thing she's got to a son. Since he's resting right now from all his work, she asked him to come stay with her for awhile. Anyway, Cousin Jeanna has mentioned Nancy Moncleave a whole bunch of times and seems to really respect her."

But that doesn't automatically mean that Willis is respectable, Elaina silently argued. *Lots of respectable people have relatives who are rakes.*

"I also know something else!" Anna declared.

"And what is that?" Elaina hoped Anna's next words didn't involve matrimony.

"He's the person I'm going to marry." She leaned forward.

Elaina suppressed a groan and remained sedately focused upon her sister.

"He's the one, Elaina," Anna whispered, her dark-smudged eyes glistening with wonder. "It was love at first sight. It was just like I told you it would be. I knew within minutes."

She imagined Anna marrying Willis in a week, only to discover some dreadful secret that made her miserable for life. Elaina, fighting for control of her rising panic, squeezed all alarm from her voice and tried to sound reasonable. "Are you sure you weren't so carried away by his looks that you interpreted surface attraction for something deeper?"

"Oh, Elaina, Elaina, Elaina." Anna shook her head and observed her sister as if she were a romantic nincompoop. "Sometimes I wonder if you'll ever fall in love. If you don't watch out, you'll wind up like Bryan Brixby, old as dirt and still single."

"Bryan Brixby is not old as dirt," Elaina asserted. She started to add that she had her first clue he was a man of character when he began attending their church and participated in communion as well as altar prayer. Whether Willis Kenney would prove to be of good character or not was still unanswered.

"Besides," Elaina added, "Willis looks to be about thirty. If that's how old he is, that would put him only five years behind Bryan."

"Oh whatever," Anna huffed, "let's don't even talk about Bryan." She rolled her eyes as if the mere mention of his name was a burden.

"Didn't Mom tell me he came to the church to examine your ankle?" Elaina asked and adjusted her glasses.

"Oh yes," Anna said. "And then we went to the outpatient clinic for x-rays."

"He took you?"

"No, no, no. He followed Willis and me there." Anna scooped a section of hair across her shoulder and began petting it. "He wouldn't let me ride with Willis unless he followed in his car. Can you believe that? He's acting like I'm twelve and he's my father." Anna tugged on a section of hair.

"Well, I'm glad he followed you," Elaina said. "At least there was somebody there for you if Willis decided he wasn't going to behave like the decent sort."

"But he *is*, Elaina!"

"I'm not saying he isn't," she countered. "I'm just saying that you had only just met Willis. It isn't wise for a woman alone to get into a vehicle with a man she just met—especially if he's driving and she's injured and can't defend herself."

Anna covered her eyes with her forearm as if she had withstood as much of Elaina's logic as she could stomach. "And this from the woman who met Ted Farris on Thursday night and drove two hours to Oklahoma City with him Friday morning."

"But that's different," Elaina disputed. She clasped her hands and covered her exasperation at Anna's sharp observations. "We're nearly related!"

"Oh, and no woman in the history of mankind has ever been hurt by a relative or a near relative?"

"I'm not saying that," Elaina shot back. "It was just a completely different situation—that's all. Besides our being near relatives, *I* was the one driving, and I *didn't have* a preexisting injury." *Also,* she thought, *I knew I could trust Ted.* But Elaina didn't dare voice the comment because Anna had declared the same about Willis. The real issue was that Elaina had faith in her own judgment and none in Anna's.

"Well, I think you and Bryan should just skip being parents and go for being grandparents," Anna grumbled. She lowered her arm. Her eyes still closed, she turned her head toward the couch back. "You both act like you're ninety and it's 1850—at least where *I'm* concerned. The rules seem to be different where *you're* concerned."

"Maybe we just care enough about you to not want to see you get hurt," Elaina said and ignored Anna's cut.

"Let's change the subject, okay?" Anna snapped.

With a sigh, Elaina rose and moved toward the fireplace. She clasped her hands behind her back and reveled in the warmth that sank past her cashmere sweater and knit slacks.

What a contrast to Anna's freeze out, she thought and peered toward her younger sister. Eyes closed, Anna jutted out her bottom lip as if she wouldn't ponder another syllable of Elaina's advice.

"Would you please do me one big favor?" Elaina questioned, and she wasn't surprised when Anna didn't even bother to turn her head or open her eyes. "Anna, would you please not do something rash and just haul off and marry the guy next week or anything like that? At least give it some time before you—"

"How much time is enough in your books, Elaina?" At last, Anna opened her eyes and glared fire-laden arrows at her sister. "Twenty years?"

"Now you know that's not what I meant." She lifted her hand and tried to stop her shoulders from tensing. The effort was wasted. "A year would be nice. It's a reasonable enough time to give you time to really get to know him. I just don't want you—"

"I know what you meant, and I know what you want," Anna snapped. "You would love nothing more than for me to dance to *your* tune and do exactly what *you* say, so *you*," she pointed at Elaina, "can control *me*." She jabbed her index finger against her chest.

Elaina's mouth fell open.

"It's just like your trying to force me to go to college. You'd like nothing more than for me to become an Elaina clone! Well, I am *not you*, nor will I ever be! And while I'm on the subject," Anna balled her fists atop the afghan, "it's none of your business if I pay cash for one car or a whole fleet of cars."

"Anna!" Elaina tucked her hair behind her ear and noticed her fingers were trembling. "I never meant...I never intended—"

"You may have been able to boss me around when we were kids, Elaina Woods." Anna narrowed her eyes. "But it won't work now. I'm an adult. I am not thirteen. I will marry whom I please when I please, and I don't have to ask *your* permission or Mom's permission, for that matter. Thankfully, Mom approves of Willis." She lifted her chin. "At least *she* respects my judgment."

The doorbell's merry chime sliced through the room's tension. Elaina, choking in an ocean of dismay, welcomed the reprieve. "I'll get it," she mumbled and hurried from the fireplace.

"Oh heaven help me," Anna complained. "That's probably Bryan. He promised to come over this evening and check on me. That's the *last* thing I need right now."

Fully expecting Bryan herself, Elaina marched toward the front door. Still scowling in the aftermath of Anna's tongue-lashing, she yanked open the door as if she were a general invading enemy territory.

Ted Farris stood on the porch. He bore a trio of golden gift bags stuffed with silver tissue. Before Elaina could overcome her shock enough to utter a word, Ted's welcoming smile wilted into uncertainty. His eyes shifted as if he were sure he'd committed the gravest of errors.

"Didn't you invite me over for dinner tonight?" he queried.

"Yes...yes...oh yes," Elaina stammered. "It's just that..." The sound of firm footsteps neared the entryway. She looked over her shoulder.

Willis emerged from the formal dining room and cast her a smile that had probably stopped leagues of feminine hearts. He lifted a bottle of ibuprofen and a glass of Pepsi. "I got them!" Willis exclaimed and glanced past Elaina to Ted before walking into the living room.

"Maybe I shouldn't be here," Ted said. Elaina swiveled back to face him. A red flush crept up Ted's cheeks as ire sparked his dark eyes. "It looks like you already have a guest."

Elaina, still so exasperated with Anna she could barely gather a coherent response, shook her head. "No...no...oh no!" She leaned forward and hissed, "He belongs to my sister."

A sheepish smile replaced Ted's frown. "Oh, sorry," he stammered and glanced down.

She peered toward the sun-kissed yard where golden leaves proved far more warm and inviting than the chilling fireside indoors. "I—I think I need a walk," Elaina declared.

"Huh?" Ted asked, his gaze blank.

"A walk," she explained. "I need one."

"Oooookaaaaay," he dragged the word out as if she were speaking Japanese and he was clueless.

Without further explanation, Elaina snatched her leather coat from the rack, stepped into the bitter chill, and snapped the door shut behind her.

Fourteen

"Besides all that," Elaina added and paused near the wicker settee on the porch, "seeing your gifts for Anna made me remember I brought a bag of goodies for her myself, but I left them in the backseat of my car."

Ted lowered the bags to his side. "Is everything okay, Elaina?" he asked as a wisp of icy breeze danced across her cheeks.

"No, it's not." She sighed, looked down, and blinked against an unanticipated sting in her eyes. "My sister has essentially just told me to get out of her life and stay out." Elaina inserted her hands into her coat pocket, toyed with her keys, and swallowed a lump in her throat. She gazed toward the biggest oak in the yard. A lone squirrel preparing for the night's slumber scurried up the trunk as if he were running from a shiny-fanged canine.

I know how you feel little guy, she thought.

"Sheesh, I'm sorry." Ted deposited the gift bags on the wicker table. He neared Elaina, squeezed her arm, then awkwardly stepped away as if he had been going to hug her but backed out.

Elaina blinked away the sting and wished he had gone through with the hug. "I guess she thinks I'm trying to boss her around," she explained. "But..." Elaina stepped toward the porch's edge and rubbed her finger along the white railing. "I'm just concerned about her, I guess. That guy you saw in there—she just met him yesterday, and she's already talking like she'd marry him next week." Elaina balled her fist against the railing. "She doesn't even know anything about him. He could be a shameless womanizer for all we know."

"He's got the looks for it," Ted acknowledged and stepped beside Elaina.

"He's a model." She glanced up at him. "Remember that Dr Pepper ad last summer you saw every time you turned on the TV?"

"Yeah!" Ted shook his head as recognition ignited his features.

"Him in the flesh," Elaina said. "It's not that I mind her seeing him or anything. I just don't want her to jump into something she'll regret for the rest of her life just because she's met a man who, in her immortal words, is drop-dead gorgeous."

"And when you told her all this, she—"

"Essentially threw a modified fit and told me I was trying to control her."

Ted draped his arm around Elaina's shoulders and offered a gentle squeeze. "She'll come around," he comforted. "She's got to realize sooner or later you wouldn't say anything if you didn't care."

"Right," Elaina mumbled. "I just hope it's not after he rips her heart out." She hesitated before making the next statement, but the distant hum of a car's engine seemed to incite Elaina to release her thoughts. "If only all men could be like you, Ted."

"Like me?" he bleated and moved his arm.

"You know, honorable and trustworthy. The kind of man who keeps his word."

"And how do you know that for sure about me?" He averted his gaze and tugged on the neck of his sweater as if he were suffocating.

"I see the same thing in your eyes that was in my father's," she explained. "Over and over again I watched my dad keep his word, no matter what—right up to his deathbed." Elaina tried to leach all traces of bitterness from her voice. At times she wondered if her father might have been a little too conscientious when it came to his will.

"Correct me if I'm wrong," Elaina continued, "but I'd wager you'd stand by your word regardless of circumstances."

"You're right," Ted rasped as if the words tasted bitter. Never once did he pull his attention from the distant unknown.

Elaina wrinkled her brow and studied Ted's profile. He stared across the road, into the pasture, as if an image on the horizon were threatening to drag him under. His mouth settled into a line, straight and hard. Elaina didn't realize she gripped the porch rail so tightly until arrows of pain penetrated her cold fingers. She released the rail and looked down at her reddened fingertips. As Ted continued to brood, Elaina wrestled for something to say to break the awkward moment.

Finally she quipped, "You're early," and checked her watch. "Thirty minutes to be exact," Elaina continued with a smile. "It's only four-thirty."

"Is that okay?" Slowly, he turned from the horizon, placed his elbow on the banister, leaned into it, and watched her with a saucy grin. "Are you going to call the dinner patrol and have me arrested?"

"No." Elaina looked down and tapped at the freshly painted porch with the toe of her short-topped boot. She didn't even try to stop the smile. Ted's mild teasing and gentle nature was already soothing her overwrought emotions. Whatever had thrown him into that black reverie must have been swift in passing. Elaina relaxed and decided it must not concern her.

She inclined her head sideways and cut him an encouraging glance. "Want to walk to the car with me? I need to get Anna's present before my nose freezes off." She rubbed the end of her nose.

"Oh sure," Ted agreed and nabbed one of the gold bags before stepping off the porch with her. They neared the house's corner, and the scattering of leaves crunched beneath their shoes in a crackling staccato rhythm.

"I brought gifts for your mother for having me over for dinner and your sister because she's ill." He lifted the bag. "I didn't figure I should leave you out."

Elaina halted near the ornamental cedars at the house's edge. She covered her opened mouth with her fingertips. "Oh my word, you didn't have to do that!"

"I know." Ted extended the bag with a shy grin. "But I'm especially glad I did now, since I acted like a jealous jerk when you first opened the door. I mean, are we adults or am I in junior high?"

She accepted the gold foil package and infused her gaze with a generous dose of grace. "Well, at this point in our…relationship, I guess maybe we're both a little unsure of things. I mean, I might have reacted the same way if I arrived at your mom's home and there was a—a beautiful woman in the background."

An odd mist clouded Ted's eyes. "I feel a little goofy, actually," he admitted and looked past her. "I mean, here I am an—" Ted ended his words, focused on the ground, and slipped his hands into the pocket of his gray woolen coat. The black reverie nibbled at the corners of his mouth once more.

"I just feel goofy, that's all," he repeated.

"Mind if I go ahead and open your present…*Goofy?*" Elaina asked and sneaked a peek past the silver tissue paper.

"No, not in the least," Ted encouraged. "Here. Let me hold the bag while you get out the present." He drew the handles from Elaina and pulled the bag wide open.

Eagerly Elaina pushed aside the silver tissue. She peeked into the bag at the same time her fingers encountered a cold, circular object. Elaina pulled out a snow globe that featured an open book with a feathered pen and manuscript inside a bubble of water. When she shook the globe, gold glitter filled the water and swirled around the pen. The setting sun added a special radiance to the gift that warmed Elaina's heart despite the frosty breeze.

"I love it!" she exclaimed and focused upon Ted.

"Good." Ted rubbed his sideburn. "I was worried you might already have something like it," he said as if he wanted her to end his fretting.

"No, not at all," she said. "It'll be perfect on my desk in my office." She examined the trio of miniature books the globe sat upon and gasped, "Look!" She pointed to the top one. "It says *Sense and Sensibility*."

"Yep," Ted drawled.

"Oh my word! That's my favorite Jane Austen novel."

"You mentioned that in class a few weeks ago, I believe," he said with a triumphant lift of his chin.

Elaina turned the heavy globe over to see if it featured a music box like so many of them did. Her expectations were not disappointed. She twisted the stem and released it, only to enjoy a rush of pleasure when she recognized the tune: "I Only Have Eyes for You." Elaina's giddy gurgle threatened to become a giggle, but she halted before she began sounding like Anna.

"When I saw it in the gift shop, I couldn't resist," Ted explained. "Here." He snatched the globe from her, grabbed her hand, and hurried toward her car. Without a hint of his intentions, Ted placed the globe atop her Honda, swung Elaina into his arms, and twirled her around the parking area.

She reveled in the invigorating move and gladly fell into step. Once again, her everyday clothing was transformed into a ball gown. Her short-topped boots became glass slippers. And stardust filled the Oklahoma sky.

When the tune slowed, Ted nudged Elaina into a slow dip. His face inches from hers, he whispered the final lyrics as his gaze wandered to her lips. Breathless, Elaina peered up at him, framed by the darkening indigo sky. The twittering of birds accompanied her being swept away in a river of longing deeper than anything she had ever experienced. Ted's focus trailed every inch of her face as if he were memorizing it. His breathing uneven, he finally encountered her gaze. His black-brown eyes became fathomless twin seas swirling with ardor and a masculine awareness that sent tingles through Elaina's limbs. He lowered his face to hers, and Elaina closed her eyes while welcoming the inevitable kiss.

A raucous honk erupted upon the evening. Ted jumped. Elaina scrambled to keep from falling to the pavement, and he struggled to catch her. They both straightened and watched a sea-green Town Car cruise up the driveway, followed by a cream-colored Lexus.

"Cousin Jeanna," Elaina stated and had never been so exasperated by the woman's presence. "Looks like she might have Noah with her this time."

"Do you think they live in an ark?" Ted quipped.

"No." Elaina playfully hit his arm. "Noah's her husband, you idiot."

The last three times Elaina visited her mother, Jeanna had arrived for an impromptu call. Sunday, Elaina asked Anna if a day went by without the woman's visit. Anna had wearily verified that Jeanna was becoming a fixture in their home.

"She drives me crazy," Anna had added as she walked Elaina to her car. "All she ever talks about is Bryan and what a fine catch he's going to make some lucky woman. Heaven help us, Elaina, Noah is so much like her they act more like brother and sister than husband and wife."

"Isn't that the doctor's car behind her?" Ted asked. "The one I met last time I was here? What's his name?"

"Yes, it's Bryan Brixby," Elaina supplied and wondered if the visitors had realized she and Ted were in a clutch when they drove up. As a waterfall of embarrassment threatened to take her under, she offered a limp wave toward the Town Car. For the first time she noticed that she and Ted were standing in the generous space between the Jaguar and her Honda. After a quick assessment, Elaina calculated that most likely none of them had been able to deduce what she and Ted were doing—just that there were some people on the other side of the car. All her embarrassment evaporated.

"I guess I should get what I came out here for," Elaina mumbled and didn't try to hide the disappointment.

"I, uh, sorta threw a wrench into that little operation, didn't I?" Ted asked with a sly twist to his words.

"Hhhmmm…you can throw a wrench in my plans any time," Elaina shamelessly mumbled and could only imagine Anna's sardonic comment if she were present.

Ted leaned closer and bestowed a fleeting kiss upon her cheek. "That's a promise for later," he whispered against her ear, his warm breath weaving a trail of expectation in its wake.

Fifteen

"Elaina, has your sister ever shown signs of rash behavior?" Bryan Brixby's unexpected voice sent a shock through Elaina.

She jumped and sloshed a puddle of coffee on her mother's kitchen island.

"Hey, I'm sorry," Bryan said. "Let me clean up the mess." He grabbed a dish towel from the cabinet and sponged at the moisture.

"It's okay." Elaina eyed the kitchen door gently swaying with the aftermath of Bryan's entry. "I guess I was so preoccupied I didn't hear you come in." She examined the doctor's muscular frame from head to toe. "You're awfully light-footed for the hulk variety," she teased and noted that he was dressed, as usual, in a tailored sports coat and slacks.

"So I've been told." With a sheepish smile Bryan tossed the towel onto a pile of soiled china stacked on the kitchen cabinet. "I keep giving my new nurse a heart attack. Can you believe she's actually accusing me of purposefully sneaking up on her?"

"No way," Elaina mocked.

"I know it's hard to believe," Bryan shrugged, "but there you are."

She returned his smile and relived the last couple of hours. The minute Bryan Brixby and the Harleys entered the cottage, Margaret extended her dinner invitation to them. While the Harleys were quick to accept, Bryan wavered. He claimed that his arriving at the same time as the Harleys was a coincidence and that he simply wanted to take a look at Anna's ankle. After kind pressure from everyone except Anna and Willis, Bryan had agreed to join the dinner party. Elaina agreed to share hostess and cleanup duties for the expanded guest list. She had just stepped into the kitchen to retrieve Noah Harley some after-dinner coffee when Bryan invaded her space.

Figuring the doctor would enjoy a mug of coffee himself, Elaina retrieved another cup from the cabinet and placed it beside Noah's.

"Anyway," Bryan continued, "I—I'm concerned about your sister—about her potential for doing something, well, rash."

She stopped filling the second mug and looked at Bryan while trying to buy time. She hated *saying* something rash that would mar her sister's name. "You mean like rushing into the kitchen, scaring somebody half to death, and then tossing out a loaded question?" she wryly asked.

"Well..." Bryan hedged as the corners of his mouth quirked down, "something like that, I guess."

"Why do you ask?" Elaina questioned. Although Anna had slighted Elaina all evening, she despised speaking ill of her sister—even if the statement were true. Elaina set the carafe on the wooden island that her mother had insisted upon during her minor remodeling venture.

"I'm highly concerned, I guess, because she reminds me so much of my niece."

"Your niece?" Elaina queried and recalled his saying Anna evoked memories of another young woman who was dead.

"Yes. My brother and sister-in-law adopted her when she was only two." His lips drooped and accented the tiny laugh lines from his nose to mouth. "They live in Fort Worth, Texas. She's sixteen now. Last fall she disappeared."

"Oh my word. I'm so sorry." Elaina's grip on the carafe handle tightened as she imagined the horror of Anna's disappearing.

Bryan rubbed his fingers along the edge of the island. "We've done everything we know to do—including hiring a private eye. Either she's run away and thoroughly covered her trail or…" He averted his head and worked his jaw muscles.

Elaina, caught in the fervor of his emotions, stood mute and without a clue as to what she should say. She recalled a recent television documentary about a serial killer who confessed to the murders of thirty-three young women and revealed their graves to the police. After years of anguish, the victims' distraught families were finding answers.

"Anyway," he finally said, "my niece—her name's Macy—is so impressionable and thoughtless. She's also every bit as pretty as Anna. I could see her being…seduced by someone like this Willis character," Bryan explained. "It makes me concerned about your sister."

And highly jealous, Elaina added to herself while scrutinizing the torment in Bryan's eyes. She observed the soiled pots and pans cluttering the counter. The leftover smell of her mom's roast and cherry pie did nothing to stimulate Elaina. Only the coffee's aroma could tempt her satisfied appetite, but the brew was out of bounds. The kitchen clock's incessant ticking pressured Elaina into voicing a comment.

"You hesitate," Bryan added. "Have I insulted you?"

"I guess my reluctance stems from loyalty," Elaina explained with a slow smile. She leaned against the island's butcher-block top. "I hate to say anything against my sister."

"I understand," Bryan said, "but I still feel that I need to express my concern. I just hope she doesn't haul off and marry that guy…or move in with him," he cautiously added. "I would hazard to guess he may have been around the block a few times," Bryan said as if Elaina hadn't noticed.

"Oh, I don't think Anna would just move in with him," Elaina quickly defended her sister. "I'd be the first to admit she's not the most mature person on the planet, but she's as committed as I am to biblical standards."

"But what about marriage?"

Elaina looked down and didn't respond. All she could think about was Anna's claiming that Willis was her future husband. "I guess that would take two people," she observed.

"So...are you saying you doubt Willis would commit?"

"What do you think?"

"I'm not sure you want to know exactly what I'm thinking of that—" He stopped and balled his fist atop the island. A dark veil crept across Bryan's face as he stomped toward the pair of French doors that opened onto the back deck. While he brooded, Elaina took time to gather her thoughts and choose exactly what more she wanted to say.

In support of Bryan's observations, Elaina couldn't deny that Willis Kenney's debonair methods seemed too smooth for comfort. After assisting Anna in hobbling to the dinner table, he had systematically enchanted her, her mother, and Jeanna. By the time the final bite of cherry pie slid down her throat, Elaina deduced that Willis had probably been charming women since he was three.

Finally, she decided to just be honest with Bryan. "If we're going to talk about Willis," she said, "you've introduced a subject I feel I can speak on." From the corner of her eye, she noted Bryan's swiveling to face her. "If you want the truth—"

"Nothing but," Bryan inserted.

"Then I agree with your concerns about him." Elaina looked him square in the eyes. "About everything except Anna moving in with him."

Bryan blinked and jerked back his head. "I was beginning to think maybe he'd snowed you as thoroughly as he had Anna."

"Not by a long shot," Elaina stated and tapped the spoon lying on the silver-plated cream-and-sugar tray. "I have to admit he's way nicer than I thought he would be. Before I met him, I figured he would be a conceited, self-centered jerk, to put it bluntly. Then, when I met him, I began to think that he might even be good for Anna—especially in influencing her toward an education. At least he does have that going for him. He also doesn't seem to be even a little bit conceited. But—"

"I don't think it would matter if he were at this point." Bryan sighed and looked toward the door that led to the dining room. An explosion of laughter suggested that Noah and Jeanna were as boisterous as ever.

"If I didn't know them better, I'd say those two were drunk about half the time." Bryan shook his head.

"Maybe just drunk on life," Elaina supplied and finished pouring the coffee. "They seem to immensely enjoy laughing about everything."

"The wild part is, I genuinely like them." Bryan stroked the first signs of a dark-blond goatee and walked back toward the island.

"I just wish they weren't so set on marrying everyone off," Elaina admitted. "I think now that Willis is on the scene they've decided he and Anna are a good pair, so they're probably more determined than ever to see us down the aisle."

"That would never do," Bryan drawled. "We'd be the opposite of the Harleys—the quietest, most boring couple on the planet."

Elaina smiled. "Unlike you and Anna who would be perfect together. Right?" While she replaced the carafe on the hot plate, Bryan cleared his throat.

When Elaina glanced back at him, he was studying his shoes. "I'm making a fool of myself, aren't I?" he mumbled. "She's thirteen years younger than I am and doesn't care if I fall off the side of the earth. What am I thinking?" He slipped his hands into his pleated trousers and shook his head.

"I keep telling myself…" he grimaced, "but it does no good."

"Want this coffee?" Elaina picked up the mug and extended it toward him.

"Sure." He took the gift and sipped the black liquid. "Besides," he added with a mischievous twist of his lips, "if you and I got married what would Ted do for a wife?"

"What's that supposed to mean?" Elaina asked and wondered at her own inane statement. She ducked her head and stepped toward the stack of china. Her back to Bryan, Elaina began furiously scraping food off the plates and into the garbage disposal.

Ted opened the kitchen door, stepped across the threshold, and braced the door's closing. His pleasant smile stiffened as he looked from Elaina at the sink to Bryan who watched her. Somehow Ted had assumed that Bryan must have gone to the restroom—not into the kitchen with Elaina. Neither of them realized he was in the room. Ted narrowed his eyes and tried to resist the second bout of jealousy he'd endured this evening. Never had he experienced such possessive urges with a woman. The irony was Elaina wasn't his—nor would she ever be.

That's the problem, he thought. *I can't have her, and it eats me alive to think somebody else might.*

He stopped the scowl before it started. All during dinner, she and Dr. Brixby had exchanged light conversation. Twice, the two of them quietly enjoyed a joke nobody else got—not even the Harleys. If the doctor were looking for someone he had something in common with, Ted deduced he should look no further.

He imagined Bryan moving toward the sink, wrapping his arms around Elaina, and kissing her neck. As Ted's wayward mind played out the scenario, Elaina reached up to stroke Bryan's face with her left hand. The ring finger bore a golden band. When he envisioned her turning in Bryan's embrace, Ted pictured her waistline thick with child.

He bolted backward and bumped into the door. The thing whisked open and then banged against his body. Elaina and Bryan both turned to face him.

"Oh hi!" Elaina said with a welcoming grin Ted hoped she intended to be as special as it looked.

Ted examined her slender waistline and mumbled something about everyone now wanting coffee. He hoped his words were coherent. The winds of caution whispered a dire warning to Ted. The last thing an independent woman like Elaina would want was a boyfriend so jealous he projected romantic hallucinations onto every male she talked with.

"I think my mom's big service tray is on the middle shelf in this bottom cabinet," Elaina said. "Why don't you get it out, and we'll see if we can't load it down with several mugs and everything else we need. I'll pour what's left of the coffee in the silver urn and then make a pot of decaf for those of us less fortunate," she added a smirk.

"Okay," Ted said. "I can handle that." Walking to Elaina's side, he rubbed his hands together as if he were about to embark upon a major project. "Let's see…bottom cabinet, middle shelf." He squatted, snapped open the door, and stared into a conglomeration of kitchen paraphernalia.

Elaina chuckled.

"What?" Ted looked up at her. She stood over him, hands on hips, as if she were the queen of the kitchen.

"You have the most lost look on your face of any in the male species I've ever seen."

"Now she's going scientific on me," Ted grumbled. "Whatever happened to the right-brained chick who teaches lit?"

"Looks like the two of you have things under control," Bryan said. "I'll mosey along."

Ted glanced toward the doctor in time to see him offer the thumbs-up sign to Elaina. The tense knot inside him unraveled. Maybe the two of them were nothing but friends.

Elaina knelt beside Ted and peered into the disorganized cabinet. "Mom keeps her kitchen about as neat as Anna keeps her clothes closet. I think their idea of organization is to open the door, throw it in, and shut the door before all the stuff falls out on them."

Ted barely heard Elaina. He was more interested in drinking in every inch of her profile and reliving that near-kiss two hours ago. When she reached to tuck a strand of bobbed hair behind her ear, Ted beat her to the task. Elaina riveted her attention from the cabinet to him. Her eyes widened and then glowed as she registered his intent. Ted inched his hand to the back of her neck and decided he would take his kisses where and when he could get them.

"I'm not sure this is the right time or place," he mumbled, his heart pounding, "but I'm going to die of frustration if I don't get to kiss you soon." When she didn't resist, Ted continued, "I've wanted to kiss you ever since your mother's move. Even after every class I've been tempted to wait for you in your office and—"

"Stop talking," she said and arched one brow in a sassy invitation. "Time is wasting." She glanced over her shoulder. "We've probably only got a couple of minutes before somebody else comes in here."

Feeling like an adolescent sneaking a smooch at recess, Ted didn't wait for a second invitation. With a triumphant growl, he moved in for the prize.

Sixteen

When his lips were within centimeters of Elaina's, Ted's cell phone emitted a series of beeps. Elaina jumped. Ted closed his eyes and rested his forehead against hers. "Let's ignore it," he rasped as the thing beeped again.

"Okay." Elaina's single word exuded all Ted's impatient hunger.

But what if the caller is Lorna? he thought. She and her friend went to Dallas this weekend for a shopping trip. She promised to call when they arrived in their hotel room. Ted could hear himself trying to explain why he hadn't taken her expected call, *Sorry I didn't answer. I was kissing another woman.*

"I've got to get it," he groaned. Ted backed away and reached for the phone hanging from his belt loop. One glance of the tiny screen validated his fears. His fiancée was on the line. He schooled his features into an impassive façade, stood up, and pressed the send button.

While he was saying, "Ted speaking," he discreetly stepped through the back door and onto the spacious deck. The faint tinge of chimney smoke greeted him. A floodlight released a silver beam that dispelled the ghostly shadows. Figuring the light must be motion sensitive, Ted suppressed a shiver that his wool sweater did little to deter.

"Hi, Teddy," a breathy southern voice floated over the line. "It's me. Darlene and me made it to the hotel room all safe and sound."

"Great!" Ted said, his breath a white mist. Involuntarily, he began comparing his fiancée to the woman he'd nearly kissed. As Lorna chatted about their plans to go to the mall, Ted peered into the kitchen. Elaina had retrieved the silver platter and began arranging mugs on it. Her red hair, shining like copper in the fluorescent light, made Ted's fingertips warm at the memory of the feathery texture. While Lorna's pale green eyes and dark hair might turn a few more heads than Elaina's looks, he was beginning to wonder if she were the female version of Willis Kenney—all charm and fluff and beauty with not much potential for character and depth.

A seizure of panic made Ted forget the night's chill. He leaned his forehead against the door's window, absorbed Elaina's every move, and then stroked the cold pane with unsteady fingers. Her back to him, Elaina picked up the mug-laden tray and manned it through the kitchen door.

"...she don't think we're going to find the dress this weekend, though," Lorna continued. "I say we will. I hate to use up all your money, Ted darlin', just lookin' for the dress. We've got to have somethin' to live on once we get married, now don't we? 'Course, I guess you're gonna tell me to just enjoy myself and not worry."

"Uh, yeah," Ted mumbled and wondered how he could have ever allowed himself to forget all the reasons he broke off their first engagement. After he recovered from being enamored with her radiant beauty, Lorna's lack of intellectual abilities had topped the list of his objections when he was twenty-two and she was nineteen.

Even more so now, he thought. While her incessant rambling continued, Ted forced himself to relive the night she fell sobbing into his arms. Never had he been so overtaken by pity and remorse. The sight of her porcelain skin marred by ugly bruises had nauseated Ted. Lorna's insisting that if he hadn't broken their engagement she would have never been in that abusive relationship had violently slung him into self-incrimination.

Now he peered into the empty kitchen and watched the door sashay to a close in Elaina's wake. The damp, cold night seeped all the way through his soul. Keeping his word had never tasted so bitter.

Elaina stepped into the dining room to the approved greetings of their guests. Immediately, she noticed the absence of Anna and Willis and figured her sister had hobbled back to her fireside couch.

"There's our woman!" Noah Harley exclaimed.

Elaina offered a friendly nod. As always, she noticed how much Noah reminded her of a beardless Colonel Sanders. Elaina bit the end of her tongue and tried to balance the bulky tray.

"Let me help," Bryan offered as Margaret shoved over a pair of pie plates to make room for the tray. He placed his own mug on the cherrywood table and relieved Elaina of her burden.

"We thought the kitchen had swallowed you whole," Noah continued. He relaxed in his chair as if he had stuffed every inch of his stomach, bulging beneath his green sweater vest.

"Oh dear!" Jeanna said. "Whoever heard of a kitchen swallowing someone? Now, that would be a mean house indeed!" She giggled and then whistled. "Kay-Kay, oh Kay-Kay, where are you darlin'?" A soft woof from near the massive china hutch announced the dog's waddling toward her mistress.

"There you are!" Jeanna bent and scooped up the Pekinese. "Come to Mamma," she crooned. "I can't let you out of my sight. This house eats people!" She twittered at her own joke and offered the dog a sliver of her pie crust.

Kay-Kay gobbled the treat, and Jeanna said, "I was more worried about Elaina leaving and not coming back. If I were her age and single, I'd lure all these delightful single men into the kitchen and see if I couldn't get one to elope."

Elaina exchanged resigned glances with first her mother and then Bryan.

"Never have I seen so many eligible bachelors at one impromptu dinner party." Jeanna stroked Kay-Kay's head. "And that Willis Kenney!" She lifted her hand as if she were on the verge of a shouting spell. "Why, it's enough to—"

"Careful Jeanna!" Noah pretended to pinch her cheek. "You're going to make me jeeeeaaaaalous," he chimed in a singsong voice.

"Oh would you stop it!" Jeanna merrily hit his hand. "You know you're the only man for me." She patted his face and followed through with a saucy kiss on his round cheek.

"Oooo weee," Noah said and jiggled his shoulders. "I think I'm getting a buzz!"

Elaina shook her head and told herself the couple wasn't funny enough to merit laughter. She laughed anyway. So did Bryan.

"Here you go, Noah," Margaret said through a snicker. "I believe Elaina has your mug of coffee ready." She picked up the steaming, fragrant mug from the tray and extended it to Noah. "Drink this and maybe you'll get an even bigger buzz."

"Ha!" Jeanna arched her back and laughed toward the ceiling. "A bigger buzz! Oh what a *hoot* you are, Maggie!" Her moo-moo stretched across her massive chest as she heaved for air.

"You should know nothing gives me a bigger buzz than Jeanna's kisses!" Noah boisterously claimed. "Even after all these years."

"Now, all we need is for Elaina to settle on who'll be her buzz-kisser for life!" Jeanna said. Margaret extended a mug of coffee to Jeanna. She accepted the cup and held it to her lips. "Tell us, my dear," Jeanna drawled over the mug's rim, "does your buzz-kisser's name start with a B or a T? Which will it be?"

Elaina and Bryan shared determined stares. "We aren't—" Elaina began.

"Oh, Jeanna," Noah exclaimed after a gulp of coffee, "now you're rhyming."

Jeanna set down her mug and turned toward her husband. "I believe I *did* just rhyme, didn't I? A B or a T. Which will it be?" she repeated and then opened her red lips for a rowdy squeal. Kay-Kay wagged her body and yelped. "Oh...oh...oh...my side is hurting," Jeanna said as Ted entered the dining room.

Elaina gently took the coffee urn from her mother and focused upon filling the remaining mugs with the dark liquid. Her head ducked, she hoped no one noticed that her expression had in any way altered with Ted's arrival. Her face chilled, then warmed. All that consumed her was their near kiss and the expectation of its fulfillment before the night's end.

"There's T now!" Jeanna blurted.

"Oh yes, there he is!" Noah agreed. "We were just trying to guess which man would be Elaina's buzz-kisser. The one whose name starts with a B or a T. Can you tell us which one it will be?" Noah said as if he were reciting a Dr. Seuss book.

"Buzz-kisser?" Ted mumbled, a bewildered wilt to his features.

Bryan sputtered over a sip of coffee and Elaina couldn't deny that Ted's blank stare evoked humor. As he looked to her for some scrap of explanation, Elaina wondered how she would react if she stepped into a room with someone talking about buzz-kissing. She kept her lips firm and denied the mirth.

Before she could embark upon some form of explanation, Jeanna began a new conversational vein. "You know," she sobered and turned to her husband, "I wish your niece was here tonight. It would certainly be good for her. We've got one too many gentlemen here."

"I know!" She turned and gripped her husband's arm. "We'll see which one of the guys Elaina decides on tonight and we'll have a dinner party and introduce Lorna to the other one. Yes! That would be perfect!"

"But don't you remember?" Noah admonished. "Last time she visited, Lorna hinted that she's engaged."

"Yes, oh yes!" Jeanna waved her hand. "But you know she must have been stretching the truth. She said their engagement was a secret. Now, what kind of an engagement is *ever* a secret?"

"I think she's telling the truth," Noah claimed with a decisive nod. "She has a ring and hasn't asked us for a dime since she left that awful husband of hers. Somebody is paying her bills. You know she's never worked a day in her life."

Jeanna propped her elbow on the table and then placed her forehead against her palm. "I sure hope you're right," she said, more sober than Elaina had seen her. "Bless her little heart, she is Noah's sister's daughter. After her mother died, Noah didn't do the best with keeping up with her. It wasn't until after her father died that she contacted us. I think it was because she really didn't have any other place to go. I love it when she visits but she would drive me crazy if she asked to live with us again. The whole time she was with us before she got married, she never stopped talking."

The plump matron raised her head and looked at Elaina. "Can you imagine anyone talking all the time?"

"Uh…" Elaina hedged.

Imagine that! Margaret mouthed from across the room.

Elaina merely shook her head in the negative and managed to remain straight-faced. She fully expected Ted to join the silent mirth but noticed that he was too busy going pale. He gripped the top of a high-backed dining chair and stared at the table as if he were trying to keep himself from collapsing.

Knitting her brows, Elaina laid a hand on his arm. "Are you okay?" she questioned.

Jeanna's renewed lamentations cut off his reply. "I hope I don't sound like I'm criticizing poor Lorna," she continued and looked to her husband for approval.

"No, dear, I don't believe you are. I understand."

"And I do feel so sorry for her. Poor thing, her mother died when she was born. Uterus ruptured right on the spot," she said and didn't flinch at offering such intimate details. "And then her father died of that toe infection when she was just twenty."

"A toe infection?" Elaina questioned before she realized any query would only encourage more details.

"Oh yes. He was a diabetic and just wouldn't take care of himself," Jeanna explained. "His toe got infected, and he didn't go to the doctor like he should have."

"Killed him," Noah supplied, shaking his head.

Elaina expected Bryan to insert some remark validating the complications of such a problem, only to realize that the doctor had left the room. She strained to peer into the entryway and caught sight of him leaning against the wall, his attention firmly fixed upon the living room. From the tortured set of his profile, Elaina deduced he must be watching Willis and Anna. Momentarily, she tuned out the Harleys and wished she could pour a heavy dose of common sense into her sister's frivolous mind.

"That left poor little Lorna with not a soul in the world." Noah's claim drew her back to the conversation at hand.

"She was an only child," Jeanna said. "And she's not the smartest woman I've ever met and just wouldn't ever make it through college. I thought when she got married right after her father died that she'd done the right thing. And then boom!" Jeanna clapped her hands together and Kay-Kay released a bark. "Earlier this year, her husband filed for divorce and Lorna said he was a wife-beater and a womanizer. Never been so shocked in my whole life!"

"We've offered her help since then," Noah explained, "but she always refuses. She's got an apartment east of Oklahoma City now and hasn't even been to see us but once in six months. That's the reason I think she really is engaged. Otherwise, she'd be camping on our doorstep."

He shook his head. "You never met a prettier thing in your whole life, but she's not much use when it comes to holding down a job. Not much at all. We've been concerned about her ever since her visit. I just hope if she *is* engaged it's not to somebody whose going to hurt her again."

"Oh well, so much for our family troubles," Jeanna sighed. "How did we get off on all that anyway?"

"I don't know," Noah rubbed the top of his balding head, "I guess it's just heavy on our minds."

"If you'll excuse me," Ted said with an abrupt step toward the dining room doorway. "I'm going to have to leave now."

"But...what..." Elaina stammered as he swept past her without so much as a glance or a goodbye.

"I'm sorry," he mumbled over his shoulder. "All of a sudden, I'm not feeling very well at all. I think I need to lie down."

Elaina hurried after him.

"Oh no," Margaret's voice floated behind her. "I hope there wasn't something wrong with the roast."

Ted stopped by the front door long enough to retrieve his wool coat.

"Ted?" Elaina questioned. "Do you want to lie down here? Mom has an extra room."

"No," he snapped. "I need to go."

"Bryan's a doctor. Maybe he could—"

"No," he repeated.

His white face rigid, Ted refused to look at Elaina. He whipped open the front door, stepped through, and attempted to close it. But Elaina followed close behind and stopped the door from shutting. The clap of Ted's shoes on wood echoed across the dark countryside as he ran off the porch.

Elaina raced to the porch's edge and gripped the railing. "Ted?" she called, her breath forming a white cloud. Elaina stiffened herself against an inevitable shiver. A mist of confusion wove among myriad questions.

His car door slammed. The engine revved. Ted turned the vehicle around and whizzed out of the driveway as if a pack of demons were after him. When his taillights faded in the distance, Elaina worried that perhaps she had done something to anger him. What, she couldn't decide. One minute the man was trying to steal a kiss and the next he was running out the door. Idly Elaina wondered if the phone call had brought some disturbing news.

"Everything okay out here?" Bryan's kind voice floated from the doorway.

Elaina hugged herself against the cold and walked toward the door. "I don't know. Ted just ran out and left. He said he wasn't feeling well and needed to lie down."

Bryan nodded as if Ted's behavior didn't surprise him in the least. "There's been an awful bug going around. Gastro-intestinal problems. Nasty stuff. Makes you feel like you're going to die right at first. Hits out of nowhere. I've seen about a dozen people this week with it."

"He *did* turn white before he left." Elaina admitted. She followed Bryan back into the house and clicked the door shut. The home's heat dispelled the goosebumps beneath Elaina's cashmere sweater.

Bryan nodded. "Poor guy probably thought he was going to barf."

"He could have barfed here," Elaina said.

"Oh, now that would have been really romantic." The doctor rolled his eyes.

"Right," Elaina agreed. With a thoughtful nod she decided to call Ted tomorrow. "I can't say that I lie awake at night dreaming of barfing at Ted's house myself."

"For a mere Ph.D., you catch on to medical stuff really fast," Bryan said, his face impassive.

"Thanks," Elaina said and never cracked a smile. "I can sleep easier tonight knowing you approve."

"You know, I still think I see some hemlock in your future," Bryan said.

"Go ahead, make my day," Elaina said.

But the whole effect was lost upon Bryan. He had already walked past the laughter-infested dining room and was moving back to his post by the living room.

Elaina decided a peek at her sister might not be out of order. Somebody in the family needed to keep an eye on Anna. As she tiptoed behind Bryan, Elaina's mind turned back to Ted. He might need her to make a trip to the store for some medicine tomorrow. She planned to also take him some broth.

She peered around Bryan's shoulder and shamelessly spied on her sister and suitor. Willis' mellow voice mingled with the crack and pop of the fire. He read from the book of poetry Elaina noticed earlier. The poem was one of Poe's she had memorized long ago. Willis' voice caressed the final line of the first stanza as if they bespoke his heart, "And this maiden lived with no other thought than to love and be loved by me."

Willis stopped there, laid the book on the table, and slipped to his knees. Like a connoisseur of fine jewels, he hovered over Anna, his face inches from hers. Willis stroked Anna's hair away from her forehead, his expression as passionate as Ted's had been in the kitchen.

Elaina, hard pressed to denounce her protective sisterly instincts, teetered on the precipice of indecision. Despite herself, she nearly acted on the impulse to rush into the room and break up the tête-à-tête. Then she wondered what would stop Willis from kissing Anna tomorrow or the next day when she wasn't there to stop him. Anna's earlier tirade sealed Elaina's decision.

I'll stay out of your love life for now, Anna, she thought, *but I hope I don't live to regret it.*

As if he were waiting for Elaina's mental ascent, Willis' lips brushed Anna's in a gentle caress that left Elaina wincing.

"I can't take this," Bryan snarled under his breath. He bolted from the scene and didn't temper his steps as he marched back to the front door.

Elaina, scared of being caught spying, plastered herself against the wall. With her cold palms pressed upon the paneling, she silently witnessed the second man of the evening grab his coat and storm out of the cottage.

Seventeen

Anna had always imagined what being in love would be like… all the way, irrevocably in love. The few times in the past she fancied herself in love, the new emotion wore off in a few weeks, and she lost interest. But not this time. Not with Willis Kenney. At last, Anna determined that life without Willis wouldn't be worth living. He was her destiny…the fire in the center of her soul.

As Thanksgiving came and went, the flames of her devotion blazed brighter. With the dawn of December, she recognized the same fervor in Willis' eyes. Hardly a day went by that they weren't together. He even postponed going back to work in order to stay by her side. Fortunately, his generous aunt, Nancy Moncleave, insisted that he continue to lodge in her mansion a mere five miles from the Woods' cottage.

The first Friday night of December, Anna stood inside the front door of Jeanna and Noah's sprawling home, just up the lane from their cottage. Jeanna had invited numerous acquaintances to enjoy her annual tree-lighting ceremony and finger-food feast. After the eats and tree-lighting, Jeanna planned a night of board and card games. Already the great room buzzed with the sounds of neighbors and friends enjoying the first serving of wassail, which tinged the air with the smells of apples and spice. But no amount of revelry could distract Anna from her vigil by the front door. Clutching her ankle-length cape, she peered through the floor-to-ceiling windows for any sign of Willis' headlights to pull into the winding driveway.

At last her tenacity was rewarded. In the final traces of twilight, Anna recognized the ebony sports car as it purred into Jeanna's winding driveway. With a giggle, Anna hurled her wool cape around her shoulders and rushed into the arms of winter.

She trotted along the sidewalk leading to the concrete parking area as if she were an eager child on Christmas morning. The full moon rose from the east and oozed a honey-like glow across acres and acres of the estate. The glacial air nipped at her nose, and Anna imagined the whole countryside covered in glistening white frost in the morning. Never had she so reveled in winter's freeze.

Once she arrived at the sidewalk's end, Anna lifted her face toward the blue-black sky speckled with dots of light like a million rhinestones scattered from heaven. While she twirled, Anna celebrated the trees' bare limbs...the long arctic nights...and especially the cold rain.

"I will go to my grave loving you, cold rain," she declared. "Because you were with me when I met Willis."

The Jaguar's engine stopped purring. The car door opened and then slammed. Anna could wait no longer. She ran through the maze of cars toward the man who held every inch of her heart. Willis opened his arms and picked her up. With a delighted chuckle, he spun her around and then pressed his lips to hers. Anna withheld nothing from the kiss. She celebrated the minty taste of Willis' mouth...the smells of his citrusy cologne and leather jacket...the feel of his curly hair beneath her touch.

Finally the kiss ended, and Anna spoke her heart. "Oooh I missed you," she cooed against his lips.

"We were only apart three hours," he teased and showered her face in a series of tiny pecks.

"Too long," she whispered as if she were a toddler caught in the throes of separation anxiety.

Willis' lustful growl bespoke his own anxiety. "What am I going to have to do to get you to spend the weekend with me at my place in Tulsa?" he asked. "Or better yet, we could go to New York and stay at the apartment my agency rents for me while I'm there. We could just let ourselves go crazy," he mumbled against her ear, his voice thick with passion.

Anna backed away from the clutch and looked into his eyes. Willis had been hinting about their becoming intimate for the last couple of weeks. Until tonight Anna had possessed the strength to resist. Now with the moonlight's reflection in his liquid brown eyes, Anna could barely recall the reasons she'd so faithfully denied him. The feel of her parents' diamond ring cooling against her finger infused her with a new surge of strength.

"You know I can't," she whispered and trailed her index finger along his cheekbone then toward the corner of his mouth.

"Woman, you're going to kill me, but hopefully I can make it until..." he moaned and tugged her fingertip into his mouth.

Anna, aware of Willis' growing urgency, backed away and lowered her hands to rest on the front of his leather jacket. She held her breath, waited for him to finish his statement, and prayed that it would involve a proposal.

"Did you know that Aunt Nancy is thrilled that we're an item?" Willis asked.

"Huh?" Anna blinked and tried to connect with his logic.

"Oh yes, she's heard so many good things about you and your mother and sister that she's thrilled her sole heir is involved with a woman of such quality."

"You're her sole heir?" Anna questioned and pictured the imposing rock mansion that she'd heard so much about. Even though she had yet to visit the estate, Anna envisioned the interior must be as majestic as the exterior. She marveled in Willis' new information and wondered what other wonderful tidbits time might reveal.

"I think the time has come for the two of you to meet," he explained. "It's very important that my future wife and my aunt get along well."

"Your future wife?" the question squeaked out like treasured hope long held captive.

"Oh yes." Willis pulled her close. "I can't wait until our wedding night," he whispered. "Tomorrow morning, I'll be at your house at ten. There's a certain little box I need to pick up to make it all official." He pulled back and gazed into her eyes. "That is, if you agree."

"I couldn't agree more," she breathed and pressed her lips against his for an ardent demonstration of her acceptance. Rejoicing in the extended kiss, Anna imagined herself the mistress of Willis' life by January—just as she had originally hoped when she first met him. She planned a simple wedding, with just the minister, her mother, herself, Willis, and his aunt. She had barely spoken to Elaina since the day the two of them had words. Therefore Anna possessed no intent of inviting her to the wedding. Still, she determined it would be the most romantic moment of her life. A glorious Cancun honeymoon would seal their union.

The purr of a vehicle rolling up the lane announced another visitor on the way. The sudden beam of twin headlights demanded the lovers pull apart. But nothing could dampen Anna's rising spirits. She bolted forward and pulled Willis' hand. He followed without restraint. When they paused by the massive brick home's front door, Anna wrapped her arms around Willis and pressed her lips to his again for a spontaneous kiss, brief yet potent.

"I love you. I love you. I love you," she whispered. "I loved you from the moment I saw you. I can't *wait* until we're married."

"I love you, too, Anna," Willis declared and rubbed his nose against hers.

"Let's show the world tonight," Anna challenged.

"Let's do."

As Willis reached to open the door, Anna hoped that boring Bryan Brixby finally got the message that she irrevocably belonged to Willis Kenney. He had yet to stop his regular visits, which made Anna feel like a cell under an obsessive scientist's microscope. A few times she had been tempted to tell the old codger to get a life. While she wished he wasn't on Jeanna's guest list tonight, Anna didn't fool herself into believing he would be left out. Jeanna and Noah had invited the whole neighborhood and then some.

The second the door popped open, Anna noticed a movement by the window where she had been waiting earlier. Only a brief glimpse of short, red hair indicated who the spy might be.

"Did you just see that person?" Anna asked.

"You mean your sister looking out the window?" Willis questioned with a devil-may-care tilt to his lips.

"It was her, wasn't it?"

"Yes, indeed."

"Ooohhh! She makes me so mad!" Anna fumed. "She's just jealous because she and Ted didn't make it."

"They broke up. Really? When?" Willis asked.

"I'm not sure. And you'll never hear it from *her*," Anna said. "She doesn't tell Mom and me a thing. But he hasn't been back to Mom's for dinner, even though she's asked Elaina to invite him. I haven't seen them together again—not at all. And she's been down lately. Of course, some days you couldn't get a smile out of her if it would save a life anyway. She's so grave."

"I think she and that Dr. Brixby ought to get together," Willis said. "Best I can tell, he's about as dull and boring as they come. It's no wonder he's not married yet!"

"Yes, he and Elaina would be the only couple who never smiled *or* spoke to each other. The perfect match!"

When Anna stepped into the great room full of guests, she spotted Elaina a few feet away. Her sister was focused upon a portly, balding man who seemed interested in what he was saying, even if Elaina didn't.

While Willis released their coats to the doorman, Anna narrowed her eyes and fought the temptation to tell Elaina she didn't appreciate being spied on. But she shoved aside the irritation as swiftly as she experienced it. Anna absorbed the ambiance of the brightly lit room...the ten-foot tree commanding the great room's corner...the mammoth rock fireplace crackling with merry flames...the yards and yards of garland draped as a border near the ceiling. Jeanna and Noah's home would make six of her mother's cottage. According to Jeanna, every room was decorated with a different motif to celebrate the holidays.

Anna lifted her nose, refused to waste another second scrutinizing her sister, and told herself she was choosing the higher ground. There was too much to see, the holiday music was too cheerful, and the night was too young to ruin it all with Elaina's petty problems.

Elaina didn't have the foggiest idea who was talking to her or what he said. Someone had introduced them shortly after she turned from watching her sister throw herself all over Willis. The middle-aged man, his words, the music, the crowd all became a blurring irritation in the background of her mind. She was so distraught over Anna's borderline risqué behavior that she was hard-pressed to maintain an indifferent profile. Even though Anna had always been carefree, Elaina never remembered her hurling herself so pointedly at a man. For the first time, Bryan's worries about Anna's moving in with Willis nagged at Elaina.

A smiling waitress dressed in a traditional black-and-white uniform walked by carrying a tray laden with wassail. Elaina accepted a cup and found her escape when the sweater-clad man started chatting up the waitress. After catching Anna throwing her a spiteful stare, Elaina moved in the opposite direction. Never had Anna stayed mad at her so long. Although Anna usually became miffed at Elaina several times a year, she normally recovered within a week. After a solid month, Anna showed no signs of coming around.

Elaina, her head lowered, targeted an alcove lined with books near the fireplace. The plethora of joyful guests through which she navigated cared little for solitude and books. The stretch of floor-to-ceiling bookshelves that mastered the corner remained unoccupied. Feeling disconnected from the crowd's festive spirit, Elaina paused at the shelves, turned her back to the group, and scanned the volumes. While her gaze registered words on the books' spines, her mind did little to comprehend titles.

She sipped her tart wassail and enjoyed the soothing cinnamon liquid as it slipped down her throat. However, the warm drink did little to cheer. Anna's behavior, while discouraging, had only added a new tinge of gray to Elaina's already dark spirits—a result of the last four weeks without Ted in her life. Aside from the death of her father, the month of November had been the hardest days Elaina had ever endured. Another death had occurred. The death of a relationship—a relationship Elaina had prayed would be permanent.

Eighteen

After skimming over several books, Elaina's saddened heart latched onto a title that served as a balm to her forlorn soul: *Sense and Sensibility*—one of her favorite novels. She barely registered the merry jingle of Jeanna's Christmas music as she stroked the worn spine. Her fingers curled around the top of the book, and she jiggled it from the other titles' tight hug. Elaina set her cup on the shelf, opened the book, and began skimming the first few lines, as if by ingesting the beloved text she could somehow diminish her heart's ache.

> The family of Dashwood had been long settled in Sussex. Their estate was large, and their residence was at Norland Park, in the centre of their property, where for many generations they had lived in so respectable a manner as to engage the general good opinion of their surrounding acquaintances....

Contrary to Elaina's original hopes, the classic words she had read dozens of times did nothing to ease her pain. Instead they heightened her memory of Ted's gift—the music box globe with *Sense and Sensibility* scrawled upon the miniature book that served as base. Mere days after she unwrapped the present, Elaina rushed into her office, grabbed the globe from her desktop, and unceremoniously plunked it into the bottom drawer. While refusing to submit to the tears, she had slammed the drawer and hoped years passed before she heard the tune "I Only Have Eyes for You."

"Ooooohhhhhhh...there you are, Elaina!" Jeanna's high-pitched exclamation floating from the room's center grated along Elaina's nerves.

Elaina resisted the urge to hunch her shoulders and run. The last thing she needed was Cousin Jeanna's matchmaking. Elaina had already met a delightful match, but he didn't have the decency to break up in person. Instead, he'd scribbled a cryptic note and attached it to his test—and that after not returning her calls inquiring about his health. When Ted placed the message in Elaina's hands, he hadn't even bothered to look at her. He had avoided eye contact with her in class ever since.

Thankfully the final exam was just next week. Otherwise Elaina didn't think she could withstand the sheer confusion of Ted's actions. One minute he was threatening to kiss her. The next he was racing from her mother's home, his face as pallid as death. Then the note! A few times Elaina had been tempted to use her professor status as a means to force him into a conference in which she would demand an explanation. Instead she had silently floundered in uncertainty and done nothing.

The faint jangle of tiny bells accompanied another of Jeanna's singsong calls, "Oh Elaina! I've got someone I want you to meet!"

Elaina closed the novel, slid it back onto the shelf, retrieved her cup, and guzzled a generous gulp of wassail. For the first time in her life, she considered drowning her sorrows. She scowled at the apple juice concoction and doubted its ability to assuage her agony. Pasting on a tense smile, Elaina swiveled to face her hostess.

Cousin Jeanna, dressed in a red velvet moo-moo with gold-toned bells on the hem, hurried forward as if she were about to announce royalty. Elaina glanced behind the rouged matron. An ethereal beauty trailed close. The young woman's brunette hair, piled atop her head in carefree grace, framed a set of pale green eyes that had probably caused a few men to have wrecks...or heart attacks. The angel's green taffeta pantsuit heightened the allure of flawless skin tinged with a light application of cosmetics.

Not accustomed to surges of insecurity, Elaina adjusted her narrow-rimmed glasses, glanced down at her nondescript, black knit pantsuit, and touched the base of her bobbed hair. Under normal circumstances such a specimen of feminine perfection would not have bothered her. After all, she was confident in who she was as a woman and what she was about. Long ago, Elaina's goals to be an intellectual and even look like an intellectual had blotted out any desire to become a blazing beauty. But Ted's letter a month ago ushered in an onslaught of vulnerability that time intensified:

> Elaina,
>
> I know this is going to disappoint you, but I can't help it. We can't be an item. I've been a fool. One day soon, you'll understand.
>
> Ted

From the minute she read the missive, Elaina had silently endured a crisis so severe she couldn't voice it for fear of losing all composure. Presently, she even doubted her ability to ever attract any man. But another side of her didn't care. *Ted's the man I want*, she thought while trying to concentrate on Jeanna and the newcomer.

"I'm *soooooo* glad I found you! I've got someone I want you to meet," Jeanna repeated. "I think the two of you could be the best of friends." Jeanna laid her hand on Elaina's arm. Tugging on the angel's hand, she created a cozy circle of three.

"Elaina, this is my niece, Lorna Starr," Jeanna said. "You might remember me talking about her at your mother's about a month ago." The matron's meaningful gaze bore into Elaina's, and she recalled every word of Jeanna and Noah's concern for an orphaned niece who had endured an abusive marriage.

The story's cruelty canceled the power of Lorna's heavenly splendor. Elaina's insecurity disappeared. Her heart went out to Lorna, and she momentarily forgot her own grief.

"Hello," Elaina said and extended her hand. "It's nice to meet you. I'm Elaina Woods."

"My aunt has told me a whole bunch about you," Lorna explained, her southern voice every bit as sweet as her looks.

"I hope it was all good," Elaina joked.

"Nothing but the best!" Jeanna claimed.

"I understand you're a professor?" Lorna questioned and removed her hand from Elaina's after a brief shake.

"Yes, at Southern Christian University."

"How nice." Lorna's eyes took on a hard glint that disappeared as quickly as it came.

Elaina stopped a frown and decided she must have imagined the woman's silent challenge.

Jeanna waved toward a cluster of guests who hailed her to join them. "I'll just leave you two to enjoy each other. You're very close to the same age, and I'm sure you'll have so much in common," she said before scurrying on to her next mission.

For lack of anything better to do, Elaina sipped her wassail. A passing waitress extended a silver tray toward them, offering some bacon-wrapped delicacies on a toothpick.

"Hmmm," Elaina said, "these look scrumptious." She slid her styrofoam cup onto the bookshelf, accepted a napkin, and took two of the hors d'oeuvres. "Are you going to indulge, Lorna?" she asked.

"No," Lorna shook her head, "I'm watchin' my figure."

Elaina glanced down at Lorna's tiny waist and figured the femme fatale weighed about thirty pounds less than she. During the last month of mourning Ted's loss, Elaina had indulged in Hershey's Kisses a few too many times. When she slipped on her pants that evening, the waist had been snug. She shrugged and didn't even try to conjure a care.

"I haven't had dinner," Elaina explained. "My stomach is growling too much for me to worry about my figure right now." She offered a smile.

Lorna smiled back with so much ease that Elaina was convinced she really had invented the tense moment. "Okay," the beauty agreed, "I guess you've talked me into it. What are these lil ol' thangs anyway?" she asked while choosing an appetizer from the tray.

Elaina bit into one and rolled her eyes as the taste of bacon and something sweet pleased her pallet.

"They're dates wrapped in bacon and baked to crisp perfection," the rosy-lipped waitress explained.

"I'll have a couple more." Elaina scooped up another pair without a trace of guilt.

"One's fine for me." Lorna began nibbling the end of her date and talking at the same time. Elaina, recalling Jeanna's complaint about Lorna's talking, soon realized that her part of the conversation required no mental energy. An occasional nod and a "Really?" or a "Hmmm," was all Lorna required.

By the time the overhead bulbs were dimmed and Noah plugged in the mammoth Christmas tree's lights, Elaina had discovered much of Lorna's history—including her mother's death at her birth, her father's death ten years ago, and the tragic marriage she'd fallen into months after being jilted. In the middle of it all, Elaina began to wonder if Lorna might be operating in victim mode. She received the firm impression that the blazing beauty was singing "poor me" and insisting that the world share in her pity. While Elaina did hate that Lorna had endured such tragedies she couldn't quite bring herself to fall into the cesspool and wallow with her.

Once the lights were low and the tree offered the room's only illumination, one of the fifty guests began singing "Silent Night," and the rest of the group joined in. Elaina, desperate for some silence of her own, edged away from Lorna toward the broad staircase that led upstairs. She knew from past visits that a restroom was near the balcony that overlooked the great room. Granted, there was a restroom downstairs as well, but Elaina was trying to put as much distance between herself and the talker as possible.

After staying in the bathroom as long as she figured was decent, Elaina opened the door and peeked out. The coast was clear. She merged onto the balcony, which featured several rooms opening onto it. The cathedral effect made the house seem as large as a monstrous sanctuary. Elaina moved to the balcony railing and skimmed the crowd below. The crowd no longer sang "Silent Night." Someone had put on a Christmas CD which was blaring forth "I Saw Mommy Kissing Santa Claus."

A playful squeal drew Elaina's attention to Anna and Willis under the mistletoe near the front door. Willis swung Anna for a low dip and planted his lips firmly on hers. A small audience of young adults shared in the revelry with wolf whistles and clapping. While Noah and Jeanna joined the hoopla, Elaina's mouth tensed. She grieved her sister's lack of restraint with a man she'd only known a month and hoped she wasn't destroying her reputation.

Anna's excessive giggles and flushed cheeks when she came up from the liplock made Elaina even wonder if her sister had imbibed some alcohol. While she had never seen Anna drunk and Jeanna was serving no intoxicating beverages, Elaina wouldn't be surprised to learn that Willis arrived with his own flask. Frantically, she searched for her mother, in hopes that maybe the family matron would notice Anna and *do* something about her behavior.

Elaina finally spotted her mom standing beside the Christmas tree. The gold beads on her scarlet sweater sparkled nearly as brightly as the thousands of lights glittering midst the limbs. Elaina stood on her tiptoes and raised her hand to get her mother's attention. Before she began gesticulating, Elaina noticed the person who was talking to her mother—an angelic creature dressed in green taffeta. Elaina lowered her hand.

"Nuts," she whispered and glanced from her mother to Anna and back to her mother. The last thing she wanted was for Lorna to spot her again. Helplessly, she watched her sister and Willis exchange a hug so tight she nearly blushed. After weighing the sacrifice of listening to Lorna another hour against saving her sister's reputation, Elaina decided she had no choice but to make the sacrifice.

Forget just getting Mom's attention, she thought. *I'm going down to talk with her.* She inched away from the balcony when a familiar masculine voice stopped her.

"She's twenty-two, Elaina. There's nothing you can do." Bryan stepped beside her.

She darted him a glance from the corner of her eyes and said, "Where did you come from?"

"I sneaked up to get away from the crowd. Same as you, I'd guess."

"Yes."

Bryan looked down upon the crowd. "She's got to make her own decisions," he continued. "And you've got to let her."

Elaina leaned into the banister, crossed her arms, and continued to observe Anna. When "Jingle Bell Rock" floated over the home's speakers, Anna and Willis began a conga line. Elaina gripped the back of her neck and stopped herself from bolting down the stairway to break it up. Skeptically she watched the pair leading a long string of twenty-somethings around the room's edge. The more mature crowd jovially made room for them and didn't seem to think twice about the merrymaking. Elaina observed her mother once more. Margaret, finally noticing her younger daughter, pointed toward her. Laughing, she spoke to Lorna, who shook her head as if she didn't quite know what to think about the wild bunch.

"Come on, Mom!" Anna's gleeful call echoed off the ceiling.

Elaina's mouth dropped open when her mother trotted to the end of the conga line and dragged Lorna with her. "So much for getting Mom to talk some sense into her," Elaina mumbled and realized she had balled her fists.

"Oh, a conga line is harmless," Bryan chided.

"I guess as long as she stays in the line, she'll be okay," Elaina said. "I'm mainly worried about all this kissing and hugging and… and…clutching in public."

"Hmmm," Bryan said. "I'm not fond of seeing that, either."

"But you're right. There's really nothing I can do about it." Elaina raised her hand in resignation. "She's twenty-two and won't listen to a word I say. I—I guess I still want to mother her like I did when she was seven and I was twelve." Elaina tore her attention from the conga line and turned toward her friend.

"That's understandable." Bryan stroked his full goatee, and Elaina wished Anna would recognize how distinguished the young doctor was.

"It's not that I *dislike* Willis," Elaina admitted. "He's terribly nice. But something just keeps telling me I can't trust him." Elaina laid her hand on the arm of Bryan's black sports coat. "I wish she'd wake up and see *you*, that's what I wish."

The doctor hunched forward, placed his elbows on the rail, and stared into the milling crowd. "I'm just a heartbroken old fool at this point," he admitted with forlorn gravity. "I've loved and lost. What would a vivacious woman like Anna want with a leftover like me?" He stared straight down as if he were watching an old movie rerun from another life. "Although I *do* believe I could make her happier in the long run than that rat ever could."

Elaina turned her back to the railing and rested her weight against it. The nearest bedroom, alight with Christmas decor, rendered a welcome reprieve from worries about her sister. Outside the room's entry, a sign in Old English script read "Bearville." Elaina caught sight of a small Christmas tree covered in tiny teddy bears and wooden beads. Nearby a poster bed featured a row of bears dressed in Santa suits. The smell of gingerbread candles invited everyone to enter and enjoy the quaint atmosphere.

Elaina continued to wait for Dr. Brixby to expound about his loss at love. After observing him for several seconds, she discovered the man was not going to elaborate.

Instead he straightened and looked her squarely in the eyes. "I expected you to have Ted with you tonight," he said.

"T–Ted?" Elaina stammered.

"Yes, you know, the tall guy who's supposed to eat up the piano." Bryan's green eyes warmed even though his expression remained impassive. "I figured by now he would have changed his name to Mr. Elaina Woods."

"Oh, go clean your stethoscope or something," Elaina groused and ducked her head in an attempt to hide any suffering her eyes might reveal. "You're starting to get nosy."

"And you aren't?"

"I'm not prying am I?" she retorted.

"But we want to, now, don't we?" Bryan's attention trailed back to Anna.

"You're just good at telling half stories, that's all." Elaina straightened and pressed at the zipper on her pantsuit's jacket. She had a hunch that Jeanna probably knew all of Bryan's past, including the name of the woman Anna reminded him of. While Elaina wasn't normally inclined toward digging into people's history, her curiosity about Bryan was demanding the details.

"Maybe we've both lost at love then?" Bryan's intuitive question left Elaina grappling for an answer. "One day maybe I'll tell all," he absently added. "But tonight I just don't have the heart for it."

A cell phone began playing Beethoven's Fifth and invaded Elaina's curiosity. Out of habit, Elaina reached for her cell phone in her sling bag and then remembered she'd left her purse with the doorman. When Bryan pulled a narrow phone from his belt holster, she exclaimed, "I thought that was *my* phone. We've got our phones set on the same ring."

"This is getting scary," Bryan said with a grimace. "What if we're really twins separated at birth?"

"Nope." Elaina shook her head. "You're *way* too old!"

His brow heavy he feigned a friendly frown and answered his phone. Mere seconds had lapsed before his features stiffened, turned to disbelief, and then shock. "No way!" he exclaimed. "You mean she—she's alive?" His fingers clenched the balcony until they turned white.

"Yes…yes…I can go." He nodded and looked at Elaina as if he were trying to communicate through mental telepathy. Bryan checked his watch. "I can be there by eleven o'clock. We'll spend the night on the road, and I can have her to you by mid-afternoon tomorrow."

Elaina, responding to Bryan's surge of energy, stood straight and clamped her fingernails into her palms.

The instant he ended the phone call, Bryan proclaimed, "Never underestimate the power of prayer." His face beamed with more assurance than Elaina had yet seen in the man. "That was my brother," he explained and bounded toward the stairway. "They just found my niece—Macy—the one I told you was missing!"

Nineteen

The next morning Elaina walked up the country lane that led to Jeanna and Noah's home. The cold air entered her lungs with invigorating crispness as she pumped her legs in rapid rhythm. Before Elaina left her duplex for the party last night, Margaret had called and asked her to spend the night at the cottage. Elaina agreed and had shamelessly enjoyed her mother's pampering this morning—right down to the homemade biscuits and fresh-squeezed orange juice. The taste of blackberry jelly and decaf coffee still lingered on her tongue. The smell of chimney smoke tingeing the air increased Elaina's sense of well-being.

She gazed across the rolling hills and trees. A thick frost glittered in the eight o'clock sun like powdered sugar sprinkled with fairy dust. A lone red bird sat on one of the wooden fence posts that marked the Harleys' vast land holding—an inheritance from Jeanna's parents. The bird chirped and then fluttered in front of Elaina, its red feathers radiant against the snowy frost.

Elaina had been up since six-thirty and was showered and dressed and in her sweat suit by seven. Anna's door hadn't even been open when Elaina went downstairs for breakfast. She vaguely remembered hearing her sister's bedroom door bumping closed at two o'clock in the morning.

What Anna was doing out so late was anybody's guess. And Elaina was guessing some things that would have made their father ill. Part of Elaina hoped Willis would do the honorable thing and marry Anna. Then reason set in. *Even if he marries her, will he stay true?* Elaina suspected that Anna, in her romantic frenzy, would be furious to know that her sister even doubted Willis' constancy. But Elaina had seen too many female gazes linger upon him last night. A few times Willis looked back.

As good-looking as he is, women probably ogle him all day long, Elaina thought, *and he probably eats it up.*

The longer she dwelled upon her sister, the more uptight Elaina became. Finally, Bryan's wisdom pierced her exasperation: *She's got to make her own decisions, and you've got to let her.*

Elaina focused ahead. The brick posts that marked the driveway to the Harley's sprawling brick home stood twenty feet ahead. When Elaina reached the posts, she pivoted and began the half-mile trek back to the cottage. With the turn, Elaina purposed to dismiss all thoughts of Anna. There was nothing she could do. If she said anything else to her sister it would only make her more angry.

With that decision, Elaina's mind began to wander to Bryan's phone call last night. She idly wondered where they found his niece and hoped Macy hadn't gotten involved in drugs or porn as so many runaways did.

The sound of a vehicle cruising close prompted Elaina to look over her shoulder. The sea-green Town Car's honk accompanied someone wildly waving from the passenger seat. Elaina waved back and detected the passenger was Lorna Starr. Suppressing a groan, she suspected that Jeanna's car must have been close when she turned at the brick posts. Elaina had been so engrossed in thoughts of Anna she had missed it. Yanking her jogger's jacket close, Elaina stopped and awaited the vehicle's halt.

As soon as Jeanna rolled down the window, Kay-Kay hung her paws over the glass and Elaina detected a hint of sweet musk perfume. Lorna squealed her remarks before Jeanna had the chance to open her mouth, "I thought that was you, girl, the second I saw you. I told Aunt Jeanna, I said, 'Aunt Jeanna, that's Elaina. I recognize her red hair!'"

With a smile she hoped hid her desire to be alone, Elaina touched the top of her head. "This red hair makes it hard for me to hide, doesn't it?"

"I was just taking Lorna down to the cottage," Jeanna said. "I called your mom, and she said to come on over." The sunshine blared into the Town Car and accented Jeanna's over-made cheeks and lips. "I wanted to show Lorna what all your mother has done with the place. I must say, she's spruced it up so much it almost makes me wish I'd never sold it."

"Yes," Elaina said with a pleased grin. "My mom was born to be a homemaker. She's really got the talent. I'm not good for much except my books and lectures. When I leased my duplex, I should have had Mom and Anna do the decorating. Anna is as gifted in that area as my mother."

"Do you want to ride to the cottage with us?" Jeanna asked and looked at Elaina as if she couldn't imagine why a young woman would be out walking.

"No thanks." Elaina shook her head. "I'm trying to get some exercise. I've been hitting the chocolate a little too heavily lately." She patted her abdomen.

"Oh, you're just like Lorna," Jeanna scoffed, and her double chin rolled. "Skinny as a rail and worried sick you're going to gain a pound."

Elaina chuckled. "I think we can all say Lorna's figure is much cuter than mine," she said and meant every word. "I'm just glad to be mentioned in the same sentence with her."

Lorna beamed from the passenger seat, and Elaina noticed she hadn't bothered with cosmetics this morning. Unfortunately, Lorna was one of those women who looked as good without the stuff as with it. After Ted's treatment, Elaina had begun to feel that she looked as drab with it as without it, so she hadn't bothered this morning, either.

"If you don't mind," Lorna said, "I'll join you. I haven't worked out all week. Jeanna and me have been eatin' all sorts a goodies! I'm probably goin' to—"

"Gain a half-pound!" Jeanna interrupted and placed her hand against her forehead. "Oh heaven forbid!"

Lorna popped open her door, hopped from the car, slammed the door, and bee-bopped to Elaina's side. Her cropped jacket left a view of a pink jogging suit hugging her slim curves. Elaina felt like a Hershey's Kisses junkie. Every muscle in her face went stiff. With a resigned wave Jeanna merrily gassed her Town Car down the lane. Elaina, left in the company of the angel, examined her dislike for Lorna. She normally didn't fall into such petty behavior. When Lorna began the chitchat, Elaina wondered if she was allowing her recent breakup with Ted to cloud her judgment.

Perhaps Lorna's only sin is that she's beautiful, Elaina thought as her sneakers crunched against gravel. She stole a peak at the vivacious woman and recalled thinking that Lorna was swimming in a cesspool of self-pity last night. This morning the young lady appeared to be the image of bubbly emotional health.

Maybe she just likes to talk about herself, Elaina thought, *or somehow felt safe talking about her life to me, or just needed to talk about it. Who wouldn't after all she's been through?* Lorna's chatter blended with the frequent squawk and cheep of blue jays and red birds as they pecked, hopped, and fluttered. In the spirit of the cheerful morning, Elaina decided to give poor Lorna another chance. She could almost hear her mother—the queen of friendship—applauding her decision.

I have no desire to look like her or have her figure, Elaina told herself. *I'm an accomplished woman. I'm comfortable with who I am.* Jeanna had said a month ago that Lorna would never succeed in college or hold down a job. The lack of an intelligent spark in Lorna's eyes strengthened Elaina's security.

"And I just don't know what I would do now if it weren't for my fiancé." Lorna's words broke through Elaina's reflections. Without slowing her stride, she examined the other woman.

"Yes, Jeanna mentioned something about your engagement awhile ago."

"Oh did she now?" Lorna darted Elaina a speculative glance and laid her hand against her chest. Her engagement ring conspicuously sparkled in the sunlight.

Elaina nodded and wondered why she hadn't noticed the two-carat solitaire last night. "She said she was very glad for you."

"Well, it's good to hear that's what she's a sayin' behind my back. I certainly thought she might have her doubts when I told her."

"Well, you know Jeanna," Elaina claimed, "she wants all the details or she gets bent out of shape."

Lorna huffed and her breath formed a misty cloud that blew back in her face. "Bless her heart. She's just so curious. And… and…" Lorna touched her temple, "she absolutely *never* stops talkin'. Would somebody please tell me what makes somebody *do* that?" She looked at Elaina in blank scrutiny.

"I wouldn't know," Elaina hedged.

"Anyway, my fiancé has just taken care of everythang since my divorce. I don't know *what* I would do without him. Me and him have something so special. See, I'm not like you and so many other women," Lorna continued. "I just never could get into the college thang, so my chances of gettin' a job are—"

"But there are plenty of jobs out there for people who don't go to college," Elaina said. "My sister is a secretary, and she's never—"

"I *desperately* need a man for those things." Lorna wrinkled her nose as if the thought of supporting herself were despicable. "I just *hate* havin' to go to a job."

"Sometimes I do, too," Elaina admitted. *Would that we all could just be princesses,* she thought and hid a sarcastic smirk. "I think a lot of men could probably say the same thing if they were brutally honest. But we all have to eat, and—"

"Oh I know. And I did try it. I worked at a library eight years ago, before I got married. I absolutely *abhorred* it. All those books!" Lorna flipped her ponytail as if she were trying to rid her mind of the recollection. "I felt like I couldn't even breathe," she continued. "That's where I met my husband. He asked me to help him in the reference section, and me and him were married two weeks later."

"Two weeks?" Elaina croaked and nearly tripped over a dip in the uneven lane.

Lorna nodded. "Yes, I was so torn up—remember last night I told you my fiancé had jilted me?"

"Yes," Elaina said.

"Well, that had only been a few months before my father died. Then when he died I was left with almost nobody. I was still so upset about my fiancé and my father and I thought Geoff would make everything okay. I thought he would take care of me like he said, but…but…he started drinkin', and…" Lorna looked away, and the simple-minded woman's grief swept aside Elaina's exasperation. Her childlike willingness to blindly believe a man she'd only known a few weeks reminded Elaina of Anna's romantic whims. She pledged anew to befriend Lorna. She, like Anna, probably needed someone in her life with the ability to reason.

"Oh anyway," Lorna waved her hand and sniffed, "my fiancé now understands all that. Mainly because he's the same one who jilted me all them years ago. Even then our engagement had to be a secret."

"Really?" Despite last night's pledge of disinterest, Lorna's story finally snared Elaina. She was now as curious as she was about Bryan's past.

"Oh yes. He was the first one I went to when I found Geoff with that other woman, and then Geoff beat me up so bad. Oh, he'd hit me a few times before, but this time it was just *awful!*" Lorna stroked beneath her eye as if it were still swollen. Elaina could hardly imagine the flawless skin marred by bruises.

"I didn't really know *what* to do," Lorna said. "Both my parents was dead. I don't have any brothers and sisters. All I could think of was him and how I never stopped lovin' him."

"He must be a very special man," Elaina admitted, and she wondered why Lorna hadn't called her aunt and uncle. They seemed truly fond of her and probably would have helped.

"Best of all, he welcomed me with open arms. He understands me, and—and my needs. He helped me through that awful divorce my husband filed for. And then he rented my apartment for me and has paid for everything since. He even gives me an allowance. He knows I just couldn't *stand* the thought of goin' to some ol' job everyday."

"That's wonderful," Elaina managed to say. "It's always good to have an understanding fiancé." *Who also has money,* she thought. Elaina gazed across the pasture and considered how much she had thought Ted understood her. The cold air seemed to seep into the center of her soul. Never had she been so hurt by a man.

Lorna grabbed Elaina's arm and halted. Caught off guard, Elaina jerked to a stop and examined the beauty for some signs of an emergency. All she encountered were pale-green eyes alight with urgent desperation. "Oh, Elaina, I've *got* to tell you. I've just *got* to. I'm goin' to explode if I don't tell someone who I'm engaged to."

"But I thought it was a secret," Elaina said.

"It is!" Lorna stomped her foot. "But I know you won't tell a livin' soul. I knew last night that I could trust you. I just knew it! You won't tell anyone, will you? Not even Aunt Jeanna and Uncle Noah. My fiancé wouldn't be happy if he knew I was tellin' you."

"I won't tell," Elaina said and tried to convince herself she should take the high road. "But Lorna, if it's a secret for some valid reason, you *must* honor his request. After all, his name will probably mean nothing to me anyway, and—"

"Oh but you and him already know each other," Lorna said.

"W—we do?" Elaina asked, and her inquisitive mind suggested she should ignore the high road this time.

"Yes, you do. He really respects you, I do believe." Lorna looked down at her hands, resting upon Elaina's arm. "He's one of your students," she continued.

"He is?" Elaina wrinkled her brow and began a mental roll call of her male pupils.

"Yes, it's Ted Farris," Lorna whispered as if she were afraid the trees had ears.

Stunned, Elaina stared into Lorna's wide-set eyes and once again detected the hard gleam from last night. Like last night, the effect disappeared as swiftly as it occurred. For a wrinkle in time, Elaina even wondered if Lorna might be lying. She couldn't imagine Ted—the sensitive, intelligent, musical genius—being cuffed to this shallow woman for life. But the determined set of Lorna's full lips bespoke truth. Elaina felt as if she were being sucked into the vortex of a suffocating whirlpool.

Never had her ability to maintain her composure been so strained. Somehow Elaina feigned a passive expression that hid her turmoil. While she wanted to drop to her knees and bellow, Elaina only allowed a slight nod.

"Yes, I know Ted," she said. "He seems like a very nice man."

Lorna's right brow arched. Elaina suspected Lorna would have preferred a more impassioned reaction from her. Immediately she sensed Lorna had more mental abilities than she'd credited her. Elaina also deduced that Lorna's revealing the name of her fiancé had nothing to do with a need for a confidante. Her charitable desires to befriend Lorna crashed to a gruesome death.

"I guess since I'm bein' honest, I must tell you that my aunt told me she's seen Ted at your mom's cottage not once, but twice," Lorna said as if she had caught Elaina in some sin. "Of course," she continued, "my aunt had no way of knowin' that him and me are engaged. It's funny actually. She said she would have introduced us if I wasn't engaged. You know how Aunt Jeanna is, always tryin' to marry people off."

"Yes," Elaina said.

"Anyway," Lorna's fingering the collar of her powder-pink jacket reminded Elaina of a self-satisfied feline, "Aunt Jeanna told me Ted helped your mama move and—"

"Yes, he did." Elaina inched away from Lorna and crossed her arms. The feline's pleasure required a blow. "We're almost related."

"You are?" Lorna questioned and wrinkled her brow.

"Of course," Elaina continued, and Lorna's confusion only fueled Elaina's ability to maintain her composure. "His sister, Faye, is married to my half-brother, Jake. When my father died a few months ago, Jake and Faye inherited the estate. Ted even helped his sister rearrange a few things while he was there that weekend. The first time I met Ted I was twelve and he was fifteen." Elaina didn't bother to tell Lorna that until this fall she hadn't seen him since.

"Oh!" Lorna squeaked out, her lips remaining in a pucker. "Well, he never told me that."

"That's odd," Elaina purred, "especially since the two of you are so close." She smiled and figured it lacked as much warmth as her heart now did.

"Maybe he did," Lorna touched her temple, "and I've just forgotten. I'm sure he must have." She lifted her chin.

"Must have," Elaina agreed.

"Oh well," Lorna acquiesced, "when I mentioned you to him, he seemed so...so...I don't know...I thought—" She resumed her walking as if the very action would dismiss the need to finish her sentence.

Elaina stepped back into pace beside her and refused to allow the other woman that pleasure. "What exactly *did* you think, Lorna?" she pressed.

"Well," Lorna sniffed, "I'm so jealous, and I know how Ted can make a woman feel, you know," she shrugged, "attached." Lorna slid Elaina a calculating glance that suggested she really hadn't wanted to avoid this part of the conversation. "He seems to have a special touch with women. Some men just draw women, I guess, like that man your sister had with her last night. I think every gal in the room was lookin' at him."

"Including you?" Elaina suggested.

Lorna's eyes widened. "I didn't mean it that way," she snapped.

"Of course not," Elaina soothed with a satisfaction she didn't even attempt to check. Before Lorna could say more, Elaina asked, "Now, why was it that you and Ted can't announce your engagement?" They rounded the corner and the cottage came into sight.

"Oh, his mother," Lorna readily admitted. "She wants him to marry someone from 'society.'" She mimicked a snobbish expression. "Ted said if we shock her she's liable to disinherit him. She's threatened a time or two over his piano career."

"That wouldn't do, now, would it?" Elaina asked.

When Lorna shot her a hard stare, Elaina maintained an innocent expression. The defensive line of Lorna's mouth softened.

"Ted said it would be better to wait until he's done with this second master's degree. Then him and me can get his mama used to the idea. At first we were goin' to announce it in December. But he's gonna take me to his mom's as a friend during the holidays, and then we'll go from there."

"Sounds like a smart plan to me," Elaina quipped, the solace of her room beckoning. When her shoes encountered the cottage's paved driveway, she upped her pace. "I don't know Mrs. Farris that well at all. But if she's anything like my sister-in-law, Faye, she'd have you for dinner before you knew it."

Lorna's cheeks, pink from the cold morning, took on a pallid hue. "Really?" she asked.

"Oh yes," Elaina assured and patted her back. "Beat you to the porch!" she called before racing toward the house.

Twenty

Elaina hurried into the cottage with Lorna close behind. The warm air, still mellow with homemade biscuits, enveloped Elaina and heated her numb nose. She checked the dining room and spotted Jeanna and her mother in the throes of coffee and small talk.

"I need to go upstairs," she said and didn't give either of the doe-eyed women time to make an inquiry. Elaina was halfway up the staircase before the front door's click announced Lorna's entry.

Oh great, Elaina thought and decided to give Lorna no reason to suspect her shattered heart. "Nice talking with you, Lorna," she called over her shoulder and offered a merry wave. "I just need to go upstairs for a few minutes."

"Sure!" Lorna agreed with a relaxed smile that didn't hint of their former tension. "Take your time."

I will, Elaina thought as she ascended the stairs. *I'm not coming down until you leave.*

The second Elaina closed the door on the guest room she began pacing. The trek from the claw-footed bedside table and around the poster bed to the table's twin became her pathway. Last month's events unfolded in her mind, and finally she began to find answers for her questions. Elaina recalled Ted's odd expression the night she told him he must be a man who kept his word. That same night, he ran from the house after going pale. Elaina assumed he was ill, as Bryan suggested. But Jeanna and Noah had been discussing Lorna minutes before Ted left. *After that, he refused to return my calls and then passed me that awful note,* Elaina thought.

Sitting on the edge of the eyelet-covered bed, Elaina yanked off her walking shoes and allowed them to fall where they may. She resumed her walking, this time back and forth at the end of the bed. Every time she passed one of the carved cherry posts, she wrapped her fingers around it and squeezed as if the bed could somehow infuse her with strength of heart.

"He must have been falling for me," she whispered. "No, I *know* he was falling for me. He acted like he was—like he might be—" Elaina stopped beside the bedpost, hung on with both hands, and laid her cheek against the wood.

"We were falling in love," she admitted. *And then when Jeanna and Noah started talking about Lorna, he must have realized he couldn't break his promise to her.*

"He must not have known Lorna was related to Jeanna and Noah." Elaina narrowed her eyes. "Probably because Lorna didn't want him to know she's got someone who could help her." She stared at the beveled mirror framed in brass hanging behind the bedside lamp. The night Ted left so abruptly, Jeanna had even said that Noah hadn't kept in touch with his niece and brother-in-law after his sister's death. So there was no reason Ted would know about the rich relatives, even during his first relationship with Lorna.

She examined her initial dislike for Lorna and wondered if a sixth sense had been at work, warning her that Lorna was the enemy. "I didn't like her the minute I met her," Elaina rasped, "at all. And I don't see how Ted could ever be attracted to her."

She moved to the mirror and peered at herself. While the blue-eyed reflection with smart-looking glasses wasn't bad, Elaina could never fool herself into believing she would ever be as pretty as Lorna. "Okay," she admitted, "I know why he was attracted to her in the first place. But why can't he see her lack of depth?"

Elaina shed her jogging jacket and slammed it against the bed. She sat back down across from the petite bathroom snuggled in the room's corner. *Maybe he did see,* she thought, *and maybe that's the reason he jilted her the first time.*

With a groan, Elaina removed her glasses and dropped them on the nightstand. She covered her face with her hands and pondered Ted's character. Unlike his sister, the man was gold through and through. When Lorna landed on his doorstep, her bruised face and crushed spirits probably sucked him into a tailspin of compassion that insisted he must restate his original matrimonial vow. Elaina doubted the man detected one shred of Lorna's manipulative tactics. Ted Farris would now keep his word—no matter what.

"Even if he's in love with someone else," she whispered. With a whimper, Elaina crawled to the bed's center, buried her head in the quilted pillows, and silently wept.

⁂

Anna paced her bedroom from mirror to mirror to make certain her appearance was perfect. In her dresser mirror, she examined her hair and makeup. After washing and drying her hair, she had brushed the straight locks until the sunlight pouring through the lace sheers melted into it like honey. Anna hurried to the full-length mirror in the room's corner. She adjusted the mahogany-framed glass until she was happy with the angle. Frowning, she pivoted and examined every inch of her scarlet sweater and black velvet pants. The outfit clung to her size-four curves as if it were handmade for her.

"Willis is coming! Willis is coming! Willis is coming!" she whispered. With a tiny squeal, Anna doubled her fists and ran in place. Her hair swished around her shoulders and she stopped.

"Oh no!" she shook her fingers as if her nails were wet. "I messed up my hair!" Anna ran back to the dresser, grabbed her brush, and carefully arranged her hair into a flawless veil.

"Okay," she whispered to her reflection, "everything's perfect." She held her left hand in front of her and imagined what her engagement ring would look like. *It will be huge, of course,* she thought with a satisfied nod. *Any man who drives a Jaguar won't give his fiancée a tiny diamond.*

She moved to her unmade bed and settled upon the rumpled cotton comforter. Anna checked the emerald-studded wristwatch her father gave her for Christmas last. "Five till ten," she huffed and eyed her collection of American Girl dolls lining several tiers of bookshelves. She'd started the collection when she was ten. Even though she hadn't added to it in five years, Anna still cherished the dolls as her dearest friends.

"Girls," she said, "I'm about to become Mrs. Willis Kenney. And it's a good thing, because things are heating up really fast!" She snickered as she recalled last night's urgent kisses. "Ssshhh!" she admonished. "Don't tell anyone."

Anna rose and twirled around the room as if she were at a ball. After several rotations, she stopped and shook her hands once more. "Oh shoot!" she exclaimed. "I messed up my hair again."

The second she picked up her brush, the doorbell rang. Anna gasped, gaped at her flushed cheeks, and then raked the brush through her hair for the final time. On her way out the door, she tossed the brush into the bed's center and ran to the stairway. She gripped the railing, paused, and took a deep breath.

Oh why act calm at a time like this? she thought and bounded down the stairway. When she hopped off the bottom step, her mother opened the front door. Willis stepped inside, and his gaze fixed upon her.

Anna's heart pounded so hard she thought she might faint.

"Well hello there, Willis," Margaret said with a special beam just for him. "I wasn't expecting you this morning."

"Hello, Anna," Willis said without acknowledging Margaret.

"Hi," Anna breathed and rubbed her damp palms against the front of her sweater.

"Here, let me help you with your coat." Margaret fussed with helping Willis shed his leather jacket. Beneath it he wore a snug-fitting cotton sweater that accentuated his lean muscles. Anna recalled last night's heated encounter and could hardly wait until their wedding night. If not for the promise she made to her father and mother when she was fourteen, Anna would be on her way to New York with him the coming weekend. But by some miracle, she had continued to stand firm by her promise, even though her yearning heart told her to abandon herself to Willis' wishes.

"Believe it or not, you just missed Jeanna and her niece, Lorna," Margaret said as she hung Willis' coat on the coatrack. "They left an hour ago to go do some shopping. I'm sure they would have been delighted to see you."

"Well, I just came to see Anna," Willis mumbled.

Anna examined his slacks pockets for some sign of a small box. She detected no evidence and wondered if he'd slipped the ring into his pocket without the box.

"Would you like some tea or coffee?" Margaret asked.

"No, no, thanks." Willis shook his head and never once pulled his attention from Anna.

"A cola?"

"Uh, no."

"Mom, do you mind if we have some time alone in the living room?" Anna requested.

"Oh!" Margaret looked from her daughter to Willis and back to Anna. "Oh no! Of course not," she babbled. "I'll just...I'll just go...go upstairs and check on Elaina. She never came back down awhile ago, not even to see Jeanna and Lorna off. It was the oddest thing. She called my house number from her cell phone in her room and just told me she wasn't feeling well and to pass on her apologies to Jeanna and Lorna. I checked on her after they left, and she was in the bathroom. I hope she's okay."

Forget Elaina, Anna thought. She'd been so excited this morning she sprang from sleep at eight—after only six hours sleep. However, Anna hadn't dared go downstairs for fear of being interrogated by her elder sister. Instead, she spent the morning in her room, grooming herself for this big moment.

The minute Margaret scurried up the stairs, Willis reached for Anna's hand, and she lunged into his arms. "Oh I missed you so much!" Anna breathed against his neck and curled her fingers in his thick hair. His clean smell both warmed and invited.

"Anna..." Willis hedged and inched away, "let's go into the living room. Okay?"

"Okay," she agreed. Anna hurried forward and pulled him along with her. Exuberance pounded through her veins, leaving her like a birthday girl not certain which package to unwrap. Anna debated whether she should settle onto the couch where Willis had first kissed her or plop at the baby grand piano and begin playing a special love song just for him.

"Let's dance," she gurgled and stepped toward Willis. Ready to sway around the room, she placed her hands along his shoulder. "I think the jitterbug would probably be the most appropriate."

He frowned over the words and stepped from her grasp.

Anna's smile faded. For the first time, she noticed the indecision in his eyes. Willis stepped toward the fireplace, aglow with embers. He turned his back to her and lowered his head.

"Anna," Willis choked out.

"Willis?" She walked toward him and then stopped. She wrapped her arms around her midsection and felt as if her world were shaking. "What's wrong? Aren't we... Didn't you..."

"No, we aren't." Willis faced her. "We can't. Not now."

"But—but why? What about the—the ring?" She rubbed the base of the finger a diamond should now claim.

He shook his head and looked past her. "I'm sorry," Willis whispered. The dark circles under his eyes and the haggard wilt of his mouth added a haunted misery to his words.

Anna stood perfectly still and tried to comprehend this turn of events. At first she told herself that she was having a nightmare...that Willis hadn't even arrived...that any minute this whole scene would be replaced by a glorious reception of an exquisite ring that would link them for life. She held her breath and waited for the horrid dream to end. But it didn't. Neither did the wretched look in Willis' eyes.

"I'm leaving my aunt's now," he continued. "I've already packed."

"L–leaving?" Elaina rasped and grasped her throat.

Willis nodded. "She's gotten angry at me over a...a misunderstanding." He shook his head. "It's nothing to concern you. She's throwing a fit and tossing me out. She's even saying she's going to disinherit me."

"Disinherit you?" Anna repeated.

"Yes. And—and until all this is straightened up, I can't offer you—" He raised his hand. "It wouldn't be fair."

"Oh, but Willis..." Anna flung herself forward, wrapped her arms around him, laid her head on his chest and squeezed tight, "I don't care about all that. I love you. You've got your modeling income. We'll be fine on that."

Willis draped his arms around her and rested his cheek on her head. The expectant beat of his heart enticed Anna into believing she had convinced him.

His next words disintegrated that assumption. "It's just not that simple, babe," he mumbled. "I only wish it were."

"But—but we'll stay together until—until—"

"I'm afraid I'm going to have to leave for New York this weekend. I've got a new job lined up, as you know. After that, I don't know when I'll be back to Lakeland. With Aunt Nancy in such an uproar it might be awhile."

"Since when am *I* worried about her?" Anna backed away and looked up into tormented eyes. She framed his face with her hands. "This is *us* we're talking about. Not *her*."

His gaze, alight with desire, trailed her face and settled upon her mouth. Anna, once again sure she had made a conquest, awaited the seal of their undying love. But Willis' lips hardened. He gripped her arms and pushed her away.

"No, Anna," he choked. "I can't. Not now. I've got to go." He strode toward the doorway.

"But…but…but…" she stammered.

"I'll be in touch," Willis called over his shoulder.

"In touch?" Anna echoed and realized he had never given her his phone number or home address. All she had was his aunt's phone number and an e-mail address from a message he sent last week.

Willis' footsteps tapped upon hardwood as he stepped into the entryway. Within seconds, the front door slammed. Anna rushed to the bay window where she'd told Elaina she would know the love of her life the instant she met him. She rested her knee on the padded seat and swept aside the striped drapes.

"Willis," she whispered as he marched toward his Jaguar. Her eyes stung. A sob erupted from her soul.

Without a backward glance, he opened the car door, slid inside, slammed the door, and cranked the engine. He sped from the home as if he couldn't get away fast enough. The Jaguar rolled onto the road. The powerful engine roared, and the tires screeched.

"Willis!" Anna screamed as if she'd stumbled upon his corpse. "Willis!" Hysterical wails overtook her as she backed from the window. "Willis!" She wept anew and stumbled into the piano. Her hand slammed onto the highest notes. The instrument responded with a cacophonous clang. Anna crashed onto the bench.

Twenty-One

Five days later, Elaina sat in her office chair, holding the globe Ted had given her. She turned the treasure over, allowed the glitter to float toward the top, and then righted it. The sparkling bits cascaded downward, covering the feather pen and manuscript in gold dust.

Elaina stared at Ted's present until the globe blurred. The memory of the day he presented the gift overtook her. Ted had whisked her around the cottage's parking area until she was dizzy with anticipation. Not even the frigid breeze could chill her heart, warmed by the adoration in Ted's eyes. Looking back, Elaina realized she was falling—and falling hard. Only Jeanna's honking had stopped the kiss that would have celebrated the beginning of new love, a love that could have taken a lifetime to unfold.

She shook her head. Elaina used her short-topped boot to kick the drawer from which she'd retrieved the gift. The drawer banged shut just as Ted had slammed the door upon their love. Elaina plunked the globe in the center of her desk and glared at the thing.

After indulging in her cry last Saturday, Elaina felt as if she were a vessel emptied of all contents. Due to Anna's upheaval and her mother's grief over her youngest daughter, Elaina hadn't shared her own despair. Besides, she'd promised Lorna she would keep the secret. Even though Lorna didn't top her list as a favorite, Elaina was a woman of her word. By Tuesday night, the first sparks of anger marred her desolate soul. The anger now insisted she ask Ted Farris two questions.

"What were you thinking?" she whispered. "And why did you do this to me...to us?"

The globe offered no answers, but Ted would. Elaina stood, gathered the class' final exams, shoved them into her briefcase, and marched out the door. The time had come for some answers.

As she rounded the corner and strode down the hallway, Elaina planned her strategy. When Ted turned in his final exam, she would ask to see him in her office after class. As his professor, Elaina would give Ted no option. The rest of the class wouldn't suspect a thing.

She glanced down at her golden watch that her father had given her Christmas last. Class was supposed to have started three minutes ago. Most likely every student had arrived by now—including Ted. She hurried down the hallway, swept into the classroom, and didn't bother to observe her students. Elaina plopped her briefcase in the center of her desk, unlatched it, and retrieved the tests from atop half a dozen composition blue books. A swift perusal of the pupils indicated twenty-one present. None were absent.

Before shutting her briefcase, she shot a question to the room's back window. "Did everyone remember to buy blue books?" She raised her brows and waited for someone to respond in the negative. All she received were anxious stares. Elaina didn't bother to look at Ted. As exasperated as she was, if he'd admitted to not having a blue book she might have told him he could find one elsewhere.

"Okay, good," she said. "Then we'll begin." She checked her watch again for no other reason than nervous energy. Nevertheless, Elaina refused to reveal even a thread of her true emotions. She wasted no time distributing the one-page exams that would generate two hours of essays. As the students read over their tests, the coughs and shuffle of papers couldn't cover the room's rising tension and the silent cries of "I should have studied more!"

Elaina proceeded back to her desk where she claimed her chair. The smells of chalk and notebooks that had invigorated her the first day of class now only weighted her weary spirit. Who would have ever guessed that fulfilling her goal of a professorship would have led to such heartache?

She sneaked a peak at Ted. While many of his companions were still skimming the test or peering into space, Ted was bent over his blue book already hard at work. The man had the highest average of the class. Not only was he a brilliant musician, his literary analyses lacked nothing. The overhead lights put a sheen on his straight hair, slicked away from his face. That, plus his jeans and sweatshirt made Ted appear to be nothing more than an average college student.

A very attractive college student, Elaina added to herself with a regret that nearly knocked her to the floor. Given his love of casual attire and his unassuming air, she doubted that any students suspected Ted had played for the president of the United States.

She scowled at her briefcase, popped it open, and scrounged past the spare blue books until her fingers rested upon the final papers from her Advanced Composition class. This semester Elaina discovered that she hated grading papers with as much passion as she loved teaching literature.

She retrieved the research papers and disciplined her mind to tackle the chore. However, the pupils' written commentaries became a hazy monologue as Anna's problems barged in upon Elaina's. After her traumatic reaction to Willis' departure, Anna had gone to her room and spent the rest of the weekend in solitude. She refused to talk to Elaina Saturday and only offered a muffled goodbye through her door when Elaina left for home. As of Sunday night Margaret Woods reported that Anna was recovering from the shock and had mentioned that Willis said he would be in touch.

Always the hopeful romantic, Elaina thought. As far as she was concerned, reason insisted that Willis was done with her sister. Despite his promises, the man had done exactly what Elaina suspected. He had used Anna then dumped her. Logic suggested Willis had probably taken more from Anna than she would ever admit to their mother or Elaina. After all, Anna and Willis had been out until two Saturday morning, and Jeanna's party broke up at eleven. Elaina didn't fool herself into believing Willis wasn't sexually experienced. Men of his background didn't stay out with a woman until two so they could sniff daisies. Now her sister was reaping the heartache. The whole scenario made perfect sense. Willis got what he wanted and then disappeared.

Elaina thought about asking her mother if Anna had confided any hint of physical intimacy between herself and Willis. However she dashed aside the thought as soon as it entered her mind. Margaret Woods, ever the loyal mother, would never suspect her daughter of such sin and would never insult her with such a question.

In a fit of big sister sympathy, Elaina wanted to rush to Anna's side, wrap her arms around her, and hold her until her pain was all better, just as she had when Anna was twelve and skinned her knee. *But Anna is still so shut off to me, she probably wouldn't even offer a distant hug,* she thought. Elaina rubbed her forehead and didn't bother to inhibit the discouragement that spilled into her disillusionment.

Her wayward gaze trailed to Ted. Her eyes narrowed. She looked at the bisque floor tiles between them and wondered if Ted and Willis had attended the same heartbreaker's training camp. While Willis' tactics may have been more earthy, Ted's behavior hadn't been any less deplorable. In a fit of furor, Elaina was tempted to write "ALL MEN ARE PIGS!" on the blackboard in big block letters, but she couldn't bring herself to commit to the slur. Elaina had been too close to her father to smear his whole gender. Furthermore, she refused to feed a prejudice against all men based upon the behavior of only two.

There are a lot of good guys out there, Elaina told herself. *Whether or not Anna and I will find one is still up for question.* She thought of Bryan Brixby. *Now that man is going to make somebody a good husband.* She considered giving her sister a good shake.

Fleetingly she wondered how Bryan's niece was faring. She hadn't heard a word from him since he received the phone call and rushed from Jeanna's party. He hadn't even attended Sunday services. Elaina had considered calling his office a few times but chose not to. She didn't want to seem nosy or pressure him into divulging painful details. His niece had been gone for months. *No telling what situation they found her in,* Elaina thought.

She focused on the research paper. Without realizing it, Elaina had bent and rebent the top corner so much it was about to fall off. With a determined glower, she purposed to direct her energies toward the task at hand. Elaina was getting no papers graded brooding over Ted Farris, Willis Kenney, or Bryan Brixby and his family issues.

As the class progressed, the students began to hand in their blue books and leave. Every time a blue book landed on her desk, Elaina checked to see if Ted were attached to it. Finally, all but one of the blue books was in the pile—the one belonging to Ted. Initially, this struck Elaina as strange because Ted was usually one of the first pupils finished at test time. Soon she understood that his tarrying was no accident.

When the last student stepped out of the room, Ted picked up his test, gathered his notebook, and approached the desk. For the first time since he nearly kissed her in the kitchen, Ted peered into Elaina's eyes. Once again, his tortured artist soul beckoned her to draw near. When her defenses softened, Elaina reminded herself that while Ted might be in torment, he had wounded her as well. She stiffened her back.

"Mr. Farris—"

"Elain—I mean, Dr. Woods—" He looked toward the doorway.

"Was there something you needed?" Elaina asked, using extra effort to keep her voice disinterested.

Ted dropped his blue book in the pile. "I was wondering if we might be able to talk." His dark eyes added a silent "please."

Elaina covered a tremor. "Actually, I was about to ask you to step into my office," she admitted.

"Good. We need to talk."

"Yes, we do," Elaina agreed, her voice firm. She snatched up the blue books, shoved them into her briefcase, and dropped the term papers atop the pile. With the latches clicked into place, she hauled the case from the desk and strode from the room with Ted close behind. On the brief trip to her office, Elaina's mind ticked through the possible reasons Ted would want to talk with her.

When she rounded the corner, she thought, *Surely the guy doesn't think we can make up.* Elaina stopped at her office door and heard Ted pause behind. The second she opened the door she wondered if he and Lorna broke up. The globe in the desk's center teased her into thinking that was the case. When she dropped her briefcase beside the desk and faced Ted, she understood that the globe was as cruel a teaser as the man who bought it. Ted's pained expression offered only regrets—no hint of good news.

"Elaina, I couldn't leave this semester like—like this." He looked down as if her desk were covered with words from which he might choose.

"Would you please close the door, Mr. Farris," Elaina requested and applauded herself for keeping her voice so poised. The instant the door closed and Ted turned, Elaina placed her flattened palms on the desktop.

"I met Lorna last weekend," she said without blinking.

"L–Lorna? Ted stammered.

"Lorna Starr. According to her, the two of you have been engaged for months." Elaina's tone in no way revealed her rising passion.

Ted stared at Elaina as if she were speaking Vietnamese. "What were you *thinking?*"

"Thinking?" he repeated.

"Or were you even thinking?" she questioned.

"Was I even thinking?"

"Why did you do this to me...to us?" she reasoned, maintaining her feigned composure.

Ted blinked. He laid his notebook on her desk, placed one hand on his hip, and used the other to massage his forehead. "I—I don't know," he said and shook his head. "I don't know."

"You don't know," Elaina repeated and her rigid arms relaxed a fraction.

"No, I don't know." Ted lowered his hand and looked past her, his stunned face blank. "It just happened. I didn't mean for it to happen." He blinked. "I wasn't looking for it to happen."

A need to know his heart urged Elaina to her next statement. "Please define *it*."

"It?" Ted focused on her. "From what I understand that word is a pronoun." A tiny smile tugged at the corners of his mouth.

Elaina's first reaction was to return the smile. She didn't. "I'm in no frame of mind to—"

"Look, Elaina," he said, "I didn't come in here for this."

"Why *did* you ask to talk with me?" she softly challenged.

"I just wanted," he shrugged, "to apologize and to—to explain about—about Lorna."

"So go ahead." Elaina sat on the edge of her chair and tried to stifle memories of their carefree weekend...of the times Ted nearly kissed her. Elaina observed the globe and schooled her face into an impassive mask.

"Lorna and I...I fell for Lorna hard when I was younger. Her father was my first piano teacher. Even though he had no formal education, he was a brilliant pianist and taught me everything he knew from the time I was in grade school until I graduated from high school. So Lorna and I were thrown together often. I had an awful crush on her my whole senior year."

"Humph," Elaina said, "I wonder why."

Ted's eyes narrowed, and a long pause followed. Elaina refused to look away.

"So we became an item," he continued. "By the time I was twenty-one we were engaged. I knew we had to keep our engagement a secret because of my mom. Even then she was pushing for me to marry someone with, well," he stroked his sideburn, "someone moneyed.

"Lorna was fine with the secret for awhile. Then she started pushing to announce our engagement. At that point I suspected that I had been using my mother as an excuse to put off the marriage. Then after Lorna threw a fit one night, I woke up the next morning and realized I wasn't in love with her." He shrugged. "So I broke up with her."

"She told me you jilted her."

"What *didn't* she tell you?" Ted asked.

"She only left out one tiny detail," Elaina admitted and saw no value in hiding the truth. "The fact that she's manipulating you into marrying her."

"What?" Ted questioned as if Elaina had lost her mind.

"Think about it, Ted." Elaina adjusted her glasses and decided if he was too blind to sort the clues nothing she could say would convince him. "Think about it long and hard."

"What does it matter if she is?" he asked and lifted his hand. "I gave her my word. I already broke her heart once. I don't have the conscience to do it again—especially not after she married that jerk on the rebound from me."

"But that marriage was *not* your fault," Elaina argued. "She made her own choices. Lorna didn't have to marry that guy."

"No, but she wouldn't have if I had kept my word to her. Then when he beat her up and slept with other women and filed for a divorce, she was left without a place to go or anyone to fall back on. She's an only child, and her parents are dead. Her father left her almost no inheritance. By the time she paid off his debts, she had pennies left. If I had turned her away, she would have probably landed on the streets."

"Good grief, Ted, you didn't have to offer to marry her to help her!"

His brows drew together.

"Besides all that, she had her aunt and uncle—Jeanna and Noah Harley. Those two have so much money they practically use hundred dollar bills for wallpaper. Jeanna's family is drowning in oil!"

"I never met them until the other night at your mom's home."

"And why do you think that is?"

He offered no answer, only silently observed her desk.

Finally Elaina said, "What's less honorable, marrying a woman you don't love or breaking your word?"

"How do you know I haven't grown to love her?" he questioned, his eyes hard with a belligerence she never expected.

Rattled, Elaina said the first thing that came to her, "Because you were falling in love with—" she stopped herself from saying "me." Elaina gazed at the globe. The silence said everything she couldn't. Suddenly she felt as if she were a bigger romantic fool than Anna. Maybe Ted did love the beautiful airhead, and he had simply used Elaina as a plaything before he announced his engagement. Perhaps he'd always fantasized ensnaring his professor in a secret relationship and then ripping out her heart. She stood, wrapped her fingers around the globe, and extended the gift to Ted.

"Here," she said, "I don't need this anymore. Maybe Lorna can find a spot for it in your new home."

Without making eye contact, Ted accepted the globe. He scooped up his notebook from the desk and exited the office. The door's click penetrated her spirit like the final note of a favored melody forever silenced. Elaina stared at the closed portal until her head began to pound. This time she refused the luxury of a cry.

Twenty-Two

"I think that's an absolutely remarkable idea! Don't you, Elaina?"

Gripping the fireplace poker, Elaina halted her attack on the sparking log in mid-jab. Earlier she blocked out her mother and Jeanna's conversation and Lorna's continual talking to Anna. Elaina had spent the last fifteen minutes trying to figure out how to abandon this Sunday lunch party without creating suspicion. She'd done everything from praying that her cell phone would ring to wishing for a health emergency.

As usual, Elaina had followed her mother and sister home from Sunday services to share the noon meal with them. But this time Jeanna and Lorna arrived minutes after Elaina stepped into the home. Given Margaret's surprised yet gracious greeting, Elaina deduced that the visit had not been planned. Jeanna and Lorna agreed to join them for lunch. Margaret insisted on calling Noah with an invitation. Lunch was warming while they awaited his arrival.

"I'm sorry, Mom. I wasn't paying attention." Elaina cast a covert glance toward Lorna, who examined a perfectly manicured nail. Eyeing the fireplace poker, Elaina wondered how much damage she would do to her toe if she dropped the pointed tip on the end of her shoe. If she smashed her toe just right, perhaps she could go home to "rest" while still being able to drive herself. With a resigned sigh, Elaina propped the poker in the iron holder. She offered her mother an apologetic smile.

Margaret returned the grin with a luster in her eyes that both cheered and comforted. The last few months Elaina had been thrilled to watch her mother emerge from a mourning widow into her own woman. Her classy blue suit dazzled her complexion and made her coppery hair shine. Margaret poured a cup of mint tea from the large urn on the service stand. Elaina couldn't remember what she'd done with her tea. Only the faint trace of peppermint testified to her recent sip.

"Jeanna has just suggested that we join her at her condominium in Oklahoma City for Christmas," Margaret said. "Noah is going on an elk hunting trip in Colorado and won't be here."

Elaina slipped out of her square-toed pumps and slid a glance toward Anna. Her sister, while still distant, had at least stopped shunning Elaina. Presently, she was busily embroidering a holiday design onto a white tablecloth as if the existence of Christmas depended upon her work. Anna offered no sign that she registered Jeanna's invitation.

Since Willis' departure a week ago, Margaret reported that Anna poured all extra energy into embroidering. According to their mother, she had finished two pillowcases last week. Anna hadn't embroidered since she was twelve, when she and her friend, Natalie, started their own two-member sewing club. Elaina thought this new venture was as odd as a cat barking. She hadn't dared express her observations for fear of Anna ostracizing her for life.

"So what do you think?" Margaret prompted.

"Huh?" Elaina refocused on her mother.

"About Jeanna's invitation?" Margaret restated.

"I just thought it might make this Christmas a little special for you." Jeanna sympathetically eyed Anna. Elaina suspected their cousin knew every detail of her sister's recent breakup with Willis.

Anna leaned more intensely into her embroidering, and Elaina wondered if she really thought she was duping anyone into believing she wasn't aware of the conversation.

"Lorna will be there, too," Jeanna continued, "so you young ladies will have someone your own age to do things with. There's plenty of shopping, and—"

"Oh yes!" Lorna injected. From her place on the couch near Anna, she scooted to the seat's edge. "I think it's a wonderful idea!" She hopped up and moved toward Elaina. Her expensive perfume preceded her, and Elaina wondered how much of Ted's money the stuff cost. She discreetly examined Lorna's snug jeans on flawless hips, the wide belt, and the clinging, ribbed sweater. The beauty dressed much like Anna, which made her look nearly ten years younger than Ted.

Lorna sidled up to Elaina as if they were the closest of confidantes. Stifling a groan, Elaina tugged her sweater vest around her torso and wished it were an iron shield. The last thing she wanted was to spend Christmas with Ted's fiancée. As expected she hadn't heard a peep from Ted since their tense conversation mere days ago. Nor did she expect him to communicate with her ever again.

"I'd love it!" Margaret sat her cup and saucer on the coffee table with the clink of china and looked to Elaina for support. "I think it would be perfect. What good is it for the three of us to sit around here anyway? Aside from Jeanna, the only relatives we have in this part of the country are Faye and Jake." She paused. "But I seriously doubt they'll want to get together."

Elaina didn't question her mother's claim. They had heard nothing from Jake all fall but an occasional e-mail decrying the horrid expenses involved in remodeling the mansion. *Otherwise we might get the idea that he should honor his promise to Dad and share his wealth,* Elaina thought. After Jake's guilty glances during her mother's move, Elaina wouldn't be surprised if her half-brother purposefully avoided them for life.

"So we'd have as much time as we wanted to take in the city life," Margaret continued. "There's the civic theater," Margaret began tallying the options on her fingers, "the flotilla at the lake, the tour of homes, the church's Christmas pageant, the Christmas bash for underprivileged children. Don't you remember the year Joseph played Santa?" she recalled, her cheeks aglow.

With a twist of guilt, Elaina wondered how she could let her loss at love blot out her mother's needs. Margaret Woods had been stripped of her home. While she could have moved to a smaller place in Oklahoma City, she left her circle of friends and the life she had known to live closer to Elaina. The first Christmas without her husband was going to be the most difficult to endure. Elaina had already struggled through her share of dreary days due to her father's absence. The stay in Oklahoma City would put her mother in the middle of all her old acquaintances, which was probably exactly what she needed.

"Well…" Elaina hedged. She observed the baby grand piano and analyzed the invitation for any obstacles. While she detected none in her own life, she pondered her sister's. "I'm free, of course, because college is out for Christmas. But what about Anna? She's got a job. She can't just—"

"Oh, but I quit my job." Anna lifted her head. Her hands grew still. She looked at Elaina as if she should already know this piece of news.

"You quit?" Elaina questioned.

"Yes," Margaret said and toyed with the chain that held her reading glasses. "She did. She just wasn't happy. The singles minister was always on her about being on time. And Anna just couldn't—it was so stressful right now I told her to just turn in her notice. It's not like she's starving. The church graciously allowed a short notice. Friday was her last day."

Anna laid her handiwork in her lap and stared into the fire as her mother spoke for her.

Lorna moved back to the couch and plopped beside Anna. "I just *hate* workin'," the green-eyed brunette whined. "They're always after you if you're even one second late." Lorna rolled her eyes and shook her head. Her loose curls swung around her cheeks. Elaina recalled seeing a few models on TV with the exact hairdo. "I think you did the right thang, girlfriend," Lorna said. "Some of us just weren't made to be trapped."

No, you were made to trap unsuspecting men into marriage, Elaina thought, but her aggravation couldn't blot out her concern for her sister.

Lorna's comment tipped Jeanna into a diatribe against the ills of holding down a job, something the pampered matron had never been required to submit to. While Jeanna carried on, Anna offered Lorna a lifeless smile and nothing more.

The faintest sound of a car engine drew Anna's dismal gaze toward the window. Elaina recalled the phone ringing when she entered the cottage. Anna had stood in the hallway and stared at Margaret until she was certain the call was not for her. Then Anna hurried to the study to check her e-mail. After she changed into her jogging suit, she checked it again.

The years Elaina wished her sister would compose herself and mature now mocked her. She longed for the hollowed-eyed shell of a woman to disappear and the old flighty Anna to return. Even when Anna was miffed with Elaina over Willis, at least she still had a personality. Elaina ached for her sister's plight even more than for her own tangled situation. As she had been all week, she was haunted with the implications of what Willis might have taken from her sister. The clues pointed to the worst.

I just hope she isn't pregnant, Elaina worried.

As she stepped away from the popping fire, she realized her mother's concerned attention rested upon her younger daughter. "Anna," Margaret coaxed, "do you think you'd enjoy staying at

Jeanna's condo through New Year's? I think it would be a great break for all of us. Don't you?"

Anna observed her mother. "Sure," she said with a listless shrug. "I'm for whatever you want."

Margaret turned her anxious focus upon her other daughter. Elaina suspected that her mother was less in need of the trip than she pretended. "Let's do it," Elaina said with an optimism she was far from feeling.

While Cousin Jeanna cackled, Lorna squealed and clapped her hands. "Yes, yes, yes, yes, yes! She tapped the tops of her knees with her fists. "We're gonna have *so much* fun!"

The doorbell's chime announced a new guest's arrival. "That must be Noah." Margaret stood.

"I'll go ahead and start setting the meal on the table," Elaina offered and welcomed the solitary reprieve. She hurried past her mother's welcoming the new guest and entered the kitchen filled with the delightful smells of roasted chicken and apple pie. Elaina's stomach rumbled, and she decided that even tolerating Lorna might be worth the reward of her mother's culinary efforts.

She hurried toward the electric stove and began to remove the aluminum foil off of several vegetable dishes left to warm on the top. When the kitchen door whisked open, Elaina expected her mom.

Jeanna Harley's quiet voice ended that assumption. "Elaina," she uttered as she moved toward the stove, "I'm worried about Anna."

Unaccustomed to a soft-spoken Jeanna, Elaina nearly missed what she said for surprise at her manner. However, the genuine concern vibrating from the matron spoke as much of her message as her quiet words.

Elaina paused before lifting the foil from the top of the chicken platter. "So am I," she admitted.

"It's not like her to be so quiet," Jeanna worried.

"I know."

"And whoever heard of her embroidering?" Jeanna grimaced as if Anna were participating in the most degrading activity known to mankind. She leaned nearer Elaina and gripped her arm. "It's just too weird," she hissed, her hazel eyes bugging.

Elaina would have seen the humor in Jeanna's antics were she not equally concerned. "Anna used to embroidery when she was in junior high," Elaina explained.

"But now?" Jeanna squeaked. "It's all because of that Willis meany, isn't it?" she continued. "Your mom mentioned that he let her down."

With a resigned nod, Elaina observed Jeanna and vowed not to divulge another detail. "Yes, but please don't mention it in front of Anna. She's terribly upset and—"

"Oh my goodness. I would never," she gasped as if they were discussing a top-secret bomb threat.

"Good."

"I just wish we could find her someone else."

"I wish she'd wake up and see Bryan," Elaina mumbled before she realized she was actually disclosing her inner thoughts to Jeanna Harley, the last person she needed to share with.

"Poor, poor Bryan," Jeanna sighed.

Elaina finished uncovering the chicken and cut a sideways glance at Jeanna. Her growing curiosity tempted her to see what Jeanna might know of his elusive past. "He seems to have a few secrets," she mused.

Jeanna moved to the kitchen counter. "I know he had a bad experience," she said as she removed the cellophane wrap off a vegetable tray. "I think there was a child involved." Jeanna popped an olive in her mouth and chewed.

"As in..." Elaina encouraged, her mind conjuring all sorts of scenarios.

The moo-moo clad lady snitched several more olives and scurried back toward Elaina. "As in a love child," Jeanna whispered in scandalous fashion. "That's the best I can gather. Her name is Macy. His brother and sister adopted her. She's visited him a few times. I've seen them together. Bryan treats her like a daughter—

not like a niece. I even once heard him say he's saving for her college. I'm not sure of whatever became of the mother."

Despite her commitment to avoid gossip, Elaina couldn't halt the tide of interest. While she had expected a story of heartbreak at the hands of a woman, she never imagined Bryan Brixby would father a child out of wedlock.

Yet Jeanna seems so sure, Elaina thought as Jeanna babbled on about Bryan still being a good catch.

Soon their neighbor popped the rest of her olives into her mouth and meandered back toward the veggie platter. But *since when has Jeanna been an authority on other people's business?* Elaina demanded.

In a fit of self-disgust, Elaina realized she had just fallen prey to the very vice she detested. Long ago she admonished Anna against the pitfalls of secondhand information. Resurrecting her commitment to the factual, Elaina decided to trust her instincts over Jeanna's supposition. She told herself that she and Bryan's growing friendship would eventually ensure that he share his story. Until then, Elaina pledged to patiently wait and think no undue ill of him.

She scooped up a dish of green beans and headed for the dining room. "Jeanna, would you please carry that veggie platter to the table?" Elaina requested in a voice that insisted the Bryan Brixby subject was officially closed.

Twenty-Three

Somehow Elaina survived Christmas with Lorna without a verbal slip. From the day they stepped into Jeanna's exquisite condominium she silently suffered through Lorna's perpetual monologue involving Ted. After Lorna's Christmas tryst with Ted, she lost no opportunity to flash the new ruby dinner ring that complemented the diamond solitaire on her left hand. Of course the two met and exchanged presents in secret lest Ted's family learn of their alliance. Even so, Lorna claimed that they would be announcing their engagement as soon as Mrs. Farris was warmed to Lorna. Elaina attributed her ability to withhold all cutting comments to divine intervention. Nothing nauseated her more than a manipulative woman with matrimonial designs, especially when she was manipulating Ted Farris.

By New Year's Eve, Elaina decided that if Lorna confided one more morsel about her and Ted she wouldn't be able to withstand the final few days at Jeanna's condominium. Thankfully, several congregations in Oklahoma City were joining together for a New Year's Eve party in Trinity Community Church's massive gym and fellowship hall. The evening would culminate with midnight communion in the sanctuary. The party offered a perfect diversion for Lorna, who forgot to talk about Ted for a whole afternoon.

While Elaina looked forward to bringing in the New Year with reverence, her plans for the party were simple. The first opportunity that arose, she would lose Lorna and disappear into the sizable crowd. After settling into an empty nook, Elaina would pull a book from her sling purse and spend the evening in blissful solitude...without Ted's fiancée.

Anna, claiming a migraine, had refused to attend the party, despite the coaxing of a fretful mother and a concerned sister. Elaina considered staying home with Anna, but she went to bed before they left for the party. Regardless of the holiday's festive activities, Elaina watched her sister gradually fade into her shell. Dark circles marred eyes that were red-rimmed every morning. Despite Elaina's loving attempts to talk with Anna about her crushed spirits, her sister repeatedly refused.

As Elaina pulled her Honda into the parking place beside Jeanna's idling Town Car, she remained trapped in her own thoughts. Elaina wondered if Lorna had finally told Ted that Jeanna and Noah were her wealthy aunt and uncle. Since Lorna had been with Jeanna the whole Christmas season, Elaina didn't know how she could keep the relationship from him. Little did Lorna comprehend that Elaina had already educated Ted about the affluent relatives. Elaina gazed across the crowded parking lot and smiled. Lorna wasn't the only one with secrets.

"Okay, what gives?" Margaret asked from the passenger seat.

"Excuse me?" Elaina put her car into park and faced her mother.

"I know that smile," Margaret claimed. Her sequined sweater sparkled in the street lamp's glow.

"What smile?" Elaina questioned and attempted to hide every hint of her thoughts. She had yet to burden her mother with even a nuance of her romantic disappointments.

"Don't give me that, Elaina Woods." Margaret shook her finger at Elaina's nose. "I'm your mother. I know you like I know the back of my hand." Her sweater winked with every move.

Elaina shut off the engine. The loss of the heater's warmth allowed the cold to seep in. She looked down at her simple brown pants and rust-colored sweater that still bore a new smell. Once again she wondered if she'd underdressed. "Then maybe you could tell me why I wore this outfit," she groused.

"So you could blend in," Margaret quipped. "It fits perfectly with your plan to get lost in the crowd and not let Lorna find you until after communion."

Narrowing her eyes, Elaina inspected her meticulously groomed mother. "How did you know—"

"Know what?" Margaret tilted her head, and her gold earrings sparkled. "That you'd rather eat live leeches than spend the evening with Lorna Starr?"

"Mother!" Elaina exclaimed as if she were sixteen and her mother had just read her diary.

"What is it about Lorna that you don't like?" Margaret quizzed.

"Well…" Elaina adjusted her glasses and wondered how this simple trip to the church had morphed into an interrogation.

"Does it have anything to do with Ted Farris?"

"Ted?" Elaina gulped.

"Yes. The best I can tell, you and he are no longer an item. Are you?"

"I don't guess we ever were an official item in the first place."

"Well, whatever," Margaret wiggled her fingers, "I know an item when I see one. Then Lorna appears on the scene claiming to have this secret engagement. I didn't think much of it until last week when she told Jeanna that they were so close to announcing their engagement she could at least tell her the man's first name. Jeanna says it's Ted."

"Oh well, you know there's a Ted on every block," Elaina hedged.

"That's what I figured you'd say." Margaret shook her head. "I've got one daughter who reveals all and another who reveals nothing."

"Mother!" Elaina repeated the exclamation.

"Well, it's the truth." Margaret patted the back of her spiral curls. "You are just like your father. If anything was bothering him I'd be the last person he'd worry with it."

"Okay, Mom," Elaina sighed, "Ted and I aren't...you know." She shook her head. "We never really had an understanding, so I guess I hoped a little too much." Elaina pressed her thumbnail into the steering wheel's leather casing. "As far as Lorna's engagement, she has told me her fiancé's name but I've promised not to tell."

"And you'll keep your word even when you can't stand the person you promised."

Elaina gazed toward the brightly lit fellowship hall.

"Just like your father," Margaret repeated. "Just like him. The only thing you got from me was my hair and my eyes."

"Ouch! I hope you didn't need them anymore," Elaina teased.

Margaret snickered. "You're just really funny, aren't you?"

"Well, I made *you* laugh. Didn't I?"

"I just wish we could get Anna to laugh." Margaret frowned and looked out her side of the vehicle. Elaina followed her gaze toward a small, lighted pond where stood a statue of Christ. The white marble reflected upon the water's glassy surface to create a double image of comfort.

"Me, too," Elaina offered.

"Did you know she's been e-mailing Willis every day since he left?"

"I suspected as much. I'm assuming he hasn't responded?" Elaina released her seatbelt with a click.

Margaret shook her head. "She told me last night that he doesn't check his e-mail very often."

"So you think she's still hoping he'll call or show up?" She removed the keys from the ignition and dropped them into her sling bag.

"Yes, I do."

"And if he does…"

"I'm beginning to hope he doesn't." Margaret gathered her purse from the floorboard.

Elaina started to open the car door but hesitated. She had been wanting to ask her mother if she thought Anna might have gone too far with Willis. Elaina had held off because of a lack of opportunity and for fear of offending her mother. Her fear was at an all-time low tonight, and the opportunity had just posed itself.

"Mom," Elaina began, "I've really been worried about Anna. Do you know if they had any kind of…understanding about marriage at all? I know she didn't have a ring yet, but—"

"I don't know," Margaret admitted while placing her purse in her lap.

"If they *did* have some sort of understanding, do you think she might have…" Elaina paused. She hated to place doubts in her mother's mind about Anna. Nevertheless, she couldn't contain her uneasiness another day.

Margaret turned to her daughter, drew her brows, and searched her face as if struggling for Elaina's meaning. Elaina silently observed her mom and hid nothing from her expression.

"Oh no!" Margaret vehemently shook her head. "I don't believe Anna would do that—not before marriage!" she continued. "She promised her father and me, just like you did."

Using her thumb, Elaina rubbed the band of the diamond ring that claimed her right hand. She had worn the ring every day since she was fourteen, and every day it had been a reminder of the vow she made her parents. They had given her the ring the hour of the covenant. Like Elaina, Anna had gone through an identical pledge at age fourteen.

"I hope you're right," Elaina mumbled and felt her mother's hackles rise. Her skin prickled with the rising stress. Grappling for a way to ease the moment, Elaina finally said, "It's not that I'm trying to slur Anna, Mom." She reached to squeeze her mother's hand. "Please don't get upset. I guess this is more a statement about my lack of trust of Willis than of Anna." Simultaneously, Elaina thrilled in the fact that she hadn't suggested that Anna might be pregnant. Given her mom's reaction, that might have pushed her into full-blown fury.

"I hope you haven't discussed this with anyone," Margaret snapped.

"Of course not," Elaina soothed. "I just—"

A ceaseless tapping on the driver's window invaded the tense moment. Elaina turned to stare into Jeanna's inquisitive face, within inches of hers. "Are you ladies going to sit in there and talk all night?" she bellowed through the closed window. "Lorna and I are freezing to death waiting on you!"

Elaina peered past Jeanna. Lorna bopped behind her aunt as if she were at a fifties sock hop.

"How could we have been so thoughtless?" Margaret asked as if the strained conversation never occurred. She and Elaina popped open their doors, stepped out, and embarked upon a plethora of apologies. With an arctic breeze urging them forward, the quartet of women hurried through the star-crested night toward the fellowship hall.

Her head bent, Elaina pulled her suede jacket close and fell in behind the older ladies with Lorna at her side. She hoped Lorna didn't embark upon her nonstop prattle. At first, Elaina thought her hopes would be fulfilled. But when the two were only ten feet from the doorway, Lorna wrapped her fingers around Elaina's forearm and leaned closer.

"Did I tell you that Ted's going to be here tonight?" she whispered.

Elaina thought she had bolstered herself against any surprise the beauty might spring. She hadn't counted on this one. Elaina halted before she considered the implications. Fortunately, her mom and Jeanna abruptly slowed their pace to allow a group of rowdy teens access to the building. Elaina covered her reaction to Lorna's news by faking caution on behalf of the imposing young people. Nevertheless, her plans for an evening of quiet reflection melted into a disillusioned heap.

"I don't recall your mentioning that," Elaina claimed.

She encountered Lorna's gaze, deceptively guileless, and wondered if Ted's fiancée had purposefully withheld this tidbit until now. "Oh yes, him and his whole family—his brother and sister and mother are comin'. His mother goes to one of the churches that's comin' tonight. Ted said she asked him to play."

"As in the piano?" Elaina questioned and felt as if her soul went numb.

"Yes. He asked me not to wear my engagement ring even," Lorna wiggled her left hand to reveal no solitaire in place, "so his family won't get suspicious. I'm hopin' they'll really like me, and me and him can come out of the closet soon. I'm so tired of all this secrecy," Lorna pouted.

Elaina didn't realize that her mother and Jeanna had already entered the building until the glass doors sighed to a close. Elaina hurried forward as if Ted's presence were of no consequence to her.

Lorna scurried after her. "He's openin' the whole party with a mini concert. He said he's gonna do some sacred stuff and some fun stuff. Have you ever heard him play?" Lorna queried without pausing for breath.

Elaina opened the fellowship hall's door and lambasted herself for not staying home with Anna. "Yes, just a little," she admitted. "From what I understand he's quite good." The smells of hot cocoa and finger foods sent a nauseous tremor through Elaina's stomach. The door closed behind them, and she glanced around the crowded room. A portable stage claimed one end. On the stage sat a baby grand piano. Ebony, of course.

The first day of class, Elaina had been tantalized by a fantasy involving Ted, herself, a stage, and a grand piano. The fantasy teased Elaina anew. She imagined Ted wearing an exquisite black tuxedo. His slicked back hair hung in a simple ponytail at his neckline and added a debonair dash to the whole suit. The man walked onto stage, settled upon the piano bench, found Elaina in the audience, and offered a flirtatious wink. Then, a rapt audience held its breath as he stormed the piano.

Elaina didn't realize she was short of breath until Lorna's voice invaded her reverie. "I remember when my dad used to teach him. He would go on and on about how Ted could make it big if he wanted to. I sure wish he would."

"You do?" Elaina asked and skimmed the crowd for any signs of her sister-in-law and brother. She touched her forehead and wondered if Anna's migraine might have been contagious.

"Uh huh," Lorna absently agreed as she perused the crowded room. "I think it would be so cool for him and me to travel all over the place together."

"But is that what *he* wants?" Elaina prompted.

"Oh, he'll come around." Lorna lifted one eyebrow, and Elaina fleetingly wondered if Delilah was a brunette with pale-green eyes, a cashmere sweater, and spike heels. She imagined Ted's sleek hair being shaved against his will, and Lorna wielding the shears.

The disturbing image nearly made Elaina miss the first glimpse of Faye and Jake. Faye walked toward the stage with Jake in her wake. *Following along like a good little puppy,* Elaina thought. Why her half-brother had ever let Faye's money blind him was anybody's guess.

Elaina began to plan her escape route when Ted Farris appeared behind Lorna. "And...how are you ladies?" he questioned. As soon as the words left his mouth, Ted's attention fell upon Elaina. His eyes widened, as if he somehow hadn't realized that the redhead talking to Lorna was Elaina.

Every lesson Elaina's father taught her about self-control was pressed to the limit. She fought the urge to simultaneously stomp her foot and cry and run. Instead of acting out her urges, Elaina casually shifted her sling bag from her shoulder, slipped out of her jacket, and watched as Lorna stopped short of wilting all over Ted.

"I'm just fine, Teddy," she oozed. "And how are you?"

Teddy? Elaina thought as he pronounced himself equally well.

"And you, Elaina?" Ted prompted as if they were nothing more than distant acquaintances.

"I'm fine, thank you," Elaina addressed the lapel of his navy sports coat and covered every clue that her heart was racing.

"This is my brother, Robert," Ted continued.

Elaina switched her gaze from the sports jacket to a burgundy ribbed sweater on broad shoulders. Her gaze trailed across a sculptured jaw-line, a prominent nose, and settled upon a pair of masculine eyes, every bit as dark as Ted's. Vaguely Elaina recalled a tall, dark twenty-year-old at Jake's wedding. Of course, Elaina had been twelve and considered him as old as Anna did Bryan Brixby. Now she acknowledged that Robert probably had turned a few more heads than Ted. However he lacked the artist's sensitivity that so drew her to Ted in the first place. Briefly Elaina wondered how Ted and Robert got all the looks when their sister got none.

"Nice to meet you, Robert," Elaina mumbled as Lorna cooed a greeting his way. Robert barely acknowledged Elaina and focused upon Lorna as if she were prime beef and he hadn't eaten in a week. Elaina nearly laughed out loud. Robert had a cruel awakening coming when he learned the angel in disguise was his brother's fiancée.

"I saw Faye by the stage as well," Elaina said to the lapel.

"Yes, Mom's here, too," Ted acknowledged, his voice undisturbed. "They came to hear me play."

"Nice to have such support." Her knees unsteady, Elaina perused the crowd. Several hundred people meandered toward the rows of chairs in front of the stage. "I guess I'll go find a seat. I hear the musician is really good." Without another peek at the lapel, Elaina strode around the chairs and found one on the back row in the farthest corner.

Only at this distance, did she allow herself a full view of Ted. His focus rested solely upon Lorna and something she was saying to Robert. Never had Elaina felt more a fool. All she could think of was their conversation in her office and Ted's statement, "How do you know I haven't grown to love her?"

"Obviously, you have," Elaina mumbled. Lorna said something with a witty smile, and Ted and Robert joined in a round of hearty laughter. Lorna's face glowed as if she'd just recited the most brilliant prose of the century.

Elaina stared at the piano and allowed herself to admit the painful truth. She was not at the start of falling in love with Ted. Neither was she in the middle of falling in love with Ted. *I have fallen all the way in love with him,* she thought and gripped the edge of her chair. Thoughts of his spending the rest of his life with Lorna nearly made Elaina collapse to her knees.

Oh Father in heaven, help me, she pleaded. *Their marriage is going to kill me!*

Twenty-Four

"Hello, Elaina," a familiar voice broke into her gloom.

Elaina gazed upward to see Faye and an older woman who resembled her. "Hello, Faye," Elaina responded with a stiff smile.

"Have you ever met my mother, Pearl Farris?" Faye asked, her gray eyes as cold as snow clouds.

"I'm sure I must have when I was younger." Elaina debated whether or not to stand. A perverse voice suggested she shouldn't. Then she could have vowed she heard her father whisper, *It never hurts to be nice, Elaina, even when you're being mistreated.*

She rose and extended her hand. "But it's been so many years since we met. Maybe we should just start over," she added with as much mercy as she could muster.

Mrs. Farris looked down her pudgy nose. After a condescending pause, she blessed Elaina with a brief handshake as limp as a comatose ferret. "Pleased to make your acquaintance," she said as if Elaina were grit beneath her feet.

"Likewise," Elaina responded with dignity, despite feeling as if she'd been jabbed in the eyes.

"Ted has told Mother all about you." Faye crossed her arms and eyed Elaina as if she were a ground rattler.

"Oh really?" Elaina casually propped her knee in the chair where she'd been sitting. She estimated that the women's knit suits, carefully paired to coordinate without being identical, probably cost more than her whole clothing budget for the year.

Her father's sage advice from childhood faded in the face of such blatant hostility. "He's told me a few things about the two of you as well," Elaina responded with an artful grin. She wasn't in the mood to play games tonight. Her heart hurt too much. If these well-dressed canines wanted to be tough, she could do the same.

Mrs. Farris rose to her full height, which Elaina estimated at nearly six feet. She imagined Pearl Farris sitting on a throne, holding a scepter, and announcing the decapitation of some poor soul unfortunate enough to scorch the evening's soufflé. Elaina estimated that her crime was having the audacity to befriend Ted after she had been monetarily demoted. Neither of the ladies seemed to realize that her relationship with Ted was officially over.

"There you are, Mother!" Ted's mellow voice floated into the growing tension like a summer zephyr off a glistening lake. Then the man himself appeared. Elaina stopped herself from grabbing Ted's arm and leaning against him. She was so relieved she forgot to focus upon Ted's lapel. Instead she looked into his soul.

With a sympathetic smile, Ted extended a cup of soda toward Elaina. "Here's your soda," he said as if she'd asked him to retrieve her one. Ted looked exclusively at Elaina as if to say, *Follow my lead here, okay?*

"Thanks." Thrilled with his interruption, she pretended right along with him. Elaina observed the dark liquid and figured it was loaded with caffeine.

"It's Caffeine-free Diet Coke," Ted supplied. "Didn't you tell me that was your favorite?"

"Oh, yes—yes, of course." Elaina gulped the soda, welcoming the burn and fizz as it swelled down the back of her throat.

"I see you've met Elaina, Mother," Ted continued, and Elaina deduced that he must have recognized her plight and come to her rescue. She nearly wilted with gratitude.

Pearl Farris' haughty expression softened in the face of her son's smile. "Yes, we were just getting to know each other," she replied as if there had been no intimidation tactics underway.

"Who's that woman talking to Robert?" Faye asked. She craned her neck to peer around Elaina.

"Oh that's Lorna Starr," Ted supplied.

Elaina stopped short of grinding her teeth.

"She's certainly a pretty thing." Pearl scrutinized Lorna through her bifocals.

"And she certainly has Robert's attention," Faye continued.

Elaina didn't bother to look.

"Oh every female has Robert's attention these days," Pearl snapped. "He started dating the very day his divorce was final. I have no idea what possessed him to marry that money-hungry vixen in the first place. It was enough to make me lose my religion."

I'm just glad to know you had some to start with, Elaina thought.

"Does this Lorna Starr come from a good family?" Faye asked.

Elaina didn't have to strain to catch her meaning, and it involved money.

"Well," Ted began, "her father was my piano teacher until I was a senior in high school. Remember Duke Starr?"

"Yes, of course," Pearl said and refocused upon Ted as if she were dismissing Lorna altogether. "Now I remember her." She suspiciously eyed her son. "If I remember correctly, you had a crush on her."

"Yes." Ted stroked his sideburn and looked past his mother. "She's also the niece of Noah and Jeanna Harley. Jeanna is the daughter of Blake Harley, you know, the oil tycoon?"

Elaina gulped another mouthful of soda and nearly choked on the liquid. Ted had undoubtedly done his homework and was trying to make Lorna look as monetarily advantaged as possible.

"Ah yes!" Pearl shook her head and graced Lorna with her attention once more. "Well, good. I think we should meet Ms. Starr." She cast a "we've wasted our time here long enough" look at Elaina. "Don't you agree, Faye?" Pearl asked.

"I do," Faye crooned. "Want to introduce us, Ted?"

"Oh, of course." Ted checked his watch. "And then I've got to head toward stage. They want me to start playing in three minutes."

"That's long enough to make a new friend," Faye said without another glance toward Elaina. "You just introduce us, and we'll take it from there."

"Okay, good!" Ted rubbed his hands together and led his mother and sister toward his fiancée.

Elaina deposited her cola on the floor, flopped back into her chair, and glared straight ahead. If she hadn't just declared herself desperately in love with Ted, she would have been thankful there was no question of marrying into that family. But she couldn't. As the tide of love roared across her soul, she vowed that she could put up with Faye and Pearl's worst antics if she could just have Ted.

Out of the corner of her eye, Elaina noticed a movement on the end of the row. When she looked up, she encountered a small procession with Ted in the lead and his sister, mother, and Lorna close behind. Lorna smiled at Elaina as if she'd just won a trip to heaven and back. Faye cut Elaina a spiteful glower. Mrs. Farris didn't even bother to acknowledge her. Elaina watched in disbelief as Pearl and Faye escorted Lorna to the front aisle. Robert followed in their wake as if he were groping for more time with his latest female acquaintance. *Will Lorna ever see that Pearl and Faye are favoring her in order to slight me?* Elaina thought. She also wondered what poor Robert would do when he learned that Lorna would soon be his sister-in-law.

She chuckled and then bit back a sob. For the first time since this whole fiasco, Elaina felt as if she wanted to act like Anna—crawl under the covers and not come out.

Soon Ted stepped onto the stage and settled upon the piano bench. The few who remained standing all found their seats. Elaina spotted her mother and Jeanna on the other side of the room as they hustled toward two empty chairs. They held drinks and plates laden with all sorts of morsels. Both women giggled at some joke as if they were a pair of teenagers. Elaina thrilled in seeing her mother completely enjoying herself.

Ted leaned into the mic, and his silvery voice floated over the speakers. "From what I understand, this is supposed to be an informal evening for everyone to just relax and enjoy themselves. I was asked to put together a mini concert to start off the evening. I hope you aren't disappointed in the songs I've put together. This first piece is actually one I arranged."

He nudged aside the mic and addressed his keyboard. The second his fingers descended upon the ivories, Elaina felt as if she were transported into a secret room in Ted Farris' heart...a room covered in praise and adoration for his Holy Creator. His rendition of "To God Be the Glory" built into a crescendo of complicated note patterns that would have impressed Bach.

So enraptured was Elaina that she nearly forgot about Lorna and Mrs. Farris and Faye. As Ted moved from a crashing finish of his first song into the flowing melody of "Amazing Grace," she even lulled herself into believing that they were about to announce their engagement and that Ted was playing just for her. All she needed to complete the fantasy was the wink.

After a series of sacred tunes, Ted phased into a round of love ballads that reminded Elaina of the day in the cottage when he waltzed around the room with her mother...and then her. Only his voice in the mic could break through Elaina's reverie.

"This last song I'm playing for a very special someone tonight. You know who you are." His gaze roved the back of the audience, settling upon Elaina for a mere wrinkle in time.

She gasped and curled her toes. Elaina recognized the very first notes of "I Only Have Eyes for You." As the mellifluous number filled the room, her simple sweater and slacks turned into a ball gown. Her slippers were glass. And Ted and she floated around the room, lost in the love binding them for eternity.

When the final notes echoed from the piano, the audience erupted into applause that brought them to their feet. Elaina, caught in the emotion, rose as well. Whistles and cheers mingled with the clapping that begged for more. Ted stood, bowed, and waved to the exuberant group. He then walked from the stage and stopped near the front row.

Elaina looked down. Her ball gown had disappeared. A pair of low-backed loafers replaced her glass slippers. As the crowd dispersed, she caught sight of Ted bending toward Lorna whose ethereal face shone with approval.

She thinks the song was for her, Elaina thought. She came within a breath of denying the possibility and then asked, *What if it was for her?* A hurricane of confusion swept through her. She retrieved her cup of soda and considered how Ted had come to her rescue half an hour ago.

Apparently, he must care for me, she thought. *The song had to be for me. It was our song!* Elaina snatched up her jacket and sling bag and stepped away from her chair. Her attention riveted back to the klatch near the stage. Nothing had changed. All of Ted's energies were still directed toward Lorna.

Elaina jerked away from the scene and began searching for a trash can in which to discard her cup. All the while, her mind dwelled upon the possibility that Ted Farris really was nothing more than a less sleazy version of Willis Kenney. She found a garbage can near the food bar and dropped her half-empty cup into the collection of soiled paper plates. The second the soda splattered, Elaina decided that Ted enjoyed the manipulation game as much as his sister and mother. There was no other explanation for his searching her out in the audience and then oozing all over Lorna after the concert.

How could I ever have allowed myself to fall in love with him? she demanded. *This is not even reasonable.*

A dull ache assaulted her temples and radiated across her forehead. Elaina had enjoyed as much of this evening as she could stomach. With Lorna firmly entrenched in the Farris' good graces, she sought out her mother and requested that Margaret ride back to the condominium with Jeanna. Elaina far preferred bringing in the New Year alone than in Lorna's triumphant shadow.

Twenty-Five

Anna sat near the window of the ultra-modern living room awaiting Willis' arrival. Jeanna's ground floor condominium at the end of the complex's cul-de-sac couldn't have been more strategically placed. The dwelling was perfect for a lover's rendezvous. Anna rubbed her clammy palms along the front of her black velvet pants and then sipped the Pepsi she'd found in Jeanna's refrigerator.

After a triumphant giggle, she swallowed the bubbly liquid and placed the bottle back on the glass-topped table. Anna stood, paced toward the brass-trimmed gas fireplace, and backed into the warmth. Seconds later, she hurried to the picture mirror near the front door and examined her reflection. Worriedly, she touched the corner of her eye and hoped the concealer hid all traces of grief.

She twirled away from the mirror and plopped back on the polished cotton sofa, the color of fresh snow. Anna had hardly believed her eyes this afternoon when she read Willis' e-mail on her laptop.

Sorry I haven't responded sooner, Anna. I guess we need to talk. I will come by Jeanna's condo tonight at the address you gave me in your last e-mail. Is nine okay?

Yours,
Willis

Like a toddler whose emotions vacillate from sobs to hilarity, so Anna had beamed while the tears evaporated from her cheeks.

"All my prayers have been answered," she now whispered. "My Willis is coming back."

She held out her left hand and imagined her ring finger weighted with a diamond no one could miss. "He's going to bring the ring," she squealed and shook her fingers. "I just know it!"

Nervously, she smoothed down the front of her scarlet sweater and double-checked to make certain her outfit was as meticulous now as it had been the last time she anticipated a ring. Anna had purchased this set to wear when she became officially engaged. She'd been wearing the slacks and sweater the last time she saw Willis.

"Oh no!" Anna shrieked. "I hope he doesn't remember!"

Kay-Kay hurried onto the living room's champagne-colored carpet, looked at Anna, and worriedly wuffed.

"Kay-Kay," Anna called. The canine wagged forward. "I'm okay. I'm just happy…happy…*happy!*" She leaned down, cupped the dog's face in her hands, and goo-gooed as if the dog were a baby. Kay-Kay yelped and licked at Anna's hands.

New laughter spilled from Anna like fresh rain upon parched land. "What will Elaina and Mom think when they come home?" she asked the dog. "Huh, baby? Just what do you think they'll think?"

Kay-Kay barked. Her eyes sparkled. Her ears twitched upward.

"They'll be so shocked they won't know which end is up!" Anna reveled in her own sneakiness. The ploy to remain home alone worked more smoothly than Anna ever imagined. No one had suspected that she was faking a headache—not even Elaina.

Anna abandoned Kay-Kay, rested her chin on the back of the couch, and strained for any sign of Willis. Her efforts were not wasted. Twin headlights ensconced in a sports car neared the condo. The bright street lights revealed the car was ebony.

"It's him! It's him!" Anna panted. She jumped from the couch and raced to the front door. By the time Willis was stepping from the Jaguar, Anna ran into the night, welcoming winter's cold sting upon her cheeks.

"Willis!" she shouted, as if he were the only man alive. Anna met him in front of his car, threw herself against him, and wrapped her arms around his torso. "Oh, Willis," she breathed. "I've missed you so—so much!" The smell of woodsy cologne, his warmth beneath the leather jacket, the steady rhythm of his heart against her cheek all insisted that he had come home to her. And this time, he would stay.

"Anna," Willis firmly stated. "Let's go in and talk, okay?"

Anna stiffened and realized he was not returning her hug. While Willis gripped her shoulders and untangled himself from her arms, she noticed the vehicle's engine still hummed. Confused, Anna gazed into the front seat. The street light's radiance cascaded onto a cloud of white-blonde hair surrounding an exquisite, feminine face. The woman observed Anna as if she were bored with the whole scenario.

"But…but…" Anna cried. Her stomach rolled. Her head buzzed. She felt as if the sky were caving in on her.

"Come on." Willis grabbed her arm and steered her back through the condo's doorway, still open.

The living room blended into a blur of glass and brass, white and cream. Willis snapped the front door shut with the finality of a jailer closing a prison cell. After the invigorating chill, the room's warmth now seemed stifling.

"You're not—you're not—" Anna shook her head. "What's going on, W–Willis?" she begged and wrung her hands. Still, a desperate hope insisted she must have misinterpreted the whole situation.

He reached inside his jacket and pulled a letter from a hidden pocket. "I've explained everything here. Please, Anna," he continued, his eyes void of all emotion, "stop e-mailing me. I'm married now. So," his shoulders lifted, "we're through, okay?" His lips settled into a straight line before he whirled around, whipped open the door, and rushed into the night. The door's slam felt like a slap to her face.

Anna gaped at the door for several minutes before the finality penetrated her mind. With a garbled sob, she collapsed against the wall, where hung a trio of mirrored sconces. One sconce crashed to the floor seconds before Anna landed beside it. She fell on her side, wrapped her arms around her knees, and hugged them to her chest. The cottony carpet caressed Anna's cheek as her tears puddled upon the pile.

"No, no, no, no..." she moaned and shook her head before a wail rent her soul.

With a worried whine, Kay-Kay trotted from the living room. Mere inches from Anna's face, she settled onto her haunches and began to howl.

Elaina steered her Honda into the last parking place near the cul-de-sac. With a weary sigh, she turned off her ignition and observed Jeanna's condominium. The living room lights blared forth; the drapes were wide open. Elaina frowned. When they left for the party, only a single lamp burned in the living room, and the drapes were closed.

Anna must have gotten up, Elaina thought. "Maybe we can rent a movie or something," she mumbled and welcomed the possibility of time alone with her sister. They hadn't really connected for two months—not since Anna got miffed over what Elaina said about Willis.

As Elaina stepped from her vehicle and locked the door, she created a mental checklist of immediate things to do. Taking some aspirin for her headache topped the list. Then she would consult with Anna and maybe order a pizza to go with their movie. The whir of city traffic coupled with the crisp air created the illusion that the whole world was driving off and leaving her to freeze—with Ted in the lead, of course. A dog's mournful howl added an ache to Elaina's hollow soul. Fleetingly she wondered if she should cut her holiday visit short and go back home tomorrow.

"I've had about all of Oklahoma City I can stand," she grumbled and inserted the key Jeanna lent her into the doorknob. Before she had the chance to turn the key, another soul-wrenching howl floated upon the night. Elaina winced and then realized the dog's tone sounded familiar and the bellow was coming from inside.

Her heart thumped. Her hands grew clammy. A sixth sense insisted that something dreadful must have happened to Anna. Kay-Kay didn't usually do anything but yelp in glee.

Growling, Elaina wrestled the knob only to discover it was unlocked. She flung the door inward, and it banged against the doorstop. Kay-Kay barked and then croaked into another lonely yowl. Elaina's attention riveted upon the woman on the floor. Anna lay in the fetal position, her dark silky hair covering her face. Breathless, Elaina conjured the worst and searched for signs of blood against the pale carpet. After a stunned second, she slammed the door and collapsed to Anna's side. Her sister remained motionless.

"Anna!" Elaina shook her and waited while the room's heat chased away the chill bumps along her arms.

When Anna didn't respond, Elaina swept aside her hair. Rivulets of tears streamed from Anna's closed eyes onto the carpet. Her lips quivered over a whimper.

"Anna?" Elaina breathed again. "Are you okay, honey?" *Now that was a really bright question,* Elaina thought. *If she were okay, she wouldn't be lying on the floor crying.* "Has someone hurt you?" she pressed. "Was there an invader or—"

She searched the apartment for signs of a struggle. Except for a single sconce on the floor, Jeanna's condo remained the same, right down to the scent of rain-forest carpet freshener. Elaina's pulse slowed while her concern rocketed. Anna had not been herself ever since Willis and she parted company a month ago. Several times, Elaina worried that her sister might be slipping into clinical depression. She scrutinized Anna anew and noticed a piece of paper crumpled in her right hand. A torn envelope lay near Kay-Kay.

"Oh, Elaina," Anna moaned and began to rock back and forth, "you were right."

"About what?" Elaina fumbled in her suede jacket's pocket and retrieved a tissue. She stroked her sister's drenched cheeks.

"About Willis." Anna opened her bleary eyes and shoved the crumpled paper toward Elaina who accepted the note. "I've been a stupid fool," Anna choked and covered her face with her hands.

Elaina glanced to the bottom of the note to confirm Willis as the author. She was transported back in time to the day when she was fourteen and Anna was nine. A neighborhood bully tried to pick a fight with Anna. Elaina stood up to her and sent her running home. Now she was overcome with the same primeval desire that had driven her to action all those years ago. Elaina was ready to find Willis Kenney and cheerfully do something dreadful to him. Nobody hurt her little sister like this and got away with it!

She gripped both sides of the crushed letter and began reading the words that lashed at her heart:

> Anna,
>
> I'm sorry if something I have said or done has made you think we should have a permanent attachment. I have been deeply disturbed by your continual e-mails to the point of finally seeing that I must clarify our relationship. I thought of e-mailing this but decided that a hand-delivered letter would be the best. This way, you

can see that I mean what I say and understand that I want to leave our past in the past.

As of last week, I am now a married man. I can't have any old girlfriends beating on my door. My wife has been as annoyed by your messages as have I. Please stop!

Willis

Anna's broken voice pierced Elaina's astonishment. "He's married, Elaina!" She struggled to sit up. Elaina, striving to absorb Willis' emotional brutality, assisted her sister.

Finally Anna leaned against the wall, pulled her knees to her chest, and propped her chin on her knees. She made no attempt to check the flow of tears while Kay-Kay licked her hands and whined.

"Oh, Anna," Elaina breathed, "I'm so sorry." She dabbed at her sister's cheeks again.

"It's just that—just that—I—I thought—" Anna propped her forehead on her knees and sniffed.

"I know you did," Elaina assured. Grace insisted that now was not the time to say "I told you so." Furthermore, she resolved there would never be a good time for those words. Instead, her whole spirit ached for her shattered sister.

"He *told* me the last time I—I saw him…he said he was bringing an engagement ring that morning."

"Oh, Anna," Elaina repeated. She settled next to her sister and wrapped her arms around her. Anna snuggled into Elaina's embrace as if she were six.

"Why would he say those horrible things in the letter, after—after—" she wailed.

"Because he's a selfish jerk," Elaina snarled.

"I s–saw her…" Anna shuddered.

"Who?"

"His wife. She was in—was in his car."

Elaina rested her cheek on Anna's head and closed her eyes. She pressed her tongue to the roof of her mouth and refused the verbal storm demanding release.

"Do you think he was married all the time?" Elaina questioned, her own assumption evident in her voice.

"N–n–no." Anna pulled away and vehemently shook her head. "I really don't think so." She snatched the letter from Elaina. "See," Anna pointed to a line, "he says his marriage only happened last week."

"I know." Elaina nodded. "But what would have stopped him from lying to you? I mean, what's lying to a man who would treat a woman so cruelly?" she reasoned.

"But he was with me all the time. We were together almost every waking hour for a month." Anna's red-rimmed eyes shone with candid certainty. "Wouldn't she have known—"

"That's a good point." Elaina removed her glasses and rubbed her eyes. Her fingers came away with a trace of flaking mascara. The day had been long. Her head hurt worse now than when she entered the condo. "That is, unless she was out of town."

"No." Anna shook her head again and rubbed at her cheeks with the back of her hand. "His aunt would have known. She was asking to meet me."

"What if he kept the marriage a secret?" *Secretive attachments seemed to be all the rage these days,* Elaina caustically thought.

"I really think the marriage is new, Elaina. I'm not trying to defend him at this point," she added, "but it's something I'm just sure of."

"Well, okay," Elaina said. "Whether it happened last week or a year ago really doesn't change how you feel or the horrible thing he's done to you."

"I'm just so glad I didn't—" She stopped and observed her right hand propped against her thigh. The diamond band on her third finger twinkled as if applauding Anna's admission.

"You didn't?" Elaina wilted against the wall.

"No. I...he wanted to."

"Yes, I could see *that*," Elaina quipped.

"But what man wouldn't?" Anna wailed. "I threw myself at him!" She covered her face with her hands and shuddered over a new sob. "I am so embarrassed," she bleated. "I have been a fool!"

You aren't the only one, Elaina thought. She slid her glasses back on and slipped out of her jacket. "I think everybody feels that way at one time or another," she soothed. "I…" Elaina hesitated. While she didn't want to break her word to Lorna, she needed to comfort Anna. "I know I've felt the exact same way you do for pretty much all the same reasons."

"You?" Anna raised her head and looked at Elaina as if she were daft. "Ha!" she mocked, and all the resentment from months past twisted her lips. "What would *you* know?" she challenged. "You've never even let yourself go enough to fall in love."

Elaina's eyes widened. Her mouth sagged. As the silence expanded into a cloud of hurt, Elaina wrestled with a reply. None came, only her eyes' telltale prickle.

In the face of Anna's accusations, last month's events crashed upon her as if each were a fresh occurrence. Tonight's incidents posed themselves as the sharpest and most brutal…Faye and Pearl's heartless treatment…Ted's transparent fixation with his fiancée…Lorna's triumphant procession to the front row.

Ted's claim from a month ago echoed through Elaina like a mantra of agony. And with it, a mocking confirmation of his true affections: *How do you know I haven't grown to love her. How do you know, Elaina? I love her…I love Lorna, not you.*

Anna's watery eyes rounded. She stared at her sister as if she were seeing her for the first time. "Oh my word," she breathed and clutched Elaina's hand.

"You don't—don't have a corner on suffering, Anna," Elaina choked out as a hot droplet seeped down her cheek.

"I am so sorry," Anna whimpered. "I shouldn't have—I've been so—so—"

Elaina could control her emotions no longer. She coughed in a last attempt to stop the tears. They refused abeyance. Elaina stumbled to her feet and tripped across the wide living room.

When she entered the hallway that led to the guest rooms, the blockade behind which she'd hidden her broken heart crumbled. Only one option remained—dealing with a grief that stripped her of all dignity.

Twenty-Six

The next morning at eight, Elaina balanced a silver-plated tray laden with breakfast goodies and gently tapped on Anna's bedroom door. When no answer came, she twisted the knob and eased open the door. Her sister lay snuggled under satin covers that hugged her slender figure. Elaina tapped the door closed with her foot. She welcomed the slightest whiff of Anna's floral perfume, carefree as a sweet-sixteen summer. Somehow the scent seemed to testify that all would be well soon. Elaina could only hope that was the case.

She deposited the tray on the desk. Behind the desk, a picture window opened onto the complex's pool and tennis courts. The weak morning sun filtered through clouds to offer a mellow christening upon the luxury bedroom's sedate shades of rose and cream and sage. The feminine appeal was completed with carved oak furnishings that fit Anna well. While Jeanna might not know when to stop talking, Elaina had long seen that the woman possessed great taste in home decor.

She lifted the silver urn and poured two mugs full of hot water. The powdered cocoa followed. Soon both cups were steaming and ready for consumption. Elaina picked up one and moved toward the bedside.

"Anna," she whispered and touched her sister's shoulder. "Anna," Elaina repeated and gently shook her.

Her sister stirred and her eyelids drooped open. "Hi," she rasped.

"Hey," Elaina said. She settled onto the side of the bed and extended the cup. "Want some hot chocolate?" she asked. "I made both of us a cup. I've also got some croissants and fruit, if you like."

"Sure," Anna said as if she had dough in her mouth. "What time is it?" she mumbled over a yawn.

"Eight."

Anna scooted up in bed and Elaina helped her plump a couple of cool satin pillows. She accepted the cup of steaming liquid and said, "Wow! Since when do I get the Queen Bee treatment?" The vague smile didn't match the sorrow in her swollen eyes.

"I just figured we both could use something a little special this morning." Elaina retrieved her cocoa from the tray and enjoyed a sip of the sweet liquid. She had taken extra care with her makeup and hoped Anna didn't suspect that she cried off and on until well after she heard Jeanna and her mom arrive home from the party.

Anna took a swallow. "Hmmm, this is good," she said and eyed her sister. "Are you okay?" she questioned.

"I'm fine," Elaina said and offered a bright smile that felt brittle. "I was more worried about you. I guess I just left you high and dry last night, didn't I?"

"It's okay," Anna said. "I'm a big girl. I went right to bed like you did." She pulled on the neck of her pink cotton pajamas, as if they were evidence of her claim. After a frown, Anna rubbed her eyes. "I guess there's no use trying to hide the fact that I cried half the night." She studied her mug.

"I'm so sorry," Elaina said and picked at the fringe on her sweater's sleeve.

"And I'm sorry as well." Anna observed her sister. "At about three I started thinking that you were everything I should have been, but all I gave you was a cold shoulder and plenty of grief." New tears puddled in her eyes.

"Stop!" Elaina held up her hand and tried to sound firm despite her wobbling voice and stinging eyes. "Don't start crying again, Anna. We'll both go down in blubbering fits."

Anna giggled, but the attempt at mirth sounded shrill and phony. "Okay," she agreed and stared past Elaina as if her mind were entering another dimension. The vacant gaze, full of agony, did nothing to comfort Elaina. Her concern for her sister's emotional health had not diminished. If anything, the night intensified her worries.

She settled back onto the edge of Anna's bed and grasped for ways she might be able to cheer her. "How would you feel about going back home this morning?" Elaina questioned.

"You mean now?" Anna asked.

"Well, as soon as you can get a shower and get packed." Elaina took a mammoth swallow of her cocoa. She didn't think she could stomach another day of having to chitchat with Lorna. The princess usually slept late. Elaina figured that if she and Anna were gone by nine then she wouldn't even have to face Lorna.

"I think that's a good thing." Anna nodded. "There's no way to keep what's happened a secret. I'll have to tell Mother. If I tell her, then Jeanna is sure to find out. I have no desire to sit around here and have her make a fuss over me all day and stuff me with olives half the evening." Anna rolled her eyes.

"She really means well." Elaina stood and stepped toward the croissants.

"Oh I know," Anna admitted. "I guess I'm just tired, and I don't want to have to put up with her. Do you think Mom will go with us?"

"I don't know. She and Jeanna have really gotten close again. They had planned to go down to the outlet mall today and try to catch some of the sales."

"They're open on New Year's?"

"Yes. From what I understand it involves some kind of special holiday sale." She eyed the tray and picked up a piece of honeydew melon. After nibbling the edge, the sweet treat lost its appeal. Elaina placed it back on the tray.

"As much as I appreciate your bringing all that breakfast stuff," Anna said, "I'm really not hungry. This hot cocoa is enough for me."

"Me, too." Elaina looked past the beige sheers toward the low-hanging clouds. The dreary weather perfectly fit her mood.

"Elaina," Anna hesitated, "you and Ted..."

Her fingers tightened on the mug. Her shoulders stiffened. Elaina fought the compulsion to fall to her knees and begin sobbing anew.

"We aren't," she supplied. "And I guess we never really were—not officially anyway."

"But you cared for him?"

"Yes." Elaina lowered her head.

"A lot?"

"Yes."

"As much as I cared for Willis?"

Elaina nodded.

"I'm sorry," Anna whispered. "I feel so selfish."

"There's no need for any of that." Elaina stroked the urn's handle.

"If you ever want to talk about it..." Anna offered.

"Thanks. I can't right now. But maybe one day..." Elaina inserted the tip of her tongue between her teeth and pressed.

The tap of a mug against wood preceded the whispering of sheets and Anna's footfalls upon plush carpet. Elaina swiveled toward her sister and placed her cup back on the tray. She barely glimpsed Anna's teary cheeks before she wrapped her arms around Elaina for a tight squeeze. Elaina hung onto Anna and buried her head against the warmth of her rumpled hair.

"I love you," Anna whispered.

"I love you, too," Elaina returned.

"More now than ever."

"Me, too."

A knock instigated the sisters pulling apart. "Come in," Anna said and Elaina cringed with the idea that the person might be Lorna. She turned from the doorway and pretended interest in a Monet print near the window.

"There you two are," Margaret said.

"Oh hi, Mom!" Elaina turned toward her mother, dressed in a blue silk robe and matching slippers.

"Well, hello to you, too," Margaret offered with a glorious smile. "And happy New Year." She observed Anna, and her smile diminished. "Is everything okay?"

Elaina picked up her cup of hot cocoa and waited for Anna to expound. Finally Anna stepped to the nightstand, pulled out the drawer, and retrieved Willis' crumpled note. Without a word, she extended the letter to her mother and collapsed into bed. As Margaret read the message, Anna covered her head and released a muffled sob.

Margaret looked up from reading the note. She and Elaina shared a wealth of silent communication until Margaret said, "We need to go back home today."

"That's exactly what I thought," Elaina agreed.

After settling on the bed, Margaret began offering all the condolences and comfort of a loving mother.

As Anna's lamenting gained momentum, Elaina hustled toward the bedroom door in order to shut it. When she was inches away, the door swung inward. Jeanna stepped into the room, her concerned face pale without her rouge.

"I thought I heard someone crying," she said, her attention riveted upon the bed.

"I'm afraid Anna has had a…disappointment," Elaina hedged and noticed that her mother had dropped the note on the end of the bed. She moved to pick it up when Jeanna snatched the note from the covers. Elaina pressed her fingertips in the center of her forehead and denied her moan.

"Oh no! Oh no!" Jeanna squealed after reading the note. "What are we going to do? This is just beyond—beyond awful." She began flitting around the room. Kay-Kay scurried in, hopped after her mistress, and yelped her approval of all the action. Soon Elaina grew certain Lorna would be awakened.

Once again, she attempted to close the bedroom door, only to discover Lorna sashaying down the hall in a pair of red shiny pajamas. Elaina scowled. She adjusted her glasses and wondered how someone could look so good first thing in the morning. She was beginning to understand that the woman's external beauty had been the sole contributor to overriding Ted's common sense.

"What's going on?" Lorna asked through a yawn.

Elaina stepped into the hallway and closed the door. "Willis broke up with Anna last night," she stated. "She's pretty upset."

"Oh that." Lorna trailed her fingers through her mane of mussed hair, and her diamond solitaire mocked Elaina. "I figured that was old news. He hasn't been around all month."

"Well, Anna was still hoping," Elaina explained.

Lorna gripped Elaina's forearm. The triumphant smile followed. "Did you see how Faye and Mrs. Farris took to me last night?" she asked. "Wasn't that just the coolest?"

"Oh yes…the coolest," Elaina dryly agreed and wondered how Lorna could be so self-focused. She hadn't given Anna's problems even a minute of consideration.

"I told Ted that him and me should go ahead and announce our engagement. I think everything'll be fine," she elaborated. "He's been worried his mother would disinherit him if he doesn't marry who she chooses. The way things are lookin', I'd say she's choosin' me." Lorna strategically laid her left hand against her chest. Her engagement ring dared Elaina to dispute her claim.

"Let's hope you're right," she mumbled and stepped past Lorna. "From what I can gather, Mrs. Farris can be a shrew." She strolled the few feet to the restroom and continued talking. "I really do believe the woman is capable of disinheriting her son. And then where would you be?" She paused inside the restroom doorway and observed Lorna without a trace of sympathy. "You might even have to get a job."

Lorna's eyes narrowed. "Teddy would never let that happen," she argued. "He can take care of me even without his mother's money. He'll go on tour and make stacks of money." She snapped her fingers.

"And has he agreed to that?"

"Well, of course." Lorna straightened her shoulders as if she were the authority on the subject.

"What if he decided to get a job as a minister of music at a small church somewhere instead?" Elaina asked. "Everybody knows ministers of music in small churches are just *loaded* with money." She rolled her eyes.

"What are you talkin' about?" Lorna placed her hands on her hips.

"You mean Ted hasn't told you?" Elaina asked.

"Told me what?" A red flush touched Lorna's cheeks.

"That's what he really wants to do." She looked Lorna squarely in the eyes, and all her suspicions were founded. Despite her claims of ardent loyalty, Lorna's love for Ted was only as deep as his pocketbook.

"And who told you that?" Lorna shot back.

"*Ted* did," Elaina responded.

Lorna's face grew scarlet. "What else has he told you?" she demanded, her green eyes darkening into those of a monster.

Elaina shrugged, turned down the corners of her mouth, and offered no new insights.

"A fine friend *you* turned out to be," Lorna huffed before flouncing toward the living room.

"Were we ever really friends, Lorna?" Elaina mumbled to herself.

The other woman stopped on the living room's threshold and glared at Elaina as if she were considering snatching her bald. "What did you just say?"

"Never mind." Elaina shook her head. "It doesn't matter." She walked into the bathroom, locked the door, sat on the tub's rim, and trembled for ten minutes. Never had she been so enamored with the prospect of going home.

Twenty-Seven

By noon, Elaina had helped Anna carry her luggage into her bedroom at the cottage. Both sisters were looking forward to the light lunch their mom was scrounging from the freezer. On the way in, Elaina offered to help her mother with the meal, but Margaret wrinkled her nose, shook her head, and whispered, "Go help Anna!"

Elaina dropped Anna's final suitcase on the end of her bed. Without a word, Anna unzipped the luggage and began to unpack. Elaina busied herself with removing her sister's clothing from the garment bag and hanging them in her closet.

When she turned back around, she noticed Anna tossing a red sweater and velvet pants into the trash can. One pant leg dangled from the marbled receptacle and flopped onto the oriental rug.

"What gives?" Elaina held up the flawless sweater and observed her sister. She had been encouraged this morning after Anna showered and applied makeup. Her sister looked far less desolate and puffy-eyed.

"I don't want it," Anna forlornly declared. She turned her back on Elaina and began slamming a stack of sleepwear into her drawer.

"And you don't want to give it to the mission?" Elaina struggled for Anna's logic.

"I don't want anyone else to have it, either," she said. Anna ducked her head, and her next words were barely audible. "It's what I was wearing last night."

"Oh," Elaina said, and decided not to press the issue. She dropped the sweater back into the trash can, and the doorbell's chime halted any more comments. "I'll go get that," Elaina offered.

By the time she trotted down the stairs, the visitor had rung the bell again. Margaret rushed into the entryway at the same time Elaina gripped the doorknob. "Oh you've got it," she said, wiping her hands on an apron.

The smell of a reheated casserole reminded Elaina she had opted out on breakfast. "Yes, and whoever it is," she whispered, "I hope they don't stay for lunch. I'm famished and want to eat it all."

"I've got plenty for everyone," Margaret said with a merry twinkle in her eyes.

Elaina peaked out the peephole. Bryan stood on the porch, his hands in the pocket of his overcoat. "It's Bryan," Elaina whispered. "He eats like a horse," she continued but was glad for the sight of their friend.

"It doesn't matter," Margaret returned. "I'll cook for him all day long if he'll help take Anna's mind off of things."

Elaina opened the door and offered a bright smile. "We haven't seen you since Jeanna's Christmas party."

"Hello, Elaina." Bryan's easy smile couldn't hide the dark circles under his eyes or the wariness in his gaze. The last words she had shared with Bryan came after a hurried phone call that announced his niece had been found. She now wondered if the story were grimmer than she ever imagined.

"It's good to see you." Elaina opened the door wider, and Bryan stepped over the threshold.

"We've missed you these past few weeks," he said while bestowing chaste hugs upon Elaina and her mom.

"We?" Elaina questioned and squelched an unexpected onslaught of guilt because she discussed Bryan's past with Jeanna Harley, of all people.

"Of course," he simply stated. "The whole neighborhood. We had a meeting last night and voted that you aren't allowed to leave for more than two nights ever again." His eyes' humorous spark communicated his intent.

"Oh you!" Margaret hit at his arm as Elaina relieved him of his overcoat. "I'm warming up some leftover casserole for lunch. Would you care to join us?"

Bryan produced an exaggerated sniff. "If that heavenly smell is lunch, then we're on."

"Okay, good," Margaret agreed. "I need to get back to it now. Elaina will get you a soda or something."

The second Margaret left them alone, Bryan leaned toward Elaina. "Sometime before this visit is over, we need to talk," he said, his mouth stressing into a grave line.

"We do?" Elaina asked.

"Yes. That's why I'm here, actually."

"Does this have anything to do with your niece?" The question couldn't be denied.

Bryan nodded, and those ghosts from the past gyrated across his features once again. "It also involves Anna," he mumbled.

"Anna?" Elaina whispered, her mind a jumble of new information.

A movement from the stairway snagged her attention. She pivoted to see her sister hovering on the bottom step. Elaina attempted to look natural and hoped Anna hadn't heard her name. Her sister's nonplused expression ended Elaina's concerns. She fully expected Anna to offer a brief greeting and then make some excuse for leaving. Therefore, Elaina prepared to cover for her sister's continual discourtesy.

The second Bryan spotted Anna, Elaina felt as if she disappeared. "Hello, Anna," Bryan said with a reverent cadence to his words.

"Hello," Anna replied. She toyed with the buckle of her wide belt.

Elaina glanced down at her oversized sweater and wool slacks and decided she would never look as good as Anna in her jeans and a cropped sweater.

"Did you have a good Christmas?" Anna continued as if she really might care.

Elaina's brows twitched.

"Yes, quite good. I spent it with my brother and his family in Fort Worth. My parents were there as well. And you?"

Anna observed his loafers and offered a dispirited smile. "It was okay, I guess."

"Oh man!" Bryan pressed the heel of his palm against his forehead. "I can't believe it! I brought a couple of fruit baskets for you guys and left them in the car." He retrieved his overcoat from Elaina, shrugged back into it, and dug his keys out of the pocket.

"Do you need some help?" Elaina offered.

"Sure." Bryan gazed past her to Anna and posed a silent question.

"Just let me get my coat," Anna said. "It's up in my room."

Bryan's stunned gaze followed Anna as she trotted up the stairs. Elaina thought a comment might be in order, but she couldn't come up with a single word. Soon Anna descended the stairs while shoving her arms into the raw silk jacket Elaina gave her for Christmas. Without a word, Bryan opened the door and the two of them exited.

Elaina hastened into the dining room and darted to the window. Shamelessly she parted the blinds and caught a clear view of her sister and Bryan as they walked to his Lexus. The two of them made an attractive couple with Bryan's sandy hair contrasting against Anna's dark locks, his muscular frame as attractive as her slender curves.

"What are you doing?" Margaret asked.

Elaina cast a cursory glance behind and whispered, "Anna has gone outside with Bryan to get the fruit baskets he brought."

"Oh goodie!" Margaret dropped a stack of styrofoam plates on the dining room table and scooted to Elaina's side. She enlarged the peephole and gaped at her younger daughter. "I've liked him since the minute I met him," she admitted. "Jeanna kept saying she thought you and he had a thing going."

"No," Elaina declared. "We're good friends, but there's no chemistry."

"That's what I told Jeanna. Really, I thought I could see some chemistry between him and Anna. Well, on his side anyway."

"How?" Elaina queried.

"Well, because—" Margaret looked at her daughter and smiled. "You got me again, didn't you?"

After a clever simper, Elaina continued the vigil. As far as she could tell, Bryan and Anna didn't exchange a word until they began managing the oversized baskets.

"Those are for us?" Margaret questioned.

"Yes, both of them."

"They must have cost a hundred bucks apiece. I hope Anna can carry one by herself. Think she needs help?"

"No, no, no." Elaina playfully hit at her mom's arm.

Margaret chuckled. "Here they come," she hissed the second Bryan and Anna turned from the vehicle. Both Margaret and Elaina allowed the blinds to snap back into place and straightened as if they were sneaky children.

"Help me set the table," Margaret instructed. "That way, we'll look natural."

"Good idea." Elaina assisted her mother in the task.

After Bryan and Anna placed the fruit baskets in the kitchen, they wandered toward the dining room. Elaina mentioned something about helping her mother finish lunch and stayed out of their way. Soon a Beethoven classic floated into the dining room and attested to Anna's playing for the doctor.

For the next hour, Elaina and her mother silently elated in the amount of time Anna chatted with Dr. Brixby. By the simple lunch's end, the shadows in Bryan's eyes had faded. Even though Elaina's curiosity still demanded details of their upcoming conversation, Bryan acted as if he'd never referenced wanting to talk with her about Macy and Anna. Instead, he looked as if he'd been given the keys to paradise. He hardly took his gaze from Anna the whole meal, and his awed expression chased away the haggard look that plagued him when he first arrived.

Elaina, eager to further Bryan's agenda, pursed her lips in a silent message and nodded to her mother. "I think Mom and I will make some coffee."

Margaret's blank gaze lasted only seconds. "Yes, that's a splendid idea!" she said and winked at her eldest daughter. "And I've got a lemon ice box pie, too, that I can get out of the freezer."

"Does anyone have a preference of decaf or regular coffee?" Elaina questioned.

"You know I never drink the stuff," Anna said, "unless it's been turned into a cappuccino."

"I'll take whatever you make." Bryan dabbed the corners of his mouth with his paper napkin and laid it atop his plate. He scooted his chair away from the table and rubbed the front of his cotton sweater as if he were stuffed.

He'd probably drink muddy water right now and never know it, Elaina thought. She stood and began gathering their plates.

"You know," Anna said over a yawn, "I'm really tired."

Elaina scrutinized her sister's pale complexion. Despite the fact that she had treated Bryan with polite friendliness, empty sorrow still spilled from blue eyes that had once been radiant with life. Elaina pressed her thumbnail into the foam plate and still wished she could share an opinion or two with that womanizer Willis.

"If you guys don't mind, I think I'm going to go up for a nap. I didn't sleep really well last night," Anna said and peered at her glass of iced tea as if she were viewing a scene only visible to her.

"Of course, dear," Margaret agreed.

Anna scooted back her chair.

Bryan stood as if Anna were royalty. Elaina, her hands full of disposable plates, paused at the end of the table and watched her sister leave the room. She balanced the plates with one hand, bit the end of her pinkie, and winced. Even though Anna had been polite to Bryan, a cloak of depression still suppressed her every action and word.

After seeing Lorna with Ted, Elaina wasn't feeling chipper herself. *But at least I've been able to get a grip on myself,* she worried.

The second Anna left the room, Bryan turned toward Elaina. "Can we talk now?" he asked, his intelligent eyes growing heavy with a dire message.

"Okay," Elaina said and welcomed the oppportunity to finally discover the reason for Bryan's visit. "Let me toss these plates first."

"I'll take them, dear," Margaret said and smiled at Bryan. "You two go on into the living room. I'll bring your coffee and pie to you."

"Mom, you don't have to wait on us like you're the maid!" Elaina protested.

"No, I insist!" Margaret's brows arched. "Now shoo, shoo, out with the both of you." She motioned them from the room like a southern matron who expected her orders to be followed without question.

Twenty-Eight

Once they entered the living room, Bryan strode to the fireplace, alight with the burning logs Margaret had ignited upon their arrival. He rested his arm on the mantel, hung his head, and gazed into the flames. The sweet smell of burning oak bespoke the joys of the homecoming Elaina had so anticipated. She moved toward the antique couch that Faye had coveted. Before she could sit, Bryan walked within feet of Elaina. He peered at her with a desperate wretchedness that both stunned her and prepared her for his next statement.

"I have a lot to tell you," he began. "Some of it, you'll need to share with Anna. We better sit down." Bryan dropped onto the sofa, and Elaina joined him.

Bryan rubbed the top of his knees and paused as if he were debating where to start. Finally he said, "Do you remember my telling you that your sister reminds me of someone I once knew?" He focused on the baby grand piano. "She even plays the piano like Liza," he whispered.

"Who?" Elaina, her back stiff, scooted to the edge of the sofa. Despite her commitment to the high road, Jeanna's insinuations bombarded her anew. Maybe their neighbor had a better handle on the truth than Elaina wanted to admit. Many men of character had been known to fall.

"When I was eighteen, I fell in love," Bryan began. "All the way, completely, head over heels. You know," he shrugged and cut her a sideways glance, "like all the songs say."

She nodded and gazed into the fire. Despite her curiosity about Bryan's past, she imagined the flames were swaying to Ted's playing "I Only Have Eyes for You."

"Yes, like all the songs say," she repeated.

But Bryan was too concerned with his story to notice Elaina's remarks. "Her name was Liza. Her family was wealthy—as in filthy rich." Bryan turned his hands upward and examined his palms. "Mine weren't."

"I understand," Elaina said, squeezing all negative emotion from her comment.

"My father was a hard worker." Bryan stroked his palms. "He and my mom sacrificed to put my brother and me both through med school. She was a secretary, by the way."

"Both of you went to med school?" Elaina questioned.

"Yes." Bryan nodded. "My brother became a neurologist. I'm just a general practitioner. I guess that makes me the flunky." He observed Elaina with a mild hint of humor nibbling at his mouth.

"You look like a flunky to me," Elaina chided.

He nodded and continued. "Anyway, all that is to tell you that I was essentially raised on the wrong side of the tracks. When Liza brought me home from college to meet her parents, the first thing they asked about was my family. When they found out my father worked in a lumberyard, they threw a fit. They could see Liza and I were already deeply in love—even though we were so young. And, well," he shrugged, "they demanded that she break up with me."

He propped his elbow on his knee and rested his forehead against his palm. "She was so scared of her father, she did what he said. I'll never forget the night I begged her not to end our relationship. I even offered to quit college and get a job to support her while she finished." He lifted his head and shook it. "I'm sure my parents would not have been happy campers if I'd followed through, but I was in love and desperate to keep Liza any way I could.

"I thought I had her convinced at first," he continued. "But the bottom line was she was too scared not to do what her father said."

"Parental manipulation and control," Elaina ground out and thought of Pearl Farris.

"Oh, I know." Bryan nodded. "Believe me, how well I know. And really, I understand her parents and mine being cautious and not wanting us to get married so young, but we didn't even think about hauling off and getting married until her parents tried to force us apart. We were originally planning to wait until we finished college.

"Anyway," Bryan lifted his hand, "when I went back to college after Christmas break, Liza had transferred to another university closer to her home in Georgia."

"How convenient," Elaina said and folded her arms.

"Exactly." Bryan stood and marched toward the fireplace. He turned his back to the flames and looked straight ahead.

Elaina, caught in the story, relaxed against the back of the couch and began to expect that perhaps Liza was Macy's mother.

"Liza was so much like your sister it's not even funny," he mused. "She looked like her and was just as carefree and innocent as Anna is. The first time I saw Anna, I nearly fell over. It was like Liza had stepped from the grave." Bryan's face grew ashen. "It was the oddest experience I have ever had."

Pinching the couch's seam, Elaina ached for the big-hearted man before her. Now that she had lost Ted, she couldn't imagine having to attend his funeral as well. She pulled a throw pillow onto her lap and mashed the fringe between her forefinger and thumb.

"So, anyway, I went on through school—me and my broken heart. I turned every scrap of energy I had toward my education and made my parents proud. Little did they know I was dying inside." He clasped his hands behind his back and studied the floor.

Elaina's mind raced with where the pregnancy must come in.

"The next time I heard from Liza, I was beginning my junior year of college at Old Miss," he explained. "She called me late one night. Her voice was slurred and she was crying." He moved toward the piano and absently caressed the ivories, as if recalling Anna's playing.

"Like I said," he persisted, "she was crying and blubbering something about a baby and her parents and that she needed me. I managed to get the name and address of the place where she was staying in Atlanta. I caught the first flight out and found her in a cheap motel with a little girl who was two. The child looked too much like her for me to deny the implications. Liza was drunker the day I found her than she had been the night before. The baby was hungry and crying. And my Liza," Bryan's face grew tense, "was so eaten up with drugs and alcohol she barely recognized me." He swallowed hard and turned his back on Elaina.

The fire's crackle filled a silence that lamented the loss. Elaina, thrown into a fit of full-blown self-incrimination, despised herself more today than she had the day Jeanna implied Bryan had fathered a child out of wedlock. She suppressed the compulsion to apologize to Bryan for having doubted his integrity and debated whether or not she should step forward to comfort him. She decided his pain was simply too private for her intrusion.

"I did the best I could to get her medical care and to take care of Macy, her little girl," he choked out.

"Macy?" Elaina questioned and began kneading the pillow. "That's your niece's name."

Bryan, his eyes red, faced Elaina once more. He nodded. "And yes, it's the same girl." He settled onto the piano bench, propped his elbows on his thighs, and clasped his hands. "Liza died within a month of my finding her. When Liza's parents found out she was pregnant, they had disowned her so they didn't want anything to do with Macy."

"Would that we all had parents like hers," Elaina said and tossed the pillow to the end of the couch. "Sounds to me like they were looking for a reason to disown her. Do you think they threatened to do that when they saw she was in love with you?"

"Of course," Bryan said. "And I might as well tell you that there are pieces of this story I don't have. I know that when Liza and I were together she was chaste. I never touched her in any way indecent, and she didn't act like she'd had experience. All I can figure is that sometime after she and I broke up, some smooth talker must have seduced her."

"You mean somebody like Willis Kenney?" Elaina asked.

Bryan's face darkened. "If I find out that cad laid a hand on Anna, I'll—" He stood and stalked toward the bay window.

Elaina started to explain that Anna had denied any physical intimacy with Willis, but Bryan, intent upon finishing his story, picked back up with Liza.

"I have no idea what all she did to make ends meet after her parents kicked her out," he continued. "I can only imagine. I didn't ask. I just tried my best to take care of her and to love her at the end. She had AIDS," he rasped, his attention firmly fixed out the window.

"I am *so sorry*," Elaina breathed. When he didn't answer, she decided she simply could not leave him to suffer alone another second. Elaina rose from the couch, strode toward Bryan, and laid her hand on his shoulder.

Bryan covered her hand with his and then grasped it between his palms. "You're a good friend, Elaina." An appreciative gleam intensified his green eyes.

"You are, too," Elaina responded.

"Anyway," he continued and gave Elaina's hand a final squeeze, "I said all that to explain Macy's place in our family, and maybe so you'll understand why I reacted to Anna the way I did."

"Yes, I can understand that," Elaina said. "I'm not sure I would have done as well as you if I were in your situation."

"It's been...interesting, to say the least," he admitted.

"So, I'm assuming your brother adopted Macy?" she prompted.

"Yes. Before she died, Liza signed over custody of Macy to me. My brother and sister-in-law had one child and wanted another one. She looks a lot like Liza, by the way. Ironically not as much as Anna does. But there you have genetics."

Elaina settled on the bay window's settee and traced a burgundy stripe along the velvet upholstery.

"Like I already told you," Bryan said, "Macy had been missing for months, and you know they found her right before Christmas."

"Right," Elaina responded.

"She was in a hospital in Tulsa. She'd had a baby and didn't know where to go. Some people at a mission talked her into calling home."

"At least you found her alive," Elaina said and winced at her own insensitivity.

"Right. And at least she doesn't have AIDS."

"I'm sorry," Elaina said. "I shouldn't have—"

"No, it's okay." Bryan encouraged her with an assuring gaze. "Really."

After she was certain he really meant it, Elaina posed a question: "How old is she again?"

"She turned sixteen last month." Bryan supplied. "She was fifteen when she got pregnant."

"Holy Toledo," Elaina whispered. "I can't imagine! What about the father? Is he the same age, or—"

"Try thirty-one," Bryan stated the age as if the words tasted like bile.

Elaina stroked her temple. "That is really sick," she mumbled.

"It makes me nauseous. I'm thirty-five, and I can assure you I have no desire to—" He shook his head.

"It's statutory rape, isn't it?"

"Yes."

"Did you find the father?"

"Oh yes, we found him. We didn't have to look far. He actually has a relative around here." Bryan's keen expression hinted that he was about to release more shocking information.

"Do I know him?" Elaina croaked, already suspecting the answer.

"Yep." He leaned against the window's side and crossed his arms. "Anna knows him really well," he drawled. "It's Willis Kenney."

"What!" Elaina stood erect and balled her fists. "Are you certain?"

"Yes."

"How did *that* happen?" she demanded.

Bryan's face settled into a sarcastic mask.

"You know what I mean." Elaina placed her hands on her hips. "How does she know Willis?"

"The short version is, she met him one day when she was visiting me and he was visiting his aunt. While I was at work, she went for a walk. He saw her and offered a lift. She lied about her age—told him she was twenty, which she looks every bit of. Anyway, Willis told her if she was ever in Tulsa to look him up. When she ran away, she and a friend arranged for fake driver's licenses and social security cards. Willis was the first person she called."

"Sounds like Willis majors in offering 'rides' to women. That's essentially what he did with Anna," Elaina mused.

"Exactly," Bryan agreed. "From what I can gather, he swept Macy off her feet as thoroughly as he did Anna. They were a hot item for awhile. When he found out she was pregnant, he gave her enough money for an abortion and told her to stay out of his life. She decided not to get an abortion and used the money to live on for awhile. When the money ran out and she wound up having to go to bed with the pregnancy, she tried to contact Willis but apparently he got unlisted numbers and moved the day he got rid of her. She nearly lost her life and the child. That's when the mission stepped in. After the baby was born, they finally convinced her to contact home."

Elaina slumped back onto the settee. "I wonder if any of this has anything to do with his dumping Anna and getting married so quickly," she mused. "He was here the morning after you got that phone call. He had promised to bring Anna an engagement ring that day. But he wound up telling her his aunt was disinheriting him and that he had to leave town."

"It had everything to do with my niece's situation," Bryan said. "As soon as Macy told me the name of her baby's father that night, I contacted his aunt. I told her everything and asked for Willis' cell number. Nancy Moncleave is a respectable woman. She wasn't blind. She knew her nephew was a long way from being perfect. She told me that he far preferred to lean on the allowance she gave him rather than work. The reason she was so glad about Willis and your sister was because she had heard good things about your family and hoped Anna would be a good influence on him. She had even promised to give him part of his inheritance once he got married."

"That would explain why he was so quick about proposing to Anna." Elaina stood and began marching toward the doorway then back to the fireplace. She stopped only long enough to occasionally glance at Bryan as he continued the story.

"By her own words, Mrs. Moncleave never imagined Willis would stoop so low to abandon a woman carrying his child. She got so mad at him she immediately cut off his allowance and axed him out of her will."

"You know..." Elaina fumed. She stopped and glared at Bryan as if he were the culprit. "He could be sent to prison for this."

"Yes, I know." He crossed his arms and squared his feet as if he were preparing for battle. "And don't think my brother and I haven't sat up many long nights discussing the possibility. A week ago we decided to press charges, only to find out from Macy that he really did think she was twenty. In that one regard, he was innocent. Furthermore, she's been through so much that she begged us not to drag her through court. So we've settled out of court. Willis has agreed to pay hefty child support until his son is eighteen. Macy is seriously considering allowing my brother and sister-in-law to adopt him. That will probably be the best option."

Elaina narrowed her eyes. "Willis just went to see Anna last night and told her he was married."

"He got married right after signing to pay child support."

"His wife must have money."

"Oodles," Bryan said.

"Makes perfect sense."

"From what I can gather from some investigative work I've done," Bryan stepped back to the fireplace, "Willis Kenney is a sought-after model, but he only works when he feels like it. And that's the way he likes it."

"That explains why he was able to take off from work and romance Anna for a solid month."

"Elaina," Bryan doubled his fists, "you know your sister way better than I do. Do you think that rake—"

"No!" Elaina joined him at the fireplace and shook her head. "I started to tell you a minute ago, but you cut me off. I think it was obvious that he wanted to, but Anna drew the line with him."

"Thank you, Jesus!" Bryan closed his lids, and the lines of exhaustion around his mouth made him look ten years older. He rubbed his eyes. "I haven't slept well in a month. I've been worried sick about my niece and worried sick about Anna."

"With all due respect, you don't look so hot."

"Thanks," he said with a sad smile. "I love you, too."

"Good. I've always thought I was the lovable sort," Elaina dryly quipped.

"At least Ted Farris thinks so." Bryan winked.

Elaina began to stutter over correcting Bryan's assumption when her mother stepped into the room bearing the promised pie and coffee.

Twenty-Nine

Two weeks later, Elaina decided the time had come for an apartment makeover. During the last months she had grown to despise the hodgepodge effect that had overtaken her living quarters. An after-holiday restlessness insisted she do something to alter her world even though a voice within whispered that the restlessness stemmed from other sources. Never had she anticipated the impact of a Thursday night class without Ted. Even though all the faces were changed, she still caught herself looking to his seat and expecting him to be present. His absence from class increased the distress of his absence from her heart.

So Elaina tackled her apartment. The first thing she decided to do was paint. That choice resulted in her arriving home Saturday morning, her backseat lined with cans of paint and primer and paraphernalia she hoped she could wield. She had invited Anna along as a color choice expert. When Elaina was writing the check for the colonial red paint, she began to doubt the wisdom of consulting a vibrant person about color. But Anna insisted on colonial red and wouldn't hear of Elaina ruining her walls with blasé dove gray.

Once they took the lid off the paint bucket and stirred, Elaina glanced at her sister. "So what do you think now?" she hedged and seriously considered a compulsory trip for the dove gray.

"Perfect." Anna nodded and gazed around the room. "It's going to really bring your furniture to life and brighten up this place like you can't believe."

"But red?" Elaina questioned. She scrutinized her couch and love seat, covered in a red, blue, and green stripe that would have gone so well with dove gray.

"It's not just red!" Anna grabbed a paintbrush from the oversized paper bag. "It's *colonial* red." She waved the brush at Elaina's nose as if she were her mother. "It's all the rage these days. You'll love it once we get it on. Let's put the lid back on the red," she said without ever stopping for breath. "We've got to do the primer first—that way it'll cover any stains and even out tone for us," she said. "Then we put on the color."

With a final rejection ready on her tongue, Elaina stopped. Even though Anna's eyes lacked intensity, she had been more alive this morning than she had since New Year's. According to their mother, Anna had slept more and eaten less these past weeks. She had also refused any outing—even church—on the basis that she just didn't feel well. Even her interest in embroidering had dulled. Still worried about clinical depression, Elaina included Anna in this project in hopes of piquing her interest enough to instigate a gradual recovery.

The paint's strong smell accompanied Elaina's sage shrug. She decided that if having red walls would help her sister overcome her loss then she'd have red walls. "Let's get busy!" Elaina retrieved her own paintbrush, and the sisters began tackling the job.

During the two hours of spreading primer, Elaina debated the best method of telling Anna about the information Bryan had shared regarding Willis. While she had been given several opportunities to talk with Anna during the traditional Sunday afternoon meals, Elaina had worried about weighing down her sister with more dark information. Simultaneously, she was beginning to fear the gossip mills. Considering Willis' aunt lived near the cottage, she concluded that Jeanna would soon be privy to the information. Elaina despised Anna learning the truth via rumor when she could lovingly soften the blow.

While they were side-by-side washing their brushes at the kitchen sink, Elaina decided now was as good a time as any. "Anna," she started and then paused while rehearsing a trio of openings.

"Hmmm?" Anna, shaking her brush free of moisture, didn't even look up.

Elaina allowed the cold water to stream over her paint brush. The last traces of primer flowed away like thinned milk. She snapped off the water and shook her brush. "There's something I've been wanting to tell you," she explained and retrieved a pair of hand towels from the drawer next to the dishwasher. She extended one to Anna.

"Thanks," she said and dabbed at the end of her nose. "The water splashed on me."

"You've got a streak of primer on your cheek, too." Elaina lightly touched Anna's left cheekbone.

She scrubbed at it with the towel. "I'm glad I didn't bother with makeup," she said and shoved at the bandanna holding back her hair.

"And I'm glad I didn't wear any good clothes." Elaina looked down at her worn sweats, already dotted with white.

"You act like this is your first paint job or something," Anna said. "I mean, you didn't even know what I meant by a drop cloth."

"Well maybe because it *is* my first paint job." Elaina admitted.

Anna shook her head. "Sister, sister, sister," she chided. "You should have visited the cottage more often. Mom and I have painted everything but the doghouse in the backyard." She pulled out the tail of her oversized denim shirt, pointed to streaks of paint, and named the room each color had been used in.

Elaina chuckled. "You're too much."

"I'm a pro, now," Anna wiggled her brush under Elaina's nose, and she delighted in seeing a trace of her sister's former verve. Elaina even considered putting off the bad news a few more days. She hated to ruin their day.

"Let's go tackle some red," she suggested and led the way back toward the living room.

"So what was it that you wanted to tell me?" Anna questioned when they passed through the dining area.

Elaina halted beside the round marble-topped pub table and gripped the top of a tall wrought-iron chair. "Oh," she hesitated and floundered for a means out of this now that she'd started it. Elaina peered out the window toward the veil of rippling clouds that promised the beginning of the snowy winter the weatherman predicted. Elaina dreaded the thought of stacks of snow as much as she dreaded telling Anna about Willis. So many people in rural Oklahoma just didn't know how to drive on the stuff.

"Does it have something to do with Willis?" Anna asked.

Elaina searched her sister's soul and decided the moment really had come. "Sit down, Anna," she said and pulled out one of the elevated chairs.

"What's happened?" she whimpered, her face crumpling. "Has he been killed or—"

"Oh heavens no!" Elaina rested her hand on Anna's shoulder. "Nothing like that. As far as I know, he's fine. I just thought you needed to know a few things that Bryan told me a couple of weeks ago."

"You've known two weeks?" Anna squeaked.

"Well," Elaina adjusted her glasses, "yes. I really just didn't know how to tell you. I certainly didn't want to tell you anything that would make you more depressed, and I—"

"When are you going to stop treating me like I'm twelve, Elaina?" Anna slumped onto the chair's edge and laid the paintbrush and towel on the table. Her head drooping, she propped the heel of her sneaker on the elevated chair's rung.

"I'm sorry," Elaina breathed and laid her paintbrush beside Anna's. "I'm just so worried about you, I—"

"I'm going to be fine." Anna lifted her chin, but her sunken eyes denounced her claim.

"Well, okay," Elaina dubiously agreed. "Then I guess I'll tell you. This involves Willis' integrity and some…things he's done that aren't honorable—not in the least."

Her face impassive, Anna gazed into the living room and listened while Elaina detailed the bad news. When she finished, Anna offered no response or movement. Only a lone tear trickling down her cheek suggested she had absorbed the information.

"Anna?" Elaina questioned and laid her hand on her sister's.

"So I guess he didn't love me at all," she squeaked. "I was just a tool he could use to get to his aunt's money."

Elaina remained silent. The whistle and gust of the cold wind whipping around the duplex building seemed the confirmation of Anna's observation. "I can't speak for Willis," Elaina finally said and decided maybe now was the time to put in a good word for Bryan, "but I know someone else I think is already halfway in love with you. Someone who's ten times a better man than Willis Kenney will ever be."

"You mean Bryan?" Anna sniffled and shoved at her tear with the heel of her hand.

Nodding, Elaina pulled out the chair near Anna and sat in it. "I've noticed you and him chatting a few times. Do you feel anything at all for him?"

"Right now all I can feel is sorry that I was so rude to him last fall," Anna explained. "I treated him nearly as badly as I treated you." She offered an apologetic smile. "But really, Elaina, I don't know if I'll ever love again—not the way I loved Willis."

Grappling for something to say, Elaina remained helplessly silent.

"Elaina?" Anna tentatively questioned. "Have you ever put someone in the place of God in your life?"

After searching her soul, Elaina decided to be honest. "I think that's a pitfall we all face at one time or another." She scrutinized her feelings for Ted and found her Lord still ranked where He belonged. "Thankfully, I don't think I'm there now," she admitted. "But maybe I have been in the past. For me, I think it was all about the pursuit of my desires at one point rather than the pursuit of a man."

"Well, I think that's what I did with Willis—or maybe with the concept of Willis, if that makes any sense."

"You mean the whole ideal of a handsome prince sweeping you away on his white steed?"

Anna nodded. "I've never been so low in my whole life," she admitted. "I feel as if something has died inside of me. And—and I don't know how to get God back where He belongs." She fidgeted with the bandanna tied at the base of her neck, and Elaina battled for a good reply.

"I wish I could fix it all for you, Anna." She covered her sister's hand. "But sometimes the answer is in you, and…"

"That's what I figured you'd say."

"I *do* believe you'll sort it out if you keep trying, though," she encouraged.

"I just wish I knew where to begin." Anna turned her hand up and squeezed Elaina's fingers.

"Why don't you just forget Willis," Elaina lightly encouraged and knew the advice was lame when it left her mouth.

"And could you follow your own advice?" Anna questioned, her blue eyes sharp with new-gained wisdom.

Elaina's gaze faltered. "What's that supposed to mean?" she asked and wondered why she posed the foolish question.

"You know what I mean," Anna said, wretched certainty in her tone. "Have you forgotten Ted? Whatever has happened between you—will you ever forget him?"

"I…" Her back stiff, Elaina stood and clutched the side of the table. Despite her attempts to block it from her mind, Lorna's recent e-mail sprang into her thoughts. Lorna began the message with friendship goo that nearly nauseated Elaina. Then she bragged about how much the Farrises enjoyed her company. Lorna said Faye had even invited her to the mansion. She further stated that Ted and she were so elated that they were going to announce the engagement soon. Lorna was convinced Pearl Farris wouldn't disinherit Ted after all, given the grace and reception she had extended Lorna. After the e-mail, Elaina wondered if perhaps the Farrises really were taken with Lorna. When they first showed her deference, Elaina assumed it was to spite her. Now she saw no reason for Faye and Pearl to extend kindness to Lorna unless they really did enjoy her company.

The three of them probably have a lot in common, Elaina thought.

Presently she couldn't imagine ever forgetting Ted, his engagement to Lorna, and the agony the alliance had caused.

"Elaina?" Anna prompted. "I–I'm sorry. I—"

She focused on her sister. "No, *I'm* sorry," Elaina insisted and wondered what her expression must have revealed. "I guess I shouldn't have said that about your forgetting Willis," she admitted. "I'm just worried about you, and—"

"I know." Anna stood and settled her arm around her sister's waist. No trace of resentment marred her features, only the hollow loneliness. "I guess that's what having a big sister is all about."

"Maybe so." Elaina picked up her paintbrush. "We've got some red to spread," she declared with more gusto than she felt.

"I promise you're going to love this color!" Anna chirped like a cardinal announcing spring's latest bloom, yet her tone sounded more forced than melodious.

Elaina stepped around two artificial ficus trees Anna had plopped on the room's edge. She picked up the red paint, hauled it onto a drop cloth, removed the lid, and inserted her brush. *Here goes,* she thought. While the telephone's ring halted her brush's first stroke, Anna tackled the job with vigor.

Her forehead wrinkling, Elaina studied the first strips of red while stepping through the clutter. Absently, she picked up the cordless phone from the maple end table. Out of habit, Elaina examined the caller ID window and temporarily forgot her concern over red walls.

The sound of her half-brother's voice on the line convinced Elaina that the caller ID hadn't malfunctioned. In the past five years her brother had only called about five times. Elaina had assumed he didn't even know her current number. Once Anna realized who was on the phone, she stopped painting and widened her eyes.

"Listen, Elaina," Jake said after the greeting. "I'm in Lakeland today on some business." His voice held the grim doom of death. "I was wondering if you were going to be home. I'd like to swing by in about fifteen minutes or so. There's something we need to discuss."

"Sure," Elaina agreed as a shroud of apprehension crept up her spine. "As long as you don't mind paint fumes. Anna and I are painting my living room."

"Not a problem," Jake said. "I've been sniffing paint fumes for weeks. Faye has been remodeling the mansion ad nauseum."

"All right then." Elaina eyed her living room. She and Anna had scooted every piece of furniture near the wall to the center. She decided they should sit at the dining room table. "Do you need directions here?" she queried.

"No, I can find it. You're just a few blocks away from SCU, right?"

"Yes."

"But is everything okay? I mean with Faye and you? Is someone ill or—"

"No, nothing like that," Jake confirmed. "I'll explain everything when I get over there."

"Okay," Elaina agreed. She hung up the phone and studied her sister's concerned expression.

"What is it?" Anna asked.

"Jake's coming over." Elaina stepped over an ottoman.

"That's odd," Anna said. "Did he say why?"

"No." Elaina moved toward the dining room entryway. "He said everything was fine with him and Faye. But he still sounded like something awful had happened." She ambled into the dining room. "Go ahead and keep painting if you want, Anna," she called over her shoulder. "I'm going to rinse my paintbrush and heat water so we can all have a cup of something while he's here."

Thirty

True to his claim, Jake arrived within fifteen minutes. Elaina poured three mugs full of hot water and offered her sister and Jake choices of instant coffee, hot cocoa, or herbal tea. Elaina immersed a bag of mint tea into her water and waited for Jake to arrive at the reason for his visit.

Seeing Jake next to her sister brought back poignant images laced with pain. Both looked so much like their father. Jake even had their father's keen brown eyes. Elaina wished for the dad from her childhood who had grown into the friend of her adulthood. Forever a man of his word, he would have understood Elaina's plight in keeping her word to Lorna.

"Well, the reason I'm here..." Jake began. He hesitated and stroked the arm of his Armani sports coat with pomp importance.

Elaina stopped stirring her tea and shared a glance with Anna.

"...is because of some awful news we've just received from Ted. I wanted to tell you in person because..." He cast a sympathetic gaze toward Elaina, and she was shocked to see the genuine concern on her brother's face. Long ago she had assumed that the man really didn't care if she lived or died. His not following through on his promise to share his inheritance had validated that supposition.

He looked into his steaming mug of coffee. "There are actually several reasons I came in person," Jake continued. "But first, let me tell you the news."

Anna leaned forward on her elbow.

"Sometimes I wonder if my brother-in-law has a screw loose." He rubbed the side of his nose in a gesture that made Elaina recall her father anew. "He's got the talent and contacts to be an international star, but he refuses. And now—" Jake scowled as if Ted had become the basest of criminals.

Elaina leaned back in her chair and caressed the spoon near her cup. She no longer looked at Jake or Anna, for she finally understood what bit of news her brother was bringing. His hints, coupled with Lorna's recent e-mail, validated that Ted and Lorna finally went public.

"Believe it or not," Jake said, "that imbecile told Pearl Farris last night that he's engaged to Lorna Starr, of all people, and that they're getting married March the first."

"What?" Anna squeaked. "You mean that halfwit who stayed with us at Jeanna's?"

"Yes," Jake confirmed.

Elaina picked up her spoon, slid her fingers down the length, turned it over, and repeated the action. A peculiar relief swept upon her. She no longer needed to harbor the other woman's secret. Simultaneously, Elaina struggled to hide her broken spirit. As long as Ted hadn't announced the engagement, there was still the tiniest chance that the engagement wouldn't stand. Now that they had revealed their matrimonial designs, she doubted Ted would turn back.

"You don't look surprised, Elaina," Jake said.

With an empty smile, she lifted her attention to her brother and allowed it to slide to Anna. "I've known this for almost two months."

Anna's mouth dropped open. "Why didn't you *say* something?"

"Really!" Jake lay flattened hands on the table and looked at Elaina as if she were the traitor of the century.

"Because I promised Lorna I'd keep the secret," she explained.

"But this is *family* we're talking about!" Jake accused.

"I'm a woman of my word."

Jake gazed at the ceiling fan. "There are times when it's okay to break your word! For cryin' out loud, Elaina, this was something my wife and mother-in-law should have known the minute you found out."

"And all this time you've—you've known?" Anna asked before Elaina had the chance to respond. Anna placed her palm atop her head and slumped against the chair's back. "Even when you were staying in the same *house* with her?"

Elaina nodded and shifted the spoon up and down at a more rapid rate.

"How could you remain so calm?" Anna shrieked. "When you—when you feel the way you—" She glanced at Jake and covered her mouth with her fingertips.

"Who said I was calm?" Elaina queried. She sipped the warm tea and wished the balm of peppermint could erase her burden.

"You look calm to me," Jake said and took a deep draw on his black coffee as if he were sealing a million-dollar business deal. "Calm as a frozen cucumber."

"Looks can be deceiving," Elaina said and pinched the edge of the marble-top table.

She felt Anna's steady appraisal but didn't make eye contact. Instead Elaina gazed toward the low-hanging clouds and wondered how they had managed to scatter into her heart.

Even though Jake continued talking, Elaina barely registered his words, until he said "disinherited." She snapped her focus back to Jake. "What did you just say?" she questioned.

"Last night Pearl said she's had all of Ted's belligerence she can stand," Jake repeated. "She's at her lawyer's office right now changing her will and cutting off Ted's allowance. From what I understand, she's also pulling the plug on his trust fund. The account is set up just like Faye's and Robert's—with Pearl as the primary holder."

"At first that's what Lorna said she and Ted were afraid would happen," Elaina affirmed. "But I just got an e-mail from her last week. She seemed to think Mrs. Farris and Faye really liked her and that—"

Jake muttered an oath. "They felt sorry for her!"

Elaina was hard pressed to imagine Pearl and Faye feeling sorry for anyone.

"They never imagined she would take advantage of them like this. Pearl is furious! She went ballistic last night when they told her. It was during dinner, and she emptied a bowl of mashed potatoes in Lorna's lap."

A brief giggle escaped Anna. She ducked her head and indulged in a slow sip of hot chocolate.

Elaina shifted in her chair and traced the rim of her cup with her index finger. "Too bad for Lorna," she mused.

"Too bad is right!" Jake affirmed. "Pearl has even forbidden Ted to ever set foot in her house again."

"I know I wish our mom was more like her," Anna drawled.

"I don't think Pearl is so off base," Jake asserted.

Studying her brother, Elaina wondered how he could have made such a statement. Faye's sharp features superimposed themselves upon Jake. Elaina wondered no more.

"I mean, here Ted is, a musical genius," he waved his hand, "and he's throwing his life away on pursuing a ministry and marrying a penniless woman who can't count to ten!"

"But he's *thirty*," Elaina explained. "He should be allowed to make his own choices."

"Not when he's making those choices on somebody else's money." Jake stuck out his bottom lip as if he were the lawyer, jury, and judge. "We also found out he's been supporting that little hussy for months now!"

Elaina considered reminding Jake that every penny he possessed came from his mother and father's hand and that Joseph Woods had allowed him to marry a woman he didn't approve of. But Elaina soon realized the irony in convincing Jake that Ted should be free to choose his mate. She didn't agree with his choice any more than Faye and Pearl did.

"All that is to say," Jake continued, "Faye asked me to tell you that, in her opinion, she would have been far less unhappy if Ted had decided upon you rather than this Lorna woman."

"So," Elaina bestowed a humorous glance upon Anna, "I guess I'm the lesser of two evils?" Her smile faded.

Anna's unmade cheeks grew pink. Her eyes hardened. She tapped her index finger against the marble-topped table. Elaina barely nodded and frowned a discouragement. Anna clamped her lips together and stood.

"I need to go to the restroom," she said, her words like precisely aimed bullets.

"Sure," Jake said as if he hadn't a clue of Anna's ire. His cell phone emitted a high-pitched blast that reminded Elaina of a sci fi movie's theme. "That's probably Faye," he explained as he pulled his phone from his belt loop. "She knew I was coming over here and said she wanted to talk to you."

"Really?" Elaina adjusted her glasses.

He examined his phone's petite screen and nodded. "Yep. That's her."

Elaina, tempted to make her own exit to the bathroom, bolstered her courage.

"Hi, honey," Jake crooned into the phone. "Yes, she's here," he replied and covered the mouthpiece with his hand. "She does want to talk to you." He observed Elaina as if they were confidantes, bound by mutual suffering.

She placed the phone next to her ear and extended extra effort in tempering her tone. "Hello, Faye."

"Has Jake told you!" Faye demanded, her voice shrill.

"You mean about Ted and Lorna?"

"Yes, that's exactly what I mean. Isn't this the most awful news you've ever heard? My mom thinks he's losing his mind!" she shouted. "I think that wench just has him blinded. Oh, 'Laina..." she continued.

Elaina winced. No one but her immediate family ever shortened her name, and she hadn't heard Jake use the endearment in years.

"How I wish Ted had chosen you! I know the match wouldn't have been the best, but it would have been far better than this creature he's dragged up from eighth grade. I just can't imagine my Ted being chained to someone as shallow, ignorant, and capricious as Lorna Starr. Here we were being nice to her because we felt sorry for her. I mean, once we learned that she wasn't Jeanna and Noah Harley's heir, we pitied her because she's just too ignorant to support herself." Faye paused for a huff. "Then we found out Ted had been supporting her for months!

"Even if you don't have a fortune, at least you do have *some* intelligence, Elaina! And a job! You actually have a job. What a concept!"

Elaina's eyes narrowed. She shoved at her cup of tea. Fleetingly, she wondered since when achieving a Ph.D. ranked as "some intelligence." "Well, thanks," she said with a sarcasm she couldn't expunge.

"You're welcome!" Faye babbled. "I just knew you'd understand. And my mother—she's beside herself and says as far as she is concerned Ted was never even born. She can't stand the sight of him right now."

"That's too bad," Elaina said and silently thanked God her mother's love and support wasn't the conditional variety. Faye fumed another five minutes about the ills of Lorna and the lesser ills of Elaina. About the time Elaina's attitude was close to irrevocably souring, Faye released her. Elaina couldn't remember a recent time when she had been so relieved. As she handed the phone back to her brother, Elaina wondered if Ted might be even more relieved to have finally broken his mother's control.

Thirty-One

The next Friday, Elaina entered her office and dropped her briefcase in the center of her desk. "I think this week was eight days long," she groaned to herself. She hadn't slept well one night. Several students even asked if she was getting sick. This morning, Elaina took extra care with her appearance in order to camouflage her haggard state as well as lift her spirits. While her external appearance had improved, her spirits were as dreary as they had been last Saturday after Jake's visit.

She and Anna had wordlessly taken a vow of silence regarding Ted and Willis. The two sisters worked the rest of the day and finished painting the living room. Elaina could now say she was a "lady in red." The wild part was, she loved it.

"Anna, you were right as always," she said as if her sister were present. "At least when it comes to home decor." Elaina plopped into her chair, rested her head on the cushioned back, and examined the rows of books lining her shelves. Every volume was a trophy…a testimony to Elaina's academic success.

I'm a bookworm extraordinaire, she thought, *but I don't have what it takes to get my man.* Elaina closed her eyes and locked her jaw. *Ted, why did you have to go and get yourself engaged?*

A tap on the door interrupted her misery. Fully expecting a student, Elaina opened her eyes and frowned. She was in no mood to explain a grade or assist with an assignment. The person knocked again. With a resigned grimace, she straightened in her chair and attempted to erase all heartache from her expression. Elaina stood and snapped open her briefcase.

"Come in," she casually called and took a stack of research papers from her case.

The door swung inward and a familiar face smiled his greeting. "Is Dr. Woods in?" Bryan Brixby asked.

"Hi there!" Elaina exclaimed and dropped the papers atop her desk. "What brings you here?" She rounded the desk, and they exchanged a hug.

"I was going to call but happened to be in your neck of the woods and decided I ought to just stop in. I've never been to your office." Bryan gazed around the room. "It's nice and…bookish," he said and approached one of the shelves.

"Well, what did you expect?" Elaina questioned. "That's what I do for a living—talk about books."

"Somehow, I expected more of you," he teased and removed a volume from the shelf. "'Sir Gawain and the Green Knight,'" Bryan mused. "Aaahhh, I love this book. The first time I read it I was in high school English." He turned the treasure over and examined the back as if it were gold-plated.

"That's one of my favorites, too," Elaina explained. "I read it about once a year just for fun!"

"The green knight is my favorite character," Bryan claimed. "He's like hulk—"

"Only better!" the two finished in unison.

"Oh man." Bryan laughed, and Elaina couldn't remember ever seeing the doctor so jovial. "I can tell you're on today," he said.

Elaina settled to the desk's edge and removed her glasses. Wearily, she rubbed her brows and sighed. "Really, I'm exhausted," she confessed. "I haven't had that great of a week."

"And what woman would in your position?" Bryan placed the title back on the shelf.

"And what position is that?" The question popped out before Elaina's tired mind deduced that Bryan must know of Ted's engagement by now.

"The rumor mills are hot and fast these days." Bryan slipped his overcoat off, and Elaina was surprised to see he wore surgery scrubs. "Pardon my attire," he said and looked at the blue shirt and pants, "some days I just can't make myself do the dress clothes thing. This is as close as I can get to sweats and get away with it."

"I hear you." Elaina peered at her bulky sweater that covered baggy wool slacks with elastic in the waist. The weatherman had been threatening snow for a week. Yesterday, a cold rain dampened the whole day. Elaina had no desire to trudge through snow or more rain in heels and a suit.

"Anyway," Bryan leaned against the door jamb, "Jeanna tells me Ted is engaged to Lorna Starr. Is that correct?"

Elaina bent to retrieve a misdirected paper wad and tossed it into her metal trash can. "Correctamundo," she said as if she were agreeing to eat earthworms.

"Jeanna has talked to me about Lorna several times. By her own admission, her niece is flighty and, er, shallow at times."

"Hmmm," Elaina responded and wondered where this conversation was going.

"I understand that Ted's mother is so dead set against the marriage she's essentially kicked him out of all participation in the family fortune and that he's finally sticking to his guns to become a minister of music."

"For one so quiet, you know so much," Elaina said as if she were a prophetess of wisdom.

"I try," he affirmed.

Elaina wiggled the phone cord and debated if the good doctor possessed some sadistic need to emotionally torture people. Several times, he had hinted that he knew of Elaina and Ted's romance. *Surely the guy knows it kills me to talk about all this,* she thought.

"Meanwhile," he rubbed his hands together as if he were cooking up the deal of the century, "I've got an offer for him. There's a country church about ten miles north of my home that is in desperate need of a minister of music. The pastor and I are good friends. I mentioned Ted to him yesterday at our community men's prayer breakfast, and he jumped all over the idea. I've got his name and number here." Bryan fished in his pocket until he pulled out a yellow slip of note paper.

He extended the paper to Elaina. "The salary is modest, but they do offer a nice brick home along with all utilities paid and a small car allowance."

Elaina accepted the note and then questioned Bryan's motive in sharing the information with her. "Why are you telling *me* this?" she asked and held the paper by the corner. It sagged away from her fingertips.

"I hardly know Ted," Bryan explained. "From what I understand, the two of you have been known to be…" his brows quirked, "…close. I thought maybe the suggestion would come better from you." His kind eyes hinted at a soft challenge.

"Me?" she squeaked and examined the paper as if it were poison.

"Yes. I think the information should come from a friend. You know, someone who understands how important such a position will be to him…*and* to his fiancée." The challenge settled into his every syllable.

Elaina narrowed her eyes. After reading the name and number, she vaguely recognized the reverend as someone Jeanna had mentioned in passing. Bryan's silent dare began to take on credence.

"Maybe you're right." Elaina leaned toward her briefcase and tucked the note in an interior pocket. "I guess I should be the one to share the information."

"Good." Bryan stood and picked up his overcoat. "And you know," he added with a conniving smirk, "these days everyone is so into all these impersonal communication devices like cell phones and e-mail and voice mail, I think this information should be delivered in person. Don't you?"

"In person?" Elaina repeated. Like a mouse mesmerized by a cunning cobra, Elaina realized what she had just agreed to. She jumped away from Bryan and bumped into the wall.

"Wait a minute...wait a minute...wait a minute," she protested and held up her hands, palms outward. "I'm not sure I'm the one here." She recalled every contour of Ted's face, every nuance of his expressions. Elaina pictured herself in his apartment, face to face with the man she had loved and lost.

Bryan really must be trying to torment me, she thought. *Besides all that, what if Lorna's there?*

"I think today would be a good day to do this." Bryan examined the ends of his blunt fingernails as if Elaina had never protested.

"Why is that?"

"Lorna is visiting Jeanna."

"How do you *know* all this stuff about everyone?" Elaina demanded and relaxed against the wall.

"Jeanna," he simply stated. "What can I say? She calls me several times a week and even makes her maid bake for me. She's convinced I'm desperately lonely and starving to death because I don't have a wife. I think she's adopted me." His face softened.

"Anyway, I just thought you might, er, enjoy a little chat with Ted. You know, before he gets married." The shrewd glint returned in his eyes. "Think about it. If you don't think so, then call me. I'll make other arrangements to make sure Ted gets the info." Elaina watched as he shrugged back into his overcoat and stepped toward the door.

"See ya," he said with a wink, then exited the room and snapped the door closed.

Elaina suspected that he well knew what her decision would be. She dropped into her chair and retrieved the note from her briefcase. Elaina examined the name and number and considered the opportunity to see Ted one more time before he married Lorna. She contemplated the money-hungry dame who had insisted that Ted would eventually go on tour. Elaina wondered if Ted's actually accepting a ministry position would make Lorna break off the relationship. Bryan had said as much without ever verbalizing the conjecture. For a few seconds, he nearly even convinced Elaina.

But who would support Lorna then? Elaina thought. Then she determined that while Lorna would be disappointed by Ted's sudden lack of wealth she would never break the engagement.

"He's still her meal ticket," she declared. *Lorna might not be the smartest woman on the planet, but she knows a good thing when she sees it.*

She fingered a strand of her cropped hair and wondered if Ted had possessed the foresight to save some money in his own account. All week Elaina hoped he wasn't left without a means to the basic necessities of life. *Maybe I should offer him a loan,* she thought.

Elaina stroked the note as if it bore some treasured sonnet, penned for her alone. The idea of talking to Ted…of seeing him one last time…of memorizing every detail of his apartment would provide Elaina with a special memory she could treasure forever. And when Ted was out of her life, she would have those cherished moments she could always remember.

Lord help me, she prayed, *I'm so hopelessly in love I'm grasping for any means to spend time with him.*

She glanced at her gold watch. Four-thirty swiftly approached. Elaina placed the note back into her briefcase and sealed her final decision.

Thirty-Two

Within ten minutes Elaina hovered at Ted's apartment door and tried to scrounge together the courage to ring the bell. She knew he was home. His Corvette claimed a parking place near the building's entrance. The sight of the red sportscar eased Elaina's worries about Ted's finances. Obviously he hadn't been forced to liquidate his possessions.

The second story hallway looked much like Elaina's apartment building during college, except the wider staircase, mahogany banisters, and fashionable color scheme suggested the rent was decidedly higher. Nevertheless, the attractive decor offered no encouragement to fulfill her goal. The faint scent of oriental food attested that someone had recently returned with some take-out. The tantalizing smell did nothing to tempt Elaina's quivering stomach.

She fingered the note in her suede coat pocket, and panic swept over her. *This is crazy,* she thought. *What if Ted doesn't want to see me? What if Jeanna dropped Lorna off here this afternoon? Bryan may have some informational tidbits, but he's not omniscient.*

The cruelty of seeing Lorna at Ted's place proved too big an obstacle. Overcome by a current of fear, Elaina backed away from the door. Without another glance at Ted's apartment, she rushed the few steps toward the stairway.

I'll give the information to Jeanna, she thought. *She'll be glad to tell him.*

A swish and clunk preceded Ted's doorknob clattering. Elaina, perched on the top step, squeezed the handrail and hunched her shoulders. The door sighed open. Footsteps entered the hallway.

"Elaina?" Ted's sonorous voice echoed down the stairwell.

She looked over her shoulder. Dressed in a pair of sweats, he stood two yards away. His socked feet suggested he hadn't been going out, which didn't logically fit his opening the door…unless he somehow knew she was there.

"Hi, Ted," Elaina pressed the greeting past her tightened throat.

"Hello," he replied as she gradually faced him.

"I…" Her gaze faltered toward his feet. Her silent question floated between them.

He wiggled his toes. "I saw you drive up," he admitted. "I was looking out the window to see if it was snowing yet. They've been predicting it all day, and they say it's supposed to be pretty bad."

"Yes."

"After I saw you drive up, I…looked through the peephole until I saw you on the landing."

His soft admission unleashed a sea of warmth within Elaina. She swallowed and prayed she could catch her breath.

"Would you like to come in?" he asked, his voice laden with curiosity.

"Well, I…" Elaina considered handing him the piece of paper and dashing away like an embarrassed schoolgirl passing a love note. Instead, she feigned a calm demeanor and focused just past Ted's shoulder. "That would probably be the best thing at this point," she said.

Ted moved back into the apartment and swung the door open in a wide greeting. "Welcome to my humble abode," he said.

Elaina walked past him and into an oversized room which featured a baby grand piano as the center of focus. The black-and-white decor accented the ebony instrument's glossy finish, and the whole effect created a reverent appeal. As Ted snapped the door shut, Elaina pictured Ted laboring at the piano, absorbing the ambiance of a melody hidden in his heart.

"Well, this is nice," she squeaked out while thankfully noting an absence of Lorna...or poverty.

"Thanks. I've enjoyed it."

Elaina, terrified to look into Ted's eyes, observed her loafers. The strong smell of oriental food verified that Ted was the one who'd just enjoyed take-out.

"Want me to take your coat?" he babbled. "I was just opening my dinner. I went to the corner for some Chinese. Do you want to join me? I've got plenty. You know how those restaurants always give you enough for an army." He pointed through a doorway.

She glimpsed a black-lacquered dining table that beckoned her to enjoy a meal with Ted. Her hands still in the pockets, Elaina clutched at the nylon lining, and the note crumpled against her palm. "No," she hurried, "that's okay. I won't be here long. I just..."

After extracting the note from her pocket, she extended it toward Ted. "Bryan Brixby came by my office this afternoon," she explained as Ted accepted the piece of paper. "He said this pastor is looking for a full-time minister of music." She studied the note and refused to look elsewhere. "The church is only about ten miles from Bryan's place. They're not big, but they do offer a house and all utilities, along with a moderate salary. Bryan also said something about a small car allowance."

Ted opened the paper and read the man's name and number. "Wow! This is great!" he said. "I was getting ready to send out résumés." He pointed toward a compact computer desk tucked in a corner behind the piano. A scattering of papers validated his words.

"I was sorry to hear about your mom and the way she—" Elaina pressed her jacket's zipper tongue between her forefinger and thumb.

"So you've already heard?"

"The grapevine is swift," she explained, "especially when your brother-in-law is my half-brother."

Ted nodded. "Actually, I'm relieved about what Mom did."

The nuance of Ted's voice insisted she make eye contact. Elaina's gaze melted into the inky depths of his eyes. All she encountered was honesty laced with desperation that hinted he loved her as much as she loved him. No trace of Lorna clouded his soul. None.

All the past was swept away, and Elaina perceived that no matter why Ted implied he had grown to love Lorna he had not. *That song New Year's Eve really was for me,* she thought. The conviction would not be denied.

Overcome by the impact, Elaina nearly fell to her knees and started begging, "Please don't marry Lorna, Ted! You don't have to! She doesn't love you. Not really! I do! I do! Not Lorna! Please, please don't marry Lorna!"

Instead, Elaina stoically responded to his last statement. "I wondered if you might be relieved."

Ted narrowed his eyes and inched his head forward as if he were trying to decipher her meaning. For a second, Elaina wondered if he might be as disconcerted by their meeting as she.

Then a cloak of understanding settled upon his features. "For the first time in my adult life, I'm free. Do you know how good that feels?" He spread one arm as if he were an eagle preparing for flight.

"I can only imagine." *I only wish we could be free together.*

"Looking back, I can't believe I let Mom get away with a lot of the stuff she did. I guess," he tucked his hand into his shirt's front pocket, "I guess I was just so used to that pattern of behavior

I let her continue on. That plus..." He hesitated as regret trotted across his face. "I hate to admit it, but you get used to having money. The idea of not having it can be well, not exactly attractive." He lifted one brow. "In the end, we'd be talking about 5.3 million dollars. That's nothing to sneeze at."

"I understand. I wasn't exactly thrilled with losing my dad's inheritance, either." Elaina absorbed every angle of Ted's face and vowed to keep the memory as fresh in ten years as it was now.

"Yes, that would be hard," Ted agreed.

"But thankfully, my mom did wind up with some of my Dad's personal savings. I can deal with not coming away with much, but I'd have struggled way more if she got nothing."

"I'm glad I saved along the way as well," Ted said. "I'm not rolling in dough, but I do have a solid nest egg that Mom can't touch. It's in my name. She doesn't even know about it."

"Good." Elaina took a deep breath and released it. "I've been worried about that. I was hoping you wouldn't go hungry between now and the time you get a job."

An admiring light flickered in Ted's eyes, and Elaina was reminded of the hours they'd spent together...of the moments when Ted nearly kissed her.

"Thanks for thinking of me," his quiet tone caressed her soul, and Elaina bottled her tears for a lonely night. Ted cleared his throat and examined the note as if it were written in some foreign language he couldn't decipher. "I guess, then, that I can thank you for this lead."

"No, not really," Elaina said. "Bryan just dropped by today, like I said, and I thought you might want the information as soon as you could get it." Her rising body heat suggested that either she needed to remove her coat or step into a temperature that befit layers of clothing.

"Well, I appreciate this more than you'll ever know." His gaze bathed her in a longing that transcended the ages.

Don't marry Lorna! The plea stormed her thoughts so strongly Elaina pressed her lips between her teeth to stop herself from blurting it.

"I guess that's it then," she rasped and couldn't supress the urge to run before she said something she might regret. "I'll just be going." Before Ted had the chance to respond, Elaina whipped open the door, scurried into the hall, and tackled the stairway.

When she rounded the first landing, pivoted to the right, and started down the second section of stairs, Elaina glimpsed a movement above. She looked upward to encounter Ted's appraisal. He hovered over the landing's rail and flooded Elaina with a silent vow of everlasting love. She caught her breath and stood motionless as dampness oozed from her palms. Like a woman dying of hunger, Elaina consumed every trace of his adoration and stored the memory to cherish for life.

The urge to lunge back up the staircase proved so strong that Elaina forced herself to run down the final flights of stairs. Only when she burst through the apartment entry and into the twenty-five-degree air did she halt for a startled appraisal of the scene before her. The promised snow had at last arrived. Huge flakes filled the air like millions of feathers floating to the icy ground. The wind whipped the snow into swirling columns that stung her cheeks. Dismayed, Elaina observed Ted's red Corvette, parked within touching distance. Only a tad of snow had accumulated upon the windshield wipers. She glanced at the parking lot, now dusted in thin threads of white. Elaina relaxed in knowing that driving safety wouldn't be affected yet.

She pulled her car keys from her pants pocket, hurtled toward her Honda, and scampered into the driver's seat. After dashing snow from her hair, Elaina removed her glasses and rubbed them on the hem of her sweater. When she replaced them and prepared to crank the engine, her cell phone played Beethoven's Fifth from the backseat.

"Oh great," Elaina breathed. She considered not answering and returning the call when she got home. But intuition suggested she should make the effort to answer. Elaina stretched to the backseat and snagged her sling bag from near her briefcase. Before answering the call, she noted her mother's name on the screen.

Once Elaina connected the call, Margaret Woods gave her no chance for a greeting. "Elaina," she fretted, "I'm worried about Anna."

Thirty-Three

An ominous precognition clutched Elaina, and she imagined all sorts of awful scenarios, including Anna's having fallen so deeply into depression she couldn't turn back. Thoughts of her recent encounter with Ted faded in the wake of concern for her sister.

"She left here at about two," her mom said. "She's been going to the library some this week and also for some long drives."

"Anna's been going to the library?" Elaina asked and wrinkled her forehead. "*Our* Anna?"

"Yes. She reads quite a bit. You just never see her."

"Ooookaaaay," Elaina dragged the word out and angled her head while trying to comprehend this new fact.

"Anyway, I've been glad she's going out some because at least she's not sleeping half the day away. Like I said," Margaret hurried, "she's been gone since two. She left her cell phone here after I told her to make sure she had it about three times. You know how absentminded she can be."

Elaina nodded.

"Now it's snowing, and she's not home yet!" Margaret's voice wobbled. "I just have this awful feeling that she's in some kind of trouble out there. She's not used to driving in snow."

"But it's barely started!" The icy temperature began to penetrate Elaina past all comfort, and she cranked the engine.

"In town maybe, but not out here!" Margaret said. "Remember, we're ten miles north of you. It's been snowing here for an hour. The ground and road are covered."

"Oh," Elaina said. "I guess the meteorologists were right. Looks like we're in for a big one." She flipped her windshield wipers on low. A line of snow scaled up her windshield and flaked off while hundreds more fell in their place.

"I know. And I'm worried sick. I called Bryan, too, but he hasn't seen her."

"Should he have?" Elaina asked.

"Well, they went to lunch yesterday, and—"

"They did?" she questioned. Feeling as if Anna were living a secret life, Elaina now understood Bryan's cheerful demeanor during his brief visit. "Was that the first time?" *Reading...eating out with Bryan...* she thought. *What's next? Sky diving?*

"Actually, yes, it was their first time. I was thrilled when Anna agreed yesterday. But, anyway, I thought maybe they were together again today. Oh, wait a minute," she blurted, "someone's beeping in on me!"

Elaina flipped on her heater. With the tepid blast of air chasing away her chills, she began the short drive to her home. Her mind settled upon the potential that Anna really was stranded somewhere. Thoughts of her sister caught out in the arctic air darkened her spirit past all spheres of tranquillity. She was turning out of the parking lot when Margaret's voice penetrated her worries.

"That was Bryan," she explained. "He's going out to look for Anna. He just now got home and says he's got some snow chains he can put on his tires. He said she told him yesterday that she's been going to that country store and restaurant up the road for their cappuccino. He's going to call them first and then go from there."

"Oh good." Elaina relaxed against her seat. "Look, tomorrow's Saturday. Why don't I throw some things into an overnight bag and head that way. If we get snowed in, I can just spend the night. That way you'll have someone with you until we hear from Bryan."

"Are you sure you can make it out here?" Margaret asked.

Elaina eyed the neighborhood road she now cruised down. The few cars that passed dispersed the gauze-like snow, leaving the road still safe for travel.

"It's really not that bad in town, Mom," she assured. "I'll be really careful once I start north."

"Okay then," Margaret agreed. "But call me every few minutes so I know you're okay."

"I'll be glad to," Elaina acquiesced before bidding adieu and disconnecting the call.

Anna sat in the car until the frigid air seeped beneath her coat. A rash of chills covered her body like the sweep of Father Winter's glacial fingers.

"Stupid dog," she muttered and undid her seat belt. A sash of pain darted across her chest, and Anna massaged the path the seatbelt had taken when she slammed on her brakes. Unfortunately, the snow-laden road provided no friction for her locked tires. The front of her car rammed into a ditch before Anna had time to even pray for divine assistance.

She reached into her Gucci bag's side pocket, fully expecting her cell phone to provide the solution to her problem. But her fingers encountered nothing. Anna frowned, hoisted her bag onto her lap, and pulled the pocket wide. Nothing.

"Nuts!" she whispered and dug through the purse's jumbled contents. No phone in sight. Like a haunting mantra from the past, her mother's voice floated across her memory, "Don't forget your cell phone, Anna! It's on the dining room table. They're predicting snow. Are you sure you even want to go out?"

Anna had disregarded her mother's concern, scoffing at the prospect of snow. In her estimation, the meteorologists were a bunch of obsessive compulsive whine-bags. They'd been threatening snow for a week and nothing had happened.

She whimpered. The wind shoved the downy flakes against her windshield until a mantle of white made her feel as if she were being locked inside a cold casket. Anna tossed her purse into the passenger seat, opened the door, and stepped into the approaching night. She hurried around the front of the Ford to assess the situation. Both tires were wedged into a puddle of glassy dark water that testified to yesterday's rain.

"Shoot!" Anna stewed and kicked the side of the car with her pointed-toe pump. Her big toe throbbed in protest and Anna stomped. She shoved her hands into the pockets of her raw silk jacket and looked up and down the country road, five miles from her home. No vehicles in sight. She'd taken this road because someone at the restaurant told her Nancy Moncleave's mansion was just over the hill.

This morning Anna thought that seeing the place Willis stayed might bring some closure over his abandonment. During the last few weeks, she came to realize that Bryan Brixby was one of the nicest men she had ever met. Problem was, Anna couldn't begin to fall in love with him, no matter how hard she tried. All her miserable spirit could insist was that there never would be another man for her and that life might not be worth living without Willis.

So Anna had driven over hill after timber-laden hill in desperate search of some reprieve from the past. While she had spotted several farmhouses, she encountered no signs of the grandiose mansion the restaurant owner described. Now not only was she lost, but she was stranded and freezing.

A fresh shiver wracked her body. Anna's teeth clattered, and she clamped them together. A pall of pending darkness hovered across the tree-strewn pastures like a wicked warlock ready to snuff out the life of any who protested its growing intensity. With the darkness came heavier snow. With the snow, more tremors. Anna's jaw shook, and her upper torso quivered in response.

I could freeze to death out here, she flippantly thought and then frowned as reality sank in. Every time one of these freezes occurred, there was always a news report about some poor soul who died due to a car wreck or hypothermia. Until now, Anna never anticipated herself as a news statistic. Frantically, she examined the expansive stretch of cow pastures and spotted an eastern light piercing the invasive shadows.

A gust of wind whined through the bare trees and slammed snow against her cheeks and lashes like pinpoints of ice. Anna dashed at the flakes and ran her leather glove along the top of her head. Then she pulled up her jacket hood. With her eyes shielded, she better detected the light's source.

"Looks like a yard light," she said. A surge of warm relief momentarily assuaged her shivers. Squaring her shoulders, Anna determined she must trek half a mile to the home. She followed the road until she came upon a lane with a mailbox next to it. "Yes!" she whispered and breathed a prayer of thanks.

She turned right onto the snow-covered path. Only the embankment, carved by years of use, offered a promise that Anna followed the right path. When she had spanned a fourth of the distance to the home, her feet protested the idea of hiking in spike heels. The gooseflesh along her thighs made her wish her jeans were thicker or her jacket longer.

Not much farther, not much farther, she assured herself and then stopped in her tracks. "Oh my," she cried and looked at her arms as if one had fallen off. "I left my purse!" Anna turned around and spotted her car, a smudge of red in the snowy twilight.

Without another thought, Anna surged back the way she came. When she ran from the lane and turned left onto the main road, her shoe skidded along the white-crested gravel. Anna rotated her arms to regain her wavering balance but to no avail. The ditch filled with dirty water beckoned like a conniving villain ready to take Anna in and release her only to death.

"Oh no...oh no...oh no..." Anna pleaded while toppling forward.

Her temple banged the metal culvert. She splashed into the water. The shock of icy liquid against her face and neck lasted only an instant before the shadows blotted out the last vestiges of light. Anna rolled to her side and struggled against the cloak of unconsciousness.

Her last thought before slipping into the fathomless chasm involved Willis and the question that had plagued her for weeks, *Is life worth living without him?* Numbness crept in, alleviating the annoying ability to feel, and Anna resolved that freezing to death might not be so bad after all.

Thirty-Four

Elaina sat on the bay window settee and searched the empty night for any sign of Bryan's headlights. The snow, twirling to the earth, took on an ominous aura in the porch light's beam as if each flake were a portal to doom. An hour had passed since Elaina arrived at the cottage. With that hour came a flood of anxiety so intense it rivaled every grief she had ever known.

The cheerful smell of fresh baked brownies bespoke Margaret's afternoon cooking spree and belied the room's dire milieu. The grandfather clock's incessant ticking seemed to announce Anna's imminent death. Margaret's gentle weeping from the couch strengthened Elaina's own temptation to cry. Instead, she clutched her cell phone in one hand and balled the other into a tight fist.

Bryan had called Margaret after he talked with the country restaurant and store. Sure enough, Anna had been there and drank her cappuccino. The owner reported answering Anna's questions about the locale of Nancy Moncleave's mansion. Bryan headed down the road Anna took and told Margaret he would call the second he found her.

But how do I know he hasn't gotten trapped in this mess? Elaina thought. *If he doesn't call within ten minutes, I'm calling him!* She checked her watch and noted the time: six-o-one.

Her cell phone emitted the first note of Beethoven's Fifth, and Elaina gave it no chance to continue. "Hello, Bryan?" she questioned without consulting the caller ID screen.

"Yes, it's me," he said, his voice grim. "I found her."

"You found her?" Elaina jumped up.

"Yes, but I've got some bad news."

Elaina clutched her throat and faced her gray-faced mom. "Please don't say she's dead," she begged. "I can't stand it—"

"No, she's alive," Bryan asserted. "But she slid her car into a ditch. The best I can tell, she tried to walk to the nearest house but somehow fell into a ditch and hit her temple. The ditch was full of water. She's soaking wet and unconscious. I'm certain she's fallen into hypothermia. That's not a good thing, Elaina," he said, a dreadful undertow to his voice. "I just got her wet coat off and wrapped her up in my jacket in the backseat."

"Do you think she'll make it?" Elaina asked as her mother lunged up and fell into her arms.

"Is Anna going to die?" she moaned, her puffy eyes brimming with sorrow.

"Just a minute, Bryan," Elaina rushed and then fought to brace her mother. "Bryan found her," she soothed, her voice shaking. "She's unconscious but definitely alive."

Elaina assisted her mom as she slid to the settee's edge and decided not to mention the hypothermia.

"Oh God in heaven, don't let my baby die," Margaret groaned. She hugged herself and rocked back and forth.

"Bryan? Are you there?" Elaina asked into the receiver, her voice stiff against any new show of emotion. One of them needed to be strong.

"Yes. Listen, I need to go," Bryan said. "It's hard driving in this stuff with two hands, much less holding a cell phone. I'm heading to the hospital now as quickly as I can. I've called an ambulance and asked them to meet me on the way. As a matter of fact, if I'm not mistaken, I think I see their lights in the distance."

"Okay, 'bye," Elaina croaked and disconnected the call. "He's got Anna," she repeated. "He's called the ambulance. They're meeting him on the way and taking her to the emergency room."

"Wh–what happened?" Margaret gripped Elaina's arm.

"She slid off into a ditch and got out to try to walk to the nearest house. She fell and hit her head. When Bryan found her she was unconscious." Elaina laced each word with love and assurance. "Mom, I really do think she'll be okay."

"What are you not telling me, Elaina?" Margaret mopped at her eyes with a bedraggled tissue. "And don't try to act like you don't know what I'm talking about." She clamped her teeth together. "This is not a time for games."

Elaina looked at the Persian rug. "He also said he thinks she has hypothermia and that that isn't good."

"What all does hypothermia involve?" she worried.

"I don't know much about it," Elaina admitted, "just that it means your body temperature lowers and that it can be dangerous."

"I've got to get to her!" Margaret stood.

"Mom," Elaina began, "I had to creep half the way out here, and that was an hour ago. The snow hasn't even offered to dissipate." Elaina anxiously eyed the window, now sporting a strip of snow at the base.

"I don't care if we have to call the county and pay them to come out here with a snowplow," Margaret stated. She stood on her toes. Her face grew red. And she yanked on the front of her sweater. "I'm going to the hospital!"

"Okay, okay!" Elaina adjusted her glasses and then placed her hand atop her head. "Let's think about this," she reasoned. "Maybe we can come up with a safe way to get to town. We don't want to fall off in the ditch, too, you know."

"Noah!" Margaret yanked Elaina's cell phone from her grip. "He has a four-wheeler he takes hunting with him! He'll drive us to town!" She pressed a rapid series of numbers into the phone and soon made arrangements for their transport to the hospital.

The next twenty-four hours were the most dreadful Elaina had ever lived. Even though her father's death had been heart-wrenching, his declining health prepared the whole family for the inevitable. Elaina had never been prepared for Anna's possible death. But that was exactly what she was facing—unless a miracle occurred.

Elaina listened to so many appalling reports from ICU that she dreaded the sight of the stern-faced nurse who had been on duty all day. Thankfully, Bryan signed himself in as Anna's doctor and made certain she received the ultimate care, with family reports every two hours. The ICU staff hadn't shirked their responsibility.

She checked her watch and leaned toward her mother. "We're due another report," she said.

"Heaven help us," Margaret whimpered, "every time they come out it keeps getting worse. First her kidneys aren't working right...next, her vital signs are erratic...her fever won't come down...they suspected pneumonia and then confirmed it...they had to put her on a respirator. What's next?" She pressed her puffy eyes.

Fixing her gaze upon the row of vending machines, Elaina proposed no options. She had spent a hapless night trying to doze on the waiting room's couch. The day had been filled with various people filing in and out of the ICU waiting room. The smell of stale coffee intensified Elaina's growing aversion for the room. Now night had descended upon them again. Her gritty eyes demanded she arrange for a room in the hotel across the street, but her numb mind insisted she stay near her sister.

Once news of Anna's wreck spread, Elaina's cell phone rang all day—people from the neighborhood, their friends from

Oklahoma City, and the congregation of their present church. The town had been forced to shut down due to the ten-inch snowfall they were dubbing the winter storm of the decade, so no visitors could arrive. But those stranded at home had lacked no scruples in repeatedly calling to check on Anna.

Elaina and Margaret took turns answering the phone. Fortunately, Margaret had answered when Ted called. Elaina had been eating in the cafeteria. She didn't think she could have withstood the double pressure of their strained love along with sharing details of Anna's tragic experience.

She watched the waiting room doorway, fully expecting the nurse to arrive within the minute. Right on time, a medical messenger halted in the doorway. Instead of the nurse, Bryan Brixby stopped and perused the sizable room. His haggard features and tousled hair reminded Elaina that not only had he stayed with them most of the night, he had also been on call today. Once he spotted them, Elaina stood. As he moved forward, Elaina recognized the portend of ghastly news in the depths of his green eyes.

"God, help us," Margaret prayed.

Bryan, dressed in the tired surgery scrubs from yesterday, stopped in front of Elaina. He glanced at Margaret and back to Elaina as if he hated having to share the new information with Anna's mother. "You better sit down," he finally said, his voice unsteady.

Elaina obeyed. He squatted in front of them and tugged on both sides of the stethoscope hanging around his neck. "Hypothermia can be evil," he began and concentrated on the tile. "Depending on the length of time a person has it, it can cause mild discomfort all the way to—" He stopped and worked his mouth.

"As you know, Anna's kidneys have not functioned quite right ever since she pulled out of the hypothermia. This can be a common effect. But now her kidneys are starting to show definite signs of failure," he spoke the words so quietly that Elaina barely heard him.

Margaret leaned forward. "What?" she asked.

Bryan observed Margaret with a compassion that looked as if it flowed from the throne room of God. "Her kidneys are failing," he repeated.

After clamping her fingers around Elaina's arm, Margaret silently stared past Bryan. Elaina covered her mom's hand with her own and blocked the option of another emotional release. Her mother had agonized most of the night as if Anna were already gone. Elaina suspected she was reliving her husband's death as well as laboring over Anna's plight.

"Where do we go from here?" Elaina asked, her voice reedy.

"We pray like crazy that she begins a rebound. If her kidneys completely fail, we'll think toward dialysis. I hate to do that because it permanently damages the kidneys." He eyed Margaret. "Also, dialysis is only good if—"

"Go ahead," Elaina croaked.

"If her other organs don't shut down on us as well. Her pulse is really erratic and weak. The pneumonia seems to be progressing. Right now," he labored over the final words, "we—we don't know if she'll make it through tonight." Bryan hung his head. His shoulders shook. He coughed. And then he stood. Before Elaina could ask another question, the doctor bustled from the room.

Elaina's mother slumped into the sofa's corner, covered her face with a pillow, and silently rocked back and forth.

"Mom, I'm going to see if I can find Bryan," Elaina said, "to—to ask if they'll bend the rules and let us stay with her tonight."

"Yes," Margaret moaned into the pillow.

She didn't have to go far to find Bryan. He stood around the corner near the elevators. One hand was pressed flat against the wall. His head hung, he rubbed his eyes with the other hand. Seeing him so disturbed left Elaina hard-pressed to control her emotions. She curled her fists and blinked against her stinging eyes.

Elaina waited until Bryan stepped away from the wall to make her presence known. She touched his arm. "Bryan," his name wobbled out.

He slowly turned. Placing his hands on his hips, Bryan looked at the ceiling and dispelled a long breath through puckered lips. "It's like Liza all over again," he rumbled. "I don't know what I'll do if—"

It's like Liza all over again. Bryan's words repeated in Elaina's mind and left her speechless. For the first time in her awareness of Bryan's attraction for Anna, she was stricken with the beginning of a new conviction. Why she hadn't seen it sooner or thought it sooner was anybody's guess. *Maybe because I've been so upset over Anna and Willis that I saw Bryan as such a better choice and missed the problem.*

But what if he doesn't really love Anna? Elaina thought. *Would he have been interested in her if she didn't remind him of Liza? What if his interest really is all about Liza and not about Anna at all?*

Dazed by her musing, Elaina's tired mind lacked the ability to feign composure this time. She backed away from Bryan and gaped at him as if he'd metamorphosized into a gargoyle before her eyes.

"Elaina?" Bryan questioned and neared. "You don't look good. Do you feel faint? Are you okay?"

He reached to support her, but Elaina shoved at his hand and stumbled farther away. "You don't really love Anna, do you?" she asked and slowly shook her head.

"What?" Bryan squinted his eyes.

"Anna. You don't love Anna. You still love Liza. This is about losing Liza for you—not losing Anna."

Bryan's exhausted features settled into confusion, too transparent to repudiate Elaina's assumptions. "I've lain awake at night and asked myself stuff just like that," he stated in a defeated voice. "When I was first attracted to Anna, I told myself it was just because she was like Liza, and it would wear off. Problem is," he pressed his index finger between his brows, "it hasn't. It's only gotten deeper and more intense. The more I'm with her, the more I love her."

"But do you love her as much as Liza?" Elaina queried, too tired and grouchy to pretend she wasn't full of doubts.

"Maybe more." He placed his hand upon Elaina's shoulder.

"More?" she echoed like a fatigued parrot.

"Look, Elaina," he said, "I know you love your sister more than anything in the world. I've watched you protect her like a mother hen. And I know you'd pretty much fight…" a gentle smile softened his features, "…the green knight for her," Bryan finished as a trio of nurses went by.

Elaina looked down. "It's true," she wobbled out.

"I know. I understand how you feel and why you'd feel that way. I can't say whether or not I'd have been attracted to Anna if she didn't remind me of Liza. After all, Anna is thirteen years younger than I am." Bryan removed his hand from her shoulder and stroked his goatee. "All I know is that I feel like I've found someone I can spend my life with—someone I really want to make happy. Do we always have to analyze everything half to death?" He gripped the back of his neck and hung his head. "Why can't we just accept that two people are finding each other and move on from there?"

Her eyes heavy, Elaina rubbed at them and absorbed Bryan's every word. The elevator bell chimed, the door sighed open, and a small group of people meandered into the walkway.

"For Pete's sake," Bryan continued, "I could convince myself that I'm really Anna's second choice after Willis. The brutal truth is neither one of us would be interested in the other if our first choice didn't go wrong. I mean, what about your own parents?" Bryan questioned. "Your dad wouldn't have married your mom if his first wife hadn't died. Do you think your mom in any way reminded him of his first wife?"

"I have no earthly idea," Elaina answered in a defeated voice. "I guess maybe I went off the deep end there—at least I hope I did." She stuck her tongue between her teeth and pressed.

"No." Bryan shook his head. "You want what's best for your sister. That's all. I'd do the same thing if I had a younger sister."

"And do you think she really is interested in you?" Elaina asked.

"Maybe," Bryan admitted with a mischievous lift of his chin. But his chin quivered. "We're talking about her as if we're sure she's going to make it."

"I know." Elaina stroked her forehead and gulped against the lump in her throat. "I really followed you out here to ask if you think they'd let us stay in the room with her tonight." Elaina shoved out the request and fought images of her sister in a casket.

He nodded and swallowed as if he shared Elaina's horror. "By all means. I'm going to her room now," he said. "That's part of what I came in there to tell you. In situations like this, it's good for the family to be as close as possible. There are too many reports of patients who come out of comas and say they heard their family talking to them. That and God's power might be the only things that stop her from dying. I'm no longer on call as of now. I'm planning to spend the night holding her hand. You and your mom are welcome to do the same."

Elaina backed away and pointed at him. "Okay, good. Wait for us right here. I'm going to get Mom, and we'll go with you."

Thirty-Five

A moan demanded release, but Anna could find no means. Her temple pulsated as if someone were striking it with a mallet. Trapped in a shroud of dusk, she lay motionless, unable to move against the gauze trapping her in a cloud of cotton. A constant hiss, a faint ding, the smell of antiseptic insisted she was no longer in the ditch. So did the warm lack of numbness. As Anna battled to decipher her locale, a desolate voice murmured that she shouldn't care…that since Willis was no longer in her world she should release her soul to the inevitable.

All her fighting ceased. She relaxed in the abyss and reveled in the freedom from caring. Her earthly problems grew dim as she floated ever closer to the center of peace. The shroud of dusk deepened to raven realms where images of Willis soon withered from memory. The serenity that beckoned proved too tempting to resist. A golden light, warm and captivating, wavered on the edge of the ebony realm. Entranced by the glow, she slipped ever closer to its balmy sphere and reached to embrace the Giver of Life standing in the light's center.

For years, *He* had been more important to her than anything. Anna longed to go back to the simple days before Willis…to the days when she loved her Lord with untainted abandonment. Anna urged her spirit forward to the bright image that oozed an everlasting love into every corridor of her soul. Gradually she grew nearer and nearer the light and longed for holy arms to embrace her for eternity.

Anna released the past with all its heartache. She begged the Giver of Light to forgive her wandering heart and vowed that no other person was more important. None. Only the Giver of Life, His love, and His eternal peace remained at the center of her soul. She extended her hands to welcome His embrace, only to find the chasm between them was still too great.

A deep voice, insistent and familiar, broke into her pursuits of peace and lured her back to awareness of her gauze-wrapped body. "Anna, oh Anna," the man wept. "You can't check out on me—not when I've just found you. Oh dear God, please, if You're listening, don't let her die."

Her throbbing head insisted she ignore the man, hasten toward the light, and forever escape pain and sorrow and life. A loving voice, holy and timeless, reverberated gently with a final answer she could not ignore, *No. Not now.*

"Anna! Listen to me." Warm hands, gentle yet firm, framed her face. "I'll do anything in the world for you. Anything. Do you hear me? I love you. I can't stop myself from loving you. If you die, they might as well put me in the casket with you." A sob punctuated the man's words. "Oh, Jesus, don't let her die!" he prayed.

She hovered on the precipice of the shroud of dusk and the raven realms and attempted to pinpoint the man's voice. *Willis!* she thought at first and then stopped the jubilation as soon as it occurred. *No, not Willis,* she decided.

Do I even want Willis anymore? The question blotted out the light on the horizon. Anna relived every moment with Willis Kenney, even the night he arrived with his wife and she fell to the floor weeping. *Why would I pine for someone who's so cruel?* she thought. *It makes no sense.*

The kind fingers caressed her cheeks. "I worship the ground you walk on," the stranger claimed. While his voice lacked Willis' rhythmic meter, it contained something Willis' voice never held: truth, integrity, stability.

"Anna, you've got to fight. If you don't, you are going to die. Do you hear me? Do you understand that you can't just give up on life like this? You've got too many good years left. Listen... listen to me, honey, if you would just realize how much I love you. We could get married and have a family. Anna, do you want to be a mother? Do you dream of traveling to Paris?"

Paris...Paris...I told someone about Paris, she thought. *A man... it was a man...this man. I told him while we drank cappuccino that I've always wanted to go to Paris. But who is he?*

Anna forgot the light. She forgot the lull of promised bliss. She disregarded her aching temple. She focused on one person and one alone...this man who said he worshiped the ground she walked on. *How many women dream of such a man but never find him?*

The raven realm lost hold. Vague images of the man began to swim through her mind. A full head of golden hair...green eyes that adored her every expression...broad shoulders strong enough to hold her through all life's blows yet gentle enough to cherish her forever.

I want that man, she thought. *I do want him. He's the most tender man I have ever met. I don't know why I've been so blind.*

"Good...good...Anna," his voice encouraged. "Your pulse is coming up. Your breathing is steadier. Keep on fighting, Anna. You can do it. Don't give up, honey. Listen, if you pull through, I promise I'll take you to Paris...for our honeymoon. We'll go and stay a month if that's what you want. We'll move there if you like. Just *please don't die!*"

His fingertips bit into her shoulders. Anna turned her head and winced.

The man released a stifled cry.

Her eyes sagged open, and she stared into the face of the man she now recalled so well—the countenance of Bryan Brixby. "Do you—do you pr–promise?" she stuttered.

"About what?" he cried. His wide eyes beacons of joy, he shook his head as if he couldn't remember a word he'd been saying.

"About—about P–Paris." Anna's weighted lids slid closed, and she attempted to raise one corner of her mouth.

"Yes!" he exclaimed. "Yes…yes…yes!" his voice boomed with conviction.

The rush of feet preempted the sound of an urgent feminine voice, "Dr. Brixby?"

"Go get her mother and sister—*now!* They went to the waiting room!"

~ ~

Elaina waved farewell to Bryan and her mother, who pulled away from her duplex's curb in Bryan's Lexus. Ever the servant, Bryan had agreed to drive Elaina and her mom home from the hospital since they'd arrived there at the hand of Noah Harley and his four-wheel drive. The snow, while still piled along the roadside, had melted from the streets during the night. Elaina squinted her scratchy eyes against the glare of white and knew she'd never look at snow the same again.

She stepped into her duplex and closed the door. The second Elaina turned the latch on her deadbolt lock, the dam on her emotions cracked. Rivulets of tears trickled from a soul exhausted from the vigil yet elated with Anna's miracle. She dropped her bag, lifted her hands to heaven, and spent several minutes in quiet wonder, thanking the Holy Creator.

The red walls pulsated with memories of Anna's vibrant nature and seemed a celebration of what God had done at three o'clock this morning. When Elaina's mother collapsed with exhaustion at one, Bryan had insisted Elaina take her to the waiting room where he arranged for a cot. Elaina stayed with her mother while Bryan remained with Anna. He promised to get them if her condition changed. After the nurse arrived with the news of Anna's awakening, Elaina held her mother up while she shed her final tears. This time, tears of thanksgiving. Anna had roused once more before they left for home; she even managed to smile for her mom and sister.

Never had Elaina been so simultaneously exhausted and thrilled. She considered her striped sofa's inviting cushions and decided walking to the bed was simply too taxing. Elaina counted the hours since she last awoke from a good night's sleep and calculated forty-eight. She slipped out of her low-backed loafers, grabbed an afghan from the brass quilt rack, dropped her glasses on the coffee table, and collapsed onto the couch.

After a sound season of sleep, a harsh banging invaded her rest. The ceaseless ring of a bell began the second the banging stopped. The bell halted, only to be followed by more pounding. Elaina opened her eyes and discovered herself on the living room couch. Despite the uncivil noise, she attempted to determine how she arrived here and what day it was. In a flash, every memory of Anna's contest with death replayed in her mind. With the memories came the realization that someone was at her door.

She tossed aside the covers, swung her feet to the floor, and examined her wristwatch. "Five o'clock?" she mumbled. Her mouth felt as if it were full of half-dried glue, and she tried to swallow as she stumbled forward.

The person continued to assault the door. "Elaina!" a familiar masculine voice yelled. "Elaina, wake up!"

Elaina grimaced as her hazy mind tried to place the familiar voice and tried to decide how the person knew she'd been asleep. An internal alarm's clang accompanied a new battery of doorbell chimes. *What if it's someone with bad news about Anna?*

Her fingers unsteady, Elaina wrestled with the dead bolt lock and then whisked open the door. "Willis!" she exclaimed. Her eyes wide, she gawked at the frenzied man. His eyes bugged. His short hair looked as if he'd pulled it into a fit of spikes. His chest heaved with ragged breathing.

"How is Anna?" he demanded and swooshed into her room without awaiting an invitation.

"Anna?" Her mind still dazed from sleep, Elaina gripped the doorknob and tried to comprehend the purpose of Willis' abrupt visit.

"Yes, Anna!" He grasped her upper arms, lowered his face to within inches of Elaina's, and said, "Jeanna called me this afternoon and told me she almost died. Is she okay? I went to the hospital but that...that...sorry excuse of a doctor of hers wouldn't let me see her and wouldn't tell me one blasted thing!" he roared. "I *hate* him!" The furor undulating from Willis punctuated his obsession.

Grappling to sort through Willis' presence, Elaina laid her hand on his arm. "Anna's fine," she soothed. "She really is."

He stumbled back until he crashed into her leather recliner. Willis collapsed against the cushion, and urgency slipped from his features. His heightened color diminished to the attractive tan that had so successfully turned Anna's head.

Elaina shut the door and began to piece together the reason for Willis' appearance.

"I looked through your curtains and saw you sleeping," he explained. "I'm sorry I woke you up."

"It's okay." Elaina yawned and retrieved her glasses from the coffee table. When she slid them up her nose Willis came into sharper focus. So did her former dislike of the man. Having assumed he used Anna as a mere plaything, Elaina was dumbfounded to recognize he cared.

"Do you mind if I go to the restroom and then get a bottle of water?" she asked. "I think I need some time to think here."

"No, that's fine."

"Want some water yourself?" She rubbed her temple and tried to adjust her drowsy mind to the new Willis.

"No."

After a trip to the bathroom, Elaina padded through her dining room and into the kitchen. She retrieved the bottled water, shut the refrigerator door, and turned around, only to encounter an unexpected person. Elaina jumped and yelped.

"Oh my word," she breathed and leaned against the refrigerator. "You scared me to death."

"Sorry." Willis scrubbed his fingers along his jaw. "I just wanted to see if your offer of water still stands."

"Uh, sure." Elaina extended a cold bottle to him and retrieved another. She covered a yawn and pointed toward the living room. "Want to go back to the living room and have a seat?"

"Actually, no." Willis twisted off the top of his water and guzzled it.

Elaina's tastebuds ached for a reprieve from the sleepy-mouth syndrome. She downed a fourth of her water before she attempted to speak again.

"I don't feel like sitting any more," Willis said. "I need you to agree to tell Anna something, and then I'll be gone." He shrugged out of his leather jacket and Elaina glimpsed a diamond-studded watch beneath the sleeve of his designer sweater.

A gift from his wife, no doubt, she thought.

"I need to tell you everything that happened," he began.

"I already know." Elaina never blinked. "You got Bryan's niece pregnant, abandoned her, made your aunt mad, got disinherited, dumped Anna, and married a woman with money because you need the money for child support."

"Is that all you think there is to it?" Willis demanded.

Elaina downed another gulp of water and shivered as the cold liquid slithered down her esophagus and into her stomach. "Is there more?"

"Lots more," he claimed. "As in I love your sister." While his anguished eyes suggested he was not lying, their expression didn't touch Bryan Brixby's passion.

"It's a little late for you to come to that realization, isn't it?" Elaina shoved up the sleeves of the rumpled sweater she'd been wearing since Friday morning.

"I knew the day I got married," he admitted, "but I convinced myself I'd forget Anna, and I was doing the right thing for the long run. I was just going to ignore her e-mails until she stopped, but my wife wouldn't. She made me write that letter and hand deliver it to Anna. I think she was afraid I'd—" He slammed his water on the counter. His jacket plopped to the floor.

"That you'd not mail it or something?" Elaina queried.

"She's really jealous," he ground out. His gaze took on the haunted expression of a beautiful leopard trapped in a bejeweled cage.

"You're a very attractive man. What woman in her position wouldn't be?" Elaina was tempted to feel sorry for him, but reminded herself he had abused Bryan's niece and broken Anna's heart.

"I was fine with everything at first. Sure it bothered me to see Anna hurt like that. But I told myself she was young, and she'd get over it. That all worked until I heard she nearly died, and then I lost it. I got in my car and drove here as quickly as I could—only to have that cad of a doctor refuse to let me see her. He acts like he owns her or something!"

"What good would it do for you to see her now?" Elaina asked. She set her half-empty water bottle on the counter. "All that would do is upset Anna all over again."

"But it would have given me a chance to explain," he insisted.

"So you've explained to me. Now *I'll* tell her."

Willis narrowed his eyes and inspected Elaina. "Promise?"

"Yes, I promise."

"Then will you also give her this?" He picked up his jacket, unzipped an inside pocket, retrieved a black velvet box, and extended it to Elaina.

"What is this?" she asked and accepted the box.

"Her engagement ring."

"You mean you actually bought one?"

Willis' mouth straightened. "Yes. Tell her I was going to give it to her when I said I would, but my aunt got up that morning screaming at me. She told me she was disinheriting me and cutting off my allowance. I'm human just like everyone else." Willis rubbed his chest and laid his jacket back on the counter. "I like to eat. I was used to that income, and I panicked. I'd made… friends with a lady during one of my trips to New York. I knew that all I'd have to do is give the nod and she'd marry me."

"I guess it helped that she had stacks of money?" Elaina opened the ring box and examined a one carat diamond solitaire sparkling with blue fire—the telltale signal of high quality.

"I was on the verge of a statutory rape trial," he growled. "I needed *something* to fall back on to keep my rear out of prison."

Maybe you should have behaved yourself in the first place, Elaina thought and snapped the ring box closed.

He glared at her as if he'd read her thoughts. "Do you know what that little tart did to me?" he demanded.

"Well, I know—"

"First, she lied to me about her age. I wouldn't have touched her with a ten-foot pole if I'd known she was only fifteen. Good grief!" He shoved his hand into the top of his hair and pulled straight up. "What kind of a lecher do you think I am anyway?"

"I—"

"And then she told me she'd get an abortion if I gave her the money. So I gave her the money!" he roared and shook his fists in midair. "Next thing I know, Bryan Brixby is calling me saying I've got a son and that they're thinking about filing rape charges against me. My aunt hears about the whole thing and dumps me, and I've got to have a way to come up with enough money to settle out of court or go to prison."

Ever thought of working regularly and building a savings account? Elaina wondered.

"Now, what would *you* do?" he finished.

The genuine terror marring his features stirred Elaina's empathy. The man had obviously freaked out when Bryan called him. His world as he knew it started caving in, and he reacted on the first impulse that hit him. *But that doesn't change his heartless behavior,* she reminded herself. She relived finding her sister in the fetal position, and her empathy abated.

Elaina considered the alternative to his not breaking Anna's heart. They would be engaged now…possibly married if Anna had chosen not to have a big wedding. And her sister would have pledged to spend the rest of her life with Willis. Elaina absorbed every angle of his classic good looks and wondered how long Willis would have stayed true to Anna. Too many women probably threw themselves at him, and he had proven he didn't have the character to withstand the temptation. Elaina imagined Anna with several small children and an adulterous husband who worked when he wanted and might come home at night or might not.

An unexpected surge of gratitude to Willis nearly brought her to her knees. His own impulsiveness had taken Anna out of his arms. Now Anna was free to marry a man with ten times his honor and constancy. Standing there in her kitchen, Elaina decided that whatever had drawn Bryan to Anna she would never again question his motives or his love. Life wasn't always perfect and the circumstances of everlasting love weren't always neat. Even if Bryan did still love Liza to some degree, she knew she could trust him with her little sister. He would never abandon her or hurt her or commit adultery against her. And that was worth a million times more than all the frivolous romance men like Willis would ever offer.

"You know what, Willis," Elaina said, "I'll tell Anna everything you've said." She extended the ring box back to him. "But I won't give her this."

"But—"

"No." Elaina held up her hand. "You broke up with her. You need to accept that the two of you can never be. If I give her this ring, it's only going to break her heart all over again. If you really love her like you say," she continued, "you'll take the diamond and see if you can get your money back."

He grudgingly accepted the box and opened it. Only the refrigerator's hum pierced the silence. Finally he mumbled, "You know what the wild part is?" Willis examined the stone, tilting the box as the ring caught the light. "The minute my aunt found out I agreed to pay child support, I was back in her good graces. Just like that." He snapped his fingers and tapped the lid down.

"And also back in her will and monthly allowance, I presume?" Elaina asked.

"Yes." His ginger-brown eyes reminded her of a dejected millionaire who'd just been tricked into trading all his gold for dust.

This time Elaina's sympathy didn't diminish so easily. While she was still thankful that Willis hadn't married her sister, she couldn't stop herself from pitying his miserable existence. He was paying child support to one woman, married to another, and in love with Anna.

"I'm sorry about how everything turned out the way it has for you, Willis," Elaina said. "I'll do my best to explain everything to Anna, just like I said." In a wave of heaven-sent grace, she gripped his arm in a reassuring gesture. "I *do* admire you for sticking to your child-support payments," she offered with a merciful smile.

"Thanks," he sighed and slipped the ring box into his pocket. "I haven't even seen the baby," he admitted as if he really wished otherwise, "but I signed papers to give permission for Bryan's brother to adopt him. I still have to pay child support as part of the agreement though. But at least this way the baby will have a home."

"Your wife wasn't interested in—"

"No way!" he erupted and raised his hands. "She doesn't even want any of her own children, let alone just mine!" He jiggled his leg and stroked the corners of his mouth.

"I've got to go," he croaked and retrieved his coat from the counter. "I sneaked off without telling my wife where I was going. She's out of town and will be flying into Tulsa by seven-thirty. Her mother's really sick, and I couldn't go with her because of my schedule. She's called me on my cell every few hours since she left."

Keeping tabs on you, no less, Elaina thought.

"I've got to meet her at the airport. If I'm not there it won't be pretty."

Willis shrugged back into his jacket and headed for the door as quickly as he'd entered the home. After Elaina extended a polite farewell, she shamelessly savored the sweet ambiance of poetic justice.

Thirty-Six

Within thirty-six hours, Anna was moved from the ICU to a private room. Within a week, her pneumonia was gone and she made the journey home. Elaina visited Anna every day, even after she returned home, and wasn't surprised to see a fresh bouquet of roses from Bryan every time the last one faded. While Anna didn't radiate with the exuberance she had during her relationship with Willis, Elaina recognized a more mature love awakening in her sister. For once, she decided not to question Anna about the budding relationship. Elaina and her mother simply watched with glee from the sidelines.

Once Anna's recovery was complete, Elaina recalled the promise she'd made to Willis. While she hated to invade Anna's growing happiness with past pain, she knew she must stand by her word. The opportunity came one Saturday afternoon, the last week of February. The two sisters had agreed to meet on SCU's scenic campus, enjoy a breezy picnic, and feed the ducks. The weather cooperated beautifully with clear skies, cheerful sunshine, and a sixty-degree warm spell that hinted that spring might be around the corner.

"Hard to believe it was snowing a month ago, isn't it?" Elaina asked. She tossed a snippet of day-old bread toward a mallard who dipped its beak under water and then slobbered down the treat.

"Yes, or that I was half dead," Anna said, her pink cheeks attesting to her full recovery. "I promise, I will never leave home without my cell phone again or drive in snow."

"Are you feeling okay?" Elaina asked. "Has this been too much for you today?"

"Oh, would you please stop it!" Anna playfully slapped at her sister's arm. "You're worse than Mom and Bryan put together."

Elaina fretfully tore her piece of bread into a dozen pieces and debated how best to introduce the Willis subject.

"You're dying with curiosity, aren't you?" Anna tossed her final shred of bread to the quacking ducks, zipped her windbreaker, and turned on Elaina with a silent challenge.

"Wh–what?" Elaina asked and tried to comprehend what Anna had said.

"About me and Bryan, silly," she said with a saucy grin. "But I've got to give it to you, sister dear, you haven't asked one question." She folded her arms. "Are you sick or what? This has got to be a record. This is the first boyfriend I've ever had who you haven't interrogated me about."

"Maybe it's because I approve of him," Elaina chided.

"Well, it's a good thing, because—" Anna covered her mouth, yet her blue eyes flashed with an exhilarating message.

"Because what?" Elaina insisted. She hurriedly threw her bread at the ducks and dusted her hands on the front of her denim jacket. "You've got a secret, don't you?" she demanded.

Anna nodded and removed her hand from her mouth. "Bryan and I promised each other we wouldn't tell anyone until it was official," she explained. "But if you were to guess…" She wiggled her eyebrows.

"You're engaged!" Elaina erupted.

Her sister nodded and motioned as if they were playing charades.

"You're engaged and…and…"

Anna held up her left hand and pointed to her ring finger.

"He's going to give you a ring," Elaina guessed.

"Yes, but when?" Anna injected. She touched the face of her watch.

"Next week?" Elaina asked.

Anna rammed her fingernail against her watch face, pressed her lips together, and widened her eyes.

"Next month?"

She violently shook her head.

"Sooner than next week or next month?"

Anna nodded, ran in place, and squealed.

"Today?" Elaina questioned.

"Yes, yes, yes! I just can't stand it. I can't keep the secret any longer. Yes! We've already picked out the ring together—last night. We left it to have it sized. We didn't want to announce the engagement yet because we wanted to have the ring and everything before we told everyone."

Elaina wrapped her arms around Anna and embraced her in a tight bear hug. "I'm so happy for you, Anna," she said and backed away. "Have you already set the date?"

"No. We're going to be waiting awhile on that—maybe a year or so. You know, to give us time to get to know each other better."

"Bryan is a wonderful man," Elaina said, and marveled that the sister who had planned to marry Willis the day she met him now showed the maturity to wait a year before marrying Bryan.

"I know. I just feel like such a fool that I didn't recognize that sooner," Anna admitted. "Looking back now, I think I wasted my whole fall on Willis when I could have been with Bryan. What's even more stupid is that I kept complaining about how old Bryan was, and Willis was only four years younger than Bryan. I just wish I had had the…the…uh…sense to not let Willis' good looks take over my reason."

"Ah, well," Elaina said and recognized the perfect opportunity to keep her word to Willis. "You know," she began and gazed over the shallow pond surrounded by oaks and pines. "Willis came to see me when you were in the hospital."

"He did?"

Elaina kept her focus upon sparkling water that rippled in the refreshing breeze. "Yes. He wanted me to tell you that…" She fastened the center button on her denim jacket and debated the best way to detail all the particulars of Willis' visit. At last Elaina chose to gently break the facts to Anna one at a time. Only when she finished did she look at her sister again.

Anna observed the ducks who paddled near the shore and honked for more bread. "So I guess he really did love me then," she whispered. A twist of sorrow pinched her features as she pulled her silky hair over her shoulder and stroked it.

"I guess," Elaina aquiesced. *As much as an impulsive man can fall in love in a month*, she added to herself.

For a wrinkle in time Elaina was certain Anna was going to cry. But after a hard sniff, she tossed her hair over her shoulder as if casting away all dark memories. "But I'm glad things turned out the way they did," she said with sage dignity. "I think Bryan is the better man on all fronts. Beside, I'm not sure how long my respect for Willis would have held up, knowing he got a fifteen-year-old pregnant. Ya know?"

Elaina squeezed Anna's shoulder. "That's about the smartest thing I've ever heard you say," she affirmed.

"Hey, I've got more smarts than you know!" Anna's jest erased all vestiges of the haunting past.

"I'm sure you do," Elaina countered.

"Bryan wants me to go to college in the fall," Anna declared. "He says I'm way smarter than I've given myself credit for. And I'm seriously considering majoring in nursing or something so he and I can work together. Maybe I'll even become a nurse practitioner!"

"What?"

"Yes." Anna lifted her chin. "He says I need to have an education to fall back on. I think he might be right."

"I wish *I'd* thought of that," Elaina chided. "I might have suggested the same thing."

"Now we're getting resentful, aren't we?" Anna quipped.

"Who me?" Elaina laid her hand over her chest. "No, never!"

"I'm going to get some more bread," Anna said with a sour grimace. "These ducks act like they haven't eaten in months."

"They're spoiled rotten." Elaina followed her sister up the slight incline to the picnic table. "Half the campus feeds them every day. I don't know what stops them from being the size of ostriches." After the sisters had both retrieved several slices of bread, Elaina's cell phone beeped to announce she had a voice mail.

"Did you hear my phone ring?" she asked Anna and reached toward her bag.

"Nope. You probably missed the signal or something out here in the middle of all these hills and buildings, and the phone just didn't ring. Happens to me all the time."

Elaina dialed her voice mail and listened to Jeanna Harley's urgent message. "Elaina, you are never going to believe this," she rattled, "but Lorna has eloped right here at the last minute—only a week before the wedding! Can you believe it? I'm beside myself. She called me. They're on their way to Egypt for a honeymoon. Mrs. Farris called me. She has absolutely gone berserk! I've *got* to go!" Without a farewell, Jeanna disconnected the call.

Her fingers curling into the slices of bread, Elaina collapsed onto the picnic table's bench.

"What?" Anna's demand floated from a distant land. "What is it? Elaina? Are you okay?"

Somehow, Elaina thought she would be able to deal with Ted's marriage once it happened. She had managed to resign herself to the inevitable and survive the last few weeks. However, with the nearing approach of March 1, Elaina discovered she was far more uptight than she wanted anyone to see. Now that Lorna and Ted had eloped and were taking a honeymoon in exotic Egypt, Elaina could bear the strain no longer.

When the voice mail prompted her to press three to repeat the message, Elaina mashed the button and handed the phone to Anna. By the time Anna finished listening to the message and returned the phone, Elaina had slung half of everything into the picnic basket.

"I need to go home," she said, her face as cold as the stone table.

"Of course you do," Anna assured as if it were her turn to be the elder sister, all supportive and understanding. She moved to her sister's side and placed her arm along Elaina's shoulders. "Look, just let me worry about cleaning all this up. I'll drop it off at your house later. Okay?"

Elaina picked up her bag and stuffed the phone in the side pocket, antennae first. "Thanks," she said, her throat tight. "We'll talk later then." She squeezed Anna's hand, then trotted up the hill toward her Honda. The drive home had never been so long, so desolate, and so full of what-might-have-beens.

Thirty-Seven

Ted Farris stood outside Elaina's duplex, pacing in front of her door as if he were a lion anxiously awaiting the return of his mate. He arrived over an hour ago to find Elaina not home. His desperate heart dictated that he tarry until she got home—even if he had to stay all day. He debated a dozen different things to say to Elaina and a myriad of ways to say them. None of them seemed appropriate or convincing. After all he'd put her through, Ted even wondered if she'd pay him the honor of listening. Several times a streak of cowardice sent him rushing toward the new red Toyota he'd bought after selling the Corvette. But each time Ted had walked back to her door, determined to once and for all state his heart and reveal the plan that had proved successful.

Lorna isn't the only one who can manipulate people, Ted thought with a satisfied grin.

He spotted Elaina's gray Honda cruising down the neighborhood lane toward the duplex's driveway. Ted rubbed his damp palms across the front of his striped cotton shirt and lost every word he'd rehearsed. The Honda purred into the driveway and squealed to an abrupt halt halfway up the path. Ted offered an uncertain wave at Elaina, who stared at him as if he were a specter. The Honda zoomed forward and halted next to his new Toyota.

Not bothering to turn off the engine, Elaina slung open the door, scrambled out, and looked at Ted. Her questioning eyes held her heart…and a yearning that spawned optimism.

Maybe she won't send me packing after all, Ted thought.

"Hi, Elaina," he said with another limp wave.

"Ted?" she gasped. "What are you doing here? I thought you were halfway to Egypt by now."

"No," he scratched the top of his ear, "I guess the grapevine is alive and well and is as flawed as ever. That would be *Robert* who's halfway to Egypt."

"R–Robert?" she stuttered.

"Yes. My brother, Robert. Remember, you met him at the New Year's bash?"

"Robert?" Elaina repeated. She moved away from the car. "You mean he's eloped with—with—with—"

"Yes, with Lorna," Ted finished and had never been so glad to deliver news of blatant betrayal. "I came to tell you because I… I…" The swish and whir of traffic, the touch of spring in the air, the red bird fluttering along a row of bushes all seemed to incite Ted to confess his heart. "I love you," he whispered, "and I was hoping that—"

A muffled cry escaped Elaina. Before Ted expected her intent, she surged forward and threw her arms around him. The two of them slammed against her locked front door and Elaina smashed her lips against his.

His arms flailed. His eyes bugged. And Ted was pulled under by a kiss that rocked the neighborhood. He closed his eyes, wrapped his arms around Elaina, and kissed her back with a passion long held captive. Kissing Elaina was everything Ted had ever imagined and so much more…the merging of two hearts beating as one...the meeting of two minds destined to be together.

The second their lips parted, Elaina placed both her hands on the sides of his face and gazed into his soul with a depth of emotion that matched Ted's own. "Oh, Ted," she finally breathed, "I love you, too."

Her eyes unexpectedly filled with tears. A broken sob spilled from her spirit. Elaina covered her face with her hands, rested her forehead upon his shoulder, and began to shake with the power of her emotions. A new sob ricocheted across the parking lot, and Ted patted her back and struggled in complete loss about what to do now. He'd never seen Elaina so out of control, nor had he ever expected to witness such an event during his lifetime. All Ted knew to do was stroke her back and helplessly utter something comforting which he hoped was also coherent.

"I need to go in," she finally bellowed. "I can't—I can't s–s–stop! I don't even—even know where my keys are."

"They're in your ignition," Ted said and grabbed the opportunity to do something useful. "Here, let me get them." He released her long enough to race to her car, turn off her engine, retrieve her purse, and lock the car door. The whole time, Elaina's weeping reverberated across the yard. Shaking in the aftermath of that kiss, Ted darted an uneasy gaze around the duplex complex and hoped no one thought he was harming Elaina.

"Let's get inside," he offered and managed to find the right key to her door. Elaina, ever capable, seemed to have lost all ability to do anything but wail.

The minute they stepped into her home, she dashed down the hallway, leaving Ted in the red-walled room that offered the subtle scent of new paint. He peered around, encountering the evidence of Elaina's understated taste in every choice of furnishing and decoration. Soon the lady erupted back on the scene as swiftly as she'd departed. Now she carried a tissue box. Still wearing her denim jacket, Elaina collapsed onto the couch, tossed her glasses on the end table, covered her face with the a wad of tissue, and silently shook.

"Ah, Elaina," Ted whispered, and settled on the couch beside her. "I've put you through so much, haven't I?"

With a silent nod, she rested her head on his shoulder. "I'm sorry," she wheezed. "I just can't stop."

"Oh, honey, I…I…wanted to tell you so much the day you visited my apartment but I didn't because…because…well, for one thing I was afraid that if I got started I might wind up telling you I love you and try to kiss you. Then I just knew—after how upset you were in your office that day—you'd knock me flat. After all, I was still an engaged man. But I was trying really hard not to be."

A series of slowing sniffles accompanied her lifting her head.

"After you and I had that showdown in your office, I felt like such a total fool," he admitted. "I can't believe I said what I did about having grown to love Lorna. I've never loved her," he scoffed. "I haven't even kissed her once since I met you—and not much before then, for that matter. I guess I just said what I did because I felt like such an idiot, and I somehow needed to defend my lack of insight." He pinched his bottom lip.

"You were so right about her manipulating me. She's almost as good as Mom. And I didn't even see it until that day. That's when I decided—I was determined—to get Lorna to break the engagement. I wanted to tell you about my plan New Year's Eve and the day you came to my apartment, but I decided to wait. I'd jerked you around so much already I didn't want to hurt you all over again if I wasn't able to get rid of her as soon as I'd hoped."

Elaina's red-rimmed eyes focused upon him as if his every word were gold.

"When I introduced Lorna to my brother New Year's Eve night, it was not by accident." Ted couldn't stop his cunning grin. "I had a hunch he'd really like her and that if Mom *did* disinherit me when we announced our engagement Lorna might decide she liked Robert better than me."

"And she did," Elaina said.

"Yes." Ted stroked her cheek. "When I brought you the Diet Coke that night, it was all I could do to keep from cornering you and telling you everything. I figured that if Mom and Faye saw us talking, they'd only give you more grief."

"Thanks for rescuing me from them," Elaina lowered her gaze. "They were really—"

"Being rude. I know," he assured.

"And the song you dedicated to a special someone that night?" Elaina prompted.

"For you, of course," he admitted. "Did you ever doubt it?"

New tears welled in her eyes.

His heart wrenching, Ted tugged her close. "I'm so sorry for everything," he breathed. "I wouldn't purposefully hurt you for anything in the world." He closed his eyes and savored the clean smell of shampoo. "When Mom called me awhile ago and told me Lorna and Robert eloped, I shouted for five minutes."

"Do you think she'll disinherit him, too?" Elaina asked, and inched away.

"I have no earthly idea. Problem with him is he's the president of the family aviation business. Technically Mom still owns it, but she'd be lost without him. He's already married one woman she didn't approve of, and she didn't kick him out of the money. So it wouldn't surprise me if all she did was gripe."

"That doesn't seem fair to you." Elaina scrubbed at her eyes with the tissue.

"It's not," Ted said, and his voice reflected his lack of concern. "But the thing Robert has going for him is the fact that he's always done what she wanted except when it comes to women. But me?" Ted laid a hand over his chest. "I'm the rebel because I won't do the piano thing. Add that to my choice in women, and Mom just can't take it." Ted caressed Elaina's hand and could hardly believe he had really pulled off the plan. "Mom was so wigged out over Lorna and Robert she told me today on the phone that she wanted to put me back in the will and give me my trust fund back."

"Really?" Elaina asked and tried not to imagine what life with such a mother-in-law would be like. "She's probably going to have one confused lawyer," she added.

"No." Ted pressed his lips together and tightened his hold on Elaina. "I declined."

"What?" she gasped and began to suspect that Ted would protect her from his mother no matter what.

"I've never been more free in my life," Ted explained. "I have less money than I've ever had, and I'm happier right now than I've ever been. I got that minister of music position, by the way."

"I knew you would." Elaina's face shone with approval and pride.

"Lorna was just thrilled to death, let me tell you." Ted laughed out loud.

"That was the last thing she wanted," Elaina affirmed and snuggled against the couch cushions.

"She almost had a coronary when I sold my Corvette and bought the Toyota. I figured I needed something a little more… practical for ministry," Ted explained. "She thought I was crazy."

"I don't care *what* you drive," Elaina said. "As long as I get to ride with you."

"Honey, you can ride with me everywhere I go," Ted sealed his claim with a gentle kiss on her forehead. He then slipped to the floor, humbly settled on his knees, and took her hand in his. "Elaina, would you marry me?" he asked, never taking his gaze from hers.

"Yes! Yes! Yes!" she cried and tumbled to the floor beside him.

Ted wrapped his arms around her for another kiss that rattled the room. After he pulled away and settled his forehead against hers, an uncomfortable cramp invaded his leg from his pocket area and reminded him of a tiny box he'd neglected. "My word," he said, "I almost forgot the ring."

"You have a ring?" she rasped.

"Of course." He fished in his jeans pocket until he pulled out a miniature red box. "I hope you like it," he said. "I actually bought it after I introduced Lorna to Robert. I saw it in a display case at the mall and couldn't resist." His heart swelling with pride, Ted opened the box and extended it to Elaina.

She gasped. Her eyes widened. She drank in the exquisite two-carat blue sapphire, circled in a carat of diamonds. "It's too beautiful for words," she whispered.

"It's the color of your eyes," he explained, and a warm wash of pleasure penetrated his declaration. "Part of the reason I went ahead and bought it was because I wanted to get something really special. I knew I wouldn't be able to afford something like this once Mom disinherited me. So…"

Ted removed the ring from the box and slipped it on her trembling finger. "A perfect fit," he declared.

"Just like us," Elaina breathed.

Ted held her close. "Yes, just like us," he whispered into her ear. "I'm afraid I won't be able to take you to Egypt or…or… Cancun or any place exotic for our honeymoon—"

"I don't need exotic," Elaina said, her eyes brimming with love. "All I need is you."

About the Author

Debra White Smith continues to impact and entertain readers with her life-changing books, including *Romancing Your Husband, 101 Ways to Romance Your Marriage, Friends for Keeps, More than Rubies: Becoming a Woman of Godly Influence,* and the popular Seven Sisters fiction series. She has nearly 40 book sales to her credit and close to a million books in print.

The founder of Real Life Ministries, Debra touches lives through the written and spoken word by presenting real truth for real life and ministering to people where they are. Debra speaks at events across the nation and sings with her husband and children. She has been featured on a variety of media spots, including "The 700 Club," "At Home Live," "Getting Together," "Focus on the Family," "John Maxwell's Thrive Ministry," "Moody Broadcasting Network," "Midday Connection," and Fox News.

Debra holds an M.A. in English. She is pursuing a second Master's Degree through Trinity Seminary. She lives in small-town America with her husband of 21 years, two children, and a herd of cats.

To write Debra or contact her for speaking engagements, check out her website:

www.debrawhitesmith.com

or send mail to

Real Life Ministries
Debra White Smith
P.O. Box 1482
Jacksonville, TX 75766

The Austen Series

First Impressions

When Eddi Boswick is cast as Elizabeth, the female lead in a local production of *Pride and Prejudice,* she hesitates. Dave, the handsome young rancher cast as Darcy, seems arrogant and unpredictable. Accepting the challenge of playing opposite him, Eddi soon realizes that he is difficult to work with on and off the set.

But when a tornado springs out of nowhere, Dave protects Eddi...much to her chagrin. And he is shocked to discover an attraction for the feisty lawyer he can't deny. Sparks fly when Eddi misinterprets his interest and discovers the truth he's trying to hide.

Will Eddi's passionate faith, fierce independence, and quick wit keep Dave from discovering the secret to love...and the key to her heart?